Child of the Storm

Child of the Storm

Kirk Lee Aeder

Foreword by Drew Kampion
with Editing by Jeanne Bellezzo

WRITEIDEAS

writing | editing | copywriting | creative concepts

Mutual Publishing

ISBN-10: 1-56647-966-5
ISBN-13: 978-1-56647-966-0
Library of Congress Control Number: 2011944484

Cover design by Cathy Kniess, Chrome Digital
Interior design by Jane Gillespie
First Printing, March 2012

Mutual Publishing, LLC
1215 Center Street, Suite 210
Honolulu, Hawaii 96816
Ph: (808) 732-1709 / Fax: (808) 734-4094
e-mail: info@mutualpublishing.com
www.mutualpublishing.com

Printed in Korea

Dedicated to Bart, Lyn, Jil, Timothy,
my parents,
and my wife Nita.

In memory of Chris O'Rourke, Mark McCoy, Ted Smith,
Bill Caster, and Larry 'Flame' Moore.

Contents

Crossing the Bar

"Sunset and evening star,
    And one clear call for me !
And may there be no moaning of the bar,
    When I put out to sea,

But such a tide as moving seems asleep,
    Too full for sound and foam,
When that which drew from out the boundless
    deep
Turns home again.

Twilight and evening bell,
    And after that the dark !
And may there be no sadness of farewell,
    When I embark;

For tho' from out our bourne of Time and Place
    The flood may bear me far,
I hope to see my pilot face to face
    When I have crost the bar."

Alfred Lord Tennyson, 1889

A Phoenix Forever Burning

by Drew Kampion

The lines he drew—the intelligence, vision and attitude they revealed—pointed towards a vanishing point far beyond all contemporary horizons. Some inner music seemed to draw out the young man's precocious dance—carving up under the hollows of concave wave-faces on the sharp edges of his lean little surfboard, throwing flamboyant poses in the throes of desperate hydraulic predicaments, polishing the era's classic moves with the command and assurance of a seasoned veteran. The performance was futuristic indeed, the origins and background of which reveal a much more daunting and complex story.

"Surfing is the most free and incredible form of self-expression this planet has to offer," Chris told me in December of 1978. This was nearly two years after he had been diagnosed with Hodgkin's disease, a cancer of the lymphatic system. I was in the midst of writing a piece for *Surfing* magazine about the four most prolific young surfers in the world. Chris was at the top of my list. The article was titled "The Boys," and also featured Mark Foo from Hawaii, someone who became one of the most proficient and bold big-wave surfers ever. Foo later died in 1994 while surfing at 'Mavericks' in California. Australian Cheyne Horan was also part of the mix, a highly touted wonder kid who appeared destined to become a world champion. What seemed like a foregone conclusion however never took place. Cheyne finished second four times and never tasted the glory of winning a world title. Finally there was Hawaiian North Shore soul-surfer Charlie Smith, who inexplicably later drifted away from the limelight even as pro surfing gathered momentum in the early 1980s.

For an eighteen-year-old kid with a reputation for having a chip on his shoulder, Chris's comments had left a particularly keen perception upon my mind. That chip, worn like an epaulet by surfers at virtually every wave-break on the planet, probably said less about Chris than it did about the rituals, codes and conventions of his local surf tribe.

This was especially true since his surf spot of choice was Windansea. The La Jolla beach's wave-terrain was well-mapped and occupied, the hierarchy long established before Chris sucked it up and paddled out there as a miniscule ten-year-old. A measure of his success can be read in the fact that after Bob Simmons, the near-mythic surfing innovator who died surfing there in 1954, Chris still remains the surfer most associated with Windansea—a powerful, tricky California wave zone that called forth and nurtured the spontaneous creativity apparently harbored in the young surfer's very genes.

Chris was clearly one of the best of all time but in such a different sort of way. He had a burning passion to surf, to ride waves, and to ride them always without compromise. Chris hungered to be as good as the best and was precocious at mastering the complicated and competitively charged Windansea break.

That his school chum Kirk Aeder chose the path of surf photojournalist, and was there to record his progress, ascendancy, and full arc of his personal and public life, speak to the unique fortunes of Chris' special path. The bond between the two friends grew stronger even as Chris became sicker. Because Kirk no doubt knew the same truth—that surfing was the most incredible form of self-expression Earth had to offer. He derived the highest satisfaction from photographing and experiencing Chris as he grew and developed.

Soon his friend's greater challenge took an even higher precedent, and both of them grew and developed so much more. They shared that vision, that soul-level understanding that surfing isn't just what it appears to be. There's something fundamentally different, free, and "cosmic" about it that resonated with the core spirit of both young men.

The symbiosis of their relationship as friends and creators of great surfing images remains a constant for Kirk, even close to thirty years after Chris's passing. The impact his great friend had upon him had no boundaries of time. Today Kirk still calls his media company IMOCO (first letters of In Memory of Chris O'Rourke)…and has refused to let his remarkably inspiring story fade into oblivion. It appeared that Chris' saga would be swallowed up in a vacuum of time—gone, but not forgotten. As a difference maker, however, everyone should know Chris' compelling tale is the most tragic story in the history of surfing. Yet the inspiration was equally as engaging.

Chris lived an accelerated life because he was forced to. Dying young is never a good thing, snuffing out so much light in full view of the open road and the shining path ahead. This sort of death is especially painful. The nearness of his unrealized achievements and unrequited dreams…it's a grief that's acutely double-edged with its near-full knowledge of those future gifts.

Chris O'Rourke's sweet short life established the power of a surfer as inspiration, as hero or role model, as pathfinder into the heretofore unknown. His challenge to the culture was a new one. Back then we hadn't had many notable young surfers die— certainly not the way he did. Drowning, car crashes, drugs… yes, but with an aggressive and lingering disease that required more sickness and pain, just to gain time, with little chance of an outright cure? And in the face of that disease, to put on a hockey helmet to protect his head with half a skull and paddle out to claim your rightful place in the lineup...so miraculous and frightening and stunning.

The enlightening courage of this young man, growing in stature and achievement even as the illness grew, as if the challenge of the disease required more of him and thus made him more, made him better...as a surfer, as a competitor, as a man...crawling out from under the chemo and the radiation and the surgeries, with the saucer-sized hole in his skull...crawling back out to the lineup, the wave, the peak...and then ripping the place apart in utter defiance of all the so-called inevitabilities... for as long as he could, for as long as he lasted. And the memory of that has lasted this long, till now, and will go on lasting...like the echoes that all surfers ride.

Road to the Sea

May 26, 1981

There was something about those wooden hospital doors that I never liked—large slabs that seemed more like barriers. I cautiously entered the room and saw Jil sitting alongside Chris on the bed with his older sister, Lyn. Jil's mother and Bob Andrews, a close friend of ours, stood quietly.

Lyn and Jil both huddled tightly around Chris, who appeared barely conscious. Tentatively, I stepped closer, but Jil didn't look up at me. Her hands were wrapped tightly around his, as if she were trying to pour her own good health into his depleted body. Lyn glanced over at me, her sorrowful red-rimmed eyes revealing the severity of his condition. For several minutes, though it seemed like an eternity, none of us spoke. We were all reflecting, each in our own way.

Certainly I was. Early in our lives we were two young boys with polar opposite personalities and different backgrounds. Chris O'Rourke came from a train wreck of a family. I was raised in pure unequivocal bliss. He was arrogant and confrontational; I was as obedient as they come. He was tough as nails, while I could only yearn for such resilience. Against all odds, our friendship evolved amidst such turmoil, and eventual tragedy.

Surfing became Chris's passion, and the ocean became not only his arena, but his sanctuary. Chris gravitated to the sea like a magnet to steel. His surfing defied the laws of gravity and inertia. Before long his abilities in the ocean were without peer; his boldness on land, unquestionable.

Tragically, his path would soon change. One day the clouds abruptly turned dark and his life went wickedly astray. What followed were many difficult days in the waves for the boy-prodigy sitting on his surfboard. Ultimately, a variety of factors contributed to Chris's downfall.

Finally, Jil spoke.

"Honey," she said softly to Chris. "Honey, Kirk is here."

Chris's eyes had been closed, and he was heavily sedated. But upon hearing her words, his head and upper body flinched. Clearly he understood—I was sure of that. I stared at the friend who had been such an enormous part of my life and thought of his strength and power and determination. As I stood there now watching him, helpless, it seemed like a lifetime. His lifetime and mine.

Chapter 1

A Kid at Heart

Chris and I did not meet until the sixth grade. Before then, I knew nothing about this boy from the East Coast, or about the chaos that swirled through his life. Everything had started out just fine. Then one day, the walls began to cave in.

He was born on March 16, 1959, into an affluent Irish family in New Jersey and welcomed by an intense winter storm that pummeled the Eastern Seaboard with gusting rain, blinding flashes of lightning and deafening thunder.

Chris's mother, Gloria, was a petite woman barely five feet tall. In her mid-thirties, Gloria was already three weeks late with her third child. The family was concerned, but the doctor heard the baby's steady heartbeat and encouraged them to be patient. When the moment finally arrived, Bart O'Rourke was so excited he drove off to the hospital without his wife. Several minutes passed before he realized his error and rushed back to where she stood calmly on the front porch, waiting for him to return.

Even in the womb, Chris was stubborn. Gloria endured a lengthy labor, finally giving birth to the newest sibling of her son, Bart IV, and daughter, Lyn, both of whom had stayed home with their grandmother. None of them slept a wink.

When his parents proudly brought their baby boy home the following morning, Chris briefly opened his eyes and firmly clutched his father's finger. Bart marveled over his new son's strength.

"You know something, Gloria? It's a good thing we're naming him Chris, after your Uncle Chris Decker," Bart said.

"If our youngest son grows up anything like his namesake, he will become a force to be reckoned with. I can already tell that he's going to be tough."

During the first years of Chris's life, his family was quite well off. His immediate family and all four grandparents lived together on a 100-acre farm in New Jersey. They spent summers on their twenty-five-acre lake property in Maine, and they owned an apartment in New York, where Chris's father ran a successful law business.

The O'Rourke family's East Coast roots reached deep. The son of Irish immigrants, Chris's grandfather, Bart II, had been born and raised in New York at the turn of the 19th century. In 1924, Chris's father was born there as well; many years later, he became a boxing champion while serving in the Navy. Chris's parents met quite literally by accident on a Memphis street during World War II. A naval officer, Bart was stationed in Memphis while taking flight training lessons as an Aerial Gunner. One hot afternoon he was driving with his best buddy, Jerry Paris, when they noticed a woman standing next to her car alongside the road ahead. Bart's eyes instantly lit up, and he did the first thing that came to mind: He purposely pulled up behind her car and slightly dented its bumper—just to get her name and telephone number. He also pretended to be hurt. But Gloria easily saw through his masquerade. Born in Memphis in 1925, she was a Southern girl at heart with a strict upbringing that emphasized proper manners and hospitality, and she felt sorry for Bart. Gloria invited the two men into her house and served them fresh lemonade.

Six months later, Bart and Gloria were married. Jerry Paris served as best man; decades later, he would become a renowned Hollywood television director.

Gloria never seemed to show much emotion. Her quiet Southern upbringing had taught her to show devotion to her husband and family, and obeying Bart's requests always came first. Near the end of the war, she gave birth to the couple's first child, Lyn, followed seven years later by Bart IV. Soon after, Bart left the Navy and joined a law firm in New York. He had a knack for the law, and soon went out on his own. By the time Chris was born, his father's practice was flourishing.

Chris's favorite place was the family house in Maine. His uncle had built the rustic pine cottage during the 1920s, and Chris was drawn to the large lake on the estate. Fishing, catching frogs and wading around the shoreline kept him occupied from dawn until dusk.

As an infant, Chris seemed to be in perpetual motion, and by age three he was a restless, smart and sensitive child who didn't like to sleep much. He soon became a real handful for Bart and Gloria. His brother and sister tried to help their parents with Chris, but as they grew up, they made new friends and developed outside interests. Watching their little brother wasn't a priority.

Around the same time, Chris sensed his parents becoming distant. Within the family the winds of change were beginning to blow.

At least Chris knew that he could always count upon his Grandmother Elbertine. By the time Chris was born, Elbertine had already been through more than her share of challenges. As a young girl she had survived tuberculosis, followed by the sudden death of both parents. Several years later, tragedy struck again, and within the span of two months both her husband and young son died in separate incidents. The two men had served their country together during World War II; her husband as a prolific fighter pilot, and their seventeen-year-old son as part of a tank division that had battled Rommel in the North African Campaign. Though both men survived the war, Thomas Jr. died at twenty-five after crashing the private plane he was flying. A few weeks later, terribly distraught over their son's death, Thomas Sr. took his own life. Chris's middle name, Thomas, was a tribute to them.

When Chris arrived, Elbertine saw a new opportunity to love a son. And love him she did. She made it a point to look after him, especially during those long summers on the lake. She often held his hand and walked him down to the water. A non-negotiable requirement of being an O'Rourke was learning to swim at a young age. Elbertine tried persuading Chris to take off his life jacket, but he always refused. Other family members took a different approach by relentlessly kidding him about it.

Soon he had had enough of their jokes. One afternoon, on the way home with his parents, Chris fell asleep in the back of the car. When they got home, he suddenly woke up, raced into the house, and pulled off all his clothes. Stark naked, he scampered down to the lake with the rest of the family in close pursuit.

His mother screamed. "Chris, what are you doing?"

Gloria watched helplessly as her five-year-old son hurried out onto the wood dock and, with no hesitation, plunged head first into the water. Chris swam nearly seventy yards out into the lake before finally coming to a stop.

"Bart, get in that water right now and go help your brother. He's going to drown out there!" Gloria yelled in a panic.

"Mom, you're kidding, right? Just look at him. He's doing fine," Bart said.

Hearing all the commotion on shore, Chris began to swim back. Gloria watched every stroke. His reckless stunt had caused pandemonium, but he returned to shore grinning from ear to ear. His father simply walked away shaking his head.

"You're an idiot, Chris," his brother told him.

Gloria couldn't help but ask. "Son, what on earth possessed you to do that?"

"Well, Mom, when I was in the car I had a dream that I could swim without the life jacket. So I just wanted to do it before I forgot how," Chris proclaimed excitedly.

It was simply a hint of things to come. From that moment on, keeping Chris out of the water was an impossible task.

After that, Chris swam in the lake every day. Every morning at dawn's first light, he sprung from bed and ran barefoot down the leaf-covered trail to the dock. He swam around the entire lake before returning to soak his feet in the cool, soothing mud. He also paddled a wooden canoe and sailed with his brother.

These were some of the most peaceful days of Chris's life. They gave no hint of the monstrous storm of turmoil lurking ahead.

Chapter 2

Fathers and Sons

End of summer, 1964

Toward the beginning of September, the family began preparing to return to New Jersey. It was a hot afternoon when Chris walked down to the lake for the last time that summer. He sat on the dock and dipped his legs into the clear water, watching large frogs swim by. Soon he heard his mother's voice calling him and knew it was time to go.

While Chris was fond of his New Jersey home, the lake felt more like his real home, where he could hang out with all the frogs and fish. During the cold winter months ahead in the city, he would miss it. Reluctantly, Chris took a few steps toward the house and then turned to look at the lake one last time.

"See you next summer," he said quietly.

Little did he know this would be the last time he'd ever see that lake again. Chris was a perceptive kid, but neither he nor his siblings had even a hint of the trouble their father was in. Bart was a proud man and father. His pride would not allow him to disclose to his family the horrible mess he had gotten himself into. Faced with mounting debt for the first time in his life, Bart didn't know what to do. Now it was too late, and their once solid foundation rapidly began to deteriorate.

For several months, Chris's father did his best to keep his problems secret, but by December of 1964, there were too many warning signs to ignore. In the span of a few short months, the family's lavish lifestyle came crashing down. The three siblings noticed their father was behaving very strangely, but they didn't know why. Inquisitive by nature, Chris wanted to know what was happening, but his parents remained tight-lipped. Then Lyn began to discover the truth.

In spite of his previous successes, Bart had long yearned to leave the law business behind. Worrying that he might not be able to provide for his family as well as he once had, Bart knew that whatever business venture he delved into next had to be prosperous. Unbeknownst to the rest of the family, he had borrowed a large sum of money from a group of suspicious people in order to start an ambitious importing business. It was a calculated move done with the best intentions, and up to this point Bart had been a smart man who made good decisions. Now, however, he realized that entering into a financial deal with organized crime was a very unwise thing to do. But he still felt confident everything would work out fine.

Unfortunately, the opposite happened. Within months, his import business began falling apart. To make matters worse, the shady individuals he had borrowed money from wanted it back—now. Death threats loomed over him. Bart feared for his own safety, and more importantly, the safety of his family.

In early 1965, Lyn was in her second year of college. During a weekend break she returned home to find their New Jersey house in a state of disarray. Her father looked panicked and scared. Suddenly he asked them all to come into the living room, where he announced they would be moving. Immediately.

"Lyn, get as many things as you can carry out of the house and put them in the car...now!" he demanded. "The same goes for the rest of you."

It was too late to turn back now. The rest of his family were caught up in Bart's own personal storm, and the astonished looks on their faces spoke volumes.

"Mom, what's going on?" Lyn asked.

"Just do as your father says." Her mother sounded resigned.

Chris was puzzled but remained silent. He had so many questions but very few answers.

"What's happening?" Chris asked his brother. "Why is Dad acting like that?"

"I'm not sure, but just do as he says, okay?"

With their lives now hanging in the balance, the O'Rourke family abruptly fled their New Jersey home. First they drove to the apartment where Lyn had been living to collect her belongings; her college life had become an unexpected casualty too. Peering out the car's window as they drove away, Lyn watched the city lights go by in a blur and thought about how strange it all was. Only a few hours earlier everything in their lives seemed okay. In a matter of moments their entire world had been turned upside down, and going back home anytime soon didn't appear to be an option.

Like the rest of her family, Lyn never saw this scenario coming. Now nineteen, she was amazed how quickly life could go from riches to rags. She worried over the family's future. Mostly, though, she wondered what effect all of this would have upon her little brother.

Only their father knew exactly where they were going. After crossing the state line, Chris finally questioned his father about what was happening.

"Just shut up," he was told.

For the next few days the family headed south. Back in New York, meanwhile, their grandfather quickly consolidated and sold nearly everything the family had left behind, including the lake house in Maine. He also liquidated virtually everything he owned. It was all part of a concerted effort to help save his son and family. This allowed Bart to temporarily satisfy part of his debt and provided more time to take care of the rest. In the interim, he devised a new plan that hopefully would get him back on the right track for good. That meant relocating to Sarasota Beach, Florida.

Shortly after arriving in Florida, Chris got his first glimpse of the sparkling blue ocean and began to feel better. While he deeply missed the lake where he had learned to swim, the Gulf of Mexico was by far the biggest body of water he had ever seen.

Right from the start, he felt at home at the salty water's edge. Six years old now, he went fishing by himself every morning, bringing small fish and baby sharks back home in a bucket. He would proudly display them to his mom before scurrying back to set them free again. When he wasn't fishing, Chris combed the shoreline like an expert detective, becoming a master seashell collector.

"Come on Lyn, let's go look for some new shells today," he constantly prodded his sister.

The Keys off Sarasota quickly become his new stomping grounds. During low tide, Chris and Lyn would walk out onto exposed sandbars that stretched seaward for several hundred yards. The area was a treasure trove of shells; Chris found cowries, cones, marginalias, olives, and more. Afterward they took the live shells home and placed them into boiling saltwater to help get the smell out and pry the little animals from inside. Chris then left them outside for several days to dry out.

After a few months he had a fairly extensive collection, including a very rare alphabet cone shell. Gloria saw that her youngest son had become hooked on shells almost to the point of obsession. With all that had been transpiring with his father, she was glad he had developed such a keen distraction. She bought Chris a book about shells; inside were pictures of shells found around the world accompanied by their Latin names. He migrated to that book like a moth to flame. The only time he put it down was when he went back to the ocean to collect even more shells.

While Chris's days were spent gathering treasures from the sea, his father's were far from carefree. Bart was still struggling to make ends meet, which drove the already-splintered family farther apart. Lyn had re-entered college in Sarasota, while Bart IV enrolled in junior high school. Chris now attended kindergarten. With their finances depleted, Gloria took a job at a local hospital.

As everyone scrambled to help make ends meet, no one was available to look after Chris. As usual, Elbertine was more than

happy to help out. Upon arriving from New York she immediately
went to work on him. His grandmother was always very patient
with Chris, and he was glad to have her back in his life; Elbertine
had shown him more love than anyone in his short life. She had
left school at a very early age and never completed her formal
education, yet she "schooled" Chris very well. They often sat on
the couch for hours while she quizzed him about his shells.

"Okay Chris, what's this one?" she asked, holding up a
white shiny shell.

"That's easy Grandma, it's a Florida cone."

"And its name in Latin is...?"

"Conus anabathrum," Chris replied with perfect
pronunciation.

"What about this one?"

"That's an orange marginalia."

"And its Latin name?"

"Prunum carneum," he said.

"Wow Chris, I'm very proud of you!" she told him.

Before long it wasn't even a test anymore—he had
memorized them all! Chris cherished the time Elbertine spent
with him. Around her, there was a loving atmosphere that Chris
did not feel from some of his other family members. She had a
calming effect on him.

By 1967, it appeared however that life in the O'Rourke
family had once again come to rest on an even keel. Chris was
living a happy childhood by a warm ocean. He had seen that his
father's life was chaotic and complicated, and he didn't want to
live like that. He preferred to take a grass-roots approach to life,
always striving to do things that were pure and simple.

This way of thinking would have a profound effect upon his
future. Chris knew that collecting seashells would not always
be his entire world. Something more prolific waited for him
down the road, and whatever it was, he vowed to be ready when
it came. For now, though, he was content, and it appeared his
father had extricated himself from the mysterious financial
woes that had beset them in New York.

If only it had been that simple. Chris's father had actually invested what little financial assets he had left into another dubious big money deal. This time it involved a marina project in South Florida known as Marina Mar. His partner was an art importer from New York who once again had strong connections to organized crime. By entering into another financial deal with the underworld, Bart had done the unthinkable. He had put his own life, along with the lives of his family, in serious jeopardy. And ever since, the transaction had hung over him like a dark cloud.

A few months later, things soured even more. A portion of the money had disappeared, and the specter of serious retaliation again became a reality. Family members began to notice the telltale warning signs. One evening, a mysterious figure showed up unannounced at the door. He was a rather smug, strange-looking guy who wore a suit and shiny pointed leather shoes. Bart had no choice but to let the shady character inside. Tension and anxiety quickly filled the air.

Gloria asked Chris's brother to take him outside somewhere.

"Where, Mom?" Bart asked in surprise.

"Anywhere," she snapped back.

Chris could sense that something was amiss. Before hurrying out the door with his brother, he turned to look back at his mom.

"You'll be okay Mom, won't you?" he asked her.

"We'll be fine, Chris. Now go on with your brother," she told him.

After the boys departed, their uninvited guest sat down in the living room and began speaking. His father tried to convince the man to allow him more time. Initially he appeared receptive to the idea. But the man also knew he had Bart right where he wanted and couldn't resist the opportunity to make him squirm a bit.

"Bart, what's your wife's name?" he asked.

"Gloria, but what do you care?" Bart replied sternly.

"Hey Gloria, how about fetching me a cold beer?" the man said, grinning slyly.

For Bart, these words were the last straw. All of the frustrations he had endured over the past few years came boiling to the surface. Once more he was in the same predicament as before, and he couldn't take it anymore. In a rage he picked up the man and slammed him against the wall, pinning him there. The violent impact caused a small framed painting to crash down upon the floor. Pieces of glass shattered everywhere.

"Don't you ever speak to my wife like that again. Do you hear me?" he said.

Bart formed a fist with his right hand and raised it backward. The man's forehead glistened with perspiration. Bart reasoned that, while he didn't have much money, he did have his dignity, and he badly wanted to punch the guy's lights out right then and there.

"Don't do it," cried Gloria.

"Whoa, whoa, hold on there now. Listen to your wife," the man reasoned. "You'd better put me down...right now."

Reluctantly, Bart came to his senses. Slowly he released his tight grip from the man's collar and slumped down upon the couch.

"You know something, Bart? I can do damn well whatever I want with you. You know that, don't you? So you better watch your step," the man said. "Now Gloria, as I was saying, how about that beer?"

Bart was still fuming inside. But what more could he possibly do? He had played his cards, and this is what had been dealt.

While all of this was going on, no one had noticed the small open crack of the bedroom door. Standing there in the darkness, Lyn had seen everything. Now she understood what was happening with her father. He was under siege again.

A week later the situation worsened. The ten-thousand-dollar car that Chris's father had been able to purchase after moving to Florida mysteriously vanished. Payoffs come in all shapes and forms; the mystery of what might happen next worried them even more. It was like deja vu. As the leader of the family, Bart had no choice but to pull up stakes and flee once more.

Chris loved his father. But there were other feelings, negative ones, swirling inside him. Bart realized that his youngest son was starting to resent him. He felt guilty about that but didn't know how to make things better between them. Chris didn't want to feel the way he did either. So one evening he extended his father an olive branch of sorts.

"Dad, I'm sorry for everything that's happening to you. Can I help?" he inquired.

"Thank you, Chris. I'm sorry, too, for how my mistakes have affected all our lives. But there's nothing you can do, son. I got myself into this mess. Hopefully I can get out of it."

Chris then recalled the words that his father had once told him.

"Dad, do you have a plan?" Chris asked.

His father looked at him and smiled.

"As a matter of fact, son, I do. And thanks for asking."

His father did have a plan, all right—but it was a half-baked one at best. Bart managed to borrow enough money from friends to purchase a cheap used car. He then advised his family to pack up all their belongings again. In three days they would leave Florida and be on the move once more. The three siblings knew that they were not just moving, but going on the run from something very serious. They tried persuading their father to open up to them, but he refused to discuss it. Uninformed and still too young to fully grasp the sinister implications of their flight, the brief compassion Chris felt for his dad a few days earlier was now gone, and anger rose once more. They had already been forced to leave New Jersey, and now the same thing had occurred here in Florida.

Chris didn't know what was transpiring with his father, but he did know that his dad continued to be the cause of his family's turmoil. He had horrible thoughts about his dad, the kind he never had experienced before. This proved to be the beginning of a corrosive resentment that plagued Chris and his father for the rest of their lives.

This time the family headed north toward Virginia, where they tried to blend in and stay under the radar of revenge. As much as he despised the notion, Bart started working again as a lawyer. The move did not fool the people who were after him, nor was it meant to. Bart knew they were aware of his location. Every night, returning home from work in the dark got his adrenaline going. But soon he was able to give them a little money—at least enough to keep him alive.

Chris, meanwhile, began attending a Catholic school in the neighborhood where they had settled. Yet just as he began feeling comfortable there, the family moved once more, this time back to New Jersey. His father decided that no matter where he went, evil would follow close behind. He thought placing himself back in the thick of things might actually offer the best solution and send the message that he was serious about paying back his debt instead of running. So for a short time, his creditors left Bart alone.

Despite the posturing, life hadn't become any easier for Bart. His business partner proceeded to sell his portion of the fledgling marina company in Florida, consuming any remaining financial base the family had left. Then Bart's own father passed away suddenly. While the family was attending the funeral, Chris's father looked over his shoulder and noticed two men in suits and dark sunglasses staring straight at him.

The tension finally took its toll. Bart suffered a nervous breakdown a few days later and ended up in a hospital. Throughout their years of financial hardship, Chris's grandfather had been the anchor of the family. Now he was gone, and their father was left floundering. Somehow Bart had to quickly learn how to grow up all over again. But he had no idea where to start.

The family rented a small house in a predominantly Jewish neighborhood, and Chris entered a public school. He was the only Catholic kid, but he really liked the school—until one day when he came home crying, pleading with his mom not to send him there anymore.

"Why not, Chris?" she asked him. "I thought you liked it there."

"No, Mom, no. It's terrible. There are murderers there. They said that tomorrow they are going to eat lox and beagles for lunch," he whispered quietly, as if someone might be listening.

"Lox and what?" she asked.

"Lox and beagles, you know...a dog!" he said with an astonished look.

His mother began laughing so hard that she had to sit down. With all the tension the family had been through lately, it only seemed fitting that Chris was the one to provide a moment of comic relief. At first Chris thought his mom was laughing at him.

"Chris, it's bagels, not beagles. They were talking about bread, not a dog," she said, wiping tears of laughter from her eyes.

It took Chris several seconds to comprehend what his mother had said. For a moment he felt embarrassed, then burst out into uncontrollable laughter just like she had.

"Chris, you are my adorable son. That's one of the funniest things I've ever heard in my entire life," she told him.

His father's bleak situation, though, was no laughing matter. Bart's life had been destroyed, but the rest of the family members tried to go on with theirs. Lyn was close to completing college and had moved into a small apartment several miles away. One day while visiting her family, she became distraught over what she saw. Her father just sat around, drank beer, and yelled at everyone. Chris and his brother looked really depressed, and she had seen that look of despair on her mother's face too many times before. Lyn didn't need to ask what was going on. Another move was imminent, somewhere far, far away. She and her mother went into the kitchen to talk.

"Yesterday your father spoke to a friend of his in Arizona. There is a ranch there. They grow oranges and other things. He told your father that if we come he would have a job and a place for all of us to stay," she told Lyn.

The decision to leave had already been made. Within a week they would be gone. Lyn and her mother both began to cry.

"But Mom, Arizona is so far away. What makes you think Dad's situation will be any different there?" Lyn asked, wiping tears from her eyes.

"We don't know, honey, but we just can't stay here anymore," replied Gloria. "Lyn, if you want to stay behind, it's okay. You need to finish college. Besides, they are not after you anyway. You'll still be safe here."

A few days later a neighbor friend sold their father an old yellow Thunderbird convertible. It would not be long now. On the afternoon of their departure, Chris held his grandmother's hand as she walked him to the car.

"Be a good boy, Chris. Just try and write me a letter sometime, okay?"

They were the last words Elbertine said to him before they drove off, leaving her wiping away a flood of tears in the driveway. Realizing that Chris had now become a strong-willed boy made her feel a little better. But this time he looked nervous and scared, and she was nervous and scared for him. In Arizona, or wherever else they might end up, his parents would be too busy trying to survive and would pay little attention to him.

As they made their way down the street, his mother turned and noticed Chris staring out the back window.

"Don't look back, Chris. There's nothing here for us anymore," she told him.

He continued to look anyway—at his grandmother, the sidewalk, the trees, and the house they had once lived in. Then it was all gone, the sight fading like a distant memory. Once more Chris was crammed into a car with his family and a few belongings. Only God knew where they were headed. The scene had become a familiar one, and he still didn't like it.

The family's drive across country became an eye-opening experience for Chris. As they drove through Utah, snow began to fall. Chris had seen the white stuff before, but nothing like this. For a brief time the car's convertible top remained open, and snowflakes drifted freely inside. Chris stuck out his tongue in a valiant effort to catch some. His brother noticed Chris giggling and was happy that he had something to distract him.

They finally arrived in Arizona in early December of 1967. But Bart's horrific streak of bad luck followed them. A deep winter freeze had set in a week earlier, and the orange groves and other crops on the ranch had all been destroyed. For Chris's father there was no job after all or, for that matter, a place for them to live. The family was politely informed they could stay through Christmas, but then they would have to move on. The man who invited them repeatedly apologized to Chris's father. He then advised Bart that if he really wanted to find employment, he should try San Diego.

"It's a growing city. I don't think you'll have any problem finding something there," his friend reassured him.

"Where's San Diego?" Chris asked upon hearing the news.

His father explained that it was a fairly large city in Southern California close to the Mexican border.

"Is it as big as New York?"

"No, son. It's nothing like that. But it's where we're going to live from now on," Bart stated with finality.

Chris looked skeptical. He had heard this line numerous times before. He stayed quiet, but his mother could see his anger building. So she tried to diffuse his mood the best she could.

"San Diego is right next to the ocean where there are tons of fish and shells. You'll be able to spend a lot of time at the beach there, just like you used to do in Florida," she told him.

Her words seemed to help, and this time Chris tried a different outlook. He reasoned that, since they already had come this far, going a little farther wouldn't matter, especially if it meant being near the ocean again.

Several days after Christmas they ventured onward. The family was understandably weary when they arrived in Southern California in early January of 1968. After reaching the shores of the Pacific Ocean, they had traveled west as far as possible. San

Diego was where California had first been discovered by the Spanish explorer Cabrillo a few hundred years earlier, and this blossoming city was where the O'Rourke family would make their final stand.

They rented a room at the Surfrider Hotel in the coastal town of Pacific Beach. From day one, the two brothers began exploring their new home. Since the hotel was located right on the ocean, Chris instantly began combing the shoreline looking for shells. Bart, however, glimpsed his first surfer and was captivated. Riding a surfboard on the waves looked like a lot of fun. He paid 25 cents and rented a 9'6" Hobie surfboard from the nearby Select Surf Shop.

With no prior instruction, Bart paddled out into the windblown waves. Catching a wave, any wave, seemed downright impossible. And even when he did, standing upright while balancing upon the board was even harder. He watched intently as other surfers around him made it look so easy, yet he fell off every time. Finally Bart gave up and returned to shore with salt water pouring from his nostrils.

Undaunted, he was excited about this peculiar new sport and wasn't about to throw in the towel. Renting a surfboard was okay for now, but he vowed to soon have enough money to buy his own. Bart told Chris that he had started surfing and figured that his little brother would be interested too. To his surprise, Chris barely raised an eyebrow. But Bart had seen that disinterested look before, and he knew that Chris didn't appreciate things being forced upon him. So Bart left him alone, knowing that one day he would eventually warm to the idea.

Their father had more serious matters to deal with. He began asking about the best place to live and kept getting the same answer: La Jolla. In the late 1960s, forced to start from scratch all over again, La Jolla seemed like a great place to begin.

Despite all the upheaval, Chris believed that everything was starting to fall into place. His parents rented a small house in La Jolla on Bonair Street, just one block away from a well-known surfing beach known as Windansea. With little money left from their cross-country adventure, they couldn't afford beds and were forced to sleep on the floor. Lyn mailed them a check for $125 that she had earned from her job. Though relieved to hear they had found a nice location to live, she was dismayed that nothing else had changed—and her father had yet to find employment.

Fortunately, Gloria found a job as a transcriber at a local hospital. During the summer, she earned enough money that the family was able to move to a larger house on Neptune Street with a perfect view of Windansea. From his bedroom window, Chris could see the ocean every day. His brother, now completely engrossed in surfing, loved the location, too.

Back in New Jersey, Lyn deeply missed her family—and no one more so than her little brother. Aware that the family was still in disarray, she felt guilty and selfish for staying behind. Though she had recently become engaged, she determined that her immediate family was the most important thing. Lyn informed her fiancé that if they were going to marry he would have to be willing to move to San Diego. He agreed.

Upon arriving in the fall, Lyn soon discovered nothing much had changed. Gloria often asked her husband to watch after Chris, to whom he abruptly turned a blind eye. His father's neglect was evident late one night when Lyn stopped by their house for a visit. Her father was passed out on the couch; lying next to him on the bare floor was Chris, filthy and dressed in dirty clothes. She let out a deep sigh and shook her head in disbelief. Helping to get her little brother into the bathtub, Lyn realized how no one in the family seemed to really care about him.

It was also obvious that most of the time no one knew where Chris was or what he was doing. Had he been attending school? Early one morning Lyn came to the house just to make sure. As he left for class, she noticed he wore two different shoes. Since the family had little money to buy new clothes, he just wore whatever he could find—mostly hand-me-downs from his brother.

The first thing Chris usually did after waking up was to flee the house—and his father. Before he could scramble away, Lyn forced him to eat breakfast. Chris didn't quarrel with his sister the way he did with other members of his family. He respected her and knew she was always trying to do the right thing for him.

Her brother, on the other hand, had become fairly well-grounded. A ninth grader at Muirlands Junior High School, Bart regularly hung out with several of his rich-kid La Jolla friends who attended La Jolla Country Day school nearby. As a consequence, though, his little brother had become merely an afterthought.

Chris entered third grade at La Jolla Elementary School. He made several new friends, one of whom was a girl named Rikki Pearson. She thought of Chris as a shy, quiet kid who really kept his head down when he first arrived. As time passed, Rikki noticed that he was beginning to emerge from his shell. They talked a lot and earned each other's trust, and he appreciated another female figure other than his mom and sister. Rikki had been born and raised in La Jolla, and she was a good influence on him.

In spite of the bad relationship with his father, Chris found himself in a happy place again. There were certainly worse places to be living than near the beach in La Jolla. In many ways it reminded him of Florida, and that helped ease the transition. But he wasn't about to relax just yet. The unpredictable nature of his family was still a concern, and he often reminded himself not to become too excited about this place. Life was uncertain, and Chris wanted to be prepared for whatever came next.

Chapter 3

La Jolla

Early 1968

I lived in La Jolla, too. My family moved there in the spring of 1963, nearly five years before Chris would arrive. We were the same age, but our lives couldn't be more different.

Living in La Jolla might have seemed like a godsend for most, but I was too young to realize how good I really had it. Naively unaware in the ways of the real world, all I knew was my sheltered little life. I went where my parents told me to go and did the things I was told to do. It never occurred to me to be rebellious. We lived five blocks from the beach in a coastal town with a funny Spanish name. It took me a while to learn how to pronounce "La Jolla" correctly, but at least I knew its English translation: "The Jewel."

La Jolla had been incorporated into San Diego in 1850, and over time, the tiny town started growing up. Its appeal as a seaside location grew during the century, and the area quickly became a popular West Coast destination, attracting naturalists, beachcombers, swimmers, divers, surfers—and us.

My father, Robert, was an IBM executive who had endured several corporate transfers from Seattle to Los Angeles to San Jose. One day his boss informed him that he would be on the move again, this time to San Diego. The moves didn't seem to faze him or my mom, Patricia. My two older brothers and I couldn't have cared less where we lived, as long as we each had our own bedroom.

My parents purchased a four-bedroom home with a swimming pool. It was a two-minute bike ride to a mile-long stretch of sandy beach called La Jolla Shores. I recall my father was worried about how much he paid for the house—around $48,000. Shortly after moving in I overheard him telling my mom that he would have to work day and night to pay for it. Listening to those words I felt sorry for my father. He was a prisoner of responsibility, especially where his work was concerned. It was something I couldn't fully comprehend. I was just a kid and free as a bird.

Our house felt like the safe haven it was, and everything I needed was close by. It was just a short bike ride away from Scripps Elementary school (my social center) or the beach (my sanctuary). Having quick access to the nearby shoreline and its glistening white sand was the best part. Circular white sand dollar shells littered the beach. The aqua-blue ocean teemed with fish like sculpin, sting rays, sheephead bass, and bright orange garibaldi. Extreme low tides exposed the rock reef formations and the additional sea life they harbored. Abalone, starfish, sea urchins, and lobster were readily abundant. Further out to sea were dark brown kelp beds where black seals, pods of dolphins, and migrating whales roamed the waters uninhibited.

The La Jolla community was designed around the ocean, but the sights on land were equally impressive. Tall palm trees swayed in the light winds. Radiant green Torrey Pine trees were everywhere, their sweet pine scent permeating the crisp clean air. Sandstone bluffs, with their carved fingers weathered by time, changed colors in the late afternoon sun. Foxes, possums, squirrels, rabbits, and coyotes were frequent visitors. It was truly California at its finest, but there was a tropical aura to the area as well. It didn't take me long to realize that La Jolla truly was a jewel.

And if that weren't enough, nearby Soledad Mountain provided La Jolla with a sense of privacy and exclusivity, almost shielding it from the rest of San Diego. Of the approximately 17,000 people who lived in La Jolla then, very few ever referred to it as a town. No, La Jolla was a "village." And it really did seem like that. Everyone pretty much knew everybody else.

Residents from other areas thought people from La Jolla acted too smug for their own good. But for us it was more like just a strong feeling of pride.

Just as Chris would do upon his arrival a few years later, I wasted little time in making the beach my entire world. There never seemed to be a reason to go anywhere other than La Jolla Shores. I thought everyone lived in this sort of kid-like bliss. I didn't know about things like prejudice, poverty and politics.

In the mid 1960s, those realizations came soon enough. Not long after we moved to La Jolla, President John F. Kennedy was assassinated. The worrisome looks on my parents' faces spoke volumes. La Jolla appeared safe to me, but out there in the bigger world it was an entirely different story. This was my first hint that life might not be that simple after all.

For now, though, it was. The waves at La Jolla Shores peeled over soft sand, creating ideal conditions for surfing, the new activity that was quickly captivating many of La Jolla's residents—including my oldest brother, Mark, who started surfing in late 1965. Two years later, my brother Erik became hooked on surfing, too. As the youngest sibling, I personally couldn't have cared less. Surfing looked rather silly to me.

The part of it that did catch my attention, though, was how my brothers behaved after returning home from a day in the waves. They were always excited and constantly interrupted each other about who rode the best wave that day. Each wave was analyzed and dissected as if it were a piece of gold. They sounded like a broken record to me, but they also described their excitement as being "stoked." Exactly what that meant I had no idea. But judging from the smiles on their faces it must have been good.

Everything about surfing now seemed so positive and fun. Then I found out about the ugly side. In placid La Jolla everyone seemed to get along. But there were stark divisions between its surfers who hung around the sandy beach breaks and the ones from the uptown reef breaks. I learned that a lot of hostility was caused by something called "localism." All those waves in the ocean were apparently worth fighting for. Maybe they were like pieces of gold after all, I thought.

Though I claimed to have no interest in surfing, I had to admit that it both intrigued and intimidated me. Getting struck on the head by a hard board or faced with other surfers yelling at you to get out of their way were tough points to overcome for a nine-year-old kid. But Erik told me this wasn't how most surfers behaved. Then he told me something that really mattered: I didn't need to ride a surfboard to be considered a surfer. What counted most was riding the wave itself.

Overcoming my initial apprehension, I started body-surfing. Sometimes I rode upon inflatable air mats that could be rented at the beach for 25 cents an hour. Being pummeled by even the smallest of waves really humbled me though. I was in awe over this force of nature and began to respect the power of the surf. I watched how a few surfers made it look so easy. Maintaining poise and balance atop their boards, they were able to ride each wave for a very long distance.

Clearly, surfing wasn't easy. It required dedication and talent, and I quickly changed my attitude. Although I didn't ride a stand-up board, I had a deep appreciation for the sport and those who were able to excel at it. The ocean continued to lure me, and I rode the waves on my air mat while my older brothers rode real surfboards.

During those years, life seemed stable and never changed. Wasn't this the way it was supposed to be for any young kid like me?

Chapter 4

The Dragons of Windansea

Summer 1968

Chris absolutely loved everything about the ocean but, like me, was not overly enthusiastic about surfing—yet. Everything else that went on around its shores, however, was fair game. One morning in late June, a dense fog clung to the Southern California coastline. From their house across the street, Chris could still hear the breaking waves through the wet blanket of marine layer. By now his brother had progressed to surfing the waves at Windansea, and Bart told him that a large south swell had arrived. Chris didn't care one bit. He felt Bart's passion for surfing had become obsessive.

Bart knew Chris had a keen interest in the ocean and pressured Chris for several weeks to learn to surf, but Chris was stubborn to the bone and usually did the opposite of what Bart suggested anyway. It was a personality trait that grew more evident each day.

Instead of learning to surf, all Chris really wanted to do was partake in his latest hobby—hunting for lizards. For a while he had continued to search for shells, but the ones he found here were a far cry from those back in Florida. It didn't take long for his interest to wane.

Later that morning the fog began to clear. Chris scurried off to Windansea, calling goodbye to his mom as the screen door slammed behind him. The damp humidity had given way to a warm and vibrant sun. The lizards along the sandstone bluffs above the beach would soon be emerging from their hiding places, and Chris was determined to be there waiting for them. He carried an empty metal coffee can with holes poked in the lid.

Just like collecting shells, he had become adept at finding and catching reptiles. A glass terrarium at home overflowed with the critters, and he also had a pet snake named George. Lyn would stop by the house and sometimes complain to him whenever a lizard got loose, but Chris loved his little pets and always found them plenty of bugs to eat.

With the exception of his father, his relationship with his family members remained fairly stable. But the age and social differences among the siblings were becoming more distinct, often causing rifts. Chris was becoming increasingly isolated. With little supervision he began doing what he pleased, when he pleased.

And on this day it pleased him to catch lizards. It didn't take him very long to find one either. He walked across Neptune Street and quickly descended upon the sandstone bluffs that fronted Windansea. The thick vines of green ice plant would make hunting for lizards more difficult; the reptilian critters had more places to hide from eager little boys. Chris finally spotted one sitting on a small ledge just outside its dirt hole. He snuck up quietly from behind and without hesitation snared it barehanded.

"Gotcha, ha, ha," he yelled excitedly, looking around to see if anyone had been watching.

The surprised lizard squirmed and wriggled in his hands. He placed the small dragon inside the can and looked around for more. That's when Chris noticed another young boy about his age also hunting lizards farther north on the bluff. Times like these often triggered emotional battles within Chris. He had made several new friends at school, but no one he truly considered to be his best friend. While eager to try and make a new friend, protecting his lizard hunting domain was equally if not more important. The aggressive side of his personality began to emerge. He would guard the newly caught lizard with his life.

The other boy had seen Chris, too, and began heading in his direction. Chris clutched the coffee can even tighter as the boy approached.

"Hi there," he said. "My name is Jim...Jim Neri. I just moved here. What's your name?"

Many of the events in Chris's earlier years had taught him to be suspicious of certain things —especially new people. So at first he was standoffish, but this new kid was basically the same age and height as he was and had the same long blond hair. Chris eased up on the attitude and extended a greeting.

"My name is Chris...Chris O'Rourke. I'm from New Jersey," he answered, sounding somewhat apologetic.

Out of nowhere, Jim began to laugh, and Chris's mood changed instantly. Maybe he had been right after all. Maybe this new kid couldn't be trusted either.

"What's so funny?" Chris responded, obviously irritated.

"Oh, I'm sorry, Chris. It's just that I'm from New Jersey, too."

"Now that's kind of weird," replied Chris.

After a few minutes of getting to know each other, they began to forge a connection.

"Catch any lizards yet?" asked Jim.

"Only one so far," Chris answered, shrugging his shoulders.

"I have a net, and I try and trap em' with it. But they're always too fast for me."

Chris snickered, amused that Jim hadn't caught one yet.

"I only use my hands," Chris boasted. "The first one I spotted never even saw me coming."

Chris held out the coffee can with the lizard hunkered down inside for Jim to see.

"You really caught him by using only your hands?" Jim asked in amazement. "Wow, that's great! He's a pretty big one, too."

"Yeah, I know. I don't even bother catching the little ones."

"Well since you're the expert, maybe you can show me how to catch them using only my hands," requested Jim.

They began hunting for the little beasts together. On this day at least, Chris was glad to have a lizard hunting companion.

"Hey Jim, after we're finished let's go look for some mice that we can feed to my snake, George," said Chris excitedly.

"Wow, you have a snake too?"

"Yeah, a California Striped Racer, it's a really rare snake. I caught him on the Torrey Pines golf course. I'll show him to you later," Chris promised.

This new kid is too much! Jim thought to himself.

The new friends moved south down the coast. Chris spotted another lizard hiding amid a dense patch of ice plant. He furiously attempted to capture it, but this particular dragon skillfully eluded him. Unwilling to concede defeat, Chris continued his pursuit. After a few minutes, he pulled his hands from the ice plant with the lizard wriggling between his fingers.

Jim was impressed by his new friend's determination, and they continued to comb the bluff for more reptiles. Since school was out for the summer, time was of no concern. A bright golden glow from the late afternoon sun began to light up the La Jolla coastline. All day long Windansea had been crowded with surfers hustling to catch waves, but the two boys could not have cared less. A strong friendship was blossoming between them and, consumed by lizard-hunting, they paid little attention to the lone surfer walking toward them.

"Hey, what are you kids doing over there?" he shouted.

The duo had spotted another lizard in a nearby bush and ignored his question. Perturbed, the surfer walked over to take a closer look.

"Hey you kids, I said what—" he started to ask but was quickly cut off.

"Shut up already, you shit head," Chris snapped angrily. "You're gonna scare him away."

At first the older surfer was startled by the young upstart's aggressive tone but quickly regained his composure.

Unbeknownst to Chris the guy was Eric Shelky, a close friend of his brother. When he realized what the two of them were doing, Eric couldn't help but laugh.

"You little kids are hunting for lizards?" he chuckled. "You've got to be kidding me. Man, there are a lot better things you could be doing than that. What a waste of time."

Chris wished the guy would go away and leave them alone, but Eric only continued his rant.

"Hey wait a minute, I know you. Aren't you Bart's little brother?"

"I'm not telling you," said Chris. "Just stop talking to us."

But the surfer wasn't about to do that.

"Just look out there in the ocean. Don't you see your brother out there riding the waves?" he exclaimed, pointing out to where Bart was surfing. "That's what you two kids should be doing—riding a surfboard just like him, not in here hunting for lizards and squirrels."

"Hey stupid, we're not hunting for squirrels," responded Chris, now standing up to confront the surfer.

"You guys are both dumb ignorant kids," Eric mumbled under his breath.

Figuring that his lecturing was going nowhere, he finally began walking up the bluff toward the parking lot.

"What an idiot," remarked Jim.

"Who cares about him anyway? Besides, we're done here, so let's go to my house!"

They quickly ran down the beach away from the waves. Suddenly, Chris heard the ocean roar like he never had before. Turning to look, he saw an extra-large set of waves cresting outside the Windansea lineup. The two boys were several blocks away, but they could still hear the surfers in the parking lot yelling in excitement.

Until that moment, Chris had never paid much attention to the surfers. He thought they all just looked like corks bobbing upon the water. But now, for whatever reason, strange inner forces tugged at him. He was mesmerized by that large group of waves and the reaction it had caused. He watched intently as a surfer paddled to catch one. After taking several deep strokes, the surfer rose to his feet and glided along effortlessly. For a fleeting moment Chris imagined he was on that board. But why? After all, he had never been interested in surfing before.

Chris recalled the teasing he had just endured from the older surfer. A sense of guilt suddenly overcame him. By not participating was he indeed blowing it?

"Come on, Chris, let's go," said Jim while walking away.

But Chris continued to stare at the ocean. The seed had been planted. It would not be long now.

Chris had made several friends since moving to La Jolla, but none would be as close as Jim. He was one of only a few people Chris respected, and that summer they did everything together. In the fall, they were both fifth grade classmates at La Jolla Elementary, and they soon met other boys in their class who liked hanging around Windansea: George Brolaski, Dylan Jones, Bob Andrews, and Randy MacDonald.

Chris had always been a bit shy around girls his own age. But his bashfulness rapidly began to subside. Rikki Pearson was still a favorite, and Shauna Buffington and Lori Krug soon joined the list of girls he liked in class. Their inner circle was now complete. The summer of 1968 had just ended, but for all of them, life was only beginning.

Chapter 5

The Marine Room

December 1969

Chris had settled into La Jolla quite well. He was having fun with his new circle of friends, and the next year went by in a blur. He always noticed the surfers out in the ocean at Windansea, yet there remained little interest in the activity for him. But something was about to take place that would pique his interest.

The winter of 1969 was an unusual one. Large storms in the northern Pacific brought huge waves that viciously pounded the entire California coastline. Even the most seasoned La Jolla residents hadn't seen waves this large before. Normally a safe swimming and scuba-diving area with calm and tranquil waters, the La Jolla Cove became awash in towering surf. The unusual sight sent many of San Diego's residents flocking to the shoreline to take in all the action.

Chris and Bart went over to La Jolla Cove for a look. Some of the bigger waves measured over three stories high, but out in the churning waters they noticed a few brave surfers. One of these was Rick Grigg, a noted big wave rider from the Hawaiian Islands. Watching Rick and the others in such death-defying surf, Chris became immensely inspired. Bart could see the astonished look on his little brother's face.

While Bart loved riding the waves at Windansea, he also enjoyed venturing to other local surf breaks and often brought Chris along in an effort to entice him into surfing. Someone still needed to keep an eye on Chris, and that honor had now been bestowed upon Bart. Chris didn't mind tagging along with his brother. His father was still unemployed and continued to be downright cruel to his youngest son. Chris couldn't stand being around him. On those occasions that reached the boiling point, his brother made sure to get Chris out of the house.

La Jolla Shores was easy to access and surf, and Chris began to notice that the waves there were much different than Windansea. The swells appeared longer, broader, and not as clearly defined. Most of these waves came crashing down at once for a hundred yards in each direction. At Windansea, the waves broke in a more defined peak: highest in the middle with a slow peel in both directions. His brother told him the differences between the two surf breaks were caused by the bottom contours beneath the water. The Shores was a beach break where waves peeled over sand in virtually the same depth of water. Windansea, on the other hand was a reef break where the waves passed over an uneven rocky bottom.

Chris wasn't sure exactly what all that meant, but Bart's explanation did allow him to become more astute at judging waves. The main surfing break at the Shores was situated in the middle of the long beach, near a small lifeguard tower. But the waves here appeared considerably smaller than those at the northern end. This stretch of beach was home to the world-renowned Scripps Institution of Oceanography and its distinctive pier. To the south, the wave heights decreased in size. At the southernmost end of the beach was a surf break known as the Marine Room. Fronted by the posh La Jolla Beach and Tennis Club, and named after the resort's upscale restaurant where the waves routinely crashed against the windows, the Marine Room was an ideal location for beginning surfers. The waves here were relatively easy to ride, even for someone as diminutive as Chris.

One day after watching his brother ride waves at the Shores, Chris finally felt the urge to give it a try. He actually felt embarrassed that it had taken him this long to discover surfing. It had been right there in front of him the entire time. Before he would ever paddle out at Windansea, he first had to learn how to surf, period.

The waves at Marine Room presented the perfect opportunity. Bart had begun to make and shape his own surfboards, so for Chris's eleventh birthday Bart made his younger brother a surfboard. The end result was a hideous-looking piece of equipment, but it was a surfboard nonetheless. After seeing it for the first time, Lyn immediately referred to the odd-looking shape as "the pregnant prune."

In spite of the new board, Chris switched his stance and again behaved as if he weren't interested.

"Surfing is for goons," Chris told his brother, still too hung up on his pride. He wanted to be a leader, not a follower.

Bart kept chiding him. He knew Chris wanted to try, but it was in his nature to resent anything he felt was being forced upon him. Bart was disappointed, but he also knew his little brother's character well. It was time to light the fuse.

"Yeah Chris, I figured you really wouldn't want to use it anyway," Bart chided. "And even if you did, you probably wouldn't be very good at it."

Bart knew this sort of statement would surely touch a nerve. His little brother was the most competitive person he had ever known. True to form, Chris stormed off in a pout. But a few minutes later he returned and politely asked Bart to take him surfing at the Marine Room. Bart smiled and did not hesitate.

"Here, you're going to need this too," Bart told Chris, handing him a small black neoprene wetsuit. "Spring is just starting, and the water is still cold."

The tattered wetsuit had a few holes and was hardly in the best condition. Still, the sight of it brought a smile to Chris's face. Now he was really equipped! The brothers set off for the Marine Room. They unbuckled the two surfboards from the roof of the car and walked down to the beach together. The surfboard Bart had made for Chris measured 7'2"—fairly large and heavy for such a small kid, but the extra length and flotation were ideal for a beginner. The initial challenge wasn't riding it, but carrying it to the water. As Chris trudged through the soft sand, the heavy board kept slipping from his hands.

"Try tucking it under your arm like me," Bart suggested. "Or better yet, place it on top of your head and balance it by using both your arms."

"Yeah Bart, that won't do me much good. This thing is so heavy. There's no way I can do that!" protested Chris, rankling at the tip.

"Just grip each rail of the board firmly with your hands and hold it steady."

A dubious Chris raised the board precariously over his head and, to his surprise, discovered he could carry his own board! Upon reaching the water's edge, the two of them stood there for several minutes watching the small waves. Chris just stared out into the dark ocean. The water felt cold, and he hoped the warm morning air would make up for it. Small waist-high waves gently peeled over the sand. Not a word was said between them. Bart didn't want to rush—he knew that Chris had to make the first move.

Then it happened. As if he had finally received an indication that it was now okay to enter, Chris picked up his new board and set out into the ocean. Nothing was going to stop him now. Bart trailed along a short distance behind. Chris put his new board on the water's surface and gingerly crawled onto it. He centered his body on its deck, then leaned over and began paddling out to where the waves were breaking.

What Bart saw next took him completely by surprise. He watched as Chris angled toward a small set of incoming breakers. Rather quickly, he turned the large board around and began stroking one arm at a time toward shore. With each paddle, he became less awkward. His arms plunged deeper into the water in an attempt to gain more speed. His mind raced with emotions. This was the moment he had been thinking about for a long time. Chris badly wanted to know what riding a wave felt like—and now he would find out.

As the small wave began to crest, he rose to his feet. For a few seconds, Chris felt awkward and unsure about this new sensation, but his confidence quickly set in. He found his balance and turned his board sideways along the wave's watery face. Gaining speed, he rode it all the way to the sand, as if he had done this a thousand times before. It was his very first wave.

Bart's jaw dropped. A surfer's first wave was never supposed to look that easy. Yet he was not entirely surprised. Chris always did have a knack for picking up on things rather quickly. Bart immediately joined him. It didn't matter if the surf that day was puny compared to what he was normally used to. The opportunity to finally go surfing with Chris was something he couldn't pass up.

For the next several hours the brothers surfed together. When the sun dropped below the horizon they finally came in, but only because it was so dark they couldn't see anymore. While the two had not always bonded in the past, this shared experience seemed to make up for everything. Riding the waves with each other seemed to foster a newfound respect, and Bart had an instant appreciation for Chris's fledgling ability. He had hardly fallen off his board during the entire session.

As they drove back home in the twilight, he knew from the look on Chris's face this was the beginning of something very special. Chris had obviously fallen in love with surfing, a feeling that couldn't be stopped or fought. This was pure addiction, a feeling only a surfer would know.

From the earliest years of his life, Chris had been attracted to things for their purity. He wanted simple things to stay simple and not become too complicated. This same train of thought now lent itself to his new favorite activity. On this day surfing had been a serendipitous act; moving forward, he vowed, he would ride each and every wave cleanly, with pureness and style.

But his timing could not have been worse. The specter of family uncertainty began to rear its ugly head once more. Chris again noticed some familiar signs that things with his parents were not working out. There was heightened tension, his father's regular drinking became excessive, and there was never enough money for anything.

His intuition proved to be correct. La Jolla had provided temporary stability for his father, but his financial situation wasn't any better. It was a fact so obvious to family members that he didn't even try and hide it anymore. So Chris conscientiously made a decision to create a separation between him and his father by focusing on distractions. And the biggest distraction was surfing.

That summer, Chris surfed nearly every day. Not at Windansea yet; he was still too intimidated. He stuck to the Shores and Pacific Beach, and sometimes it was hard to find transportation to get there. But his surfing ability noticeably increased each time he ventured out into the ocean. In just a few short months, Chris graduated from the Marine Room to the main peak at La Jolla Shores. Soon he began referring to the Marine Room as being for sissies.

One day Chris was surfing at the Shores when a few of his brother's buddies marveled over the younger O'Rourke's talents, including La Jolla standouts Reed and Joel Mayne, Tim Lynch, and Rusty Preseindorfer. Chris's confidence grew further after hearing their compliments, and he relished the attention of the older surfers.

Then the bad news arrived. By late summer of 1970, life started to unravel again for his parents. His mother informed him they would be leaving La Jolla and moving back to New York again. Upon hearing this, 11-year-old Chris responded with an obscenity-laced tirade that would've made a longshoreman blush. He quickly stormed out of the house, refusing to believe what he had just heard. Furious and frustrated, Chris fled to Jim Neri's house on Kolmar Street a few blocks away.

"Jim, you're the best friend I've ever had, and I don't want to leave here," Chris told him.

The two boys had long ago discovered how many similarities they shared. Jim had also started surfing, and his father was never around much either. Chris had absolutely no intention of moving back to New York. So he spent that night at Jim's house, and the night after that, and the night after that. Chris's mother knew where he was and figured it was best to let her youngest son cool down for a while.

Finally it came time to leave La Jolla, and there was nothing Chris could do about it. Despite his young age, there was already a wellspring of anger within him—certainly more than any kid should have. He couldn't understand why his life was so unstable and chaotic. The rug had been yanked out from under him once more. Why was this happening over and over again?

Chris had not yet challenged the waves at Windansea, the one place he had vowed to surf and his motivation for learning in the first place. The waves there had a powerful allure that kept beckoning him. He kept that singular thought alive in his mind, knowing that one day he would return to answer the challenge.

While Bart and Lyn remained in San Diego, Chris reluctantly returned to New York with his parents. They rented a small cottage in East Hampton on Long Island. Chris was understandably depressed. It wasn't just the waves he had lost, but all his friends, too. He walked alone along the shores of the Atlantic, staring out into a gray and stormy ocean. Chris could not believe his misfortunes. He had found his calling in life— surfing—and being here seemed like such a waste of time.

All Chris could think about were the waves back at Windansea. He visualized what it would feel like to surf there. He had come so close. One night Chris dreamed that he traveled back to California and became a famous surfer. He woke up and ran into his parents' bedroom, pleading with them to return to California. Chris was a long way from where he really wanted to be. All he wanted was a normal life. But did he even know what a normal life was?

Chris would not have many prayers answered in his life. But for once, luck was on his side. Incredibly—or perhaps typically—after being back in New York for only two months, his father announced they would be returning to La Jolla. Upon hearing the news, Chris jumped so high with excitement that he nearly hit the ceiling.

Though Chris was thrilled to be going back to California, the quick exodus from New York felt undeniably shady. The saga was one that his father still refused to talk about; his situation had gone on for so long now that it didn't seem to matter anymore. But Lyn knew that her father was still being pursued by organized crime. Returning to New York had only been an attempt to appease them.

On October 17, 1970, Chris and his parents returned to La Jolla, eventually settling into an apartment in the La Jolla Shores area. Chris didn't mind living far from Windansea. Returning to La Jolla was all that mattered. Now he could walk to the Shores and go surfing whenever he wanted.

Chris's father was aware that his youngest son's involvement with surfing had become virtually unstoppable. He issued an ultimatum.

"Chris, either you take the time to learn how to surf and compete professionally one day, or you go to summer school. It's your choice," Bart told him.

Being offered advice from his dad had been a rarity in the past. His father's latest words felt like a vague attempt to reach out to him, and he didn't need any further counsel about which road to choose.

Chapter 6

Our Paths Finally Cross

November 1970

After years of constant upheaval and moving from place to place at a moment's notice, Chris's path brought him to my neighborhood and Scripps Elementary School.

Compared to his topsy-turvy life, mine was sweet stability. Since kindergarten, I'd pretty much always had the same classmates and friends and spent most of my free time at the beach. Over the past year, I'd probably whizzed right by Chris on my bike and never even noticed him. One day, just before Thanksgiving of 1970, that all changed.

Early that morning I set off for school by taking the shortcut behind our house. The dirt path stretched through a large vacant lot, making it easy to hunt for lizards along the way. Like Chris, I liked to catch the little dragons, and they were always a fun distraction before school. But with winter approaching, the mornings were colder, and there were no lizards in sight.

I was in sixth grade. For some reason our class had two teachers—Mr. Welsh and Mrs. Harris. They were both fair people who only became strict when really necessary; it took something monumental to make them angry. Since the other kids in my class were fairly easygoing, that didn't happen very often. Today, however, would be an exception.

We took our seats as the school bell sounded. All seemed normal, until we noticed the new kid sitting over on the far side of the room. His long blond locks partially covered his sunburned face, and he stared blankly down at his desk, making no effort to acknowledge any of the other students around him. As the class settled down, Mr. Welsh introduced our new arrival.

"Okay kids, before we get started today, I would like to announce that we have a new pupil among us. His name is Chris O'Rourke. He just moved here from New York and will be—"

"Actually, teacher," the new kid interrupted in a rather condescending tone. "That's not true. I'm not really from New York. I used to live here in La Jolla. But then my parents had to go to New York for a few months. So it's not like I haven't lived here before. I just thought you might want to know that, Mr. Teacher."

Several seconds passed, and Mr. Welsh didn't say a word. Perplexed, I wondered what was coming next.

"Well, thank you for clearing that up, Mr. O'Rourke," he finally replied.

Chris appeared surprised. No one had ever called him "Mr. O'Rourke" before. But that would be the least of his concerns. Mr. Welsh had obviously been irritated by Chris's demeanor. We all knew that, if there was one thing our teacher wouldn't tolerate, it was being interrupted. He instructed Mrs. Harris to take over the class. Then he stepped outside to vent. Without realizing it, the new kid had already broken the teacher's golden rule. Watching Chris from afar, I had the distinct impression he hardly cared.

The new boy seemed so indifferent to what was going on around him. He radiated confidence, but there was a lot of arrogance, too. I was curious. Why would a young boy act like that? I would soon find out.

February 1971

Chris's next few months at my school were similar to that first day. He hardly spoke to anyone, seemed completely disinterested in class and his fellow classmates, and made no effort to become involved with activities. Remarkably, though, he achieved "A" grades on most of his tests. His daily routine never varied. He barely made it to his desk each morning before the school bell rang, and at the end of the day he was the first kid out the door. Chris always seemed to be in a hurry. He sprinted off as if his life depended on it.

Most of my friendships were already well-established; I had my gang, and none of us rode the waves on surfboards. But something about Chris intrigued me. Unlike the rest of us, he was uninhibited and didn't care what other people thought of him. On those rare occasions when he did communicate, he was either very friendly or extremely brash and self-centered. We couldn't have been less alike. Or so I thought.

After school I usually hurried home, too, to drop off my books, hop onto my bike and pedal off to the beach. I rode up and down the long boardwalk, deciding how to spend my time— playing in the grassy park, body-surfing the waves in the shore break, or combing the tide pools for shells and marine life.

One afternoon I stopped to watch the surfers out at the Shores. I parked my bike and sat down on the soft sand. Since I didn't surf on a board, I was hardly an expert on the intricacies of the sport. So I watched and tried to learn. The first thing I noticed was how each surfer had his or her own individual style and ability. Some surfers rode with their back to the wave, while others faced it. A few caught and rode a lot more waves than the others, and for a longer duration. They performed what could best be described as "maneuvers." While not exactly poetry in motion, there was definitely an art to it all.

One surfer in particular really stood out among the rest. Rather diminutive in size, he caught far more waves than anyone else and rode them faster. I truly admired how this particular surfer made it all look so easy. Body-surfing was hard enough for me; balancing on a hard, sharp-edged surfboard upon a fast-moving liquid wall of water looked downright next to impossible.

For a while I continued to stare out at the ocean, but soon the late afternoon glare of the California sun made it harder to see. A silhouetted figure emerged from the waves with a surfboard tucked under his arm and walked in my direction. As he came closer, I realized this was the same surfer who had excelled in the waves. As he approached, I suddenly realized exactly who it was—the new kid, Chris.

As he began to pass by me, I stood up. Up until that moment, we had really only said "hello" a few times at school. I knew that he recognized me, too, but he remained a bit standoffish. So it was up to me to take the initiative.

"Hey Chris, you're in my class at school," I said.

"Yep, I guess I am," he answered rather sheepishly.

"You sure caught a lot of waves out there. I was watching you."

Chris didn't respond.

"I don't know much about surfing, but you looked really good. How do you like living here in the Shores?" I continued.

"It's great as long as I can go surfing everyday," he said, wiping saltwater droplets from his face.

This time he didn't seem to be in such a hurry. Surfing kept him calm. Now he could relax. We continued talking and slowly got to know each other better. It didn't take long for him to open up to me. Chris told me how his family had been forced to move around a lot. Now he was happy to finally be back in La Jolla.

"Have you tried surfing before?" he asked.

I explained how my two older brothers were both surfers, but it wasn't something I had much interest in. I loved the beach, the ocean, and catching waves, but stand-up surfing was still not on my radar.

"Sometimes I ride the waves on my air mat," I told him.

Finding this amusing, Chris just chuckled.

"I was just like you once. I couldn't have cared less about surfing. Then my brother shaped me a board. Now surfing is all I do. Hey, maybe my brother can make you a surfboard, too?"

"Well, let's wait and see," I said, not quite ready to take that step.

"Before I moved to the Shores, I used to live up by Windansea. My brother still goes surfing up there a lot," Chris continued.

I was only in the sixth grade, but I had heard whispers of this place "Windansea" before. And to be honest, most of it wasn't good. The place was compared to the Wild West; it was home to fierce surfing locals, loose women, fights, drugs, and parties that were regularly raided by the police. Or so I was told. There was no doubt that Windansea was the cultural epicenter of the La Jolla surfing scene. Given his arrogant behavior at school, it came as no surprise that this enigmatic kid had previously lived around there. I was beginning to understand him, but I was still a bit awestruck.

"Wow! You really used to live up near there?"

"Right across the street from the beach," Chris boasted. "Our family was there for about three years. I used to go to La Jolla Elementary School and had a lot of friends there."

"Is that why you don't talk to anybody much at our school?" I asked, somewhat hesitantly.

"I don't know. I guess. All my real friends are at another school. Sitting there at that desk everyday, to be honest, all I can think about is hearing that bell ring, so I can go surfing."

"How come you had to leave La Jolla Elementary?" I asked.

Up until this point, Chris's mood had been light. But now his brow furrowed and his feet squirmed about in the sand. Was I asking too many questions? He hesitated and looked unwilling to relive whatever was going through his mind.

"We had to leave because of my dumb dad's job, or no job, or I'm not even sure anymore," he said. His voice dropped an octave. "My parents and I had to go back to New York for a little while to straighten things out. I didn't want to go, but I had no choice. Now we are back here, and that's all I care about."

"So where do you live now?" I asked.

"In an apartment a few blocks away near the 7-11. My mom told me it's only for a little while though. My dad keeps saying we're broke. But we're supposed to be moving near Windansea again soon. When that happens I'll transfer back to La Jolla Elementary."

Wanting to change the subject, Chris looked at me quizzically.

"What about you, Aeder? Where do you live?" he says.

Until then no one had ever really called me by my last name, and it sounded weird to me. At school Chris had always appeared very self-centered. Now I was a bit surprised he showed a genuine interest in me.

"I live about five blocks away on Vallecitos," I finally replied.

"How long have you lived there?"

"For about as long as I can remember," I told him.

Chris raised his eyebrows, appearing a bit mystified. Compared to all his relocations, what I had just told him must have seemed incomprehensible. I certainly hadn't known him for very long, but it was apparent he had already gone through a lot in his life. He seemed reluctant to answer some of my questions, and I decided that was why he acted so secretive at school. Explaining his life to others was something he didn't want to do—until now.

"Isn't it hard changing schools all the time?" I asked.

"Yeah, it is. But by now I'm pretty used to it."

I sensed a lot of pain in his words. Moving around certainly hadn't been the only challenge in his life; there were obviously many more. I had been blinded by ignorance. Right then I realized that not all kids grew up in a safe, stable environment as I had.

A cool breeze began to blow as the sun inched closer to the horizon. A few other surfers hurried past us on their way out of the water.

"You know, Aeder, I also like to hunt for lizards, and look for things in the tide pools," he said.

"Me, too!" I replied in excitement.

Exploring the tide pools and hunting for lizards. At least here were a few interests we had in common.

"Anyway, Aeder, it's time for me to go. I'll see you around. Let me know if you want to get a surfboard, and I'll tell my brother," he said, turning to walk away.

"See you later, Chris."

I watched as he scampered over to the showers to rinse off. I felt glad that I had finally made his acquaintance.

Over the next few weeks, we spoke to each other more and more often at school and the beach, and I sure learned a lot more about surfing. Chris had more surf stories than I could keep up with and always told them with a smile. When it came to his family life, though, he continued to keep his guard up. When he did talk about it, he spoke with a frown. I became aware that Chris had a very complicated personality with a variety of dispositions: funny Chris, angry Chris, genius Chris, frustrated Chris, unprincipled Chris, and Chris who just wanted to be at peace.

I'd had no interest before, but now I was fascinated. The way Chris spoke about surfing was captivating, as if nothing else in life mattered. I still rode my bike to the beach after school, only now I pedaled much faster. And I always spotted him out there in the waves.

The better I got to know him, the more I noticed his intense competitiveness. Chris wanted to be the best at everything he did. During our school's annual Presidential Physical Fitness Tests, I beat him in the 100-yard dash. Afterward, I walked over to him and was surprised by his reaction.

"Get away from me, Aeder. I don't want to talk to you," he said, visibly upset.

"Why?" I asked, completely dumbfounded.

Chris walked away without saying another word.

It took him nearly two weeks to get over it, and then we were friends again. I learned the true depth of his competitive nature. Whether it was catching the biggest fish in the tide pool, riding the best wave in the ocean, or finishing first in a foot race, winning meant everything to him.

At school, I was one of just a few kids he established any kind of friendship with. Doug Wiesehan, the only other surfer in our grade, was another. But Chris's polarized personality scared a lot of people away. His temperament wavered constantly and could change on a dime. Still, I tried to understand and be his friend the best I could.

Then one day at school I saw Chris hurriedly approaching. He wore a big smile and was eager to tell me something.

"Hey, Aeder," he said, still calling me by my last name, much like an older boy would. "My dad finally got a new job, and my parents found an apartment to rent over by Windansea. So I'm moving back there next week."

At that moment he was so content, as if complete order had finally been restored in his life. Something about Windansea was in his destiny. It was where he belonged, and I was happy for him. A few days later, his school desk was empty. I rode my bike to the Shores and didn't see him there either. He had finally been reunited with all his "real" friends.

After returning to his former school, Chris became even more of a wisecracker. For his new sixth grade teacher, Mr. Hollenbeck, the timing of his transfer could not have been worse. Chris drove him absolutely crazy. The teacher often stood next to the piano at the front of the class, pounding his fists in frustration. He wondered how a kid could be so brilliant one moment, and so disruptive the next.

Chris didn't care. Only a few months remained before summer vacation, and all he wanted to do was go surfing. Chris took his antics as far as he could without getting kicked out of school.

We were no longer in the same school, but it wouldn't be long until I would see him again.

Chapter 7

Initiation

May 1971

Surfing had become more than just a hobby for Chris. The sport had given him a sense of purpose like nothing before, and it was time to graduate to the next level. Living near Windansea again provided the perfect opportunity. The one-bedroom apartment they had rented was small and cramped, but it was just a stone's throw from the beach. Chris was overjoyed. Now that he was back where he really belonged, it was time to stop watching the waves at Windansea and start surfing them.

It wasn't the power of the waves that intimidated him. No, his hesitation was due to the older surfers who ruled Windansea. A young kid like him entering their domain just wasn't done. Chris was eager to break the barrier, but at what cost?

The transition back to the old neighborhood had made him tougher. His moody behavior worsened, but this only added more fuel to the fire within him. He made a vow to himself: The first time he surfed at Windansea, anyone who gave him a hard time would get a punch in the face in return, no matter how big they were.

Chris still had many friends at La Jolla Elementary, including Bob Andrews and Jim Neri. Bob noticed that this latest version of Chris was more volatile than the one who had been here before. Along with his continued use of profanity, Chris had become skilled with his fists and never hesitated to employ them in response to any perceived slight. One such incident occurred a few weeks before school let out for the summer.

Two larger boys began teasing him about his long sun-bleached hair. Chris immediately challenged them both to a fight, one against two, and beat them both into submission. The incident only reinforced what Bob and several of his classmates already knew. Chris's personality was driven by anger, and if anyone challenged him, they had better be prepared to go to the mat. He was like lightning in a bottle.

Fighting aside, he lived for the waves. I continued to look for him each time I rode my bike to the Shores; life seemed rather boring without him around.

Windansea was his stomping grounds now. At the time, only a few young kids dared to surf there. His friend Brew Briggs was one of them. Brew was a year older than Chris and just as equally taken by surfing—so much so that his skin had turned brown as a berry from constant sun exposure. On several occasions he had encouraged Chris to finally give the place a try.

One evening before sunset, Chris went to Windansea and looked at the waves. He ran into Jim, who was also building up the nerve to paddle out. They saw a set of waves go untouched as they passed the crowded lineup. The sight made Chris cringe.

"What's wrong with those guys out there?" barked Chris. "What a bunch of goons. Neri, look how many waves there are, and no one is even riding them!"

Jim just nodded in agreement. They watched as another set arrived, backlit by the brilliant glow of the sunset. Each transparent wave lit up like a golden crystal. Chris was transfixed. The time for him to surf at Windansea had arrived.

"I'm ready. Tomorrow is the day. Come on, Jim, let's do it," Chris blurted out.

"Sorry, Chris, but I can't go with you," Jim replied. "Our family is going away for the weekend, and we're leaving tonight."

Having his best buddy along would have been nice, but Chris wasn't deterred from his goal.

When he returned home that evening, he found his mom in the kitchen.

"Chris," she asked. "What happened to all your lizards and snakes?"

"I set them free," he replied.

Gloria was relieved. Their small family quarters were bad enough without mixing in a good portion of La Jolla's reptilian population. Yet her son's unusual behavior piqued her interest.

"Why did you do that?" she asked.

"Well Mom, I'm no longer interested in them. There's something more important that I need to do."

It had been a long time since Chris had shared any of his thoughts or feelings with his mother. She knew right away that a significant sea change had occurred in her tempestuous younger boy. And she had a pretty good idea what it was. She didn't necessarily approve of surfing; the Sixties' beach-bum ethic was still firmly etched in everyone's mind, especially in tiny La Jolla. But she welcomed anything that would keep Chris focused and out of trouble. If surfing was it, then so be it.

Chris went into the small converted room he shared with his brother. He closed the door and stared at all the surfing posters Bart had pasted upon the walls. Chris imagined he was one of the surfers in the pictures. No, he wasn't just one of them. He would be even better! In order to do that, first he had to start surfing at Windansea. Tomorrow would be the day. Windansea would provide him with his own special place—a location that he could make his and his alone. A home.

That night he hardly slept. Windansea awaited him, a place more powerful and treacherous than anything he had ever surfed before. Would he be ready?

The next morning Chris hurried out the door with his surfboard and flimsy black wetsuit. He didn't tell anyone where he was going, not even his brother. Moments later, he was standing at the water's edge. He noticed many new things about Windansea now that lizards were no longer his goal: the dark kelp sea beds offshore, the texture of the rocks bristling with colonies of black mussels and goose-neck barnacles, the small flocks of low-flying pelicans. Even the most visible symbol of Windansea, the palm frond thatched hut, looked different.

Chris studied the ocean carefully, gauging where and when to paddle out. Defiant to the end, he wasn't about to ask another surfer about this. While building up his nerve, he noticed Eric Shelky, the same older surfer who had once chastised him for not surfing, at his side.

"Does Bart know you're doing this?" Eric asked.

"No one does," he said.

"Hey Chris, I've seen you surfing at the Shores. I'll give you credit. You're a pretty good little surfer. But it's a whole different ball game out here."

"What? You don't think I can do it?" Chris replied harshly.

"No, it's not that at all," laughed Eric. "Actually, it's just the opposite. If anyone can do it, you can. I've seen how you can be a tenacious little bastard. Just keep in mind that the waves here have a lot more power. I'm sure you will do fine."

The two surfers noticed the ocean had calmed down. It was time to paddle out.

"Do you have enough wax on your board?" Eric asked.

"Duh, what do you think?" snarled Chris, rankling at what he again perceived as condescension from the very sort of surfer whose respect he inwardly craved.

"Fine then, see you out there," said Eric, rolling his eyes at the kid's arrogance.

Chris watched as Eric plunged into the water and began paddling out. Chris took a more cautious approach and trailed along a short distance behind. Halfway out to the main surf peak, Eric abruptly came to a halt.

"Okay Chris, right here is where you stop."

"What do you mean?" he asked, puzzled.

"What I mean is this is as far as you go. This part of Windansea is called Right Hooker. The area here is where kids like you hang out and catch their first waves. See those waves farther out there?

Those are for the big boys. You start out in here first, learn how to ride the waves, and then you can come out there."

Chris wasn't sure if he liked this advice at all. He didn't like to follow orders, but for the moment, he obliged. An hour later, however, Chris had not ridden a single wave. There were plenty that he could have caught, except that none of the more established surfers had given him a chance. Since nobody gave away waves at Windansea, he had to fight for a place in the pecking order.

Working his way into a well-established hierarchy wasn't something he was used to. When he had surfed at the Shores, he did whatever he wanted. Much to his dismay, none of his swearing or angry obnoxiousness would cut him any slack in the Windansea arena. He was forced to start at the bottom of the totem pole—and this simply made him more determined to make the place his own.

Chris began to pay closer attention to everything happening around him—the surfers to his left, the surfers to his right, and the set of waves rolling straight toward him. He positioned himself properly in the lineup. A small wave headed in his direction with no other surfer in sight. Chris turned around and began paddling, just as he would have at the Shores. But this wasn't the Shores. Rising to his feet, he suddenly felt a thick wall of water slam into his head. The impact knocked him off his board and pushed him several feet underwater. His body was pounded like a rag doll against the sharp barnacle-covered rocks below as the wave relentlessly punished him.

Several breathless moments of liquid chaos ensued. Chris finally surfaced, coughing and gasping for air. His surfboard was gone—washed into the rocks on shore. He gagged on the salt water, listening to the older guys laugh at him. He was struggling against the current toward shore to retrieve his board, recalling what Eric Shelky had told him about the power of the Windansea surf.

Chris knew it was important to rise to his feet as fast as possible. Forward momentum and speed would drive everything else he did upon the wave. But he had forgotten, and all the older surfers were in hysterics.

"Yeah, welcome to Windansea!" Chris thought.

Their laughter only inspired him more. A few minutes later he paddled back out. An empty wave approached Right Hooker and, determined to show the other guys he could do anything they could, Chris stroked for it like a madman. The wave crested, and this time he stood up quickly. His feet dug firmly into the board's waxy surface, and he slid smoothly down the liquid face. He felt his speed increase as the power of the wave crashed down behind him, but this time he wasn't going to let it land on his head! He steadied his outstretched arms, increasing his balance. And the longer he rode, the more confidence he gained.

After his first official wave at Windansea finally ended, all Chris felt inside was pure jubilation, as if his chest were going to burst. He had dreamed about this moment for what had seemed like forever. One wave at Windansea—and now he knew for certain this was what he wanted to do for the rest of his life.

Over the next few hours, he caught many more. And while Chris may have impressed himself, a Windansea surfer's initiation took far longer than one session. Walking back home should have been a joyous occasion for Chris; instead, he harbored mixed emotions. While the waves were everything he had hoped for, he seethed in anger over how the older surfers had reacted to him.

When he complained to his brother that night, Bart was proud that Chris had finally tackled Windansea but unsympathetic about how he had been treated.

"I told you about the reputation there. So why is it such a surprise? You have to earn it on your own. It's the way things are. To them you're only a little punk kid," Bart told him. "And just because you're my brother doesn't mean those guys are going to give you any waves. They certainly didn't give me any when I first went out there. Just put in your time and soon you will be one of the local guys laughing at all the new guys."

It was one of the few times that his brother's words actually sunk in. Chris was bound and determined that the next time would be different. When he returned the following day, an impressive set of waves loomed on the horizon. Chris immediately noticed how two older surfers tried to prevent him from catching one. But he had anticipated this.

"Look at the kid," one of them said. "He thinks he can get away from us."

The two surfers surrounded him, and it appeared Chris would be denied again. What they hadn't counted on, however, was the young upstart's competitiveness. Though Chris had never surfed in an official contest, he had already become quite the surfing tactician. His astuteness in the water was amazing; he read the ocean's movements better and reacted faster than just about anyone. As the surfers chased after him, Chris quickly paddled the pair into the deep water channel and away from the lineup. Suddenly Chris turned around and stroked mightily in the opposite direction. When the best wave of the set arrived, he was the one riding it. Seeing their buddies get outdone by a kid, the other surfers in the water didn't hesitate to chastise them about it.

This was a defining moment for Chris. The locals backed off, and before long he rode almost any wave he wanted. Earning further respect didn't take long. Over the next few months he was accepted into the Windansea hierarchy faster than any other young surfer before him.

As his acceptance grew, so did his ego. His bold personality fueled a formidable, constant craving for attention. Just surfing at Windansea wasn't enough. He wanted to embrace the radical ethics of localism that were ingrained into its history. His fists became part of his repertoire, and since fights at Windansea happened all the time, his reputation grew accordingly.

Chris wasn't even in the seventh grade yet. So it was astounding to see such a young kid never back down from a fight, especially since his opponents were usually older and much bigger. Driven by the need to prove himself right from the start, he quickly ascended the Windansea ladder. Soon, "the kid" could paddle out and take any seat in the entire lineup: inside at Right Hooker, or outside with the big boys.

The older surfers began referring to him as "the screamer." Each time Chris paddled out, he acted as if he owned the place, glaring and screaming loudly at anyone he didn't know.

"Kooks go home!" he shrieked at them.

The older Windansea crew who had once put Chris through a harsh initiation of his own now openly embraced him. He became the tough young kid who was willing to do the dirty work for them.

But not all of Windansea's surfers were proud of its reputation. Some of them thought that even Chris took matters too far, including Brew Briggs. As one of Chris's surfing mentors, Brew had taught him more about Windansea than anyone else. Chris greatly admired Brew's polished regular-foot surfing style; in fact, they rode the waves in such a similar manner that it was downright eerie.

One day they were surfing together at Right Hooker when Brew saw trouble coming. A surfer whom Chris didn't recognize was paddling out. Even from a distance, Brew could tell by the angry look on Chris's face that a confrontation seemed inevitable. A wave approached, and Chris paddled for it. But the new surfer could not get out of his way. A violent collision ensued.

The other surfer had ruined Chris's opportunity, and there was little question as to what would happen next. After the wave passed over them, Chris and the surfer emerged from the froth of whitewater. Chris unleashed a verbal tirade that resonated loudly throughout the lineup. They never came to blows, but the bickering between them continued for several more minutes. Eventually they had to be separated. Brew waited until the other surfer paddled away before speaking with Chris.

"Don't you realize that guy is your neighbor? He lives on the same street only about five houses away from you. Chris, you must try and settle down a bit. You can't get into fights with everyone," Brew scolded, shaking his head.

Chris had always had enormous respect for Brew. Initially he bristled at his friend's suggestion, but the more Brew talked, the more Chris seemed to calm down—or pretended to, for his friend's sake. Brew easily saw through his act and wasn't about to let him get off that easy.

"You know something, Chris? I've been thinking about it, and it's not just about what happened today. I used to get angry at others, too, much like the way you do now. But sometimes it's just not worth it. Like how we treat those two guys, Mark Ruyle and Ted Smith, so horribly. We always kick them out of the lineup and chase them in, yelling at them to go back to Pacific Beach and everything else. Who cares what they do? Mark and Ted are cousins and have always been very nice and respectful each time they come to Windansea. We are the ones—actually, you are the one who is being such a jerk. It's so wrong to do that," counseled Brew.

To Chris, this was an entirely new philosophy. His bloodshot eyes were angry, but inside he knew his friend was right. He didn't always have to act like that. Brew knew that Chris's actions were mostly a way for him to fit in. But the anger was also a release valve for the disrespect he still felt toward his father, and that wasn't about to change. Out of respect for Brew, however, Chris would give it a try.

Chris's first few months at Windansea were an equal mix of the good, the bad, and the ugly. The pairing of the turbulent young man with such a volatile environment created sparks on the La Jolla surfing scene, long one of the most venerable and colorful in all of California. Windansea had never seen the likes of Chris before. Considering Windansea's sordid history, this statement alone spoke volumes.

Well before Chris O'Rourke ever arrived on the scene, the area had a strong reputation for localism. In Tom Wolfe's infamous novel The Pumphouse Gang published in 1968, one chapter provided a vivid, albeit slightly outlandish, portrayal of the Windansea surfing culture. Epic tales of glorious surfing adventures, lewd and rowdy behavior, and run-ins with the police were regular occurrences. Unfortunately Wolfe's writings never touched upon Windansea's good aspects; the majority of the people who frequented it were actually very good-natured.

Windansea's history dated back to the 1930s when a few young La Jolla High School kids became infatuated with surfing. The first locals were known as the Plant Boys and included Woody Brown, Don Okey, Towney Cromwell, Buddy Hull, and Fred Kenyon Sr.

After World War II, new faces began to emerge: Woody Ekstrom, Bob Simmons, and Pat Curren. In 1946 the Hawaiian grass shack was constructed on the bluff fronting the surf break and soon became the most recognizable symbol of Windansea. Bob Simmons in particular would go on to have a profound worldwide influence upon the sport. He attended the California Institute of Technology where he studied hydro and aerodynamics. Bob also loved to shape surfboards, so it was only natural for him to apply what he learned to surfboard design.

Practically overnight, the new Styrofoam core he created became the most innovative in the world. Surfboards became lighter, thinner, and much more maneuverable. His concept soon allowed surfers to ride waves at locations previously thought too dangerous, one of which was an unnamed spot just north of Windansea.

On September 26, 1954, Simmons rode his last wave there. He drowned during an unusually large swell, and his body wasn't found until several days later. The dangerous surf break was posthumously named after him: Simmons's Reef. The legacy he left behind was immense. His technological breakthrough in surfboard design forever altered the future of the sport. This made it possible for a few outstanding surfers here to get their start, particularly Butch Van Artsdalen and Mike Doyle.

Butch found solace surfing a spot several hundred yards to the south of Windansea that came to be known as Big Rock. The dangerous tubular nature of the waves at Big Rock provided a formidable challenge, but it didn't take long for Butch to master them. A few years later he went on to conquer the most dangerous surf break in the world at the time: the Banzai Pipeline in Hawaii. As such, Butch established himself as the original "Mr. Pipeline."

In the meantime La Jolla had gained the reputation as "the master bedroom of San Diego County." The area around Windansea was the county's most prime stretch of real estate. Tall palm trees and impressive marquee homes were nestled together above white crystallized sand inlets. But not all of La Jolla's famous surf breaks were found along Neptune Street. Another spot nearby known as Horseshoe was so mesmerizing it was only spoken about in whispers.

Each new generation of Windansea's surfers was expected to keep the localism tradition alive. Chris had now earned his spot in the pecking order not only by being a good surfer, but also by being a good fighter. Even when he was joking around, you could sense the anger lurking just beneath the surface. It was here, amid this charged atmosphere, that he would become one of the most talented young surfers in the world.

Chris's talents were soon noticed by a prominent figure among surfing's elite. Mike Purpus was the most recognized surfer in California at the time. A fixture within organized competitive surfing, Purpus lived and surfed in the South Bay of Los Angeles. He was nearly twelve years older than Chris and already had several years of contest experience under his belt.

One of Mike's best friends had been Scott Briggs, Brew's older brother. A few years before, Scott had tragically died in a car accident during a surf trip to Mexico. Mike made it a point to take Brew under his wing ever since, especially when it came to surfing. He introduced Brew to many of his older surfing buddies from San Diego, including well-known surfers Gary Goodrum, Gary Keating, Steve Seebold, and Rusty Preseindorfer.

Late in the summer, Mike called Brew to see if he wanted to go surfing at Trestles in North San Diego County. Brew asked him if it was okay to bring along a friend. Mike had never met Chris, and he chuckled over the sight of the two young freckle-faced surfers pulling their surfboards out from the rear of his car.

Chris felt a bit out of his element at Trestles. The waves were nearly eight feet! But he still wanted to act cool.

The waves seemed gigantic to two little surfers like Chris and Brew, so they didn't catch many. But surfing with Mike had been a great experience, and Chris politely thanked him. The king of competitive surfing in California, Mike had no way of knowing that, in just a few years, "little" Chris O'Rourke would become his biggest rival.

Chapter 8

Statusphere

Knowing how all-consuming Chris's devotion to surfing had become, his parents braced for the worst when school resumed in the fall. For both of us, elementary school finally had become a thing of the past. Seventh grade meant that I would now be transferring to Muirlands Junior High School—and so would Chris.

I knew that it wouldn't be long until I saw Chris again. I ran into him during my first week at Muirlands and said hello, but he walked past as if he didn't know me. Judging by the way he acted at school over the next few days, it appeared his arrogance had intensified. He seemed very impressed with himself, particularly when hanging out with all of his surfing buddies. In between classes one day, I saw him standing in the narrow hallway close to my locker. I said hello to him again, and at least this time he remembered my name.

"Hey Aeder, how's it going? Are you still living in the Shores?" he asked somewhat condescendingly.

"Yeah, O'Rourke, as a matter of fact I am," I said, figuring that I could speak like that, too.

"Well, you won't be any good as a surfer living down there. Tell your parents to get a house over where I live near Windansea."

As if it was that easy. Most of the things he said were based on his reality and certainly not on mine. Over the next few months we mostly interacted only at school, and I knew why— because I wasn't a true surfer like he was.

But I was a good listener, and soon he opened up about his past even more. There were stories about his family, including mostly negative ones about his father. His stories of surfing at Windansea, though, always took top billing. Exaggerating to no end, Chris was a good storyteller. He had a way of making you feel that you were right there, too. His stories taught me more about Windansea than I had ever known. Growing up a Shores kid, Windansea had always been out of my comfort zone. Up until then I had steered clear of the place; now, I looked forward to going there. Each visit was more exciting than the last. Surfers in the water, girls in bikinis on the beach—the place just seemed so...festive.

Chris was definitely the fastest surfer in the water, as well as the loudest. I often heard him chiding other surfers, bragging about his rides, or jeering newcomers. He laughed a lot, too. It was apparent he had really made a home for himself here. Chris wasn't always easy to be around and even tougher to read, but I was happy that he had found his calling.

His hyperactively competitive nature hadn't changed at all. In the same amount of time it took his friends to ride one wave, Chris had already ridden four or five. By now Chris knew every surfer at Windansea. There were a few in particular whom he really looked up to: Tom Ortner, Jon Rullo, Andy Tyler, Ron McLeod, and a younger surfer named Mark Brolaski. All of them had lived and surfed around Windansea for a long time and were known for having the most soulful surfing styles there. Chris admired them, and soon they became his mentors as well.

While watching them surf, I learned that a surfer's style was "soulful" if he made it look easy. The same concept was true of dynamic maneuvers, the new moves that would become the future of the sport. Tom and Jon were the veteran examples, and a few select surfers at Windansea had perfected the style. But a younger and more dynamic Chris brought a whole new flair to the waves.

By October of 1971, being the hottest young kid at Right Hooker wasn't enough. Chris wanted to prove his competitive talents to everyone, and the only way to do that was through organized surfing contests. Amateur events were growing in popularity along the California coast, and they beckoned to Chris. In early November his brother drove him to Oceanside for his first-ever surf contest. Competing in the division for surfers age twelve years and younger, Chris rode the waves well enough for second place — a good result for his first time out. Except to him, second was as good as last. Unsurprisingly, he threw a tantrum right there on the beach.

"Second? What's wrong with those judges anyway? Are they blind?" he screamed.

"What do you expect, Chris?" Bart counseled, trying to settle him down. "You're twelve years old. I know you think you're hot shit after surfing at Windansea, but you really haven't been doing it all that long. Give it some time."

Those words sounded strange to him. Time simply wasn't an option. Chris wanted to succeed from the outset. Bart's friend Tim Lynch, who had often witnessed Chris's conceited behavior at Windansea, felt that his cocky arrogance would actually breed future success. Refusing to lose was the mark of a champion. So instead of admonishing him, Tim advised Chris to humble his arrogance and speak with his true skills.

His endless hours of surfing, however, began to have a negative effect on his family. Disappointed by how regularly he skipped school, Chris's parents gave him a stern lecture. Chris took it all in stride. A few weeks later, Bart and Gloria became engrossed with their own personal dramas. Any further supervision of their son disappeared, and the toll it took upon him was immediate.

Surfing with his older friends further eroded his tenuous relationship with the educational system. His father preached the importance of staying in school.

"Chris, you can surf all you want to. I don't care. But you have to go to school and stay in school. Even if you flunk all your classes, getting kicked out of school is not an option. Do you understand me? And rather than hanging out with those older Windansea denizens, competitions should become your focal point. If you're going to waste all your time surfing, then one day you should become the best in the world at it."

Bart also realized that his youngest son, in spite of being so obnoxious, did have some redeeming qualities: he had a high IQ, was a quick study, loved his mother, liked to help others, and surprisingly, had a very creative and introspective side.

In spite of his lackluster attitude toward school, Chris enjoyed writing poetry. Chris approached Jim Neri one day shortly before Christmas and read him a few poems he had scribed. Jim was an astute individual and more scholarly than his friend, but when he read Chris's poems he couldn't help but be impressed.

Chris O'Rourke
December 2, 1971
Social Studies

POEMS.......A BOOK
FROGS

If I was a small green frog, and I lived in a Big Brown log,
Early in the night when the light got thinner, I would go out and get my dinner.
I love to lurk in the thick grey fog, and can't survive in the deep brown smog,
Where people die and cities grog.
People die and waste away, but frogs will always be here to stay,
Compared to a dog a frog is small, but the small will live and the big will fall.

So the next time you bite into a frog's leg and say mmm!
  And how good this tastes,
Just wait a minute and take his place, think of the rest of
  his body you'll waste.

SCHOOL

School is a thing that's not for fun, it's not for play it's
  not for none.
School is a game that's hard to play, you go to school
  every weekday.
You go nine months for your education, you have three
  months for your vacation.
You go to school for just to learn, not voluntarily
  following a yearn.

THE GATE

A gate is a symbol of state, hesitate before you penetrate
  a gate.
If you violate and penetrate the gate, you may anticipate
  a terrible fate.

TURTLES

Turtles run jump splash and play, but they do it in their
  own way.
Some turtles snap, put your fingers at their mouth and
  you will get a zap.
Some are big, some are small, some are very tall.
Some are old, some are gross, just look at the Galapagos!
What goes on inside the shell, maybe they just sit and
  yell.
Turtles are nice so don't be mean, they do nothing to
  spoil your scene.
They kill turtles for their eggs, they kill frogs for their
  legs.
Anyone who would kill frogs and turtles, has got to stink,
  so take a while and think.

Chapter 9

Surf Contest Prodigy

January 1972

Eric Shelky and Tim Lynch met Chris at his house early one morning to take him to his second surf contest: The Annual La Jolla Shores Menehune event. Surfers twelve years old and younger were allowed to compete in the local event, and they came from beach areas all around Southern California. Winning the contest was an honor and a rite of passage, especially in La Jolla. Kyle Bakken and Henry Tuomola were two young local surfers who had won in the past, and Chris wanted to win it, too.

At the end of the day, he returned home clutching a small golden trophy. Chris pushed open the apartment door, and the look on his face said it all.

"Hey, Mom! Hey, Dad! I won the contest! I got first place!" he beamed.

His parents smiled wistfully upon seeing their son basking in the glow of victory. He had tasted victory, and there was no turning back now. He entered more contests and quickly learned the ropes of competitive surfing.

For aspiring surfers from California, the WSA (Western Surfing Association) was the only entity that remotely resembled a unified body of competition. Chris had begun in the lowest category possible—the Menehune division. In order to advance to the next WSA level, all he needed to do was win a contest.

He won the first WSA Menehune contest he entered, and the victory promptly elevated him into the Boys 1A division. Two months later at a contest in Pacific Beach, he captured first place again. This catapulted him into the Boys 2A division. He followed that up with another victory in April. Chris had never felt so proud, especially since his mother, sister, and brother had all come along to watch. (His father was nowhere to be seen.)

Eric Shelky continued to lecture Chris about competitive surfing strategy. Also a WSA surfer, Eric competed in the much higher Men's 4A division. He preached techniques that could win surf contests, and Chris listened eagerly.

"You have to be alert for all kinds of tactics. For example, if you are paddling for the same wave as one of your competitors, sometimes they will try and lure you into an interference call. They will pretend to paddle one direction on the wave, but at the last second will go the other way. The surfer who stands up first has the right of way," he advised. "So don't take your eyes off them, or the judges will make an interference call against you. Just try and position yourself in the lineup in order to catch the best waves possible."

Eric's words of wisdom paid immediate dividends, and as a result, Chris's meteoric rise continued. In May he was victorious again, this time at a Boys 3A event in Huntington Beach. Now thirteen years old, he had surfed his way from the 1A into the 3A in less than six months. Normally under these circumstances, if Chris were to win again, he would become eligible to compete in the Juniors category, followed by the Men's 4A division. This elite classification, however, was reserved for only the most established West Coast surfers eighteen years or older. Before Chris, no one had pushed the boundaries of success at such a young age. WSA contest officials found themselves in a bit of a quandary. They finally determined that, while Chris's surfing indeed spoke volumes, for now he would have to be content staying in the Boys 3A.

At first this didn't bother him. He knew his time would come soon enough. But as his trophies piled up, the urge to compete against the best consumed him. In June came another WSA contest at Malibu. Eric and Chris drove up together to the famed surfing break in northern Los Angeles. They were both riding on the same kind of boards shaped by Windansea surfer George Taylor. The surfboards, known as GT3s, were a single-fin pintail shape with turned-down rails.

Chris placed first again.

En route to· La Jolla later that day, Chris learned the perks of winning a surf contest. Eric decided to stop at Tamarack Surfboards in Carlsbad to see a friend. Inside were several bikini-clad eighteen-year-old girls who immediately took a liking to young Chris. They huddled around the little blond-haired surfer everyone seemed to be raving about. The girls began kissing him playfully, and one of them handed Chris a beer. Eric could live it up with the best of them, but watching Chris now he suddenly felt guilty. He hadn't meant to corrupt him. Yet to the victors come the spoils, even if the victor is only thirteen years old

That summer Chris competed in several more WSA contests and received a first, two seconds, and a fourth for his efforts. These results might have been good enough for anyone else, but not for him.

The next contest on his horizon, however, was a very prestigious one. The 1972 World Championships of Surfing would be held in San Diego, and the best competitive surfers in the world would be there. Unfortunately, Chris didn't complete the entry form in time and wasn't allowed to compete. Instead, he used the experience to evaluate the other surfers as a measuring rod for the future.

During the contest he befriended a young surfer from Hawaii named Michael Ho. Their admiration for each other's surfing was mutual, and they discovered that, in spite of their different geographic locations, they shared many similarities.

Chris's ability also caught the eye of more-seasoned foreign surfers—in particular, Australians Peter Townend and Wayne

"Rabbit" Bartholomew. The talented duo had been staying in La Jolla and ventured to Windansea, where they immediately noticed two young surfers terrorizing the waves: Brew and Chris. Although Peter was an outsider, Chris showed no resentment toward him. He could tell that Peter was a talented young surfer just like himself, and Chris liked his accent. This was Peter's first look at one of the hottest young surf kids from America, and while impressed, the Australian was equally as arrogant. They were both fixated upon one day becoming the world champion of surfing.

Chris was always happy to meet other young talented surfers from around the world, yet he treated many of his fellow surfers from California with disdain. Chris was already a hardcore competitor, and he reasoned that, in order to be the best surfer in the world, first he had to be the best in California.

His quest continued after the World Championships. Chris eagerly looked forward to his next WSA competition, and on November 4, 1972, he captured first place at the Santa Cruz Boys 3A Open held at the famous surf break known as Steamer's Lane. His first place total of 2,000 points easily won out over well-known surfers Jeff Hamilton (1,600 points), Mike Weed (1,280), and Kevin Reed (1,000).

A week later Chris finished second to Mike Cruickshank in the Pacific Beach Optimist San Diego 3A Open. The start of that event was plagued by torrential rain squalls with downpours so thick that the judges often could not even see the surfers. But there was no missing Chris's talent.

Chapter 10

Triumph Amid Tragedy

The more Chris surfed, the more the sport enthralled him. The dream of becoming the best surfer ever completely consumed him. He slept, ate, and breathed surfing twenty-four hours a day, and his future only looked brighter.

The same could not be said for his parents. Bart and Gloria had been going through continuous peaks and valleys. They had been forced to move on two more occasions, Gloria began to drink heavily, and Bart's employment situation had not improved in spite of his many awkward attempts.

Since they rarely spoke to each other, Chris had no way of knowing that his father had become very supportive of his surfing. Chris slept over at friends' houses and only came home when he had to, which made him seem like some sort of vagrant kid. Bart seldom had the opportunity to watch his son compete, and it pained him to be unable to convey his sincerity.

To make matters worse, the ghosts of Bart's blunders had caught up with him again. A shady contact from the past had tracked him all the way to La Jolla and had come with a new offer. He told Bart about a new resort "they" were opening in Costa Rica, and if Bart agreed to manage it, his debt would finally be resolved forever.

Hesitant to become involved in this sort of thing again, Bart declined. He wanted no part of the deal, even if it did mean getting him out of hot water. Reflecting on what a fiasco his life had become, he finally told the man, "Just go ahead and kill me if you want to."

The mysterious figure headed for the door and then looked back at Bart, perhaps for the last time. A faint smile crossed his smug face. After the visitor left, Bart's mind was spinning. They were never going to leave him alone—ever. The goal was to keep him squirming for the rest of his life. No one in the family knew if somewhere down the road he would be killed or forgotten.

One day he decided to do something about it and took a drastic step that devastated the entire family. Gloria called Lyn, sobbing hysterically that Bart had run off to Mexico with another woman. Shocked, Lyn begged her mom to pull herself together and asked how the boys were handling the news.

"Bart is okay, honey. But I'm really worried about Chris. He looks like dynamite ready to explode," said Gloria. "Chris is the one who found the note from Dad."

The next few months were a blur for everyone. Bart's reasons for abandoning them were all too obvious. In Mexico he could carry on an affair, hide from his pursuers, and protect his family at the same time. For Gloria, the reasons didn't matter much anymore. She was mired in her own problems, which included depression, guilt, and a far-reaching slide into alcoholism.

Despite his mother's plunge into alcoholism, Chris was able to maintain focus on his dream. He often helped her through the bad times, which in turn made him feel better about himself. One thing was certain—any parental control that had remained over Chris was now completely gone. He could do anything he wanted. The chaos in his life had become like a cancer. And left uncontrolled, cancer cells multiply.

Through surfing, however, Chris found the joy and recognition that was missing in his family life. Competitions beckoned, and winning was exhilarating. His expertise in the waves soon caught the eye of the owner of a nearby surf shop, Sunset Surfboards, and he asked Chris to join their surf team. In return he received free bars of surf wax, t-shirts, and substantially reduced rates on new surfboards. Chris didn't have much money, and he sometimes helped his neighbors clean up their yards in order to make a few dollars. This enabled him to purchase a new surfboard that he hoped would help him do even better. Yet how much better could he actually become? Chris had finished 1972 as the top-ranked WSA surfer in the Boys 3A division.

At the time only a handful of West Coast surfers had become involved in competitive surfing. The intense competition elevated their desire for a superior performance. Every contest amplifies a surfer's response to the waves and raises the bar. Philosophies of performance, finely tuned by the incentive to win, are displayed for others to investigate.

The WSA events had helped to further establish a credible ranking system for West Coast surfers, as well as judging criteria. The intent was to reward surfers for performing the most maneuvers in a controlled manner. These maneuvers had names: cutbacks, tube rides, off the lips, roller coasters, and 360s. Also, competitors could not blatantly interfere with another surfer who had established the right of way on a wave. Almost from the outset this rule became a bone of contention. Waves were forces of nature that could be ridden either to the left or to the right, and determining who had the right of way often proved debatable.

As time went on it became obvious that surf contest judging was not a perfect science. Nature operates on her own schedule, and no one knows for sure what the waves or weather will do on any given day. Most of the WSA competitions were held in exceedingly poor surf conditions, and judging mistakes were made, some more blatant than others.

But there was no mistaking Chris's talent. No other surfer in the short history of the WSA had progressed so rapidly. It took a great deal of focus and determination to succeed in surfing contests. Some were able to handle it as deftly as they handled their lives on land. Others folded and returned to the solitude of their own pond.

In early 1973 his winning ways continued with even more first place finishes. His near-invincibility was undeniable. What more could he possibly do to convince WSA officials that he was ready for the 4A? This was the closest thing to a professional division, and those who reached it displayed superior talent that separated them from the rest of the pack. The 4A included older surfers such as Mike Purpus, Dale Dobson, and Tony Staples. But even against these savvy veterans, Chris knew he could handle his own. The only obstacle keeping him from doing so was his age.

Nonetheless, throughout California the buzz about Chris O'Rourke was growing. His compatriots at Windansea bragged loudly about him, and from Santa Cruz to San Diego there was a resounding belief that the temperamental kid from La Jolla was on the verge of something very special.

WSA Contest Director Ray Allen finally admitted the obvious—that the talent gap between the 3A and 4A divisions was closing fast. California's surfing youth had served notice they were now a force to be reckoned with. Right there leading the charge was Chris, who by now had become the poster boy for the movement. Several other young talented surfers were emerging from California as well: Allen Sarlo from Venice Beach, Mike Cruickshank from Orange County, Kevin Reed from Santa Cruz, and Willy Morris from the San Fernando Valley. It took a few years until they could finally taste the fruits of success, but Ray Allen could now feel proud about the WSA and what they had accomplished. In spite of its inherent flaws, the organization appeared to have a positive effect on the growth of competitive surfing along the West Coast.

Shortly before summer, the WSA announced that the next contest would feature a mix of 3A and 4A competitors in Huntington Beach. Now Chris would finally have his opportunity. With a confident, positive attitude, he even had a brand new surfboard shaped specifically for the event.

Everything looked good, except for finding transportation. Since no one was available, Chris grabbed his wetsuit, several bars of surf wax and a few necessities and stuffed everything into a large plastic bag. He picked up his surfboard and walked out onto the street. He realized that hitchhiking all the way north to Huntington was going to be hard, but it was his only option.

The last car to give him a ride dropped him off a few blocks from the Huntington Beach pier. He had no idea where he was going to sleep, until he recalled his conversation with Ray Allen a few days earlier. Chris remembered the name of the hotel where Ray said he would be staying. Still carrying all his surf gear, he walked up and down the streets looking for it. When he finally found it, he went straight to the front desk.

"Hi," he told the clerk with a wide, innocent-looking smile. "I'm staying with Mr. Ray Allen, but I don't know his room number."

By now it was eleven o'clock, and Ray was just getting to sleep when he heard a light tapping at his door. He ignored it, but it continued. Finally, peering through the window, he made out the silhouette of a young kid holding a surfboard. Surprised, Ray slowly opened the door.

"Hi Chris, what are you doing here?"

"Sorry Mr. Allen, I just arrived here for the contest tomorrow. But I have no place to stay. Would it be okay if I could just crash out here with you?" asked Chris.

Ray knew he had to think quickly. While he was a kindhearted person who truly wanted to help Chris, he also held a respected position as the WSA contest director. He worried how letting Chris sleep there might appear to the other competitors. Fearing accusations of favoritism, at first Ray told him no.

"Please, Mr. Allen," Chris pleaded. "I know it's late, and I'm really sorry. But I don't have anywhere else I can go."

Ray knew he couldn't just let Chris sleep in the streets where he could get attacked. The kid was only asking for help.

"Sure Chris, come on in," Ray told him, ignoring the pang of guilt.

Chris was more than content to sleep in his clothes on the bare floor, using his beach towel for a blanket. At least he had a roof over his head and a bathroom. The next morning, Ray cautioned him.

"Not a word to the other surfers about you staying here, okay?"

"I have no problem with that," Chris nodded.

Ray could tell that this O'Rourke kid had tons of confidence. He had already witnessed his expertise in the water but had never spoken to him on a personal level.

"Hey, Chris, good luck out there today."

"Thanks, Mr. Allen. Thank you for everything," Chris replied.

On June 25, 1973, three months after his fourteenth birthday, Chris paddled out into the glassy waters next to the famed Huntington Pier—-and straight into his very first mixed 3A/4A heat. The competition featured a restructured format considerably different from normal WSA events: the usual four or six-man heats were replaced by man-on-man rounds, pitting one surfer directly against the other. There would be one winner and one loser. Losing twice eliminated a surfer from the event.

Chris's first heat was against 4A surfer Tuzzo Jerger from Los Angeles. Unfazed by all the pressure, Chris easily disposed of him. His next opponent was veteran surfer David Carson. Most onlookers figured the snotty La Jolla kid would finally meet his match. Yet Chris's explosive surfing easily took care of David, too.

While waiting for his next heat, Chris pondered the complexity of surf contests. Each one was a unique journey. At Huntington Beach he found himself in an unusual situation— his peers were now his competitors. As the rookie, he was the one now on trial.

The more he progressed, the harder the competition became. Although he had never faced him in a competition before, Chris's next opponent was a familiar one—-Mike Purpus, the surfer who had taken him surfing at Trestles a few years before. Mike was still the top-rated 4A surfer in the WSA. Gazing at Chris, he could only shake his head in amazement at how far the little kid had come. Mike understood that Chris represented the future of surfing in California.

At this contest, Mike figured he would cruise past Chris and straight into the semifinals. Before entering the water, Mike took one long look over Chris. His face was covered in a half inch of white zinc oxide for protection against the sun. The long-sleeved, black beaver-tail wetsuit that he wore looked way too big for his body. At that moment, Mike thought Chris looked like a little clown who was way in over his head.

"How are you doing, Chris?" Mike asked while waiting at the water's edge.

Chris was all business and didn't want to be distracted, but he answered anyway.

"Okay, I guess," he replied.

"Just okay?"

"Well, to be honest, I'll be doing much better after this heat is over," admitted Chris.

Mike watched with puzzled amazement as Chris hurriedly paddled out into the ocean before him. Had this young upstart just challenged him in some way? "No, he's just a kid. A bit cocky, but still a kid," Mike thought.

The heat lasted twenty minutes. Mike casually cruised through the lineup and paid little attention to Chris. After catching several waves, he figured victory was well in hand. He failed to notice, however, that Chris had performed blazing high-speed maneuvers while riding each wave all the way to the shore. The late afternoon shadows of the Huntington Beach Pier proved to be an ominous sign for Mike. After the heat had ended, he paddled back in and saw his father quickly coming toward him.

"Hey Mike, that little O'Rourke kid just blew you out of the water!"

"What are you talking about?" asked Mike.

"Yeah, he seriously ripped....way better than you, I hate to say," his father explained.

When it was announced that Chris had won, a stunned silence surrounded the pier. What had happened to the King of the 4A? Soon the silence became a buzz of excitement and then a roar. A new sheriff was in town.

Chris finally lost his next heat against Dale Dobson. But he had left his mark. Displaying wisdom beyond his years, he went on to place third in the contest, ahead of Mike and several other high-ranking 4A surfers. Huntington Beach had long ago turned into a melting pot of sorts for surfing. Chris's radical brand of style had just stirred that pot a bit deeper.

Chapter 11

Sheer Dominance

In the months that followed, there was a buzz, even among his competitors, over how well Chris had done at Huntington. His accomplishment was also witnessed by several influential people at the core of the surfing industry, and the aura that surrounded him continued to widen. Coincidence or not, more spectators than normal started showing up at the WSA events.

Chris had already secured the Boys 3A Championship for the second straight year, and just when it seemed there was little incentive left for him to do well, he raised the bar again.

With one minute remaining in the final heat of a contest at Malibu, Chris stroked into a glassy four-foot wave breaking to the right. He raced off the bottom of the wave to gain the speed that would allow him to perform a series of high-caliber maneuvers: a slashing roundhouse cutback, two vertical roller coasters, two more gouging cutbacks. He topped it all off with a tube ride and disappeared for several seconds behind a veil of watery curtain.

That one wave alone made a loud statement. Chris really was bigger than the Boys' division, bigger than the 4A, bigger than anything they'd ever seen. His stylish repertoire of maneuvers bordered on futuristic. The dances he performed upon the waves were a unique blend of soul-surfing and flash.

After the finals, Chris walked slowly up the beach, his face covered by wet strands of long blond hair. He noticed Bart heading in the opposite direction toward a WSA official.

"For Christ's sake, Bart, he's winning every event," the man said with a hint of disgust.

"So what's wrong with that?" Bart asked.

"It's getting rather one-sided, don't you think? It's not even a contest anymore for the rest of those guys. Your brother is so far ahead in the ratings it's ridiculous. No one else can touch him," the official responded.

"So what are you implying?" asked Bart. "You're penalizing him for being good? Just put him in the 4A permanently against the men. That's what he's been telling you for the past several months. I know for a fact that the surfing industry is looking for something to jumpstart everything. Chris is that thing. But I know why you won't do it because you know, just like everyone else, that he will beat the pants off those guys too."

"You're absolutely right, Bart. I can't do that. The 4A is only for established surfers. I can't let a fourteen-year-old kid just bypass the Juniors' division and jump all the way to the Men's," he said.

"You know something? I've never seen anything in writing that actually states that surfers in the 4A have to be at least eighteen. So where did that rule come from?"

"Okay, okay, here's what we are going to do," the man said. "Right now, let's find out how well he really stacks up against the men. We're going to hold a Super Heat with the winners of all the divisions from today. Dan Flecky won the Men's, Kirk Murray won the Juniors', Tim Flannery won the Masters', Frayne Higgason won the Seniors', and Chris won the Boys'. We'll put everybody in one heat and send them out there to see what happens."

Over the microphone came the announcement of the twenty-minute Super Heat. Initially caught off guard, Chris quickly became excited to compete once more. He stared at the ocean, intently observing its movements. Bart offered encouragement.

"I have a feeling that you are just going to annihilate these guys," he told Chris.

Unsure how to respond, Chris leaned over to retrieve a bottle of water that he had hidden in his towel. He took several swallows, allowing the drama to build.

"Thanks Bart. But actually, I've already won," Chris finally said.

Together they smiled. Chris picked up his board, its fiberglass deck covered in several layers of thick surf wax. The Super Heat proved to be a spirited affair, and not surprisingly it was Chris who stole the show. The surfers he had gone up against were certainly no slouches. Kirk Murray was a very talented surfer in the Juniors' division, and Dan Flecky was one of California's rising stars, having climbed ahead of Mike Purpus to claim the number one ranking in the 4A. But on this day nothing could stop Chris. Another barrier was broken.

After claiming the victory, Chris reverted to type. He trotted over to the judges and cornered the head official.

"You see? You see?" he spat. "You guys are so afraid of letting me surf in the 4A full-time. Yet I just went out there and destroyed all your best surfers. You guys are all such goons. When will you finally get it? I don't belong in the 3A anymore!"

While it was clear the judges did not appreciate his arrogance, there was no denying the truth in his words. Other than his age, there really were no reasons to hold him back any longer. But just when it seemed he would get his wish, several 4A surfers objected. Their point of contention was valid—they had all complied with the rules, and while Chris was obviously a very talented surfer, why should he be treated any differently?

Ultimately a compromise of sorts was reached. Chris would be allowed to compete in the 4A, but not until the start of 1974. Ray Allen had been stubborn about the decision. Despite the kid's obvious accomplishments, he still hoped that Chris would show more patience.

"One day you are going to do really well, Chris. But honestly, what's the rush? You have tons of time to get where you're going," Ray told him.

The words sounded odd to Chris. After all, why was he in such a rush?

His victory in the 3A division at Malibu that day solidified his championship for the 1972-73 WSA season. The final rankings put him as the champion with 8,745 points, Greg Clemmons in second with 6,325 points, and Allen Sarlo third with 4,406 points. Suffice it to say, Chris had blitzed the rest of the field.

His quick rise up the ladder came as no shock to fellow 3A competitor Allen Sarlo. The talented surfer from Los Angeles also wanted to be the best from California. After watching Chris, however, Allen realized he would have to settle for second. With a strong ego of his own, this was not an easy thing for Allen to admit, but he admitted Chris had a unique, almost freakish talent.

While in the company of his rivals, Chris was generally a very friendly guy. Away from them, however, he harshly criticized their individual surfing styles. His words were not intended to be personal attacks. Chris's surfing talents had been groomed in the soulful environment at Windansea, and his standards were set so high that anything less looked ridiculous.

Chris greeted his permanent entry into the 4A with joy, even if he had to wait several more months for it to happen. No one from Windansea had previously gone very far in competitive surfing. Surfers around La Jolla realized Chris was about to change all that. Older surfers became fascinated by this blond enfant sauvage and found themselves supporting him in many different ways—regardless of the occasionally disdainful attitude he displayed in return.

U.S. Championships, Malibu, September 1973

Next up on the contest schedule: The United States Championships of Surfing. As the Boys 3A champion, Chris easily qualified. The venue had originally been announced at Huntington Beach, home to the popular U.S. Championships during the 1960s. At the last minute, however, the contest was shifted north to the fabled right point break of Malibu.

In previous years, plagued by judging inconsistencies and a lack of waves, the U.S. Championships had fallen on hard times, and the WSA itself was struggling. Yet the competition was still strongly supported by the surfing industry, which wanted to ensure the event would live on.

For Chris, the U.S. Championships would be a measuring rod of sorts. He wanted to determine how he compared to the other top surfers from America. He knew the strongest opposition would come from the Hawaiian contingent that included future greats like Larry Bertlemann, Buzzy Kerbox, and Buttons Kaluhiokalani, along with his new friend Michael Ho. Chris deeply respected the surfers from the Islands and admired their smooth styles. Hawaii was widely considered to be the birthplace of the sport, and he dreamed of traveling there some day.

Plagued by inconsistent surf, lack of organization, and an overflow of competitors, the contest proved to be a challenge for all involved. In his first heat, Chris surfed against Michael Ho, Buttons Kaluhiokalani, Mike Cruickshank, and Allen Sarlo.

Allen and Chris were regarded as the most improvisational surfers on the entire West Coast, and Allen had a particular incentive to do well. Malibu was his spot; he has been born and raised in nearby Venice, where his parents owned a waterfront home, and he surfed at Malibu nearly everyday.

Chris's intuition about the Hawaiians proved correct. After several days of competition, it was Larry Bertlemann who took top honors in the Men's division. Fellow Hawaiians Buzzy Kerbox and Michael Ho finished fourth and fifth respectively in the Juniors'. Chris displayed some impressive surfing on the clean walls at Malibu but had to be content with a fifth-place finish in the Boys'. At this event he inexplicably appeared mortal, like Picasso being a mere house painter. The genius proved ordinary. His only solace was finishing ahead of Dan Flecky.

Driving back to La Jolla that night, George Taylor noticed Chris sulking in the back seat of the car.

"Hey Chris, fifth ain't bad, you know," George said. "After all, there were more than a hundred and fifty guys there. And most of them have a lot more experience than you."

Chris didn't answer. As far as he was concerned, a good loser was a consistent loser.

Fortunately, he would not have to wait long to taste victory again. On October 20, he took out his frustration by winning the Boys 3A division at Tamarack State Beach in Carlsbad. Jeff Hamilton, a surfer who by now had become accustomed to being Chris's bridesmaid, took second place.

Watching the contest from a distance was another young surfer with the same aspirations as Chris. Joey Buran had grown up in Carlsbad and was two years younger. Curious about the competitive aspects of surfing, Joey came to the contest to see what all the fuss was about.

He had his surfing heroes, too, including Hawaiian Pipeline master Gerry Lopez, along with California surfers Mike Purpus, Randy Laine, and Bobby Burchell. But Joey had also heard a lot about this younger kid, Chris O'Rourke. Pictures of him had been printed in the surf magazines, and Chris would be competing in the 4A starting next year. Joey was naturally curious. Who was this kid?

He would soon find out. As Joey watched Chris surf, he was blown away by how exceptionally good Chris was—light years ahead of everyone else.

"Whoa, this kid is truly something different," Joey thought. "I want be like this guy. I want to do what he does."

Like Chris, Joey was a mix of arrogance and confidence. After watching Chris that day, Joey knew he had his work cut out for him. Being regarded as the best surfer from California wasn't going to be easy with Chris O'Rourke around. A bitter and ultra-intense rivalry would ultimately form between them. But until that time arrived, Chris didn't give Joey Buran a second thought.

Chapter 12

School and Surfing Don't Mix

As my own interest in surfing evolved, I went to several of Chris's 4A contests. During a competition it was difficult to talk to him—he was in a zone. Even though I watched from afar, Chris always waved to me. Until now, our friendship had been confined primarily to school, but this seemed to expand its boundaries.

Chris had transformed himself into a competitive surfing phenomenon. But his hot temper was as legendary as his incredible surfing. The "gnarly" little kid known for his role in the ugly localism at Windansea was getting older, but still guarded "his" beach aggressively. At Windansea, no outsider could ever touch him. The older "enforcer" surfers would always back him up.

Eric Shelky would look after him, along with another tough surfer named Brud McGowan. When Chris screamed at another surfer, his face often turned beet-red in anger. The locals would paddle over toward him in a hurry, which caused the other surfer to make a hasty retreat.

While many other surf spots along the California coast had this same code of ethics, Windansea was undoubtedly one of the harshest. When an outsider entered the water, anything was possible. Sometimes Chris would try and pick a fight with a bigger surfer for no apparent reason. He would loudly chastise him, so everyone else in the lineup could hear. When that surfer tried to reach out and strike him, the battle was on. Chris was the instigator, the others were the hitters. The Windansea crew sometimes made the violence seem matter of fact, as if they were protecting their own family.

"Hey if you're willing to pick on a little kid, then now you're going to deal with me," Eric would tell them. "We're going in on the beach to settle this now!"

The Windansea tough guys sent the intruders back home black and blue. Chris wasn't the only young surfer they protected. Oscar Bayetto, Mark McCoy, Jim Neri, Tim Senneff, Ted Smith, and Mark Ruyle all received the same preferential treatment. Though Chris had constantly picked on Mark and Ted in the past, the two cousins had recently moved into the Windansea area and found acceptance.

There was no shortage of incidents, and Chris was usually right in the middle of them. One day a bright yellow Volkswagen beetle pulled up at Windansea. Two surfers stepped out of the car, grabbed their boards and headed for the water. A few hours later they came back thinking Windansea wasn't such a bad place after all—until they noticed their car. Several individuals, including Chris, had turned the vehicle completely upside down.

The two surfers immediately asked a few people standing around if anyone had witnessed the act. No one said a word, so they called the police, who were equally perplexed by the odd sight. A crowd of nearly forty surfers gathered in the parking lot as a boisterous commotion ensued over the identity of the perpetrators. With the assistance of four policemen, the victimized surfers' car was finally turned upright, its smashed roof looking like a crushed beer can.

Chris's surfing mentor, Tom Ortner, had witnessed the entire incident from afar. The most respected surfer in the Windansea lineup, Tom had a mellow personality that was in stark contrast to the majority of the surfers at Windansea, and he never participated in the violence. Tom was aware of Chris's growing intensity and knew that anyone who got in his way instantly became a perceived threat. If Tom had known about

Chris's turbulent family life, perhaps Chris's actions would have been easier to understand, but that still didn't make them right.

Chris always made it a point to be on his best behavior whenever Tom was around. Finally, he witnessed Chris trading blows with a much older surfer. Chris picked up his board, turned it around fin-first, and began swinging it at the other surfer's head. After the melee settled down, Tom didn't hesitate to tell Chris that he had gone too far.

"Chris, when you turn the fire on too high, people jump back. You really need to learn how to turn it down."

Whether Chris's fiery personality could in fact be tempered seemed uncertain. Tom thought Chris was a quiet and polite kid most of the time—until sudden outbursts of anger would take over.

Anger remained one of his primary emotions, but others began to emerge as well. On Halloween night, Chris and some friends visited a haunted house on Girard Street in downtown La Jolla. Even some of his closest friends, including Jim, Shauna, Rikki, Dylan Jones, and Lori Krug, felt Chris had become a little too smug for his own good. So they decided to play a trick on him. Inside the darkness of the haunted house, everyone ditched him. Several seconds passed before Chris realized he was alone. He called out, but no one answered. Feeling along the damp wall, searching for a way out, he began to cry.

"It isn't funny anymore, you guys!" he screamed at the top of his lungs.

Several minutes later, Chris finally emerged with thick tears streaming down his cheeks. Unaccustomed to being on the opposite end of a prank, he stormed off down the street and never returned. None of his friends had ever witnessed this sensitive side of him. They had certainly struck a nerve.

But his anger was never far from the surface. Scot Cherry had transferred to Muirlands Junior High from Clairemont, an inland neighborhood east of La Jolla. Clairemont surfers often tried to infiltrate Windansea, only to be rejected by the locals. Since Scot was a surfer, too, their relationship was combustible from the start.

One day the ill will that had been simmering finally came to a boil. Chris had been surfing at Windansea when Scot decided to paddle out there for the very first time. Scot knew he was from the wrong side of the tracks and had yet to gain acceptance, but when Chris saw him in the lineup, it was as though gasoline had been poured onto a fire. A line had to be drawn—and it had to be drawn now. He immediately paddled over to Scot and, without saying a word, jumped on top of him. Chris put him in a headlock and began punching his face, bloodying his nose. Finally, Scot paddled away.

Scot became a frequent target of Chris's anger. In the months that followed, Chris and Scot would tangle at Windansea, at school, and in the alley behind Nautilus Pharmacy.

But even Chris knew that he couldn't be such a jerk all the time, so he regularly participated in good-natured antics, too. At school, his free-spirited fun often kept the rest of us thoroughly entertained. Once, Chris and a few other boys decided to streak naked during gym class. After the door opened, they quickly took off running. Their plan was to run an entire lap around the perimeter of the gym building before ducking back inside. Upon returning, however, they were shocked to discover the door had been locked. The predicament left them exposed for everyone to see.

The sight caused Rikki, Shauna, Lori and several other girls to stop dead in their tracks. Hysterical laughter filled the air as the girls watched the boys prance around while trying to cover their private parts.

Chris and the others began pounding on the door. To make matters worse, the principal was making his way toward the building after hearing the commotion from afar. Finally, one of the gym coaches unlocked the door and allowed them to scamper back inside. Rikki told Chris the incident was the funniest thing she had ever seen.

Not long afterward, the two friends began dating. Chris invited Rikki to a movie at the La Jolla Cove Theater on Girard Street. He had become much more confident around girls and was intent on proving it. After entering the theater, Rikki asked Chris if they could sit up front with their other friends, but he insisted on sitting in the last row where it was dark. Shortly after the movie started, Chris put his arm around her. Rikki didn't mind, especially when she noticed that Chris was nervously shaking.

"I wonder if this is the first step to how girls get pregnant?" she thought.

After the movie ended, they went across the street to the Mary Star of the Sea Church. They sat in the pews and kissed. Rikki was charmed by the thought that Chris was her first real boyfriend. At the end of the night, he surprised her with a present: a silver Saint Christopher medal.

"I saved up some money and bought this for you," he said.

"It's beautiful, Chris. Thank you."

Rikki felt guilty, though. She noticed how Chris always wore hand-me-down clothes and never seemed to have much food. The O'Rourke family had little money, and she certainly didn't want Chris spending his money on her. She vowed to help him however she could.

He telephoned her often to "wrangle"—a term he coined for talking with a friend.

"Hey Rik, those pomegranates you had the other day at school were so good. Can you please bring an extra one for me tomorrow?" he would ask.

"Sure, Chris," she would always tell him.

Their young romance lasted a few more months, after which they returned to being "just friends." Chris felt more comfortable around Rikki than any other girl he had ever met before. He could ask her anything, even about the pretty new girl who had just transferred to school. Tall, dark-skinned and beautiful, Cha Kenyon was from the Bahamas, and she immediately caught the eye of every guy in school. She was like no girl Chris had ever seen before. One day while he and Rikki were sitting next to each other in class, Cha walked into the room. He leaned over to Rikki and whispered.

"Hey Rik, see that new girl? I want to meet her. Can you introduce us?"

Although she was still a bit jealous, Rikki didn't mind helping him out, and Chris quickly turned on the charm. He and Cha ended up dating for a while, and Chris was happy to call her his girl. Cha often went to Windansea to watch Chris surf. She was amazed by his ability to recall exactly what he had done on each and every wave he had ridden. Chris had become a highly evolved surfer, so the details of the wave, where he sat in the lineup, where he took off, and exactly what he did were etched in his mind.

"Did you see me on that one really big wave? It was the third one of the day. I did all those cutback maneuvers and got inside the tube at the end," he told Cha. With each recounting, the details would become more exaggerated, until a two-foot wave became an eight-foot wave.

Chapter 13

Bill Caster and
the WSA 4A

In early 1974, two significant developments bolstered Chris's budding surfing career—competing in the 4A division and meeting Bill Caster. Chris and the well-established surfboard shaper from San Diego bonded quickly from the moment they met. An innovative designer who had searched everywhere for a talented young surfer to ride his boards, Bill found his star pupil in Chris.

For an elite surfer, having natural talent is only half the battle. Finding the right surfboards to ride is the other half. Chris had never seen anything like Bill's unique, hand-crafted boards, and they perfectly suited his surfing style. So Chris politely thanked everyone at Sunset Surfboards, and announced he would now be riding for Bill Caster.

From the beginning, Bill's technologically advanced boards combined with Chris's cutting-edge surfing to create a lethal combination. Since the WSA had allowed Chris to compete in both 3A and 4A events, he entered as many as possible. In February, he paddled out at Huntington Beach for a Boys 3A contest as a "tune-up" for the events that would follow. At the end of the day, he finished first ahead of Mike Clark, Kevin Reed, and Bobby Burchell.

During that spring and summer, there would be numerous 4A contests held at Oceanside, Ocean Beach, Santa Cruz, Huntington, Malibu, and San Miguel, a right-hand point break in northern Baja California. Chris performed well in all of them.

But his biggest challenge that year had nothing to do with surfing. In the fall, we all took the leap into the tenth grade at La Jolla High School. Chris promised his mother that he would work harder in school. Gloria was still battling alcoholism, and after her husband ran away, she looked to her three children for inspiration, particularly Chris.

Established in 1922, the La Jolla High School campus was located just three blocks from Windansea, and during the first few weeks, Chris was absent most of the time. There was no need to ask where he was. I gave him copies of my class notes in an effort to help him out, and he seemed appreciative.

Chris finished 1974 as the WSA Boys 3A champion for the third consecutive year. It was his fourth-place ranking in the Men's 4A, however, that really caught everyone's attention. The winner of that division, Aaron Wright, was another maverick surfer from Pacifica, near San Francisco. But Wright was nearly ten years older.

By now Chris had bypassed most of California's established surfers. This didn't exactly come as a surprise; they had seen it coming for years. The surfing media was well aware of Chris's accomplishments, too. His name and photographs began to appear more often within the pages of Surfer and Surfing magazines. Since both publications were based in Southern California, it was only natural for them to recognize his accomplishments.

I could see that all of the attention Chris was getting was going to his head, and he craved more. As the leader of Windansea's brat pack, he inspired other young surfers around him. Two kids in particular who badly wanted to emulate his style of surfing were Tim Senneff and Greg Schneider—which seemed rather ironic, considering the first time they ever visited Windansea, Chris had thrown rocks at them. Both were determined, however, to break into his ranks. One day they discovered a way to get on his good side by forming the "Chris

O'Rourke Fan Club." Their motto: "Once you're in the club, you're in for life."

Membership did not come easily, but soon the club began to grow. Tim earned Chris's acceptance, as well as a bit of leverage, when the Senneff family moved into a large house directly across the street from Big Rock. Almost from the get-go, Chris made it his home, too. He always stopped by after surfing, so he could play ping-pong with Tim. Chris also knew that, if he hung around long enough, Tim's mom would ask him to stay for dinner.

In order to be Chris's friend, you had to play by his rules. These kids shared many of the same interests that he did—especially a passion for surfing at Windansea—and together they formed a tight-knit group. The legacy of Windansea had now been passed down to a new generation. Their motto was "Welcome to Windansea. Now go home." There was too much tradition to uphold, and those traditions died hard.

He found ways to get attention at school as well. Our lockers were close together, and we spoke often. Feeling the need to loudly announce his presence, he would spontaneously create bizarre-sounding shrieks and yodels. Whenever I heard these I knew right away who it was. I would turn around, and he'd be there, sporting a sly grin.

"Hey Aeder, why is it that you haven't started surfing yet? Are you still riding that air mat?" he said after one particularly blood-curdling screech.

"Yeah, I'm still using the air mat. I ride the waves at Boomer Beach over by the Cove. The waves there are pretty good, and you know what the best thing is? Surfboards aren't allowed," I told him as proudly as I could.

I knew that I was in for a heavy ribbing.

"Come on, Aeder. I know you are a jock head, too. Stop playing all that baseball and basketball. And that air mat? Get yourself a real surfboard," he said sarcastically.

Chris's mind was always on surfing. If you weren't a dedicated surfer (or a good-looking girl), he acted as if he wanted absolutely nothing to do with you. Toward me, however, his attitude seemed different. Chris saw stability in me, the kind he didn't have. There were many times when he told me personal things about his family. I always listened and offered advice, and that alone seemed to earn me some respect. I felt bad that his family's situation hadn't changed all that much. Fortunately, his future looked remarkably bright.

"I saw you win a few contests last year. You're doing really well. My brother Erik showed me some pictures of you in Surfer magazine. Just keep it going," I told him.

"Thanks, Kirk. You should come and see more of the contests sometime," Chris said, finally calling me by my first name.

"You know something, Chris—I think I will. I just started getting interested in photography. My parents gave me enough money for my birthday to buy a new camera. It would be great to take some pictures of you surfing," I told him.

"Well, time is ticking away. You better hurry up, or you'll be too late."

Just then the bell rang.

"Shit, we're going to be late for class." I told him.

Chris chuckled before casually strolling off in the opposite direction.

"Hey, where are you going?" I asked.

"Come on, Aeder. Where do you think?"

When I saw him a few days later, however, his mood had abruptly changed. He was tense and seething with anger. I asked him what was wrong, but he refused to answer. Jim Neri then told me what had happened. Chris's father had returned from Mexico, and now his mother's problem with alcohol was even worse.

Now Bart had returned looking to make amends, and this latest transgression only fueled Chris's anger toward him. Bart begged his family for forgiveness, but Chris wanted nothing to do with it.

From that point forward, Chris and his dad rarely spoke to each other, and Chris was always confrontational. Shortly after his dad returned, the entire family got together for dinner. Holding nothing back, Chris kept taunting his father and called him a jerk. Irritated by his son's behavior, Bart picked up a small teak bowl, looked straight at Chris and snapped it in half.

"Say what you want about me, son, but at least I had the good sense to always stay in school!"

Chris's truancy had always been an issue with his father. He was a bright kid, but Chris reasoned that his true education was out there in the ocean. School wasn't going to take him very far, but surfing would.

Chapter 14

Santa Cruz and the South Africans

February 1975

Unfortunately, in the mid-1970s, there really was no such thing as a "career" in surfing. Its future as a professional, competitive sport was questionable. Public perceptions of surfing were based almost entirely on Gidget movies and the music of the Beach Boys; in fact, most people didn't even consider surfing to be a sport at all. It didn't help that surfers were stereotyped as nothing more than unemployed, drugged-out beach bums; while that may have been true of some, it hurt those who were trying to take the sport to a higher level. Grass-roots movements to advance the sport were evolving in Southern California and in surf communities around the world, but they lacked the cohesion to bring the sport into the mainstream.

Surfing in the Golden State was going through a turbulent transition. The violence and territorial issues contributed to the problem. No one owned the ocean. Some surfers dreamed of the day when they could make a living off the sport. Others wanted to preserve surfing on a more a leisurely, grass-roots level.

Chris proved to be a combination of both ideals. He loved the soulfulness of the sport as well as the competition. He had no idea where the professional part of it was headed, but he was ready. And, he was eager. His bully reputation however threatened to overshadow his amazing talents and potentially undermined his rise to the forefront of progressive West-Coast surfing. People often advised him to just sit back and let it happen, but the urge he felt inside was hard to control.

Far more surf star than student, Chris was now hanging on by a thread academically. Getting suspended on several occasions hadn't exactly helped his cause either. School authorities advised him that, if he didn't get his act together, he would be expelled. But Chris knew that his father expected him to get kicked out, and true to his defiant personality, he wanted nothing more than to prove Bart Sr. wrong.

Still, WSA surfing competitions always took precedence over everything else. His progression up the ladder was nothing short of prolific: first overall in Boys 3A in 1972, 1973, and 1974; twentieth overall in Men's 4A 1973 (he competed in only one event due to age restrictions); and fourth overall in Men's 4A in 1974. One month shy of his sixteenth birthday, Chris wasn't even close to reaching his competitive peak.

The 1975 WSA contest season was about to commence. Now that he would be surfing exclusively in the 4A, getting off to a good start meant a lot to him. His commitment to doing better at school lasted about two weeks.

Meanwhile, I had finally started to take surfing photos of Chris, which brought us closer as friends and allies. Several months earlier I had begun working as a busboy at the Happy Frenchmen restaurant on Prospect Street, and I earned enough money to purchase a decent 35mm camera and small telephoto lens.

During good swells we always tried to meet up at Windansea. However, the best surf conditions always seemed to occur during school days and, being reluctant to ditch class, it was sometimes tough to get good shots of him. It came as no surprise that he gave me a lot of shit about that. Occasionally, though, he would have a change of heart and actually express appreciation that I tried to do well in school. He knew there was value in education—-just not for him.

Chris's friendship with Jim Neri ran along the same lines. Jim was an avid surfer as well but didn't see the point in missing school over a good swell. He figured the waves would always be there, but school only happened once. When Chris ditched school while Jim and I did not, we always heard about it later. Even when the waves were horrible, if you heard Chris tell the story, we had really blown it.

Chris was eagerly looking forward to the first contest of the year. A week later at Huntington Beach, he again defeated Mike Purpus and captured first place. The $400 first place prize Chris received didn't hurt either. It was the most he had won so far.

During the contest, word began to spread like wildfire about a new upcoming competition. Organized at the last minute, the event was originally not part of the WSA schedule for 1975. California's best surfers were elated to learn that a special contest would take place in Santa Cruz at the end of February: USA versus South Africa. The event had been organized by WSA President Dr. Robert Scott and South Africa Surf Rider Association President Basil Lomberg. Their concept was so unique that the event had two names: The Santa Cruz Encounter and the International USA-South Africa Team Challenge.

Steamer's Lane, the premier surf break in Santa Cruz, would host the competition. Chris couldn't wait for the contest to begin. He had a deep respect for the surfing scene in Santa Cruz. The waves were very powerful, just like those in La Jolla, and Steamer's was a place he knew well; he had competed there several times before and had become good friends with Richard Schmidt and Vince Collier, two of the best young surfers in the area.

The United States team compiled a list of West Coast 4A surfers that would compete, including Dale Dobson, Tony Staples, Jeff Smith, Steve Seebold, Clyde Beatty Jr., Aaron Wright, and Chris O'Rourke.

After surfing in Hawaii that winter, the South African contingent had agreed to make the stopover in California before heading back home. They really didn't know what to expect, except that after surfing in the warm waters of Hawaii, they counted on the fact that Santa Cruz was going to be cold.

The South Africans definitely had the stars. They were led by nineteen-year-old sensation Shaun Tomson, who had won the prestigious Hang Ten Contest at Sunset Beach just a week earlier. Other members included Peers Pittard, Bruce Jackson, Jonathan Paarman, and Shaun's older cousin, Michael Tomson. It seemed undeniable that the South Africans were the far better surfers, and few expected the competition to be close. With nothing to lose and everything to gain, the Californians eagerly awaited their arrival.

As expected, the contest was a complete blowout—but it wasn't the South Africans who dominated. And leading the American team to the upset victory was Chris O'Rourke. He navigated the changing conditions at Steamer's with an uncanny panache. The American surfers ruled from the outset, easily cruising past their South African counterparts to finish in the top ten positions. Peers Pittard, the highest-placing South African, finished eleventh. The foreigners looked a bit overwhelmed by the frigid cold waters of Northern California. Wearing full wetsuits for the first time in several months no doubt hindered their abilities, but in the end they offered no excuses.

For California's surfers, the results were truly a big deal. It proved they could compete with the best in the world. The overall individual winner was Tony Staples, who was also from San Diego. Chris finished in third place but had the high point heat (972) of the entire event after putting on an incendiary performance—and he garnered most of the media attention afterward. A few months later when Surfer magazine published an issue featuring coverage of the competition, Chris received some very strong compliments:

"O'Rourke would execute remarkable cutbacks resembling those of a water skier. He would get so laid out on the shoulder of the wave, before pulling his board back around and snapping it off the white water in full control. He was definitely impressing the large crowd on the cliff, judging from their slack-jawed expressions."

His third place finish only earned him a meager $25 prize—certainly not a lot for his effort, but he didn't care. Doing well against some of the best surfers in the world meant more to him. The contest was a measuring stick of sorts. He had placed well ahead of Shaun Tomson, regarded as the best young surfer in the world at the time, by a whopping seven hundred points! Three years younger than the talented South African, Chris figured his time was certainly coming too.

After the event concluded, Chris and Shaun talked on the bluff above Steamer's Lane. Shaun noticed that Chris was a very upbeat kid, focused, with an energetic surfing style that was fast and clean. Like so many others, he figured Chris was mainland America's surfer of the future. Their conversations were positive. When Shaun walked away that day, he knew Chris would go far.

The next day Chris and his friends made the long drive back to San Diego. Staring out the car's window, he daydreamed about what would come next. He had become more than just an incredible surfer; he was now a force of nature. Over the next three months Chris either won or placed highly in several more 4A events. On a few occasions, however, his quirky persona and reputation for localism made him a target of certain judges who frowned on such things. Getting eliminated early from a contest didn't happen often, and when it did, eyebrows were raised.

If the rumors circulating were true, there might not be any more events to judge. Ominous signs loomed for the WSA. The organization's finances had been as shaky as a California earthquake, and rumor had it that 1975 would be the final year of competition. The WSA even awarded its annual champions early. During the middle of summer, Aaron Wright was announced as the new 4A champion, followed by Chris in second place. The remaining competitions for that year would be included in a combined 1975-76 WSA season—if there was one.

Contests or not, there was no mistaking that the face of competitive surfing in California was changing. Names like Dale Dobson and Mike Purpus were no longer at the top of the rankings. As the WSA began to fall apart, Chris's efforts began paying off in other ways, like receiving free surfboards from Bill Caster. By now the shaping guru had completely taken Chris under his wing. While other sponsors provided free wetsuits and surf trunks, it was his kindred-like friendship with Bill that meant the most to Chris.

As summer slowly came to a close, Chris set his sights upon what could be his final year in the WSA. He had heard exciting rumors about a newly organized professional surfing tour that would travel around the world. He looked forward to the next challenges—one of which would arrive much sooner than any of us expected. It wasn't a surf contest, but it was the swell of a lifetime.

Chapter 15

The Monster South Swell from New Zealand

La Jolla, September 1975

Summer's end was around the corner. Two weeks into our junior year of high school, a small south swell arrived over the weekend, followed by another surge with smooth waves hovering around three to four feet. Weather forecasters predicted even more of an increase due to a powerful hurricane off Baja California. Elated, surfers at Windansea immediately prepared for the swell.

When Tuesday dawned the waves were indeed larger at about four to six feet, followed by another dramatic rise on Wednesday. Since the waves from Baja had already peaked, the origin of this new swell was a mystery.

I took a break from my homework that night and caught the latest report on television. The fast-rising surf was being generated by a massive storm in the Pacific Ocean southeast of New Zealand. Not since I was a little kid during the infamous winter of 1969 had I heard the weatherman predict such extraordinarily large surf for Southern California.

The night before its full arrival, the incoming surf was already being touted as "The Monster South Swell from New Zealand." Chris said the waves were going to be massive and begged me to ditch school and take surfing pictures. I tried to sound enthusiastic, but he easily sensed the hesitancy in my voice.

Nonetheless, early the next morning, I woke up filled with anticipation. After breakfast I gathered my school books in one arm and camera equipment in the other and climbed into my Volkswagen van. Even from five blocks away, I could hear the surf pounding the shoreline. The ominous swell had arrived. Inside me an emotional tug was fighting it out—-surf, school, surf, school. As I pulled out of the driveway, I confidently decided I would go to school and take pictures of the big waves afterward.

Driving along on Torrey Pines Road, I began to realize the sheer magnitude of this swell. The air was moist and smelled like salt water. I briefly pulled the car over at a small lookout above the tide pools at Devil's Slides and saw an inordinate amount of whitewater pounding the shoreline. As I continued on, several cars sped past me with surfboards tied to the roof, horns honking. This certainly wasn't going to be just another normal day in La Jolla.

A few weeks earlier, I had quit the high school volleyball and track teams to focus on surf photography. I had taken Chris's words to heart—I really didn't want to be a "jock-head" anymore, and shooting surf pictures had become more alluring. I kept my initial goals simple, but one day I wanted to have my photos published in the national surfing magazines.

My brother Erik, a surf photographer himself, told me the financial rewards were miniscule, and other than the two surf magazines, there were few outlets clamoring for surfing photos. I guess I just didn't care about all that. Hanging around the ocean taking pictures of waves and pretty girls might have other rewards. With my entire life ahead of me, I wasn't worried about the downside of the profession. Where it would all lead one day was a mystery, but I was willing to take the chance.

At the time there were three established surfing photographers with strong ties to the La Jolla area: Erik, Warren Bolster, and Jeff Divine. Compared to them, I was extremely inexperienced. Manually focusing a camera lens while following a fast-moving object proved difficult, and I had great respect for those who had mastered the profession. When this epic south swell arrived, however, none of them were around. This left plenty of room for a wishful surf photographer like me. The door was open; all I had to do now was step inside.

As I continued driving, the full reality of that morning began to hit me. This truly was going to be the swell of a lifetime. I decided to detour toward Windansea to look at the surf, and what I saw was breathtaking. Ten to twelve-foot waves, as smooth as glass, pounded the lineup. It was by far the biggest surf I had ever seen there.

An extra-large set of waves crashed down three hundred yards beyond the normal lineup, closer to the offshore kelp beds. Suddenly I realized that ditching school might be the only option after all. It was a classic south swell all right, but much bigger than anyone had imagined. Normally at Windansea, the waves could be ridden either to the left or right. This swell was so massive, however, that going right was next to impossible—it was a mass of whitewater confusion. Several enormous waves trapped unsuspecting surfers, breaking their surfboards and pounding them all the way back to shore.

The Windansea parking lot overflowed with cars and onlookers. Along Neptune Street, traffic backed up in both directions. I found a place to park further north and walked over to the bluff for a closer look.

Another massive set of waves loomed on the horizon, but the air was so thick with salt spray that none of the surfers saw it. People sitting in cars began honking their horns to warn the surfers what was coming, but by the time they realized what was happening it was too late. The huge surf trapped them all, with punishing consequences. Boards and bodies were tossed around like toothpicks inside a washing machine.

Undeterred, they retrieved their boards and paddled straight back out for more. The surfers at Windansea were tough guys who could pretty much handle anything the ocean could throw at them. This day was markedly different, however, and would truly separate the men from the boys.

It seemed a foregone conclusion that on this day truancies would be at an all-time high—but I would not be one of them. I got to school, and just as I gathered up my books and began walking, another vehicle screeched to a stop behind me. I turned to look and instantly recognized the classic black 1953 MGTD with two people inside.

"Hey Aeder, where do you think you're going? Have you seen the surf? The waves are huge right now," Chris said with a grin wider than a half moon.

"Yeah, man. Beyond huge really," agreed Oscar Bayetto, who was driving.

Getting out of this would not be easy. Two years older, Oscar was a senior at our school and loved surfing as much as Chris did. The two of them were compatriots, much like Batman and Robin, and were always hanging out together. Chris was always searching for an escape from the turmoil he had with his father, and Oscar provided the release valve, especially after his own father purchased a house on Nautilus Street, a mere stone's throw from Windansea. Chris had all but moved in.

A rare opportunity was staring me in the face, daring me to take advantage of it. The most advanced young surfer in mainland America wanted me to photograph him on a day when the surf was monumentally huge. If ever I was going to make a mark in surfing photography, Chris O'Rourke was going to be the one to get me there. His rising status in the surfing world meant that good pictures of him would be in demand. He needed publicity in order to attract new sponsors. Chris's high-caliber surfing, coupled with my desire to photograph him, would be the link to finally bring us together as truly good friends.

When the school bell rang, I looked over my shoulder, an action Chris noticed instantly.

"You're not really thinking of going to class on a day like this, are you? Come on, Aeder, you're joking right?" he chided.

"Yeah, I know," I stammered. "I just saw the surf at Windansea. Shit, it looks huge, but I have two tests today, and I don't know..."

"Ahhhhhhhhhhhhh!" he roared in disgust.

"There will be other good days. Besides, those big waves don't exactly look like they are going anywhere. After school I will come to Windansea and take some pictures, okay?"

While taking the studious approach had cut me some slack in the past, this time Chris wasn't buying it.

"There won't be more days like this one. You know something, Aeder? As surfers we all realize that one day a swell will come that's bigger than anything we've seen. Maybe the best we'll ever see in our lifetime. This is it, Aeder."

Noticing that I was still hesitating, he then cast his lure to reel me in for good.

"Hey, and do you know that Gerry Lopez just paddled out at Windansea right now? What more do you want?" Chris told me.

Mentioning the name of the most famous surfer in the world certainly caught my attention. Now this was something I hadn't expected. And I didn't know if he was serious, or just baiting me.

"Gerry Lopez? Really?"

Chris didn't respond. Instead he just stared at me with those Irish blue eyes as if to say "are you in or are you out?" The school bell echoed again. With one minute remaining to get to my seat, I looked over at Oscar who was shaking his head in disbelief. Chris leaned his head out of the car.

"You're a pussy if you don't do this, Aeder. A pussy! You said you wanted to be a surf photographer, right? Well, here's your chance. It won't get any better than this. See you down there. Don't be late. Let's go, Oscar."

As their car sped off toward the beach, Chris never looked back. I realized that, a few minutes later, he would be paddling out into that epic surf. Chris knew how to get under my skin. Most of my good friends were on stable ground, living their lives based on the future. Chris was just the opposite, clearly enjoying life for the moment. He even told me once, "It's best to always do things in the moment, because you never know when everything in your life will change."

I figured if anyone should know about that it would be him, especially after all the turmoil he had been through. Reluctantly I ran off to my first class, barely making it inside before the final bell rang. Catching my breath, I thought long and hard about the decision I made. When the teacher spoke, everything sounded like a blur. My mind was four blocks away. Even from my seat I could hear the surf roar and smell the salt water spray. Maybe it's not too late after all? My stomach churned as the battle of emotions waged inside me again. It's time to pick a side, I told myself—so I did.

Fortunately, my seat was at the rear of the class. When the teacher turned his back to write on the chalkboard, I snuck out the door. I had rarely ditched school before, and running back to my car brought a new, exhilarating feeling. I would just live with my decision and worry about the repercussions later. That seemed to be Chris's motto, so why couldn't it be mine, too?

I had no way of knowing it then, but skipping class that day would prove to be a defining moment in my life. Chris had influenced my destiny, and from this moment forward, I would never look back.

I couldn't even recall the few seconds it took me to get back to Windansea. I retrieved my camera equipment from the back of the car and walked to the thatched hut near the sand's edge, one of my favorite shooting spots. But on this day even the sheltered hut was being battered by the swell. Large waves crashed against the rocks, sending torrents of water over the structure.

I moved to a dry area high on the bluff, set up my telephoto lens on a tripod and scanned the lineup. Right away I spotted Chris and Oscar paddling out through the frothy waves toward other Windansea regulars: Tom Ortner, David Rullo, Andy Tyler, Bruce Byerly, Brew Briggs, Jeff McCoy, Guy Newberry, and Peter Lochtefeld. The cream of the crop had come out to ride the formidable surf.

Peering through my telephoto lens, I saw another large set of waves approaching. A surfer I didn't recognize began paddling for the first one. He glided along effortlessly, making the entire ride look easy. It was then I realized it was Gerry Lopez, the King of Pipeline and the most famous surfer in the entire world—-just like Chris had said.

"Well, what do you know? He wasn't pulling my leg after all," I muttered to myself.

I had seen a few surf movies with footage of Gerry riding the waves at Pipeline in Hawaii. But to have him suddenly appear in person at our beach on the best day in decades was almost too good to believe. As Gerry ended his ride, I was amazed by his harmonious surfing style. He was by far the smoothest surfer I had ever seen.

The next wave was even larger. A small figure took the drop and immediately began carving a series of subtle turns, and right away I knew who it was. On his first wave of the day, Chris was already making his presence known. Since the massive waves were only breaking to the left, Chris would be surfing entirely on his backside, but he didn't mind. Until today, ten to twelve-foot waves at Windansea were something he had only dreamed of.

With my finger ready on the camera's shutter button, I watched through the telephoto lens as Chris reached the bottom of the wave, performing a powerful bottom turn that sent a sheet of water flying into the air. Gaining speed, he redirected his board vertically into the wave's steep face. At the top, he smacked the watery lip forcefully with the bottom of his board. The radical maneuver once more propelled salt water high into the air. As gravity pulled him back down the wave's face, Chris managed to keep his feet connected to his board.

His favorite part was still to come—the tube ride—and Chris was ready. As the thick lip of the wave pitched outward, Chris found himself encased in several feet of cylindrical liquid. With only one way out, he calmly steadied himself and aimed straight ahead.

Chris loved riding tubes. It was a place where time seemed to stand still. He shifted his feet to quicken his foreword momentum, crouched back, and dragged his left arm along the inside wall of the peeling tube. Displaying confidence beyond his years, Chris knew he would find his way out of there sooner or later.

Inside that wave, the roar of the ocean sounded more like thunder. Chris once compared it to holding a large seashell next to your ear, only a million times louder. But this particular tube appeared as if it would now get the best of him. The small opening ahead was closing fast. For everyone watching from the beach, it looked like there was no way out.

In this fleeting moment—there on center stage expressing all of his skill and verve and audacity—Chris just wanted to stay inside that tube forever. To everyone's amazement, he miraculously emerged from the watery hole. Amid a chorus of cheers, Chris finished the wave with flair, performing several backside cutbacks and roller coasters all the way to shore. I saw him thrust his fist high into the air out of pure jubilation. Gerry Lopez had witnessed the entire ride while paddling back out in the deep water channel. Gerry had heard about Chris before coming to Windansea, and now he knew why so many people were talking about the young surfer.

Gerry had arrived early that morning on an overnight flight from Honolulu and had been surfing since daybreak. Exhausted, he caught one last wave and came ashore. Word on the beach was that he had been surfing the same large south swell a day earlier, at Ala Moana on Oahu's South Shore. He had chased the waves across the Pacific as they roared into Southern California—an inconceivable concept for the era.

Now, Mr. Pipeline was content to sit atop his rental car in the Windansea parking lot. From there he watched Chris O'Rourke take over the Windansea lineup. In the days that followed the epic swell, Gerry commented to the press that Chris did things that no one else from California was even trying.

For a few more hours, I continued to shoot photos. But things did not always go exactly as planned. Manually focusing the long lens proved to be difficult, and on the swell of all swells, I went through a lot of trial and error. I couldn't help but recognize the parallels between the rigors of riding big waves and photographing them. My hesitancy earlier that morning had cost me the opportunity to get any decent photos of Gerry Lopez. To make matters even worse, I had neglected to bring enough film along. Being forced to shoot conservatively on the most incredible day of surf I had ever seen was agonizing.

Finally, nearly five hours after first paddling out, Chris decided to take a breather. He stroked into one last wave, riding it all the way to the shore with the same fervor he'd had all day. A crowd of friends and onlookers greeted him on shore. As usual his entire face and neck were slathered with white zinc oxide, but his Irish skin had nonetheless taken a noticeable beating in the intense sun.

It seemed as if everyone on the beach wanted to talk with him. After several minutes he spotted me on the bluff and came over, smiling from ear to ear.

"I'm glad you showed up, but I knew you would," he grinned. "Hey, did you get any good shots of me? Did you get a picture of that one insane tube I had earlier?"

"I think so," I answered hesitantly.

"Aeder, I gotta go get something to eat. Then I'm coming right back and going out again, so don't leave!"

I watched as he raced back up the bluff toward the parking lot. He walked over to Gerry Lopez and gave him a friendly handshake. As they shared their respective stories over the day's action, other surfers began to gather around. Though generations apart, the two surfers from different parts of the world had the same magnetic aura. Gerry was already an esteemed legend, and Chris appeared headed in the same direction.

That memorable day was the peak of the powerful south swell. The high surf continued to linger for several days afterward, but not with the same amount of fury.

During a summer of otherwise flat surf, this memorable swell would define an entire generation of California surfers.

On my way home, I reminisced about the day: radiant smiles, cleanup sets, elevator drops, grinding barrels, and a fiery red sunset the likes of which I had never seen before. All of it did seem like a once-in-a-lifetime experience, just like everyone had said. But I was only sixteen. Surely there would be another one like it. Wouldn't there?

My mom was waiting for me at the front door. From the stern look on her face, I knew I was in trouble. She immediately asked me why I looked so tan compared to when I had left earlier that morning. I didn't even try to muster up a response. I was told that the attendance office at school had called, inquiring why I hadn't shown up. I tried hard to explain about the day's history-making swell. My mom wasn't exactly buying it, but judging by how excited I appeared, she knew that something truly special had taken place. Apparently the only thing saving me from harsh punishment was that I hadn't been the only one who ditched school that day—a record number of truancies had been issued. Fortunately my parents were pretty lenient, and I got a minimal slap on the wrist. It had all been worth it.

That night, doing my homework was next to impossible. I had never been so captivated by surfing before. I had learned how various aspects of the surfing world were related. The surfers at Windansea had welcomed Gerry Lopez, an outsider, and treated him with respect. His modern day feats at Pipeline might not have been possible had it not been for Butch Van Artsdalen, the original Mr. Pipeline who had come from Windansea a decade earlier. The ocean connected every surfer in the world.

A few months later, Gerry Lopez was quoted in a Surfer magazine article about the historic swell:

"Chris O'Rourke is the best surfer from California that I have ever seen."

Chapter 16

First Taste of Hawaii

December 1975/January 1976

One month after the epic south swell came another 4A contest at Malibu. The WSA was already far into its "second season" for 1975, and to no one's surprise, Chris sat firmly in first place. On the first day of competition, he produced a massive 750 points. By comparison, the next closest surfer had only 400. Standing on the beach watching was Allen Sarlo. As much as he hated to admit it, Allen determined Chris was far superior to everyone—-including himself.

What none of the competitors realized, however, was that this would be the last 4A contest ever. Without good organization or a decent judging system, the future of the entire association was in doubt. Chris's experience during the event's final day exemplified the issues.

The WSA obtained permits from the city of Los Angeles to run the contest and, as such, priority access to Malibu's fabled surf break. While organized surfing competitions make every effort to clear the lineup of non-competitors, not everyone obeys. With no security, it can become a free for all. And it did.

During his second heat, Chris found himself having to maneuver through a hundred or more Malibu locals. Contest organizers and area lifeguards couldn't control all the surfers in the water. The crowd ate Chris up, and all he could muster was eighty points. Allen Sarlo, who had been born and bred on these waves, scored 550 points and claimed first place. Rick Rouse from Encinitas was second, Aaron Wright from Pacifica was third, and Chris was fourth. Considering the circumstances, Chris took it all in stride.

A few months later, Surfing published an article by Brandon Wander about the event with a passage that read: "In the end the contest could only be ranked Mickey Mouse. Chris O'Rourke and Jeff Smith seemed the class of the contest, but gained little for their effort."

It was the beginning of the end for the WSA.

Being recognized as an acclaimed surfer in California was one thing, but on the larger stage Chris was still a nobody. To become famous in the surfing world, first you had to make it big in Hawaii.

Hawaii was the proving grounds for everyone, a holy place where dreams could come true—or snap like a twig. Surfing Oahu's famed North Shore had always been one of Chris's dreams. Now, it was a necessary step on the next part of his journey.

One day in early December, I saw him near my locker.

"Hey Chris, when are you leaving for Hawaii?"

"Tomorrow actually, I can't wait anymore. If it wasn't for school, I would have gone three weeks ago," Chris responded.

"Since when has school ever stopped you before?" I asked with a laugh.

"I'm doing it for my mom. She told me that, for every day I go to school, she won't drink."

"Under the circumstances, that sounds like a fair trade. I hope you get some good surf in Hawaii. Good luck over there, Chris," I told him as we shook hands.

"Thanks, Aeder. I can't wait!"

His mother's bout with alcoholism appeared to be getting better. Chris had been a positive influence upon his mom and vice versa. He didn't pray very often, except for her. Seeing his mother become stronger meant more to him than anything else in the world. It was also amazing to see him attending school more often in spite of his surfing successes.

Chris made arrangements with his teachers to get out of school two weeks earlier than normal. His recent good behavior, coupled with the promise to make up all his tests after returning, had earned him a reprieve.

He would go to Hawaii ranked as the number one competitive surfer from California. He had finished the second half of the 1975 WSA season as the new 4A Men's champion; just sixteen years old, he held a commanding two thousand point lead over the next competitor.

With Robert Mitchell, another classmate of ours, Chris left the mainland to finally get his first taste of North Shore power. Traveling with Robert was purely out of necessity. His uncle had a house near a surf break called Laniakea. Chris rode the waves at "Lani's" with relative ease, but his focus was on surfing Pipeline and Sunset Beach. Not having a car at first proved to be a major dilemma. But since the North Shore was a fairly compact place, Chris met other surfers who were always glad to give him a ride. Kamehameha Highway went right past every major surf spot on the North Shore.

The winter surf season in Hawaii was already well under way. Chris had never felt this free before—-no school, no tests, no hassles, and no father yelling at him. Soon enough, however, Robert's uncle had enough of the two boys' obnoxious behavior. He drove Chris and Robert north toward another popular surf spot called Velzyland and just dropped them off by the side of the road with their surfboards, suitcases, wetsuits and all.

Fortunately, Chris noticed a couple of friends standing nearby. They had rented an apartment near Velzyland and immediately invited Chris and Robert to stay with them. The tiny one bedroom apartment instantly overflowed with six surfers and their arsenal of surfboards. Chris and Robert were forced to sleep on the hard floor, but to them it was still luxury. Welcome to the North Shore!

Eventually they borrowed a beat-up, rusty brown Volkswagen with two broken windows from an old Hawaiian couple who lived next door and had really taken a liking to Chris. Having a car meant he could venture to other spots, too—Rocky Point, Sunset Beach, and at last, Pipeline. Robert surfed, too, but had also brought along his movie camera, and on the bigger swells he was content to film Chris from the beach.

Chris confidently rode waves far bigger than anything he had ever tackled before. His quiver of three Caster surfboards included a 6'7" purple swallowtail for smaller waves, a 6'10" round tail for medium-sized waves, and a 7'2" pintail for bigger surf.

That winter, he was one of only a few talented California surfers in Hawaii. Overshadowed by the Hawaiians and a strong international contingent of professional surfers, Chris nonetheless did his best to stand out. He had hoped to enter any of the pro North Shore surfing events that he could, but Hawaiian competitions had stricter entry qualifications than California. A pecking order existed, and due to his relative anonymity outside mainland America, Chris discovered he could only get into the events as an alternate

But in early January of 1976, Chris's luck changed—and so did the entire surfing world. The International Professional Surfing (IPS) organization announced its formation, and a professional world tour of surfing finally became a reality. Surfing events would be held throughout the year at locations worldwide, with prize money awarded by sponsors of each contest. The diversity of corporate sponsors appeared promising for everyone involved. Some, such as Lightning Bolt Surfboards, were known names in the surfing industry; others like Coca Cola had nothing to do with surfing at all. Based on a ratings system, an annual world champion would be determined at year's end.

This was exactly the kind of news Chris had been waiting for. And with all of the world's top professionals already in Hawaii, the first contest of the season immediately got under way. The IPS tour's inaugural event, the Lightning Bolt Championships, was set to kick off at Sunset Beach a few days later. But since the waves there would be too large and out of control, officials shifted the location to Makaha Beach on Oahu's western shore.

As the highest-ranked surfer from the West Coast, Chris made every effort to get into the contest, but his lack of experience in Hawaiian surf relegated him to the alternate list. Another surfer ahead of him on the list would have to drop out, and since every surfer in Hawaii jumped at the chance to surf in the contests, Chris's chances of getting in were next to impossible. Undeterred, he went to Makaha and hoped for the best.

On the beach he bumped into Mike Purpus. Mike had been to Hawaii several times before, and his tenure in competitive surfing had earned him an automatic berth in this contest. They talked for several minutes, all the while keeping their focus on the large waves breaking out at Makaha. Fifteen to eighteen-foot waves swept through the lineup.

Watching them, Chris said, "Well, Mike, maybe I won't feel so bad about not getting into this contest. It looks pretty wild out there."

Even Mike had his doubts. Mike had no animosity toward Chris and actually felt proud of him. The rambunctious kid from La Jolla would just be reaching his prime by the time pro surfing really evolved into anything.

"I gotta tell you something, Chris," Mike said. "You are the most 'radical-smooth' guy I have ever seen in my life. You're an unbelievable surfer, and you certainly can be a champion someday. God damn it, I wish I was ten years younger, so I could surf against you when the time arrives."

"Thanks, Mike. That means a lot to me," Chris told him.

His words were a big vote of confidence from someone who mattered. Mike had once been victorious at the Makaha International Championships in the Juniors' Division. Long after Mike walked away, Chris stuck around hoping to get into the event, but it wasn't meant to be.

WSA rankings meant nothing here in Hawaii, and this did not sit well with Chris. He noticed Mike's first heat included another California surfer, Mike Doyle. Rory Russell from Hawaii, along with Terry Fitzgerald and Nat Young from Australia, rounded out the field. All of them were eight to ten years older than Chris. How could he make a name for himself in Hawaii if he couldn't get into the contests?

That sense of urgency was something he had felt a lot lately. Other talented young surfers seemed content to play the waiting game, but Chris always seemed to feel he was running out of time.

A few nights later, Chris awoke to loud noises that sounded like thunder but turned out to be thunderous waves. The largest swell of the winter season had arrived in the middle of the night and unleashed its fury upon the North Shore. Chris was so excited he couldn't go back to sleep. In the dark of night, he walked the short distance to the beach at Velzyland to have a look. In the pitch black, he could see that the ocean had turned completely white.

Early the next morning, Chris and Robert took off for Waimea Bay. The Smirnoff Pro contest was about to commence, and the waves were the largest Chris had ever seen. Colossal walls of water topping thirty feet stormed across the bay. On the beach, a "who's who" of surfing had gathered in preparation. The heavyweight surfers from Hawaii prepared their boards, including Reno Abellira, the Aikau brothers, Gerry Lopez, and James "Booby" Jones. They were joined by the young Australians: Peter Townend, Mark Richards, Ian Cairns, and Rabbit Bartholomew. Along the wave-battered shoreline, ABC's Wide World of Sports hurried to set up large television cameras. Several helicopters surveyed the scene from above.

Chris walked around the Waimea Beach Park, working his way into the crowd of professionals and mingling with as many of them as possible. Mike Purpus was one of only two California surfers entered into the contest. With such large surf, several competitors were hesitant to paddle out. Contest Director Fred Hemmings, once a world champion surfer in his own right, announced he would paddle out on his own to show everyone it could be done.

Surfing such mammoth waves was no walk in the park; under these conditions, lives could be on the line. But at the end of the most incredible surfing contest the sport had ever seen, Mark Richards was the winner. A few weeks earlier, he had also been victorious during the World Cup at Sunset Beach. Ian Cairns took first place at the Duke Kahanamoku contest, while Shaun Tomson had captured the Pipeline Masters.

That winter proved that surfers from other parts of the world could compete with the Hawaiians, who were long considered the dominant force in the sport. Professional surfing had reached a turning point, and while Chris was happy to be there, he wasn't happy to be on the outside looking in. Aspiring surfers from California had regularly taken a back seat in major surfing competitions. Chris was determined to change all that.

Chapter 17

An Unguided Missile

La Jolla, June, 1976

The 1976 inaugural IPS world tour had reached its halfway point, and in the hierarchy of pro surfing, California was still at the bottom. With nearly non-existent sponsorship, representation from California was minimal even for its most established surfers. Jetting around the globe chasing surfing competitions came with a high cost. Mike Purpus made it to only a few events before finally running out of money.

Chris and a few other American mainland surfers, like Florida's Jeff Crawford, definitely had the ability to compete, but not the funds. At the time, corporate sponsorship of professional surfers by American companies was still unusual; the sport and the industry were regarded as too raw. The sport needed more than just good surfers—it needed creative marketing.

It didn't help matters that ideological divisions still existed within California. A new ethic sprang up based on loyalty to specific geographic regions. This was the sort of notoriety "soul surfers" craved, not the international spotlight. This caused a reactionary shift away from what was considered "progressive" surfing and manifested itself in ways such as wearing all-black wetsuits or riding anonymous all-white surfboards. Anything colorful or flashy was frowned upon.

On the opposite side were those eager to see surfing progress. A core of budding young talent lined the California coast: Kevin Reed and Joey Thomas from Santa Cruz, Russell Short from Ventura, Allen Sarlo and Mike Weed from Los Angeles, Tony

Staples and Chris O'Rourke from San Diego. These were the surfers touted as having the best chance to break through. In particular, Kevin and Chris set themselves apart from the rest with their creativity and innovation. Chris's backside tube riding was truly cutting edge, while Kevin's futuristic-looking aerial maneuvers left people astonished.

As fate would have it, the rise of Chris O'Rourke as California's top-rated surfer coincided with the downfall of the competitive venue he dominated. The second half of the 1975 WSA season proved to be the organization's last. Chris had achieved his goal of finishing first in the Men's 4A and had become the undeniable champion, but where would he go from here? His elite status in the WSA certainly hadn't done him any good in Hawaii. Surfers from other areas of the world were the ones receiving all the accolades anyway: Bertlemann, Ho, Buttons, Jackie Dunn, Mark Liddell, and Dane Kealoha from Hawaii; Australians Richards, Bartholomew, Townend, Mark Warren, Bruce Raymond and Michael Peterson; and South Africa's Jonathan Paarman and Shaun and Michael Tomson.

Even America's East Coast boasted three fairly progressive surfers: Jeff Crawford, Rick Rasmussen, and Greg Loehr. The trio all hailed from Florida, which only made the lack of international-caliber talent from California more glaring.

To make matters worse, no IPS contests were scheduled for California in 1976—a true indication of how badly professional surfing was suffering in the Golden State. Chris didn't have enough money or big sponsors to chase the IPS tour, and once again he sensed that time was not on his side. His goals and ambitions were slipping away, and it seemed there was nothing he could do about it.

With no contests in sight, Chris had to be content as the prince of the La Jolla reef breaks. He also began to frequent the waves at Blacks, a powerful beach break north of La Jolla Shores, as well as remote locations in upper Baja California. The only silver lining to surfing locally was that he now had more time for school. He and Oscar even picked up work as busboys at the Bratskellar restaurant on Prospect Street.

Chris had also discovered a love of music and regularly listened to his favorite tunes before hitting the waves. While the Stones and Led Zepplin ranked among his top choices, he was particularly inspired by George Benson's "Breezin." While surfing he would play it over and over in his head, matching his moves to the rhythm.

For several days the waves had been good, and I had not seen Chris at school. One day about a week before summer vacation, Chris casually strolled into our English class ten minutes late. Jim and I were sitting in the back of the room. We knew that the teacher, Mr. Ulan, would not resist giving Chris some ribbing.

"Ooooooooooh, class...there he is! Welcome to English 101, Mr. Chris O'Rourke. We are so honored you have decided to bless us with your presence today," he said with obvious sarcasm.

Chris hurriedly looked about the room, as if he had forgotten where his seat was. Mr. Ulan couldn't help but take the act further.

"Oh, and can I also get your chair for you, Mr. O'Rourke? I mean, you spend so much time on your surfboard you must be tired! So it must feel good to sit down sometimes. There are actually several empty chairs today, so please take whichever one you'd like."

When the teacher pulled one of the chairs aside and invited him to sit down, the entire class burst into laughter. Chris's face turned bright red, one of the few times I ever saw him get embarrassed, but after a few moments, he began laughing, too. Mr. Ulan was one of the few teachers at La Jolla High School who knew how to handle Chris while pulling his strings at the same time.

Chris somehow received an A in English that semester. Not that he appeared to care much. When the last day of school came to a close, Chris had only two things on his mind: surfing and sex. By now he had become a magnet for girls. If he'd had his own bedroom, it would have needed a revolving door. Instead, he would sneak through a girl's bedroom window at night and out the next morning and boast to Jim or Oscar about what transpired.

Parties around La Jolla in the '70s were infamous for rowdiness. When someone's parents left town, his or her house instantly became available for mayhem. An invitation for twenty regularly turned into a crowd of one hundred simply through word of mouth. Most parties included revelry, drinking, sex, drugs, and fistfights.

Chris was a fixture at them. Usually he was quickly besieged upon either by friends who wanted to talk about surfing or girls who wanted a piece of him. With no surfing contests on the horizon, chasing girls became more of a priority. His romantic conquests took more energy out of him than surfing. And while he had a beer every so often, he wasn't a big drinker. After witnessing what his mother had gone through, the urge for the bottle just wasn't there. Marijuana, though, was a different story.

Early one morning I met up with Chris at Windansea. We had made plans to shoot photos, but the small surf dictated otherwise. As we stood cursing the lack of waves, Ted Smith walked up. We had all been at the same party the night before, and it showed. Ted, especially, was dragging his heels.

"Hey Nob, you don't look so good," Chris said, using his nickname for Ted.

"Well I don't feel that great either. I need breakfast more than I need the waves. It looks pretty shitty out there anyway," he responded.

"The surf is so bad because the tide is too low," explained Chris. "The high tide in the afternoon should push the swell in better. I'm starving also. Let's go eat and come back later."

Chris finally had a car, so we piled into his faded yellow Datsun sedan and went to John's Waffle Shop, a popular La Jolla eatery on Girard Street. Chris knew almost everyone in there. He pretty much lived on cereal for breakfast, lunch and dinner, and I made the mistake of offering to buy him breakfast. When the waitress brought our food, I discovered he had placed two orders of steak and eggs!

After breakfast we drove a short distance to the top of Soledad Mountain, where we stood in the shadow of the large cross and gazed down upon the scenic coastline. A prime make-out spot at night, the mountain's high elevation provided unobstructed views of San Diego for miles in every direction in the daytime .

It was also perfect for checking the surf. Judging by the wave lines, it appeared the new swell had finally arrived. Chris didn't look satisfied, though.

"Now that's pretty weird," he said, puzzled. "The Shores and Blacks aren't that far apart, separated by less than a mile or so, right? But look at the angle of the approaching swells. The waves at the Shores are small and wimpy, while Blacks is big and pumping! You would never know those two places are so completely different right now unless you are up here."

Ted and I stood silent.

"Well Chris, I'm glad you have become such an astute observer of our environment," I chided him.

Chris looked at me quizzically. Usually he was the one screwing with me.

"Okay you guys, look down there again. You can see it's a straight south swell by the angle of the waves coming in. See those lefts over there at Blacks? The waves are wrapping parallel along the coast and bending back out to sea. Now look at the Shores. Everywhere south of Scripps pier is really small. During south swells, the Shores get blocked by the tip of La Jolla Cove, so the waves can't get in there as well," Chris stated.

"Tell us something we don't already know," replied Ted.

"Yeah, thank you for that educational fact, Mr. Surf Star," I said to him with even more sarcasm.

"Hey Aeder, what's with you? I've never seen you try to act so tough before," Chris said with a laugh. "All I can say is that you better have your cameras ready today, because we're going to put on a clinic."

"If Blacks looks that good, then Windansea should be even better. Let's go," stated Ted.

We hurried back to Chris's car and sped off. Getting Chris to surf somewhere other than Windansea wasn't impossible, but sometimes it felt that way. He just wanted to be where the waves were the best, and if that meant his beloved Windansea, then so be it. When it came to surfing photos, it really didn't matter to me. I was content to follow Chris anywhere.

With four surfboards tediously strapped to the car's roof, we headed off down Soledad Mountain Road in the direction of Windansea. Ted sat next to Chris in the front; I was crammed into the back seat surrounded by a pile of smelly wetsuits. Even the pungent aroma of surf bar wax failed to offset the stench. Attempting to find more leg room, I shifted my body and noticed nearly two dozen bars of wax on the floor.

"Oh Chris, do you think you have enough wax?" I joked.

"That's not all of it," he said. "There's about ten more under Ted's seat."

"Well, considering how much you surf, I guess you need it. You're like a fish," stated Ted, glancing back at me for approval.

Knowing he would be in the waves soon always excited Chris. He slipped a pink cassette tape into the stereo. As the Rolling Stones' "Hot Stuff" played loudly, he pushed down harder on the gas pedal. Almost simultaneously we started bobbing our heads in unison. Ted attempted a feeble imitation of Mick Jagger, and Chris immediately gave him shit for it.

Then I noticed Chris was looking at me in the rearview mirror.

"Hey Aeder, have you heard this song before? It's from their Black and Blue album," he told me.

"Oh come on, Chris. You think I already didn't know that?"

All of us were avid fans of the Stones, but none more so than he. In the mirror I could see Chris's baffled expression.

"There's something about you today, Aeder. You really aren't a jock-head anymore," Chris said approvingly.

I made a weird face at him while using one of his own favorite expressions.

"Well 'duh,' Chris. But just remember, I can have fun and still stay in school."

When it came to friendship, Chris always wanted to have the upper hand. Through his tenacity, I had learned to be stronger and stand up for myself. He taught me how to level the playing field, just as I was doing now. Chris had noticed the change in me, too, which made our bond as friends finally complete.

We could see whitewater from the surf along the coast ahead. Chris pushed the pedal down even harder. As we approached the bottom of the hill, we saw a perfectly arranged set of orange traffic cones. With no one in sight, the colorful array became a target Chris could not resist. He swerved and began knocking them down one by one. Watching the cones tumble in various directions behind us was hilarious, but our laughter wouldn't last for long.

A construction worker had witnessed our act. He was enormous—and irate. He stepped out into the middle of the street and wildly waved us down.

"Uh-oh. The closer we get, the bigger that guy looks," said Ted.

"Shit, you're right. That guy could play for the Chargers in the NFL. Maybe he does?" I added.

"Oh, stop being such pussies, you guys. Just watch and learn," said Chris, slowing down as if he were going to stop.

The big man continued to stand his ground in the middle of the street.

"Hope you know what you're doing, Chris," I said with apprehension.

As the car slowed further, the man moved from the middle of the road. Figuring we were cornered, he appeared ready to give us a solid thrashing.

"Is this your plan, Chris? To just stop, so we can all get our asses kicked?" asked Ted.

Chris knew there was still enough room to get around him. He stepped on the gas and swerved to the right side of the road. We flew past the angry man, sideswiping the curb in the process and dislodging a hubcap. Through the back window, I watched his reaction and was glad we had fled. Stomping up and down in the middle of the street, he threw a tantrum, hurling his hardhat violently upon the ground. As he disappeared from view, all I could see was his middle finger.

"Sucker!" Chris yelled out the window.

Finally clear of the human roadblock, our panic turned into hysterical laughter. We ventured on, pulling up a few minutes later outside Oscar's house. On Nautilus Street just a short walk from Windansea, it was the perfect hangout, and everyone kept at least one surfboard there. Oscar's father, Ruben, was a warm and friendly man born in Italy and raised in Argentina. Oscar had been born in Buenos Aires in 1957 and moved to Beverly Hills with his parents a year later. In 1968, he moved to La Jolla with his father.

Unlike many parents, Ruben welcomed the young surfers. Since Chris's parents were still mired in turmoil, he was practically living at Oscar's full-time. Chris found peace and solitude at Oscar's. He just wanted to surf without interference.

As we walked on the red brick path around the house, I heard laughter ahead. Chris pushed open the gray wooden gate, and I immediately smelled the pungent aroma of marijuana. The rest of the crew was already there: Jim Neri, Mark Ruyle, Tim Senneff, Mark McCoy, and of course, Oscar.

Within our circle of friends, only Mark Ruyle was born and raised in San Diego. The rest of us had come from elsewhere. Our lives were thrown together by circumstance, and in many ways, it felt like we were all family. Living in La Jolla, our opportunities seemed unlimited. All we had to do now was take advantage of them.

We gathered on the large wooden porch surrounded by bright pink rose bushes and tall pine trees. An array of Caster surfboards was spread across the grass lawn, a silent endorsement of everyone's favorite shaper. Since not every surfer likes the same dimensions and shapes, Bill made it a point to treat each one individually and shape their boards accordingly.

It wasn't just by coincidence that they all rode Caster boards. When Chris finished with one of his free boards, he was allowed to give it to whomever he wanted, and everyone clamored for his hand-me-downs.

Standing there passing around a joint, we began to compare surfboards. Tim picked up Ted's board, closely examining its curves and lines. Chris walked over, too.

"Hey Nob, I know that Bill made you this board, but the nose is so thick it's hideous," he said. "Does this thing even turn? How can you possibly ride it?"

"Well, it works for me," snapped Ted. "Besides, not all of us get our boards for free. I use a thicker board because I want it to last longer and not break."

Feeling deflated by Chris's remark, he muttered something unintelligible before grabbing the board from Tim's hands.

Chris had become a master of finding weird nicknames for his friends, and he rarely called anyone by their real name. Another nickname for Ted was Rapelroin. Tim was known as Neo Sennefrine, and Mark McCoy as Fishface. And it didn't take him long for him to come up with a name for me, too. He began referring to me as A-Dee-Do, which he derived from an obnoxious television commercial about a local plumbing business with the same name.

Somewhere along the way, Chris also thought up a terrible vocabulary of words that no one else knew. For starters there was shreidle and eaglebug. He would just throw those words out in the middle of a sentence and expect everyone to know what they meant. Even when surfing he enjoyed making bizarre yodeling sounds. From what anyone could tell, the noise was a warning that a set of waves was approaching.

Chris's vibrant, enigmatic persona was magnetic. He was always the center of attention, and in spite of his obnoxious behavior, we truly believed in him. We all just sensed that he was one of a kind and wanted to be there with him when everything happened.

Jim emerged from the house holding the most recent copy of Surfer magazine, which featured a few photos of Chris.

"Did you get published again, Chris?" inquired Tim.

"Of course he's in the magazine again, you knucklehead," said Oscar. "He's only the best surfer in all of California. Chris can surf circles around anyone."

It was obvious the sweet marijuana's effect had settled in. Chris waxed down his surfboard, brimming with confidence.

"The IPS pro tour started earlier this year. I heard that, other than Purpus, Flecky, and Randy Laine, no one else from California is even trying," Chris remarked. "How pathetic is that? I need to make some money and find a few more sponsors. Then next year, I will compete full-time."

"How are you going to do that, Chris? Traveling is so expensive," asked Mark.

"It's not impossible. I just have to try harder. Before every IPS contest, they have these preliminary trials. If you do well, you can get into the main event. At the end of the year, being ranked in the top sixteen provides guaranteed entries in all of the contests for the following year," explained Chris. "I don't know how I will come up with all the money. Caster said he would pay for some of it, but I need to find other sponsors, too. All I know is the drive to better myself just has to be there. Otherwise, I'll just drop off the map."

His face lit up with excitement while contemplating the possibilities. "Anyway, enough talking for now. It's time to go surfing, boys," he said.

Our Commander had spoken. Everyone picked up their boards and scurried off toward Windansea as if on a mission. Toting along my camera equipment and metal tripod, I fell behind them.

These guys were vastly different than my other friends, none of whom were surfers, and I had a ton of fun hanging out with them. I soon discovered that my personality was changing, too; being part of their gang had altered me. In addition, I had become more proficient in surfing photography. Several of my photos had finally been published in Surfing magazine, which earned me further respect and trust.

I used to be nervous about going near Windansea, but in the company of these guys, it was no problem. Becoming a surf photographer had really helped punch my ticket to enter its fabled domain. There wasn't a surfer alive who didn't like to have his picture taken.

I set up my gear in the shade of the hut while everyone paddled out. For the next hour, I photographed them catching and riding the three to four-foot waves. As usual Chris was the standout, and I captured several nice shots of him. Although he enjoyed riding larger waves further outside, every so often he paddled for a wave at Right Hooker and tucked into several small tube rides. He looked completely at home inside those hollow waves.

But the mood was about to change. Glancing toward the water's edge, I noticed two surfers preparing to enter the ocean. Though I was far from being any sort of Windansea veteran, I could tell they were not from La Jolla and had never surfed here before. None of this mattered to me, but it mattered to the locals. I sensed there would be trouble.

Mark Ruyle began paddling for a nice wave breaking toward the left. One of the new surfers paddled, too, and took off in front of him. Both rose to their feet, but when Mark turned his board at the base of the wave he instantly collided with the other surfer. Chris was paddling back out in the channel and had a clear view of the situation. As the two surfers emerged from beneath the frothy water, he saw that the other surfer's board had poked a massive hole into the deck of Mark's brand new Caster board. Mark and the other surfer began to exchange verbal insults. The sight of his friend arguing with a stranger was all the inspiration Chris needed.

"You fucking, kook. What the hell are you doing? You shouldn't even be out here. Eat shit and go home," Chris told the other surfer.

The surfer told Chris to fuck off. And the fireworks began.

His Irish blue eyes lit up like a Christmas tree, and his face turned purple with rage. He paddled up to the surfer and sprang right on top of him. Chris began wrestling with the other surfer, finally driving him under the surface of the water. Placing him in a headlock, Chris pulled the surfer's head back above water and began delivering a series of solid blows to his face. The surfer's friend, who had been watching the proceedings from afar, paddled over to help. But he was quickly intercepted by Oscar and Mark who kept him well away from the fight.

Another set of waves passed through, but Chris maintained his solid grip. To make matters worse for the surfer Chris had been pummeling, his board was now floating toward shore.

Finally, he broke free of Chris's grasp and swam away. But Chris wasn't done with him just yet. He hunted down the surfer's board and headed for the beach. Tossing it onto the sand, he found a large rock nearby and used it to hammer several deep holes into the deck. All the poor guys could do was watch helplessly.

"Get the hell out of here and don't ever come back. You hear me? Ever! And tell all your other kook friends out there in Clairemont, too," shouted Chris.

Then, as if nothing had happened, he calmly paddled back out into the surf. His personality had changed in an instant. The two surfers quickly departed, and calm was restored.

It was vintage Windansea. I was not the type to go looking for trouble, but when I was hanging around these guys, I knew something exciting could happen at any moment. I felt like wherever they were was the place to be, and I wanted to be there, too. Chris was always there for his friends, even if it meant getting into a full-scale brawl. Not that he always felt good about it; later that afternoon while we were walking back up the street, I could sense his regret. He had come a long way from hunting for lizards along these very same bluffs.

Chapter 18

Donuts at Ralphs

Late Summer, 1976

In 1976, most people still knew or cared little about surfing. But for those riding the waves, the allure of the ocean was powerful and almost spiritual. Surfers thrived on challenging a raw force of nature amidst an environment where inherent dangers were everywhere.

Every day and every swell was different, which was why Chris and so many others had become attracted to the sport in the first place. Many surfers believed their true personalities were revealed through their individual surfing styles, and the ocean provided an outlet for these personalities to come alive.

This certainly was true for Chris. He had become an artist of sorts, choreographing his every move on the waves at Windansea. Tom Ortner was particularly impressed and could see that Chris was incredibly passionate about surfing. Tom had been around a long time and never saw a truly high-caliber professional surfer emerge from Windansea—until now. He had no idea where Chris's remarkable surfing style came from, but he knew it was way beyond what anyone else around there was doing.

In addition to fueling Chris's artistic style, the waves continued to serve as a release valve for his anger. His relationship with his father continued its downward spiral. Chris might have been just a teenager, but he certainly wasn't naive. It was bewildering that a once wealthy and highly successful individual could have fallen so far. Chris knew a lot of his family-related issues didn't quite add up, but instead of taking the time to look deeper, it became easier to simply place all the blame upon his father.

Unfortunately, Chris had no idea that Bart Sr. had actually been following his surfing accomplishments and was impressed by his skills. At a time when newspaper coverage of surfing events was almost nonexistent, his father would often telephone the sports editors of the San Diego newspapers with the contest results. He never told anyone about it, so when the results were published, no one knew how they got there. He was proud of Chris, and it pained him to see how their relationship had deteriorated so completely.

Chris also realized that he was growing more distant from his brother and sister. Bart and Lyn loved their little brother, but his erratic behavior was often hard to deal with. Other than his depressed mother, none of Chris's family members attempted to provide significant guidance. Not that it would do much good. Resisting any sort of control had always been in his nature.

Although he no longer lived with his parents, Chris regularly stopped by to visit his mother. He would sit and talk with her for hours. Each time she went into the kitchen, Chris followed her, intent on making sure she wasn't pouring alcohol.

"I love you, Chris, and thanks for trying to help me," she often told him.

Chris continued to find his escape at Windansea. When he had first paddled out just a few years earlier, the older surfers had laughed at him. But nobody was laughing anymore. No one even dared look at him the wrong way. Chris was still getting into fights, often with surfers twice his size, with little or no regard for his own safety.

Occasionally out-of-towners who had previous run-ins with Chris would purposely come looking for him. But Chris always seemed to escape the potential confrontations. He compared it to how the underworld people had often stalked his father. Now Chris knew what it felt like.

That fall, we all began our senior year of high school. Jim and I began making plans for college. Ted showed little interest in furthering his education, and attending a university was the farthest thing from Chris's mind. Considering how often he still ditched school, it seemed a miracle that he would actually graduate. How he hung in there was a mystery no one quite figured out. His teachers either loved or hated him—there was no middle ground. All I knew was, when it really counted the most, Chris had allies in all the right places.

One person definitely on Chris's side was our history teacher, old Ralph Dawson. He was a surfer, too, but not just any surfer; he had been one of the first in San Diego. The educator was now in his early sixties, but during the '30s and '40s Ralph, along with a few buddies like Skeeter Malcolm, helped pioneer surfing in San Diego. Ralph had a smooth and very recognizable surfing style, along with a deep love for the sport. His exploits were legendary, so much so that a particular surf break he often frequented in Point Loma had become known as "Ralph's."

Only a handful of surfers existed in all of San Diego County during his glory days, but when too many of them showed up at the same spot, Ralph often went ballistic. Upon arriving at the Ocean Beach pier, he often complained to his friends that it was too crowded to surf —even though there were only two or three other surfers in the water! So Ralph began searching for other places to ride that no one else knew about.

Soon, he stumbled across one such place adjacent to the San Diego Harbor entrance. However, this unique surf break came with a catch. The waves ended their journey in ocean waters situated directly offshore of government land and were not readily accessible. His discovery of this previously un-ridden spot coincided with the start of World War II. San Diego's naval bases and industry were booming, and since the area was in the middle of a sensitive military location, the waves were deemed off-limits to anyone trying to access them—at least by land.

Ralph, however, figured the Navy never said anything about reaching the waves by boat. He and his friends wasted little time securing a suitable vessel, and the legend began. It soon became such a favorite of his that Ralph rarely went anywhere

Top: Chris flashing the peace sign while horsing around with a friend in La Jolla, 1968.
Bottom: The calm before the storm—Chris at age three wading into the lake at the
O'Rourke family estate in Maine. Summer of 1962.

Top: Chris at the Marine Room holding one of his first surfboards, 1970.
Bottom left: Muirlands Junior High School 8th grade photo, 1973.
Bottom right: Chris's La Jolla High School graduation photo. Fall of 1976.

Top: The inside wave section at Windansea known as 'Right Hooker.' This is where Chris built his notorious reputation. 1977.
Bottom: A fiery-red sunset at Windansea during the famous 'Monster South Swell From New Zealand. September of 1975.

Top: Chris surfing at Windansea upon a rare wave breaking to the right during the huge New Zealand south swell. September of 1975.
Bottom: Overview of the wave lineup at Windansea with the distinctive palm frond thatched-hut in the foreground. 1978.

Top: Chris's classic surfing style was more than evident on this day at Windansea. Late summer, 1976.
Bottom: The undisputed king of California surfing in 1976. Chris standing near the Windansea hut.

Top: It only seems appropriate that the road situated above Windansea is named Neptune Street. Neptune was the ruler of the sea, and so was Chris at Windansea.

Bottom: At his peak, Chris's backside surfing style had no peers from the U.S. mainland. The formidable waves at Big Rock were his playground where he showed off his amazing talents.

Main photo and inset: Chris had already been diagnosed with Hodgkin's lymphoma when these two photos were taken on the same day in late summer of 1977. He appears as healthy as ever wearing his Quiksilver trunks and Caster t-shirt in the backyard at Oscar's house, and later, tearing apart the waves at Windansea.

Top: During our day trip to a recluse surf spot in Northern Baja California known as 'Power Plants,' Chris's powerful style of surfing was on full display. February 1977.

Bottom left: On the way back to San Diego, and before passing over the international border, we stopped at a roadside taco stand where Chris mingled with, and fed, a few circus elephants that had broken loose from their confines.

Bottom right: Chris clowning around before paddling out at Power Plants.

Top: In early March of 1977 Chris received three new Caster surfboards before departing for Australia and his debut on the IPS world tour. Alongside Chris are surfboard shaper Bill Caster (lower left) and airbrusher Gary Goodrum (lower right).

Bottom: Chris surfing at Velzyland on Oahu's north shore in December of 1977. While Chris was a well-known standout surfer from the U.S. mainland, that winter he was overshadowed by all the emerging international talent on the north shore.

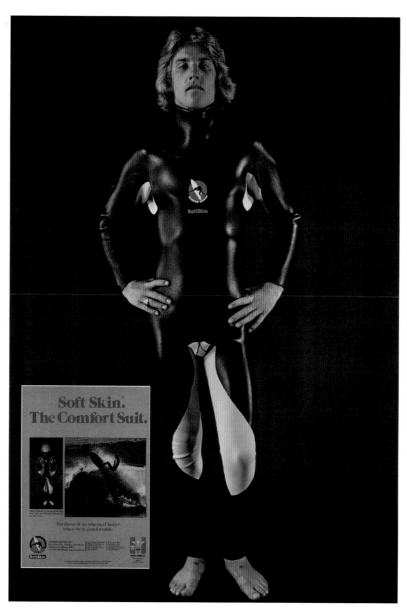

In the fall of 1977, Chris posed for photographer Larry Moore for a Surfer House wetsuit advertisement. The company was one of Chris's first major sponsors. The completed ad, which appeared in the Feb/March 1978 issue of Surfing Magazine, is shown in the inset.

Top: Several hundred yards north of Windansea, the surf break known as Simmon's Reef is where Chris excelled at front-side tube riding. It's astonishing to think that, even today, no other surfer has come close to what Chris once accomplished out there.

Bottom: Chris emerging from his spectacular, and often-talked about, lengthy tube ride at Simmon's Reef in February of 1978.

Top: This moment truly was 'a miracle day.' A few months after his cancer reappeared, and after having a significant part of his skull removed, Chris finally went surfing again at Windansea. He is seen here exiting the ocean wearing a hockey helmet in obvious pain. May 1978.

Bottom: As time went on, and even with part of his skull missing, Chris's surfing rapidly improved, much to everyone's amazement. One day I was taking pictures from the water and he narrowly missed hitting me while performing one of his patented 'off the lips.' One oddity of this photo is the distinctive cross reflecting off the top of his helmet.

Top: Eventually Chris switched to a sturdier form of head protection in the form of a yellow skateboard helmet. Paddling out at Windansea, cancer and all, Chris still felt as if he had all the reasons in the world to smile. September, 1979.
Bottom: On the same day, Chris performs a backside off the lip on a left-breaking wave.

Top left: Chris could no longer compete in professional surfing contests in the way he was once accustomed to. Competitive to the bone, this thought pained him, perhaps more than the actual cancer itself. So his friend Chris Ahrens (center) arranged a one-on-one showdown with fellow professional California surfer Dan Flecky (right) at Windansea. Chris won. September 1979.
Top Right: After being diagnosed with cancer, the two primary fixtures in Chris's life were his loving wife Jil, and son Timothy. February 1979
Bottom: Chris with his son Tim, mother Gloria, and brother Bart. January 1979.

Top: This is one of Chris's last tube rides ever at Windansea, January 1981.
Bottom: Just part of the crowd that began to gather for the scattering of Chris's ashes in the wave lineup at Windansea, early June 1981.

Top: Even though Chris passed away when he was only twenty-two years old, it felt like the two of us were friends for a lifetime. And while I regularly took many photos of him, there were few photos of us together, except this one in the backyard of Oscar's house near Windansea. Spring, 1979.
Bottom: This is one of the most memorable photos I ever took of Chris. Through all the pain he smiled while flashing the peace sign at Windansea. This image is how I will always remember him. September 1980.

else. Occasionally a military boat would pull up in the deep water channel and try to entice him to leave, but Ralph knew that the ocean was for everyone and held his ground. And why wouldn't he? The smooth, four to six-foot walls of water peeled along for several hundred yards. The stellar waves mostly broke to the right and resembled a point break more than a reef break.

He had heard a lot about Chris, who was now his student, and teacher and pupil formed a real bond. The fact that Ralph was forty-five years older than Chris meant nothing. A surfer was a surfer no matter what the age. Ralph was one of the few educators Chris actually respected.

The previous summer, Ralph had watched Chris surf during an informal competition at the Ocean Beach pier. For the first time, he was able to witness his pupil's extraordinary talents. What Ralph saw in Chris mirrored what he saw in himself. Watching Chris that day made him feel younger again, full of drive, energy, and determination. In reality he was now an old man, but that didn't stop him from living his ocean thrills vicariously through Chris. Ralph realized that Chris was not only trying to elevate his own surfing, but the entire sport along with him.

"That's a lot of weight to carry around on your shoulders, young man," he told Chris one day. "Don't let it get too complicated, or it will stop being any fun for you."

So it was safe to say that he cut Chris a lot of slack in school, especially when it came to truancies. As long as Chris showed up to take his tests, Ralph didn't seem to care if he was in class or not. If Chris was absent, it just meant that somewhere the waves were good, and he was there riding them.

Just a few weeks into the fall quarter, a late-season south swell had been brewing, and Chris, Tim, and Mark McCoy made plans to ditch school the following morning to surf at Ralph's. They would all meet at Tim's house before sunrise, which would give them ample time to get to the break. First, however, they needed to find a boat, which was much easier said than done.

Chris was the first to arrive. He walked quietly up Tim's driveway with a surfboard tucked under his arm. It was still dark, but Chris noticed the outline of a small sailboat in the side yard. Inside, he pushed open Tim's bedroom door and was surprised to see that his friend was still fast asleep. Tim finally opened his eyes, and when he saw Chris standing there, a guilty look crossed on his face.

"Hey Senny, what's going on? We're still going, right? Right? Tell me you found someone with a boat?" Chris moaned.

"I called everyone I knew, Chris, but none of them could go today," Tim sheepishly replied.

This was not what Chris wanted to hear.

"What are you talking about? I thought you said it would be easy. Come on, Tim! The waves at Ralph's are going to be insane today. We have to find a way to get there!"

"I thought George Taylor was going to come up with one for sure. Then he called me late last night and said he had to work today. So no boat, sorry," said Tim.

While Chris could see that his friend had indeed tried, he was dismayed nonetheless. Then, he recalled the sailboat. Tim saw the change in Chris's expression and knew something outlandish was coming.

"What about that boat out there in your yard? You never told me about that. Let's just take it," demanded Chris.

"No way, Chris, I can't do that," said Tim, horrified at the turn the conversation had taken. "That's my older brother Steve's boat. He'd kill me. Besides, it's way too small and doesn't even have a motor."

Just then Tim's other brother Mike barged into the room. He had overheard their conversation and, instead of dismissing the idea, surprisingly he was all for it—as long as he could come along, too.

"You see, Tim? Come on, let's do this. That boat is just sitting there begging for us to use it," said Chris. He sensed weakness and was going for the jugular.

Just like so many others, Tim found it hard to say no to his friend. After all, he was one of the founders of the Chris O'Rourke Fan Club. What other choice did he have? A few minutes later, he found himself outside staring at the boat with the rest of them.

"It's just a little sailing sabot. Not much room for four surfers in there," he protested weakly.

"It's too late, Senny. You can't get out of it now," Chris responded. "We're going."

Like a general giving military orders, the leader had spoken. The three boys picked up the lightweight boat and carried it to the front driveway. After taking the mast off, they turned the small skiff over and hoisted it upon the roof of Tim's Ford Blazer. Mark showed up just in time to go along. The group gathered up their boards, wax, and wetsuits and climbed into the car.

"I'm not sure how the four of us, along with all our stuff, are supposed to fit into that boat. I mean, look at us now—we can hardly fit inside this car!" Tim said in one last futile protest. "I want to go surf at Ralph's as badly as the rest of you, but I kind of think this is a little nuts."

"I think we're nuts if we don't try," answered Chris. "I heard the waves at Ralph's yesterday were insanely perfect, and the swell is supposed to be even bigger today. It's coming straight out of the south, the last one of the summer for sure."

With no further objections, they hit the road. That's when it dawned on them that no one had brought along any food or water.

"Duh, whose fault is that?" asked Mark. "Hey Senny, you were supposed to take care of that, too."

"Yeah, it's all my fault, again," whined Tim. "Why not just blame me for everything?"

"So what do we do now?" asked Mark.

"I'll stop at the 7-11," said Tim.

Chris spoke up confidently. "That won't be necessary, Tim. Just drive over to Muirlands. I will take care of the rest."

Chris revealed his plan. Each weekday morning, a delivery truck brought donuts and cinnamon rolls to the junior high school. Packaged together inside small boxes, the pastries were often left unguarded outside the cafeteria door. Chris knew exactly what time the truck came and went, and it was apparent that he had done this before.

The boys parked out of view across the street and waited for the prize to arrive. Right on time, the delivery truck pulled up, unloaded its bounty, and departed. Chris and Mark bolted from the car and made a beeline toward the goodies. They sneaked up behind the handball courts, close to the cafeteria door. Peering out from behind the wall, they decided the coast was clear and scampered straight for the sweets.

Watching them, Tim and Mike couldn't help but laugh. "Look at them!" exclaimed Tim. "They look more like secret agents than surfers. They must think they're on an episode of Mission Impossible or something."

Armed with two larges boxes of pastries, the partners in crime sprinted back to the car, laughing the entire way. Upon arriving at the Mission Bay boat launch, their stomachs were full of dough and sugar with plenty more for the trip.

They gathered up their surf gear and prepared to get underway—only to realize that none of them actually knew how to sail! Mike and Chris knew some basics, but not enough to get them there.

As the morning sun began its slow rise over the mountains, Chris realized the waves at Ralph's were now happening without him. It was an agonizing thought.

"I used to go sailing with my brother but I don't remember much. How hard could it be though?" Chris exclaimed.

Determined, the four boys carried the boat down the slippery ramp and placed it into the water. Mike climbed in first and rowed it over to the dock where the rest of the crew was waiting. He then pulled out two small sails from inside one of the boat's compartments and rigged it up the best he could.

"We'll be able to get a little momentum from the wind, but not much," he said.

Realizing the boat had several oars, Tim suggested they could also take turns rowing. Mark scoffed at the notion.

"Ralph's is at least five miles down the coast. That won't work," he said.

"Yes, it will. Let's stop wasting time and get going," replied Chris.

The loaded boat was a sight to behold: four surfers, four surfboards, a pile of wetsuits, a few jugs of water, and a stash of donuts. Crammed to capacity, the small craft teetered precariously as it left the dock and headed out toward the harbor entrance. Chris and Mark took the first shift at the oars.

Out in the open sea, they headed south along the coastline, surprised to find their endeavor going rather smoothly. Over the next hour, large ocean swells passed beneath them, rocking their small craft. Chris spotted a California Gray Whale surfacing jut a hundred yards away and admired how the huge beast moved so fluidly. The whale was heading in the same direction, which the crew took as a good omen. For several minutes, the mammoth whale moved along with them. It then thrust its tail skyward as if it were waving goodbye and disappeared underwater.

As they neared Ralph's, their excitement grew. They could see the waves now; crisp early morning offshore winds created plumes of salt spray that stretched high into the air off the top of each breaking wave. Each feverish stroke of their oars brought them closer to the prize. They positioned the boat in the safe open water channel alongside the surf break. And when the first set of waves arrived, it was clear their efforts had not been in vain. Under a cloudless blue sky, four to six-foot waves pounded the ocean's surface with flawless precision. Already in their wetsuits, Chris, Mark, and Mike immediately jumped out of the boat on their surfboards and began paddling toward the empty lineup, leaving Tim alone to anchor the boat.

"Thanks a lot, you guys!" he yelled as they paddled away.

But the pristine conditions silenced any further complaints. The empty lineup and long steep walls of water enabled Chris to perform one radical maneuver after another, some that he had previously only envisioned. Out here, where he wasn't wearing a contest jersey in competition, he had more freedom to experiment.

Chris was a perfectionist; if he didn't perform a particular move right the first time, he kept trying until he did. On some waves he focused on perfecting his roller coaster maneuvers. On others he concentrated on roundhouse cutbacks. And whenever the wave opened up for a tube ride, Chris would always find his way inside. The watery cages provided a brief sense of freedom, and on this day there were plenty of those to go around. Utilizing the sharp rails of his board to turn more fluidly, Chris sprayed so much water around that even the watchful sea lions seemed impressed. He packaged everything together so that his surfing exploded into a dazzling array of precisely executed maneuvers.

Morning turned to afternoon, but no one even noticed. Occasionally one of the surfers would take a short break and paddle back to the boat to fuel up on more donuts. By late afternoon, though, they could surf no more. They still had to row that darned boat all the way back to Mission Bay, but given their exhilarating experience, no one seemed to mind.

On the way back, they were too tired to even talk. But as they neared the harbor entrance, Chris suddenly blurted out, "Every time I ditch school something good always seems to happen."

When Chris was a no-show in history class that day, Ralph Dawson figured he was surfing somewhere. If the south swells were big enough, Ralph could hear the waves at Windansea from his classroom over four blocks away. Later that afternoon when all the students had left, Ralph stood silently by the window listening to the pounding surf. He took a deep breath and sighed. He had spent countless hours in that classroom. It pained him to know that the entire school building, full of classic Spanish architecture, would soon be bulldozed to make room for a more modern, earthquake-proof building—one that contained no windows.

"A classroom with no windows? Those bastards! What are they thinking?" he wondered.

Well, he would be retiring soon anyway. Ralph could put up a mean front, but inside he was as gentle as they come. He loved telling stories about the old days of surfing, and he had plenty of them. Getting him to tell one was always a good respite from our history lessons.

A few days after their adventure, Chris could no longer conceal his enthusiasm. He wanted Ralph to know where they had been and informed Mark of his intention to spill the beans.

"I'm going to tell Dawson about our surf trip. The waves were so good that he really should know about it," Chris said.

"Sure, go ahead and tell him, Chris," said Mark sarcastically. "He won't give a truant notice to you, but he will to me and Tim."

Mark begged him not to tell but realized his friend's stubborn mind was already made up. When Chris finally told Ralph how perfect the day had been at "his" break, the news brought a warm smile to the old man's weathered face, and Chris knew that Ralph was buzzing with excitement on the inside. Instead of scolding Chris, the teacher asked what size board he had used. Then followed another question Chris hadn't expected.

"By the way, Chris, how did you get there?"

As Chris recounted the entire tale, Ralph appeared honored by the monumental effort they had undertaken. And just as Mark had predicted, everyone except Chris received truancies. Ralph even seemed to look the other way whenever he saw Chris doodling waves on paper during the middle of class. And on those occasions when his chair was empty, old Ralph just nodded his head knowing Chris was out there somewhere, surfing.

Chapter 19

Surfing Always Comes First

Winter 1976/77

Autumn's arrival in Southern California brought the usual changes to the surf. Summer's warm-water south swells gave way to colder ones from the north. Most beachgoers headed inside for the winter, but surfers merely traded their surf trunks for full wetsuits and continued to ride the waves. Winter's approach usually meant larger and even more powerful swells were on the way, and the Windansea crew would be ready for them.

With our final year in high school well underway, Chris reveled in the notion that soon he would be free of the classroom. Sitting indoors in class seemed like a waste of time to him, and completing homework was next to impossible. Jim often sat down with his friend and forced him to do the work. On these occasions, he often noticed how Chris's creative mind would suddenly emerge out of nowhere, and he would become genuinely interested in the subject. Jim found this facet of Chris's personality perplexing: an intellectual's mind trapped inside a rebel's body.

I moved through our senior year with a mixture of pleasure and pain. Like Chris, I looked forward to it all being over. Yet I also realized that high school only happens once. My friendships at school ran deep, and soon we all would head our separate ways. So I gave a higher priority to some things at school more than others, especially being a member of the La Jolla High Surf Club.

Surfing wasn't even on the radar when it came to city-sanctioned school athletics. The La Jolla High Surf Club certainly didn't look like much. Ours was a rag-tag operation at best; maintaining order among a group of high school surfers proved to be a daunting task. There were elections, and with few other club members demonstrating any semblance of organizational skills, I became the choice for vice president.

Away from school, our lives revolved around the local surf spots found along Neptune Street. A few days before Thanksgiving, a solid six-foot northwest swell hit, and Big Rock became the central attraction. Chris tried persuading me to ditch school, but since I had qualified to graduate a semester early, I couldn't afford to take any risks.

However, immediately after school I ventured to Big Rock. The waves looked phenomenal.

When the first good wave rolled through, Chris was the one riding it. His 6'8" lime-green Caster surfboard was ideal for the powerful conditions. Backlit by the late afternoon sun, the waves appeared eerily translucent, each fluid wall daring the surfers to catch it. Big Rock is normally best surfed during high tide, when more water covers the foreboding reef, but as it was low tide now, the receding ocean created even more challenging conditions. One mishap could prove disastrous.

Due to the severity of the waves, only a handful of "stand-up" surfers were in the lineup. The "knee-boarders" —surfers who ride waves while kneeling on their boards—were the real standouts. Kneeboards are considerably shorter than average surfboards and also have two fins instead of one for sharper turning. This more compact style of surfing enables riders to descend the face of a wave much faster. Knee-boarders Tom Lochtefeld, Marshall Myrman, Mark Skinner, Mitchell Pelligrin, and the Huffman brothers pretty much ruled at Big Rock.

There were eight knee-boarders in the lineup, but only three surfers; Chris, Brew Briggs, and Peter Lochtefeld. Chris was unfazed by the dangerous low-tide conditions and regularly took off backside on waves breaking in only a few feet of water. Through my telephoto lens, he always appeared in control and never once fell off. His sweeping turns, deep tube rides, and slicing carves created some serious eye-popping among the surfers paddling back out in the channel.

Brew, too, was surfing with reckless abandon. Competing with other surfers had never been part of Brew's repertoire, but today a spirited battle waged between the two friends. Each wave they rode became another opportunity to up the ante. After watching Brew fade deep inside a tube, Chris made sure the next wave he caught would be even better. Their surfing styles, honed upon the La Jolla reef breaks, were strangely similar—so similar that there were whispers that Brew was actually the better surfer. Chris never openly acknowledged the possibility himself, but the mere notion made him bristle and fired up his motivation.

As the sun dropped further below the smog-ridden horizon and turned a brilliant fiery red, it was time for one last wave. Chris picked up the tempo, saving his best for last. Brew's surfing had certainly been spectacular, but Chris's aggressiveness left little doubt as to who the top dog really was. Chris had finally reached the point in his surfing at which he could do virtually anything he wanted—nothing was out of reach. Seventeen years old and still not close to his prime, his future in the sport only shined brighter.

A few days later, I went to Bob Davis Camera to pick up the Big Rock photos. There were several good ones of Chris, and I showed them to Larry Moore, the photo editor of Surfing magazine. He published two shots in the next issue. Chris and I were stoked!

A few weeks later, I learned that my parents were going out of town. The Surf Club needed a place to hold the monthly meeting, and for reasons I can't recall, I generously volunteered our house. I expected about a dozen or so surfers to show up. Of course, I should have known better. By nine o'clock there were around eighty people, many of whom I didn't even know, milling about our house. It seemed amazing to think that only a short time earlier we actually tried to commence with the "meeting." After someone showed up with several cases of beer and a few marijuana joints, any chance of holding an organized session vanished into the smoky air.

Everyone was on their best behavior, but that didn't ease my apprehension. Panic must have been written all over my face, because Ted came over to offer encouragement.

"Sorry, Kirk. But didn't anyone tell you that parties in La Jolla are hard to keep a secret?"

"Party?" I replied. "I thought this was supposed to be a meeting?"

"Ha! There was never going to be a meeting," he answered, surveying the crowd for girls.

So I figured that, until the first signs of trouble at least, I might as well enjoy it, too. But if this was a La Jolla party, then where was the Prince? Seconds later, almost on cue, the front door opened and in walked Chris. Showing up late for a party was the norm for him. He preferred to make a grand entrance after everyone else had already arrived. He just stood there for a few minutes, looking like the king of the castle, then motioned me over, and pulled a large joint from his shirt pocket.

"Hey Aeder, let's get out of here for a little while. I want to tell you about something."

Sneaking away from the mass of humanity, we holed up on the other side of the house. No sooner had we entered when Chris lit up his "spleef"—as he called it.

"Aeder, I met this insane chick," he said, taking a deep toke.

"Oh, you mean another one?" I replied with a laugh.

"No seriously, this one is all-time," he said with as much gravity as he could muster. "She's not from La Jolla—she's from Point Loma. Her name is Jil Strong, and she's so unreal and gnarly."

"Where did you meet her?"

"You know my friend David West? He knew about Jil. Last week I was at this party, and I saw her from a distance. So I asked him if he could set us up. One night we all went skateboarding together at the Community Concourse, you know, those spiral lanes at the parking structure in downtown San Diego. She is so bitchin! Now we're completely going out and everything. Jil is my new chick! I even went with her to a party last week, and she just blew away every other girl who was there. I will never go out with anyone else again. I'll introduce you to her soon," he stated proudly.

I was skeptical about Chris's bold statements but tried not to show it. Chris never had any problems with the ladies, but long relationships didn't seem to be his thing. I was tempted to give Chris a load of crap over what he had just said, but not wanting to spoil his enthusiasm, I decided to refrain. During that moment, I realized how much further our friendship had evolved. I could tell that he respected and trusted me, along with any advice I might give him.

"Well, I'm stoked for you," I said with encouragement. "And I can't wait to meet her either...you dog!"

With the effects of the marijuana settling in, we both started laughing. Then, Chris began studying a surf poster on the wall. The image was of an idyllic surf break on Maui known as Honolua Bay. One of the most iconic surf points in the world, this was a location where Chris would surely be a natural.

"Hey Aeder, you've been to Honolua a few times, haven't you? How is that place?" he asked.

"Oh, you would love it, Chris. Super-long right barrels, absolutely perfect waves. You would rip the shit out of it!"

"Yeah, someday I want to go there," he said. "Honolua Bay looks like an insane wave. For sure it's perfect for me."

"What about this winter?"

"In December I'm going to the North Shore again and probably won't have time for Maui too. I need to go where the contests are. I'm entered in the trials at Pipeline and Sunset, and I'm third in line as an alternate at the Duke event. Those events are what it's all about for me right now," he explained. "Speaking of which, you should come to Oahu, so we can shoot photos together there!"

"I won't be able to do that because I'll be graduating a half-year early. When school lets out for Christmas break next month, I will be done for good," I said. "After that, I can do pretty much whatever I want because I won't have to go to class anymore."

Chris looked stunned. "How are you able to do that?"

"Gee, I don't know, Chris," I teased. "Maybe it's because I actually attend all my classes. I also went to summer school twice and accumulated enough credits, so I could get out early."

Chris laughed, but I sensed a twinge of regret over how poorly he had performed academically. School was just not his thing. We stood there in the smoke-filled room and talked about surf. Chris was so passionate in the way he described his surfing adventures. Knowing that he was often prone to immense exaggeration, I still found his tales amusing.

"You know something, Aeder? Surfing is like a drug. It provides a kind of rush that never leaves a trace, and it's the only one you need," he said.

He never elaborated on what he meant by that, nor did I ask. A few seconds later, we rejoined the intoxicated masses.

"Just another La Jolla party," uttered Mark Ruyle, strutting by with a girl on his arm.

The debauchery continued well into the night. The next morning, thankfully, our house was still in one piece. This alone caused me to proclaim the Surf Club meeting a resounding success. Fortunately I had a few days to clean up the mess before my parents returned. And one month later, when school let out for the holidays, my high school experience had officially come to a close.

Elated to have nine months off before starting college, I decided to dedicate the time to surfing photography. The first thing I needed was better camera equipment. So I began working as the night manager for Swenson's Ice Cream Parlor on the corner of Girard and Pearl, which allowed me to save money while keeping my days free for the surf. Chris absolutely loved ice cream and came by often for my "friends and family" discount.

Shortly thereafter, Chris headed off to Hawaii again. Returning to his favorite surf spots —Rocky Point, Velzyland, Sunset Beach, and Pipeline—Chris felt more at ease in the tropical surf and easily blended into the scene. He had grown taller and become stronger as well. We didn't know it then, but he would soon need all the strength he could muster.

That winter in Hawaii marked a turning point, not just in Chris's surfing, but with the entire professional surfing scene. Around the world, other talented young surfers shared his passion and aspirations. The first real youth movement in surfing was taking hold, and a new generation pushed the boundaries like never before. And in their rush to succeed, some pushed harder than others.

Several top Australian surfers in particular had begun to cause a stir. The Australians had a different mindset than the Hawaiians; their goal was to surf the waves on the North Shore much more aggressively than had ever been done before. Their determination to elevate pro surfing to a much higher level, and the flamboyant manner in which they went about it, contradicted the low-key Hawaiian approach.

Rabbit Bartholomew, one of Australia's best surfers, had a rather brash interview published in Surfer magazine titled "Bustin' Down the Door." Rabbit openly boasted about going to Hawaii and surfing better than anyone there—Hawaiians included. His words lit the fuse of an already combustible situation.

Several of the local surfers were insulted by the foreigner's careless actions. The issue soon became a major cause for concern in the Hawaiian North Shore surfing community. Hawaii was regarded as the birthplace of the sport, and the Hawaiians regarded surfing in their waves as something to be respected. As such there were rules to follow when surfing there.

The roots of the conflict reached much deeper. In 1893, the United States military had arrested and jailed Hawaii's queen, taken over the Hawaiian Islands and essentially stripped their inhabitants of any remaining power. Consequently, relations between native Hawaiians and Caucasian or "haole" newcomers had been on tedious ground ever since—especially when it came to surfing.

That winter, professional surfers including Rabbit, Peter Townend, Ian Cairns and South Africa's Shaun Tomson were all physically attacked. Death threats were issued. Several of the aforementioned surfers went into hiding. And it could have been much worse if Hawaii's ambassador to surfing, Eddie Aikau, hadn't intervened to play peacemaker. Eddie's assistance proved vital. After a few tense weeks, and with everything now out in the open, pro surfing could gingerly take its next steps forward.

Chris, fortunately, had been able to steer clear of the controversy. As a "haole" on the North Shore, Chris was lucky to have good local friends like Michael Ho. Chris's Irish skin was whiter than white. But while surfing with Michael, he was nothing but an afterthought to those Hawaiians looking for payback.

The inaugural IPS tour concluded in Hawaii at the end of December. Australia's Peter Townend became the 1976 world champion of surfing despite not winning a single contest all year. The highest ranked surfer from the American mainland was Florida's Jeff Crawford in tenth place.

Chapter 20

Evolution Complete

In January of 1977, Chris returned from Hawaii brimming with confidence. Almost immediately he lucked into an epic two-day west swell at Big Rock; local surfers were calling it the best swell in the last five years. The goofy-foot surfers like Oscar, Jeff Toomey, and Craig Eck had a field day riding inside the cavernous tubes.

Chris had settled into consistently riding one of his favorite surfboards, a 6'5" pintail shape with a white deck and powder blue rails. This marked a turning point for him, and he began riding shorter boards more often than not. At Big Rock, one of the most dangerous surf spots anywhere along the California coast, Chris continued to raise the performance bar even higher. He was on par with the best surfers in the world, and his jaw-dropping backside surfing sent a loud and powerful statement to other American surfers.

About two weeks after the first swell, Big Rock received a hearty second dose. But Chris was nowhere to be seen. In the middle of the afternoon, Chris finally arrived, waving to me from a distance before paddling out. Usually in a hurry to get into the water, today he was inordinately slow, taking long, peaceful strokes. Upon reaching the lineup, he shook hands with several other surfers. Then, he caught his first wave and immediately tucked inside a big, beautiful liquid barrel. And every wave he caught after that was pretty much a repeat performance.

Two hours later, Chris returned to shore. It seemed as if everyone on the beach wanted to talk to him, and he stopped repeatedly to chat. Several minutes later, I walked over to him.

People were still milling around him, discussing his incredible maneuvers. Chris just smiled, taking all the attention in stride. As his fans began to disperse, Chris wrapped a thick towel around his waist and removed his wetsuit. He seemed calmer than I had ever seen him.

"Aeder, come over here," he commanded.

"Hey Chris, I think these photos are going to be some of the best I have ever taken of you," I told him as we shook hands.

"Wow, that's great! I want to see them as soon as possible. How long will it take to get them developed?"

"A couple of days at least, but I'll let you know when I get them," I replied.

It was then I noticed someone sitting inside his car. A slender girl with long blond hair stepped out.

"Hey Jil, this is my friend Kirk. He's the one who takes all those crappy surf pictures of me," he said, chuckling.

I was shocked that he had introduced me by my first name. And Chris was right about his new girl. Jil Strong was stunning and looked like a model in a magazine. They kissed, and a look of pure happiness spread across his face. Now I understood his laid-back manner. A hot girlfriend was a sort of status symbol. And while it was anyone's guess how long their relationship would last, it was obvious that Jil had already had a positive impact.

Right before he drove off, Chris rolled down his window.

"Hey Aeder, I'm competing in that new Katin contest in Huntington Beach next week. You want to go along?"

"Sure thing, Chris, count me in," I replied.

Watching them speed off, I reflected on Chris's incredible performance that afternoon. La Jolla had yet to prove to be a real hotbed for progressive surfers. Chris had certainly broken barriers while also carving out a solid competitive record. But in spite of all his accomplishments and accolades, he had received very little press coverage in return. Deliberate or not, this lack of attention raised question marks, many of which still had to do with his reputation for violence and localism at Windansea.

Fortunately, Big Rock had attracted one key visitor that day who could change all that. Using a waterproof camera, veteran Surfer magazine photographer Warren Bolster captured several amazing images of Chris. Warren was already a bit of a legend when it came to surfing photography. He could also be rather prickly, and because of his temperamental disposition, I usually steered clear of him.

I had to admit that I was quite envious of Warren's photos. But I had known this day would come; Chris had become a hot commodity for surfing photographers far more established than I was, and Warren was certainly one of those. He was among the best at recognizing exceptional surfing talent, and right from the start, he knew Chris was a standout. In order to photograph him more easily, Warren took Chris away from the Windansea crowds to remote, less-crowded surfing locations—which was great for Chris, but not for me. Over the next few weeks, there were several good swells in La Jolla, but Chris was nowhere to be seen.

Surfer then published a lengthy feature article titled "California's Emerging Young Talent." The piece focused on three surfers: Kevin Reed from Santa Cruz, Russell Short from Ventura, and Chris. The praise that Warren bestowed upon Chris spoke volumes.

"During my years as a surfer-photographer in California, Florida, and Australia, I've had the pleasurable opportunity to watch a lot of the hot young future greats (the names Jeff Crawford, Greg Loehr, and the late Kevin Brennan of Australia immediately come to mind), and I'm of the opinion that Chris O'Rourke, young in age, but sophisticated in style, is not the least of them. He's only just begun to leave his mark."

Chris was thankful for the recognition. He knew any publicity was important and went a long way toward endorsements from potential sponsors. His surfing style drew accolades from even the staunchest of pundits and disbelievers. All he had to do now was keep the momentum rolling.

The upcoming inaugural Katin Team Challenge Competition at Huntington Beach seemed like another great opportunity for coverage. This event was structured differently from other surfing contests and was an experiment of sorts; instead of competing against each other, surfers would compete together as corporate teams. Each team consisted of four to six surfers, all of whom represented their respective industry sponsors.

The mix of competitors was an odd sight, but intriguing nonetheless. Though the contest was not part of the 1977 IPS Pro Tour and no points were counted toward the individual world title for the year, the Katin contest still attracted the most highly acclaimed surfers in the world. It was the largest gathering for a pro event in California surfing history.

Chris competed for the Caster Surfboards team. We drove up to Huntington Beach together in my old Volkswagen van with four surfboards crammed inside.

"It feels like I've spent a lot of time up here in Huntington at these contests," Chris said, stepping out of the car and surveying the coastline below. Numerous top surfing professionals milled around the area. Larry Bertlemann talked quietly with Reno Abellira beneath one of the scaffolding tents. Peter Townend and Ian Cairns were surrounded by a small crowd down on the beach. Peter, or PT as he was more commonly referred to, had won the inaugural IPS World Title the previous year. Now he stood as professional surfing's reigning champion. Ian had finished in the top ten. It was generally considered that any surfer ranked in the top sixteen had to be pretty darn good—the elite of the elite. Compared to these guys, Chris was a complete rookie. Once he became established on the world tour, however, reaching the top sixteen was a goal that certainly appeared within reach.

If Chris felt any excitement right then, he kept it to himself. He wasn't in awe of these guys. I, on the other hand, was pretty excited to be standing in such close proximity to the best surfers in the world.

But while the talent was there, the waves were not. The two to three-foot swell accompanied by a cold onshore wind didn't look promising. Contest officials huddled together, discussing whether the contest would be a go or not. All surfers were on standby until the decision was made.

"I don't know, Chris. It looks pretty shitty out there to me. Do you think they will hold it?" I asked.

When Chris didn't respond, I realized he was staring hard at someone behind us. Following his gaze, I spotted Shaun Tomson surrounded by a large entourage of friends, curious spectators, and gushing girls. Basking in the attention, Shaun smiled while signing autographs.

It seemed everyone knew about Shaun. The handsome young South African was the hottest surf-star around, widely touted as the sport's next world champion. Shaun had become the first surfer in history to win the Pipeline Masters surfing backside. Yet he was also the same surfer Chris finished well ahead of in a contest at Santa Cruz two years earlier.

Chris looked straight at me, his face filled with jealousy and rage.

"Aeder, I know I belong with these guys, too. I feel like I've already proven that much. And they better fucking watch out because I'm getting tired of taking a back seat to them, simply because I'm from California," he said.

Moments later, dressed in his full wetsuit, Chris wrapped his arm around the board and hurried down to the water's edge. The official announcement was made: the contest would soon get underway, and competitors would be allowed a thirty-minute warm-up session. Chris was one of the first ones in the water. He wanted to acclimate himself to the cold conditions and, perhaps more importantly, gain a little visibility in the process.

Unlike the powerful reef breaks in La Jolla, the shifty beach break at Huntington did not create the kind of waves Chris preferred. Other than Blacks Beach and a few surf spots in upper Baja California, Chris had disdain for beach breaks. He felt that most beach breaks lacked power, and if the power wasn't there, he had no interest.

Chris's initial waves in the cold winter surf were a far cry from the six-foot barrels of Big Rock. But he quickly adapted, drawing attention in the process. His snappy roundhouse cutbacks sent large curtains of water flying. I started taking pictures and saw Peter Townend nearby. PT had not become world champion for nothing, and Chris's surfing had caught his attention, too. Peter realized he had seen this surfer before, but where? Another Australian pro asked Peter who it was. That's when it finally dawned on him.

"Well I'll be. That guy there, mates, is Chris O'Rourke," he said. "When I went to the 1972 World Contest in San Diego, I saw him surfing one day at that Windansea place. He was just a little grommet then, a snotty little grommet actually. But judging by the way he's surfing now, shit, he's really come a long way."

"Hey, I've heard of that guy, Chris O'Rourke," replied the other surfer in a thick Australian drawl. "He's supposed to be really good—the best surfer these Seppos have." ("Seppo" is a derogatory Australian term for Americans.)

PT watched Chris perform a clean bottom turn that set him up for the rest of the ride: two tenacious straight up and down off the lips, followed by three of his patented gouging roundhouse cutbacks. Chris rode the wave all the way to the shore and instantly paddled back out for more.

"He surfs like one of us," said PT. "I reckon that's got to be the best guy I've ever seen from California. During this contest we should definitely be watching out for him."

Also taking note of Chris from afar was Shaun Tomson. On that first day of the contest, while not facing each other directly, both surfers were victorious in their initial heats. At the end of the day, Chris and Shaun even had a rare chance to speak. On the surface they displayed a reasonable respect for each other. But in reality they were competitive to the bone. It was all about winning, and giving the other surfer any kind of psychological edge was strictly prohibited.

Over the next few days of the contest, Chris performed reasonably well. He won two more heats and made it through several others. Ultimately he fell victim to a competitive surfer's

152 ◆ Chapter 20

worst nightmare: a heat with literally no waves. Eliminated from the competition, Chris wasn't sure if he had shown his competitors what he was truly all about, but at least it was a start. While the focus of the contest had been team-oriented, Shaun's first place finish in the individual honors helped cement the victory for Team O'Neill, a fact that didn't escape Chris's attention.

The second year of the IPS world tour would soon commence in Australia. Chris had long since made up his mind that he was going to be there. With only a few weeks left to prepare, there was still much work to do.

Chris's mindset was firmly on the ocean. He realized that established surfers like Shaun, Rabbit, Dane Kealoha, and Mark Richards all came from wave-haven areas around the world that also had tremendous internal support for the sport of surfing. In Australia and South Africa, surfing's popularity was on par with soccer and golf. In Hawaii, surfing was part of the culture dating back hundreds of years. These geographic areas also had a consistent array of high-quality surf breaks, several times better than California. Chris would certainly be an underdog, but at least he would be ready.

The end of winter in California was fast approaching, yet solid swells from the northwest had been few and far between. Usually still prevalent this time of year, storm systems in the north Pacific had remained noticeably absent. No storms meant zero waves. Unable to surf much, Chris became anxious. The small swells that did arise coincided with bad weather. But even in the pouring rain, Chris went surfing.

One day while at Oscar's house I noticed he was coughing a lot. We talked for a while before he went outside and began changing into his wetsuit. I tried convincing him to stay out of the water. Irritated by my tone however, he essentially told me to 'fuck off.' Chris always went surfing when he was sick. His motto was that, if the waves were breaking, then someone should be there to ride them, no matter what the conditions were.

As the weather finally began to improve, a significant storm was forecasted to produce large surf along the entire California coast. This would be our last chance to shoot photos before Chris left for Australia. Late one afternoon, Chris called to say he was going to Baja the next morning and wanted me to come along.

"Why tomorrow?" I asked him. "That new swell hasn't even arrived yet."

"No, Aeder, you're wrong. There's a different swell happening right now that's not even breaking up here in La Jolla. My friend went down to Baja Malibu today and said it was six feet down there—perfect A-frame beach break peaks firing on the sand bars," he spoke excitedly.

"I don't know why that happens down there in Baja, but sometimes the swells come in at weird angles," he continued. "I have to get in some practice somewhere. Besides, you don't have to go to school anymore, so you can't use that excuse. So we're going!"

Once Chris made up his mind, there was nothing I could say to get out of it. Not that I needed an excuse this time. Chris loved to surf in Baja; it was a good way to escape the crowds and always an adventure. Spots such as Baja Malibu, San Miguel, and Salsipuedes were his favorites.

"Okay, count me in," I told him. "I also know someone else who would like to come along, too—my friend Tony Gerschler. You met him once before actually. He's the associate editor of Surfing magazine and has always wanted to shoot movies of you. This would be the perfect time."

"That sounds great! Let's meet at Jil's house in Point Loma early in the morning, and we'll all leave from there. See you then," he said.

Chris had had many girlfriends, but this was the first time was truly smitten. Jil was his pride and joy. When she came onto the scene, it changed his friendships with everyone, primarily because we didn't see him as much. But she also opened his eyes to many new things: better clothes, better mannerisms, and a sense of stability. She understood that Chris's life revolved around the ocean. And, Jil was beautiful. We were envious, but also very proud of him.

The next day at dawn we crossed the international border into Baja California. One of the greatest things about living in San Diego was the easy accessibility to surf spots along this area. Northern Baja was close, convenient, and ridiculously cheap.

But there was also an element of danger south of the border. Mexican police, or Federales, were notoriously crooked, and American gringo surfers were easy targets. I had heard some nasty stories of people getting robbed, hauled off to jail, beat up, raped, and worse. Bribing the police to escape a bad situation was often the only way out, so it was always a good idea to bring along a few extra dollars.

Getting seriously injured was also a concern, as finding proper medical assistance nearby wasn't easy. But the quest to find empty waves always seemed to override the inherent dangers.

The best surf conditions were early in the morning before the strong winds came up, and Chris drove extremely fast. Mark McCoy sat in the front next to him while Tim and I were crammed into the rear. My friend Tony followed behind. With my tripod jammed uncomfortably into my ribs, I watched eagerly for signs we were getting closer to our destination.

Having a Surfing magazine editorial staff member along was an added bonus. Tony was an avid admirer of Chris's surfing, and on this private excursion, he looked forward to capturing movie footage of him. It also made us feel safer to know we had access to two vehicles. While none of us had ever encountered any problems here before, Baja still had that "wild west" feeling where anything could happen.

With the exception of a few bottles of water, none of us had bothered to bring along any food or other beverages. Chris suggested snatching another cluster of donuts from Muirlands.

With a highly devalued peso, however, everything in Mexico was already so cheap. Chris had become a regular at the "pan" shops and always knew exactly where to go.

We headed south along the dusty coastal road, stopping only to load up on bread, colorful pastries, and other essentials. We made out like bandits: I bought several donuts, two loaves of bread, and a six pack of soda for less than a quarter. As we continued on toward Baja Malibu, the road twisted closer to the ocean. We could finally take our first look at the waves—and the extremely small surf was not what we had expected to see. Had Chris miscalculated?

"It looks flat as a pancake out there," I said to no one in particular.

Even Chris looked puzzled. He began to drive faster; the farther we journeyed, the more we could see whitewater crashing along the shore.

"You see what I see?" asked Mark.

"Yep, that's Baja Malibu," said Chris.

We pulled over onto the side of the road for a closer look. This time, the waves were everything we had hoped for. Caressed by a light offshore breeze, long perfect barrels peeled in both directions. We hooted at the top of our lungs in excitement. Chris was right after all.

We were so jubilant that no one noticed the Federales a short distance away in their police cars. They watched our every move, and once we saw them, we made sure not to do anything further to attract their attention. The police drove off a few minutes later, but we knew they could return with reinforcements at any moment.

"I have a bad feeling about those guys. That's usually how they do it, you know—make it look like they don't have any interest in you and then swoop back a few minutes later. I think we should go check out another spot close to here that might be even better than Baja Malibu anyway," said Chris.

Not knowing when the Federales could be back, the idea of changing locations sounded good to everyone except Mark.

"Are you nuts, Chris?" he asked. "Look how good it is out there. No one else is even around, and you just want to drive away from it?"

"Hey Mark, if you think the waves are good here, just wait until you see this other place. It's called Power Plants. Warren Bolster took me there one time. The waves are more powerful than Blacks. I know the conditions will be insane there."

Chris had an uncanny sixth sense for the ocean, so we agreed. Several minutes later, we arrived at the entrance to Power Plants. Surrounded by tall cactus and scrub brush, we traversed the long dusty road, finally arriving at a locked gate. This problem was quickly solved when a Mexican rancher appeared, and we gave him a few pesos to let us pass through. Several giggling children emerged from within his house and begin chasing our cars, so we stopped and handed them some pesos as well. Chris gave a new Caster t-shirt to the oldest boy.

"Regalo," he said in Spanish, explaining that it was a gift. The boy smiled from ear to ear.

Finally we arrived at the ocean. The beach was serene and empty, without another surfer in sight, and the four to six-foot surf could not have been more ideal.

"Oh my God, look at those tubes out there!" exclaimed Tim.

As we watched, a wave unleashed the water trapped inside its tube like a pressure hose, creating a powerful blast of spray that surfers commonly referred to as "spit." Back in San Diego, the surf was calm and flat. Less than sixty miles to the south, however, we had discovered a gold mine. We were ecstatic to have the entire beach to ourselves.

As the boys slipped into their wetsuits, a pod of dolphins passed through the wave lineup. Overhead pelicans flew in perfect formation.

Chris excitedly waxed up his board. I walked over to take a picture of him, and he stuck out his tongue. We both laughed. But then Chris started coughing like he was choking on something.

"Are you okay?" I asked.

"I'm fine, Aeder, don't worry about it."

He ran off to the shoreline and suddenly stopped. In order to reach the perfect waves, he had to paddle through the swiftly moving ocean currents closer to shore. Unlike rip tides that flowed out to sea, these moved sideways and looked more like a raging river. He picked up a small piece of wood and threw it into the water, watching as it was quickly swept away. Chris had only seen these dangerous currents before at Pipeline in Hawaii, and he knew paddling through them would be difficult.

A few hundred yards to the north, two electrical power plants stood next to the shore; between them, a rock jetty stretched into the ocean. Chris took off down the beach and climbed onto it, scampering out upon the large rocks well past the treacherous currents, and leapt into the water.

As he waited at the lineup, the dolphins surfaced just a few feet away. Chris watched them, smiling, then turned his attention to a large set of waves approaching. He had chosen one of his favorite Caster surfboards—a purple 6'4" pintail that he had ridden at Big Rock a few weeks earlier. Chris loved the color purple and made it a point to have it airbrushed on all his new boards.

Chris caught his first wave, then another, and another. Mark and Tim finally joined him. As the morning progressed, I rapidly changed rolls of 35mm slide film while capturing all the action. Tony had taken several reels of Super 8 movie film as well. It didn't matter whether Chris was surfing with his buddies, or in a competition. He was always the standout in any session. He took every wave seriously, as if it were his last.

These were the magical moments surfers lived for. So free and uninhibited, the ocean was like one huge water park with no boundaries. All over the world, incredible surfing locations were still waiting to be discovered. The possibilities seemed endless, which only added to the allure.

By early afternoon the wind had switched to an onshore direction, effectively ruining the surf for the rest of the day. As the water's surface began to deteriorate, Mark and Tim quickly paddled back to shore.

Chris, though, couldn't resist a few more rides. By now he had mastered the shifting lineup, and no wave could hide from him. He almost toyed with each wave, and in the process, made surfing look so easy and effortless. While riding inside the tube, instead of crouching down like most surfers would, Chris confidently stood upright. Only a handful of surfers around the world were doing this: Gerry Lopez, Dane Kealoha, Michael Peterson, Rabbit Bartholomew, and Shaun Tomson.

All of us were now eager to depart, but Chris paddled for one last wave—and he couldn't help riding it without adding a little personal flair. By now I thought I had seen him do just about everything. Wrong again! Chris took off on a five-foot wave breaking to the left. Normally his back would face the wave, but this time he assumed a goofy-foot stance. This ambidextrous style in surfing was commonly referred to as switch foot. Similar to the notion of a baseball player who can hit from both sides of the plate, very few surfers could do this with any degree of competence.

Undaunted, Chris casually descended the wave's steep face. He performed a stylish bottom turn and briefly touched the ocean's surface with his left hand. The wave opened ahead of him, and he tucked inside the liquid blue barrel. For a brief moment, I could have sworn that I was watching Gerry Lopez. The way Chris dragged his hand was exactly how Gerry surfed at Pipeline. In the end, Chris rode the entire wave switch foot.

When he walked up the beach toward us, he was again coughing hard. I figured he had swallowed some salt water and didn't give it much consideration. Everyone gathered around the cars and spoke excitedly about the surf. We had made the right decision about coming to Baja and were now counting our blessings.

"Hey Chris, you certainly made the right call today," said Mark.

We packed up our belongings and began the drive back to San Diego. Famished, we stopped at a roadside taco stand along the outskirts of Tijuana for real food. We ordered over two dozen tacos—so many that the stand's owners could have closed up shop for the day. Standing alongside the dusty road, we devoured our food as if we hadn't eaten in days.

Nearing the end of our carnivorous feast, we spotted two large elephants that had broken loose from a circus tent nearby. The massive beasts wandered in our direction, finally stopping about thirty yards away and began grazing on weeds. Though the elephants appeared subdued, their enormous size was still intimidating. Chris, however, was unfazed. He walked right up to them holding a taco in his outstretched hand. One of the elephants reached out with his trunk and snatched the food.

Surfing had become Chris's passion, but he had never lost his fascination with animals—fish, lizards, cats, dogs, dolphins, or even elephants! After the elephant finished eating, Chris grabbed a few more tacos and returned to feed them again. As they munched away, he gently stroked each creature's forehead. The rest of us stood by, transfixed. Still not satisfied, he bought a few more tacos for his new friends. No one said a word until we were again on our way.

"How did you know those elephants would like tacos?" I had to ask.

"Wild elephants mostly eat plants and grain. But those ones in the circus don't seem to be looked after too well. They just looked really hungry. That's probably why they broke loose. I know what being hungry feels like especially when you don't have any food at all, and believe me, it's not fun. So I was just trying to help them out," he said.

Even after all these years, Chris still sometimes formed stronger bonds with animals than with humans.

Chapter 21

IPS Pro Tour Bound

March 1977

Chris targeted three IPS surfing contests in Australia for his official debut on the world tour. The highest-ranked professional surfers from the previous year were already seeded into the main event, and with only a few open slots remaining, the trials would determine which contestants would round out the field. Chris received official invitations from the event sponsors to participate in the trials of each competition.

There were only four competitors from the United States: Randy Laine, Dan Flecky, Jeff Crawford, and Chris. The reasons for this were simple: financial hardship, lack of quality sponsorship, and the beleaguered state of surfing in the United States at the time. Even such established surfers as Mike Purpus were unable to make the trip. Chris, however, was fortunate that Bill Caster, along with a private San Diego restaurant entrepreneur who loved surfing and believed in Chris's talents, had provided the sponsorship money for him to go.

However, Chris wouldn't be the only surfer from La Jolla traveling to Australia. A women's version of the IPS would commence that year, too. Debbie Melville Beacham was a regular in the Windansea lineup. Just like Chris, her surfing was built around competition, and for several years, she had competed in the women's events on the WSA. In 1977 she would go on to finish eighth in the world, and in 1982, she won the Women's Pro Surfing world title. Debbie was the only female surfing mentor Chris ever had, and he respected her greatly.

Two days before his departure, though, Chris fell ill. Since all outward symptoms pointed to the flu, there seemed little need to explore further. Yet on the cusp of his eighteenth birthday, when good health should be a given, something far more serious was invading his body.

By now Chris and Jil were nearly inseparable. For the most part, they were living together. Jil's mother had a house in Point Loma, and he spent a lot of time there. Chris got along well with Jil's mom and older sister, and the three women shared a collective hand in fostering a better lifestyle for him. Chris's old hand-me-down clothes quickly became a thing of the past. Spending time in Point Loma provided other rewards, too, especially surfing the waves at nearby Sunset Cliffs.

But after getting sick, Chris figured he needed to get away for some rest. He decided to stay with his parents, who had since moved from La Jolla and now rented a condominium in Cardiff-by-the-Sea about fifteen miles north. His relationship with his father had been a bit better lately, and some of their differences had been reconciled. Gloria was still an alcoholic, but Bart Sr. was making a determined effort to be a better person—not just for his wife, but for his youngest son, too. In spite of all their family issues, Chris's parents had told him that he was always welcome at home. Even Lyn had moved back home after having marital difficulties.

On his first day back home, Chris already seemed to feel better. He noticed how everyone was getting along and how good it felt to be around his family again. This time there was no tension, only laughter. Chris couldn't even recall the last time it had been like this.

When I picked him up the next day, I watched as he stood in the driveway, saying goodbye to his parents. He gave his mother a hug that seemed to last an eternity and then shook hands with his father. Seeing him coexist so harmoniously with his dad was a bit shocking. After everything Chris had told me about him, it was nice to see them standing side by side. And from a short distance away, I overheard their conversation.

"Chris, a few years ago I recall saying that, if you were going to waste of all your time surfing, then..."

"...one day I had better become the best in the world. I know, Dad. I remember you saying that, too," Chris interrupted.

"Well, this is your time now. I know it's just the start, but be sure and take advantage of it. For motivation, just look at what happened to me. A person can make one wrong turn in life, and it completely changes everything. You can do a lot better than I ever did. So have a safe trip and good luck...son."

"Thanks, Dad," he said.

Chris turned and walked toward me appearing a bit dumbfounded—and for good reason. All I could think was, did that really just happen? It was the first time I had ever seen him interact with his father. Admitting his own failures was his father's way of reaching out to him. And while I couldn't be sure how much future bonding there would be, for now at least this was a good omen.

Before Chris and I headed for La Jolla, we stopped at the Caster shaping factory in Sorrento Valley to pick up the brand-new quiver of surfboards that he would take to Australia. If Chris was nervous about the trip, it didn't show; on the contrary, he brimmed with confidence.

I had met Bill Caster before. He was a smart, very straightforward guy who always had new shaping ideas floating about in his head. Creative to no end, Bill was regarded as one of the best shapers around.

A team of experts worked in the factory alongside him, each of whom had an important role. Bill's protégée shaper Gary Goodrum was one of those, along with Ernie Higgins, who did the airbrushing and glassing of each board. Caster surfboards had a huge following, not just in California, but in far away places like Japan as well.

Chris regularly heaped praise upon Bill calling him "the best shaper in the world by far." Whether it was competitive surfing or other aspects of his life, being "the best" meant everything to Chris, and when it came to other people that he cared about, Chris often talked about them in much the same way.

Before we left that afternoon, Bill had a surprise for him. Chris's rise in popularity had necessitated the production of the "Chris O'Rourke Model" surfboard, a new line of boards now available to the general public. On the deck of each board was a brand new logo, a small silhouette of one of Chris's favorite moves, a backside off the top. Chris was both surprised and honored.

A short time later, I dropped him off at Oscar's house and wished him good luck in Australia.

"Go kick some ass down there."

Chris removed his brand-new boards from my car with extreme care. As he walked away, I heard him coughing again. Knowing that he had been sick, I thought nothing of it. But I wasn't aware of the small lump on the side of his neck that Jil had noticed a few days earlier. She expressed concern, but Chris simply downplayed the matter. Nothing was going to interfere with the journey he was about to embark upon—especially not something as trivial as a small lump. Chris tried to deflect the issue by saying it was probably an acne problem of some sort. He always played the tough guy, and he was in a state of denial about something he should have paid more attention to.

The next day Jil drove him to Los Angeles International Airport, and Chris flew off to Australia's Gold Coast. He was so excited that he didn't sleep at all during the twelve-hour flight. At the Brisbane Airport, he was met by his affable Australian friend John Nielsen. The two had become friends a year earlier while John was on a trip in California. John's cousin was Paul Nielsen, one of the most famous surfers in Australia at the time.

Competing in an IPS contest was markedly different than the old WSA. One disparity was the waiting period allowed for each event. Whereas the WSA previously held events over one weekend and hoped for the best conditions, each IPS contest was allowed an eight to ten day waiting period to ensure the best conditions possible. With three contests at stake, Chris knew he was in for a long trip. First there was the Stubbies Classic at Burleigh Heads, immediately followed by the legendary Bells contest in South Victoria and concluding with the 2SM Coca-Cola Surfabout in Sydney.

Other than Jeff Crawford from Florida, Chris was the most highly regarded contest surfer from the mainland United States. The competition he would face here would be his initiation into the big time. Even the American media had continued to focus their attention primarily upon surfers from Hawaii, Australia, and South Africa. And until someone from the mainland United States proved they could step up, it would stay that way. No professional IPS contests were even scheduled in mainland America.

Chris yearned to change all that. The trial rounds for the Stubbies contest consisted of nearly sixty surfers who would vie for eight available main event slots. Competing in the trials was something Chris's traveling partner Michael Ho did not have to worry about. The young Hawaiian surfer competed on the tour during 1976 and had already had a taste of what the experience was like.

Burleigh Heads had a revered surfing history in Australia and was one of the best right-hand point breaks in the world. With its picturesque beach and grassy knoll, it was also ideal for spectator viewing.

Chris settled into his new environment quite nicely. Right away he learned that all the top pros made their own personal arrangements, whether it was airplane flights, car rentals, hotel rooms, or packing their surfboards. No one had an agent to take care of these things; professional surfing simply wasn't that advanced yet.

The Stubbies contest would take place from March 12-24 and would be staged over the best five days of surf within the waiting period. The main event provided a revolutionary precedent of sorts—the first professional contest ever utilizing man-on-man heats. Two surfers would enter the water, but only the winner would advance.

Unlike the main event, the trials consisted of four-man heats; the top two surfers would continue on. Surfing in professional contests usually came down to whoever caught the best waves, but when his first heat was held during a quickly subsiding swell, Chris fell victim to circumstance more than his opponents. Fortunately, by finishing second, he was given another chance. One more bad result, however, and he would be eliminated altogether.

During his next heat, he placed second again and continued to advance. He won the next heat, too. As he neared the final eight positions, his chances at competing in the main event looked good—until his luck ran out. Initially, he took his usual approach to losing and became quite angry. Michael quickly reminded Chris that surfing on the IPS was much different than anything he had faced before.

A few days later, Chris finally acknowledged he had been terribly anxious. There was a long, arduous road ahead, but he was still eager for the challenge. The Stubbies contest was eventually won by Michael Peterson, a highly revered Australian surfer. Chris watched the final heat from the beach and found himself drawn to Michael's fluid surfing style. He quickly proclaimed the Australian's brand of contest surfing the best he had ever seen.

It wasn't just Michael's performance during the Stubbies that awed Chris. More than 30,000 spectators were on hand to watch. Surfing's overall popularity within the country was obvious.

A short time later, Chris felt extremely weak and tired but wasn't sure why. With a one-week break until the next contest, Chris continued to hang around the Gold Coast and surf perfect waves. His friend John Nielsen worked as a commentator for a popular radio station in Brisbane known as Team 120/4GG.

John often showcased surfing on his radio shows. He interviewed Chris, who was more than happy to oblige. During all those years in California, winning contest after contest, Chris had never been asked for an interview. When John asked Chris how it felt to be one of only a few surfers from the mainland United States on the pro tour, his response was predictable.

"I'm not even thinking about anyone else from California," he said. "Who cares? I hate to say it, but there doesn't seem to be very many positive things coming from there right now. All I know is, I just want to win the world title someday. That is my only goal in life right now."

Considering how revered surfing was in Australia at the time, those local surfers listening no doubt snickered over the brash Californian's remarks. They probably laughed even more the next day, when a black limousine plastered with 4GG logos pulled up in the parking lot at Burleigh Heads. The doors opened, and Chris O'Rourke stepped out with his surfboard. John had arranged the limo for Chris merely as a publicity stunt. Already wearing his surf trunks and wetsuit, Chris casually walked down to the beach and paddled out into the surf.

Any Australian surfer watching no doubt wondered what was going on. After all, who did this Seppo think he was? Yet this was a country whose own surfers had the same brash attitude about surfing as Chris. Big egos had long since become part of the sport. Unfazed by all the attention, Chris confidently padded out at Burleigh and caught his first wave. He performed several solid cutbacks before pulling into a lengthy tube ride. For a moment at least, he had silenced any doubters.

A few days later, Chris and Michael paddled out together at another nearby surf spot known as Kirra. After riding his first wave, Michael paddled back out next to an Australian surfer. They watched intently as Chris stroked into a wave and began a series of spectacular maneuvers.

"Hey Michael, who's your friend there, that bloke riding the wave?" the Aussie inquired.

Upon hearing the surfer was from California, the Australian began to laugh.

"Hah, I didn't think there was anyone from there who could actually surf properly," he snorted.

As Chris neared the end of his ride, he completed a 360-degree roller coaster maneuver that sent a sheet of water flying twelve feet into the air.

"Well...judging by that, I guess you're wrong," laughed Michael.

The Australian surfer was Jim Banks, a young aspiring professional himself. A goofy-foot surfer from Sydney, Jim admired Chris's surfing and vice versa. Jim was also chasing the dream, but unlike Chris, who was full of confidence, the introverted Aussie regularly questioned his own abilities while putting himself down.

That afternoon on the beach, Chris was quick to compliment Jim's surfing. "You're a really great surfer, Jim. You do all those big turns and then, toward the end of each wave, you always whack that one big maneuver."

Chris's words proved inspirational to Jim. Until then, no one had ever really said he was a good surfer. The two quickly bonded as friends. Jim believed that Chris was very much ahead of his time and was bound to go far.

When it was time for Chris to travel on to Sydney, he and Michael decided to drive there. The stretch of scenic coastline was well known for its secluded surf breaks like Byron Bay and Lennox Heads. There was just one problem—they didn't have a car. Fortunately, John Nielsen stepped forward and gladly loaned them an old car he never used anymore.

"That's great, John. But once we get to Sydney, what do we do with the car?" Chris asked him.

"Well boys, I doubt it will even make it there. But if it does you can just leave it alongside the road somewhere," John laughed.

He then warned them about one issue: the car had no floor brakes. Only the emergency hand-brake worked. But the two desperate surfers did not see this as a problem and set off on the long journey. Driving the disabled vehicle proved challenging and required them to act as a team. Chris steered the vehicle and was responsible for the clutch. Michael was in charge of the hand brake and would constantly have to anticipate what Chris was going to do. After a few close calls, Chris determined it was best if he just yelled out "Brake!"

Soon they had the operation down pat and continued on their way through the Australian countryside. The surf at Byron Bay was big and perfect. Then, a short time later at Lennox Heads, the waves made Chris feel like he had died and gone to heaven. Except for Jil, whom he missed dearly, La Jolla had become an afterthought.

When Michael and Chris finally arrived in Sydney, it was time to go their separate ways. Michael wanted to head on to Bells Beach in Victoria to get ready for the next contest. Chris had made arrangements to visit with Jim Banks. Jim's parents were more than happy to put Chris up for a few days at their house in Cronulla, a quaint beachside suburb. With its powerful surf, Cronulla instantly reminded Chris of La Jolla.

Jim also took Chris surfing to another place he often frequented, Gary Beach. The idyllic spot was located inside the Royal National Park in New South Wales, a few hours south of Sydney. But after returning to Cronulla, Chris again fell inexplicably ill and wasn't feeling any better the next day. Jim's mom took him to a doctor who just happened to live next door. Without ever really examining him, the doctor told Chris he was fine and had nothing to worry about.

"What about this lump on my neck?" Chris asked.

The doctor took a brief look and said his lymph glands were swollen. Chris was skeptical, but other than feeling sick, what did he know?

Over the next few days, Chris valiantly fought off fatigue, improving just enough to make the journey to Victoria with Jim. The long waves at Bells Beach were the site of the next competition, the legendary Rip Curl Bells Beach Pro. Forced once again to compete in the trials, Chris got off to a good start by winning his first heat—followed by two losses and elimination.

Chris handled the matter with uncharacteristic class and a clearer understanding of what surfers competing in the trials were up against. Back in the days when he competed in the WSA, the biggest controversies revolved around judging inconsistencies. It seemed to be the same here. The judges for IPS competitions were supposed to be completely objective, but it didn't always turn out that way, especially for unknown surfers competing in a foreign country.

When the Bells competition concluded a few days later, Jim and Chris returned to Sydney. Still dealing with fatigue, Chris was nonetheless determined to compete in the last IPS event in Australia, the 2SM Coca-Cola Surfabout. The Coke event held the honor of being the richest surf contest in the world. Since it was staged along the beaches of Sydney, it attracted an enormous crowd of spectators. During the trials, Chris once again found himself up against a hungry crew of young surfers from all over the world—except this time around, he won several heats in a row. In the end, he finished a respectable eighth, but in these trials, only the top six surfers advanced to the main event. Chris had barely missed qualifying for his first IPS contest.

Encouraged by his latest effort, he showed no anger over the result. This feat in itself was progress. Chris understood he was up against the most elite surfers in the world. Coming to Australia to compete against them was only the beginning. After learning the ropes, he felt confident things would only get better. During the trip he had turned eighteen and was a few years younger than the majority of competitors on the tour. Chris reasoned that he had his whole life ahead of him, and there would be plenty of time to catch up.

The time he spent in Australia proved beneficial in other ways, too. He had gained some much-needed visibility and exposure. Chris also marveled over the Australian surfing industry, and how much different it was from California. One emerging corporation in particular caught his eye. Quiksilver was a relatively new company that began producing surf products during the late 1960s. It was founded by Australians Alan Green, Carol McDonald, and Tim Davis, who viewed surfing not just as a sport, but as an active lifestyle. The best surfers in the world were beginning to travel a lot, and the buzz was growing. Quiksilver wanted to be at the forefront when everything came together in the future—whenever that might be.

Chris had seen surfers wearing Quiksilver trunks in Hawaii and was highly impressed by the quality product; he went back to California with a few pairs of Quiksilver trunks. He sensed that Quiksilver would become a major force within the sport and yearned to one day become part of their team.

Chris departed Australia more determined than ever to make a career in surfing. On the plane ride home, he noticed that the lump on his neck had become larger, but not knowing anything about complicated illnesses at the time, he thought there was no cause for alarm.

By the time he landed in Los Angeles, Chris already had memorized the world tour contest schedule for the rest of that year. He began making plans for the next contests he would travel to and set a goal to find more sponsors. After his return, several corporate surfing companies in California began to show more interest in him. Chris was beginning to earn the respect of the surfing world beyond the boundaries of his beloved Windansea. For the first time since those summers he spent on the lake in Maine as a child, Chris felt a true sense of belonging.

If only life were that simple.

Chapter 22

Cruel Hand of Fate

May, 1977

Before Chris would compete anywhere again, he would face a much greater challenge. When the lump on his neck was still there a week after his return from Australia, Jil had had enough of his resistance and made an appointment for him to see a doctor. That night, purely by coincidence, Chris read an article in Family Circle magazine about cancer of the lymph nodes, commonly referred to as Hodgkin's lymphoma. The article perfectly described his symptoms. He was stunned.

"Oh my God," he told Jil. "I feel exactly like they do."

Upon hearing this, Jil decided Chris's situation couldn't wait. Something needed to be done now. She drove Chris to a doctor to have the lump in his neck evaluated. He was told to see another doctor at Scripps Hospital the following day.

In spite of the potentially bad news, Chris slept well that night. I'm just a young adult, he thought. Things like cancer are supposed to happen to much older people. Aren't they?

Whatever this thing was, Chris figured the doctor would take care of it, or maybe it would simply shrink and go away. He had never been scared of anything before, least of all a little bump on the neck.

The next morning, he met with Dr. Richard Anderson, a cancer specialist at Scripps Hospital. A biopsy was performed under general anesthetic. Chris awoke quite disoriented from the drugs, but he could hear people speaking across the room. They were talking about cancer and about someone having a five percent chance to live, and he knew they were talking about him. He could faintly hear Jil talking, too. She was upset and crying.

"Your boyfriend's situation is a bit perilous," one of the doctors said. "We'd like to get him into surgery as soon as possible."

Almost immediately, Chris tried to go back to sleep, hoping the next time he woke up it would just have been a bad dream. Yet there was no escaping the diagnosis: Chris had Hodgkin's disease. Even worse was the news that the cancer had possibly spread beyond the lymphatic system and into the rest of his body.

Within a few hours, the cancerous lump on his neck was surgically removed, and a few days later, part of his spleen was removed as well in an effort to eradicate as much of the cancer from his body as possible.

Though Chris's spirits remained amazingly high, the days that followed were filled with confusion and disbelief for everyone close to him. How could this possibly be happening, especially to someone in the prime of his life?

I learned the news from Tim Senneff.

"Kirk, I just found out that Chris has cancer," Tim said.

"What are you talking about, Tim? Cancer? Isn't Chris still in Australia?"

"No, he came back a week ago. He wasn't feeling good, so Jil took him to a doctor. Now he's at Scripps Hospital, and they have already operated on him a few times."

"Jesus, that's unbelievable," I said in complete shock.

I immediately jumped into my car and drove to the hospital. At the time, I had no way of knowing how familiar this trip would become. When I saw Chris, he appeared very upbeat. For a long time, we just talked about his adventures in Australia, avoiding any discussion of cancer. Chris wanted everything to seem normal, so I just played along. Then out of the blue, he asked if I had been shooting photos of other surfers while he had been in Australia. When I told him yes, he looked disappointed. So I joked with him to try and raise his spirits.

"Hey Chris, what about when you were in Australia? Don't tell me there weren't plenty of other photographers taking pictures of you," I said, trying to be lighthearted. Chris knew I was being sarcastic, and at least my words put a smile on his face.

He faced a battery of medical tests over the next few days. He looked down but certainly not out—far from it, in fact. Chris laughed, joked, and talked like everything was normal. But something had happened, something terrible.

Chris had several more procedures to detect and remove cancerous lymph nodes throughout his entire body and to determine how far the cancer had spread. With his typical resilience, he slowly began to recuperate. The most difficult part, chemotherapy and radiation treatment, was still ahead, but even worse was the anguish he felt. Why was this happening to him? Why now? During his entire hospital stay, the IPS contest schedule for the remainder of 1977 was at his bedside. Chris had now reached a stage in which life had stopped giving him things and would now start taking them away.

Finally, Chris was discharged from the hospital and allowed to go home. He rotated among Jil's home in Point Loma, Oscar's house in La Jolla, and his parents' condo in Cardiff. Now more than ever, Bart and Gloria knew it was time to rally around their son.

The reality of what had happened to him was difficult for any of us to imagine. There was some good news, though: Chris's doctors had been able to remove most of the cysts in his body. Now it was up to chemotherapy and radiation to take care of the rest. The procedures would kill both the good and bad cells within his body; the hope was enough good cells would be left over when it was all finished.

For the near future at least, Chris wasn't in any life-threatening danger. What could happen down the road, however, was anyone's guess. So he went on with his life the best he could, and in early June, he graduated from La Jolla High School. Due to Chris's illness, his teachers allowed him to study at home and make up missed tests. Until Jim coaxed him into it, Chris had no intention of having his photo taken for the annual yearbook. Jim had his own picture taken first and then loaned his dress jacket to Chris. When the 1977 high school yearbook was finally published, both of them appeared wearing the same clothes.

Long before Chris became ill, I had made plans to spend the summer on Maui. I would start college at UCSD in the fall, and spending the summer in Hawaii seemed like the right thing to do. I looked forward to a lengthy break from La Jolla and also hoped the change of scenery would further my photography career. By good fortune, I seemed to be arriving on the scene just as surfing was on the verge of exploding into the mainstream.

Perhaps, as a child, I had watched too many television re-runs of Gilligan's Island, but I still found the tropical allure of Hawaii particularly intriguing. I had been to Maui several times in the past, and as much as I loved La Jolla, the best waves I had ever seen in my life were at idyllic Honolua Bay. A surfing photo I had taken of Australian Mark Richards at the fabled break had just been published as a two-page color spread in the 1977 Surfer magazine Photo Annual.

I looked forward to heading back to Maui. But when the wheels left the ground at San Diego's Lindbergh Field, I sure as hell felt a lot of guilt inside. It was difficult leaving my friend behind. While everyone else worried about his health, all Chris could think about was the impact cancer would have on his surfing career.

At least I knew that Chris was in good hands at Scripps Hospital. The cancer center had a solid reputation; several years earlier, my own mother had been treated for breast cancer there and had made it through. A few weeks after I left, his doctors seemed encouraged by Chris's progress. The intense doses of radiation and chemotherapy appeared to be helping, too, even though they made him extremely nauseated.

While I was gone, Chris's strength continued to improve. And not even cancer would get in the way of his unwavering loyalty toward friends and family. During the middle of summer, Chris decided to stay the night at his parents' condominium. He went into the bedroom that he and Lyn sometimes shared and found Lyn sitting there in the dark. She asked Chris not to turn the lights on.

"Why?" he asked.

"Because I don't want you to see me crying."

This was the wrong thing to say to her caring younger brother. Chris didn't hesitate to turn the lights on. She was in tears.

"My God, what's wrong?" he asked.

Lyn explained that her relationship with her boyfriend had become abusive, and he was seriously mistreating her.

"He's a really bad guy, Chris. I finally got away from him, but all my stuff is in his garage and he won't let me get it," she said.

"Lyn, why didn't you tell me about this before?"

"Because you are sick and have way more important things to take care of. This is all so stupid actually," she replied.

"Does being sick make me any less human? And it's not stupid at all because this guy is being a real jerk to you. I am still human, so don't treat me like a freak," he said. "Let's go. We're going to take care of this right now. Where does this guy live anyway?"

"He lives in Leucadia. But Chris, it's 11:30 at night."

"All the better time to take care of this dude then," her brother said.

They got into Lyn's car, and with Chris at the wheel, it didn't take long to get there. Along the way, Lyn realized she had never been in a car that went that fast. When Lyn pointed out where the house was, Chris came to a screeching stop in front of the garage, jumped out, and began pounding on the front door. A few seconds passed before Lyn's former boyfriend opened the door. He was a very big guy, but Chris was unfazed.

"You better come open the garage door right now before I knock it down myself," he said.

The man finally recognized Chris.

"Hi Chris, it's cool to see you, but what are you doing here?" he asked, sensing that something was definitely amiss. Then he noticed Lyn sitting in the car.

"You know why I'm here! You're fucking with my sister, and if you fuck with her, then I will fuck with you. I'll kill you. Is that clear? Now go get her stuff and bring it out to the car. And if you even look at her the wrong way, I will beat the fucking crap out of you."

"Hey, go easy there Chris. I have no problem with you, and I'll do what you say," he responded nervously.

The guy retrieved Lyn's items and gave them to Chris. As they began to pull away, the guy cordially tried to say goodbye. Chris stopped the car, stepped out, and took a swing at him, grazing his chin.

"That's it. Do you hear me? I never want to see you near my sister again," he said.

Lyn had to admit she never was more proud of her little brother. The man was twelve years older and a hell of a lot bigger than Chris, but she realized her brother was not afraid of anything. Right then and there, he had taken care of business.

Chris wasn't finished yet.

"And if I ever see YOU near him again, I'll bring you back there and force you to marry the guy. Are we clear?" he told Lyn.

After that night, and for the rest of his life, Lyn's little brother became her big brother. Chris had stood up for her, and she would never forget it.

Other members of the O'Rourke family were fighting battles as well. As a precautionary measure, Chris was readmitted to Scripps Hospital for a brief evaluation. Gloria called Lyn at work, begging her daughter to take her to see Chris.

Though Gloria was still struggling with alcoholism, Lyn knew that her mom had made strong efforts to become sober, and she detected a positive difference in her mom's voice. So Lyn left work early and drove to Cardiff to pick her up. As Lyn pulled into the driveway, however, she watched in agony as Gloria staggered out the front door. Just a short time earlier, she had sounded so normal. Now it was painfully obvious that her mother had suffered another relapse.

"Mom, there's no way I'm taking you to see Chris in your condition," Lyn told her.

Gloria insisted she could sober up enough by the time they got there. Reluctantly, Lyn gave in. At the hospital, Lyn approached the front desk to find out which room Chris was in. When she turned around, her mother was nowhere to be seen. After searching for several minutes, Lyn decided to take the elevator up to Chris's room. She opened the door and saw Chris lying on the bed with a variety of tubes attached to his arms.

"Hey Lyn, I thought you said you were bringing Mom. Where is she?"

"Chris, I'm sorry but Mom..."

There was no need for further explanation.

"Shit, not again!" Chris said, slamming his fist down on the bed. "You know, she's such a good mom. So why is she doing this to herself?"

At that moment, the door swung open, and Gloria walked in. Chris saw her awkward movements and didn't waste any time giving her an earful.

"Get out of this room!" he yelled at her.

"Chris, you don't mean that. I'm your mom," she replied, slurring.

"I do mean it, and no, you are not my mom. Because my mom doesn't drink!"

"But son...I want to help you," she said.

Chris snickered. "How can you help me when you can't even help yourself? So what are you gonna do for me? Huh? What are you gonna do for me?"

The strength of character it took for Chris to say all this was remarkable. With tears pouring down her face, Gloria turned and slowly walked out the door. Her son's harsh words had certainly hurt, but they had also sent a powerful message.

Later that night, Gloria telephoned her own mother and her husband's mother as well.

"Please help me—I'm an alcoholic," she sobbed.

A few days later, both of Chris's grandmothers arrived. A few months later, with their help and care, Gloria finally stopped drinking for the rest of her life. Her long bout with alcoholism had come to an end—and it had taken her son's predicament to show her the guiding light.

I often called Chris from Maui that summer to see how he was faring. Always, the first thing he asked me about was the surf. But it had been a fairly uneventful summer wave-wise, and I had few surf stories to tell. However, I did meet a really good surfer from Maui, who was coincidentally also named Chris. Chris Lassen had a powerful regular-foot surfing style and also was an extremely talented artist who specialized in oil paintings. He would become an internationally recognized artist whose work would be featured in prestigious art galleries worldwide.

Having access to the best surfer on Maui helped fill the void in my photography, but I began to miss La Jolla and all my friends back home. I was glad to hear that Chris's health had been rapidly improving. He still wasn't out of the woods, not by a long shot, but he had regained his strength and was surfing again better than ever. With this in mind, I eagerly looked forward to my return.

When I returned in late August, the first thing I did was stop in to see Chris. I was thrilled to hear that he was surfing so well again. The activity was something his doctors actually encouraged, and everyone said he looked as fluid and radical as ever—as if he hadn't missed a beat. I was anxious to see for myself.

But after leaving him several telephone messages, I had yet to hear from him. Since a new south swell had arrived, I went to Windansea to have a look, but there was still no sign of him. About to give up, I finally saw his car parked further north toward Simmons's Reef. I walked over and there he was, standing on the bluff watching the waves. For someone who had recently been diagnosed with cancer, he looked very healthy to me. I couldn't see any difference at all.

"Hey Chris, let's go shoot some photos," I said.

Chris turned and gave me a lukewarm smile but said nothing in response. I wasn't surprised to get the cold shoulder. And I could hardly blame him. While I had been on Maui having the time of my life, he had been stuck in a hospital fighting for his own. Knowing that he would soon come around, I waited, and after a lengthy silence, Chris finally responded.

"I don't think so, Aeder. Not today. While you were gone, I hooked up with a new photographer, and I only shoot photos with him now. We're going over to Blacks this afternoon," he said.

"Oh yeah, Chris? What's his name?"

When Chris hesitated, I knew he was just pulling my leg. He immediately looked toward the ocean and didn't say another word. For a brief moment, I considered that maybe it wasn't an act after all. Was he really that pissed off at me? I had been so focused on going to Maui that perhaps I really hadn't taken the time to understand the seriousness of his disease and what he was going through. Yet the person standing in front of me sure looked like the same old Chris O'Rourke. And after hearing him start to chuckle, I should have known better.

"I knew you were just playing your game with me," I told him.

"No you didn't, Aeder. You thought I was serious. I swear you are so gullible sometimes," he replied with confidence.

We watched together as a large set of waves passed through the Windansea lineup. It was a beautiful day in La Jolla, but there were surprisingly few surfers in the water. I noticed a large sea lion making its way through the surf to nap on the beach. Against a cloudless blue sky, a flock of pelicans flew effortlessly in perfect formation. Simple stuff really. But it meant a lot to us.

"Does it hurt, Chris?" I finally had to ask him.

There was a long pause. "Not really," he said. "The radiation isn't that bad, but the chemo part is. They give me this one big shot that takes about an hour to complete. I just have to sit there and take it. The worst part is what happens afterward."

"What's that?" I asked.

"Most people get super sick and start throwing up everywhere. After a few hours, it usually goes away. But sometimes it lasts several days. I guess I have been lucky. It hasn't been that bad for me. Fortunately my doctors have told me that I won't have to do this much longer."

"Well that's good news! But Jesus Christ, it's a bummer you have to go through all this," I told him.

"It's all right. And at least my hair never started falling off. During my treatments I see a lot of bald people in the room. My doctor says I'm doing really well though. Just getting back into the ocean and going surfing again was a big step. It helped me get my head back together."

"So how are you feeling now?" I asked.

"Right now?"

"Yeah, Chris, right now."

"Actually super good. I just want to rip the shit out of those waves at Right Hooker right now," he said. "Did you bring your cameras with you?"

"Duh, you knucklehead, what do you think?" I responded with a grin.

"I'll go get my board then and be right back."

Chris headed off on foot up Nautilus Street toward Oscar's house. I couldn't help being amazed at his resilience. I was an optimist, but I was also young and naïve. I figured that whatever cancer remained inside him wouldn't stand a chance. For now at least, on such a beautiful day, I felt hope.

No sooner had I set up my camera equipment near the Windansea hut when Chris reappeared. Wearing a black sleeveless wetsuit top and Quiksilver surf trunks, he quickly waxed his board and took a few steps toward the ocean. Suddenly, he turned back to me.

"Oh yeah, Aeder...I forgot to tell you something. Jil and I are having a baby. The due date is early next year."

He hurried off into the ocean and began to paddle out. Dumbfounded, I just stood there speechless. What had he just said? A baby? Chris had always liked to catch people off guard and then watch their reaction. After paddling a short distance, he finally looked back at me. I raised my arms high into the air in jubilation.

"Congratulations, Chris. Way to go!" I yelled.

I had come to expect these moments from Chris, but that didn't mean I ever got completely used to them. What I did notice was that his life, with or without cancer, always had so much more drama than mine. It seemed like another surprise waited around every corner. I didn't know anyone else our age that was having children. But I was happy for Chris and Jil. Finding out he had cancer several months earlier was the worst thing Chris had ever experienced. I hoped this latest bit of news would be a positive thing for his health.

I was anxious to see if his surfing had changed, but after watching his first few waves, I noticed no difference at all. If anything, Chris looked even better than the last time I had seen him.

A short time later I spotted Jim on the beach with his surfboard. There is nothing better in surfing than a good session among friends. It's the essence of what the sport is really all about. After Jim reached the lineup, he paddled directly over to Chris. They shook hands and talked while waiting for the next set. A very studious person who always had a calming effect on Chris, Jim had been accepted at UC San Luis Obispo and would soon be leaving La Jolla. Chris would miss his pal's friendship and steady guidance, but he knew there were plenty of others to lean on.

Over the next few weeks, Chris continued to make a solid recovery. Every surf session made him feel stronger. His rapid improvement and positive attitude amazed his doctors and friends. With the chemotherapy and radiation treatments dramatically scaled back, everything around him seemed to shine a little brighter. His doctors advised him, however, against traveling long distances. Chris would hold off for now, but the winter surf season in Hawaii was only a few months away. That's when he planned to make his next move.

Then came the announcement: A professional surfing contest would take place in California at Lower Trestles in San Clemente, located just an hour to the north. Chris would not have to travel far at all. The Sutherland California Pro would draw the biggest names in competitive surfing from around the world. The event was not IPS-rated, but this didn't stop the large contingent of international competitors from attending.

The Sutherland California Pro had originally been planned exclusively for surfers from the United States. But since there was a long break in the IPS tour schedule, foreign surfers wanted a piece of the action, too. The entry list soon turned into a credible collection of pros such as Peter Townend, Mark Warren, Rabbit Bartholomew, Michael Ho, Bobby Owens, Dennis Pang, and Rory Russell.

Surfers from California included Mike Purpus, Tony Staples, Allen Sarlo, and an emerging duo from Hermosa Beach, Chris Barela and Mike Benevidez. One particular last-minute entry, however, generated a lot of buzz. Chris's bout with cancer had been well-publicized by now, and this would be his first competition since his diagnosis.

On the first day of the contest in late September, Surfer magazine writer Jim Kempton interviewed Michael Ho and asked the Hawaiian surfer whom he thought would win.

"Other than me?" Michael laughed. "The guy everyone should be watching out for is Chris O'Rourke. He's by far the best surfer from California, and in spite of his sickness, is surfing out of his mind right now."

As we drove up the freeway that morning, Chris fidgeted nervously and appeared eager to hit the water for his first heat. He was intent upon proving that, in spite of his illness, he was still one of the best in the world. The contest itself seemed like a positive sign for surfing in the United States, as professional events like these provided vast media attention and helped the sport grow.

As I exited the freeway, Chris suddenly asked me to pull over. Before I could even come to a complete stop, he pushed open the door and vomited. Then, he closed the door and instructed me to head on.

"Are you all right?" I asked.

"Yeah, I think so. That usually doesn't happen very often."

A few minutes later, we pulled in at Lower Trestles. The waves were about three to four feet in height and quite consistent. The format and judging criteria for the event would be different than a normal IPS competition; each contestant would be guaranteed a minimum of three heats. Each surfer's total points would be accumulated and those with the highest totals would advance.

In the early afternoon, Chris paddled out for his first heat. The moment was extremely emotional for him. He surfed very well and returned to the water later for his second heat. Both his performances caught the attention of other competitors.

On the second day of competition, the ocean turned completely flat, and the event was postponed. But the lull would not last long. Late in the afternoon, a significant new south swell began to push through. By sundown the waves at Trestles had quickly risen to six feet. Clearly the contest would resume early the next morning.

But while waves arrive at the whim of Mother Nature, chemotherapy appointments do not. You go when you're told to go because your life depends upon it. This was not an issue for any of the other competitors, but it was for Chris. He had a treatment scheduled for that morning, and he had to be there. Fortunately, his third heat wouldn't take place until mid-afternoon, and Chris was determined to compete, even though most people felt he would be too fatigued to surf.

Thirty minutes before the start of his heat, Chris was nowhere to be seen. Over the loudspeaker, the competitors in his heat were told to pick up their contest jerseys. And just when it seemed as if he wouldn't make it, Chris suddenly appeared. He paddled out with the rest of the competitors and, in an amazing display of determination, performed well enough to advance through to the final stages of the event. What no one on the beach knew was that he vomited twice during his heat.

While Chris had truly persevered, unfortunately this was as far as he would go. He returned the next day feeling rejuvenated and rode several solid waves while carving out an impressive mixture of cutting-edge turns and maneuvers. But when the judges announced their decision, Chris was left behind. Most of the onlookers who had been watching from the beach were stunned.

Chris took it all in stride and tried not to make a big deal about it. But inside I knew he was fuming. And if he couldn't win the event, at least he was happy that his friend Michael Ho did. Michael had surfed brilliantly throughout and earned the victory outright.

One hundred and eight of the best surfers in the world had competed; Chris had placed a respectable thirteenth. After the event, he received "The Most Inspirational Surfer" award. Finishing as highly as he did certainly raised a lot of eyebrows. Was Chris O'Rourke really all the way back?

Back in La Jolla a few days later, Chris was in vintage form, vehemently questioning the judging decision that had caused his elimination. Even Dave Gilovich, a part-time competitor and editor of Surfing Magazine at the time, later commented, "Chris got a bit of a bad call toward the end of the contest there.

And that was unfortunate, especially considering the ordeal he has been through."

A short time passed, and Chris got over it. He recalled what Michael had once told him about not letting his contest frustrations fester. Instead, he focused on getting fired up for the next contest, whenever that might be.

His complaints, however, did illustrate the divisions in judging criteria. Even in the pro ranks, at times there seemed to be little consensus. What exactly were the judges giving points for? Chris was beginning to think that stylish surfing had taken a back seat to what he called "gyrating."

Professional contest surfing was still young, and competitors and judges alike hoped that a more uniform judging system could be developed. On the bright side, the Sutherland Pro and Katin Pro-Am events had proved that high-level surf contests could succeed in the United States. Almost everyone within the American surf industry figured it was now only a matter of time until an official IPS event was staged here.

Chapter 23

Road to Recovery

By the fall of 1977, Chris cemented his reputation as the most progressive surfer from the mainland United States—cancer and all. His doctors believed that his illness appeared to be on the decline, and his main goals were to stay healthy and to improve his surfing. As most of his friends—and certainly the entire Windansea surf community—saw it, a permanent spot on the IPS tour would be his for the taking.

Several photos of Chris that I had taken earlier that year were published in Surfing magazine. I had become absolutely hooked on surf photography. Though I had started my freshman year at UCSD, I didn't need college to find out what I wanted to do with my life. I already knew.

When Chris learned that UCSD didn't keep official attendance records, he regularly tried and often succeeded in getting me to ditch class and shoot photos of him. Thanks to his new sponsorship deal with a young company known as Surfer House wetsuits and his financial arrangement with Bill Caster, Chris could finally call himself a professional surfer. So I went along for the ride.

One afternoon I received a telephone call from Larry Moore, the photo editor of Surfing. He gave me an assignment to take profile photos for an upcoming article about Chris but refused to divulge any details. This didn't necessarily come as a surprise; a fairly intense rivalry had developed between the staffs at Surfer and Surfing, and the two bi-monthly magazines kept a tight lid on their projects.

Regardless of what was going on with the magazines, I

jumped at the opportunity. I immediately telephoned Chris to arrange the photo shoot. He made a great suggestion.

"Aeder, meet me over on Playa del Sur Street. We can use Oscar's car as a background," he said.

When I arrived an hour later, Oscar was wiping down his classic MG3. Chris was already there, and we hovered around the shiny vehicle in awe.

"This is such a classic car, Oscar, perfect for cruising around La Jolla," I told him.

For the next hour, Chris posed by the car with his purple Caster surfboard while I snapped photos. His demeanor seemed uncharacteristically subdued. Over the past several months he had gone through many life-altering changes, and his illness had caused him to look at his life and mortality much differently now.

The next week, I drove Chris to San Clemente to be photographed by Larry Moore. These pictures, taken inside a studio, would be published as a full-page advertisement for Surfer House wetsuits. Larry was accompanied by Surfing's advertising director, Robert Mignogna, who strongly supported Chris and had helped to facilitate his sponsorship deal with Surfer House.

Dressed in a brand-new full wetsuit, Chris stood on a small platform against a solid black backdrop lit by umbrella lights. He was very polite and posed in the ways Larry and Bob suggested.

"Hey Chris, just look like you're the world champ. Because one day, you probably will be," said Robert.

And for a few fleeting moments, he did feel like the world champ. During the photo shoot, Chris talked a lot about surfing but said nothing about his cancer. Impressed by his good nature and positive attitude, Larry and Robert thanked him for coming.

While Chris relished having his photo taken, especially outdoors in the surf, he also enjoyed escaping to secluded surfing locations in Central California where there were no cameras. Rincon and El Capitan near Santa Barbara were two of his favorites, along with The Ranch just slightly further north. This hard-to-access surf break was situated along a privately owned stretch of scenic coastline. The Ranch provided long rides, excellent practice, and freedom from photographers. Local surfers were fiercely protective of The Ranch. Cameras and long telephoto lenses were rarely, if ever, welcomed; photographers who tried were immediately escorted away. Chris felt fortunate just to be invited there by his local friends Larry Bennett and Kit Cossart. Some of the best surf sessions of his life went unnoticed by the media, shrouded instead within a tight veil of localism and secrecy.

The ocean temperature in Central California was considerably colder than down south. Hardcore surfers were normally accustomed to surfing in whatever conditions were thrown at them, but their bodies weren't weakened by cancer. After surfing for several days in the cold water, Chris was more than ready to get back to La Jolla.

In late November, his doctors reported that his cancer had all but disappeared. The announcement could not have come at a better time. Chris was intent upon surfing in Hawaii that winter, and now there was no reason not to go.

Two days before he left for the islands, he got more good news in the form of an advance copy of the Surfing magazine that featured his story. His coverage was part of a much larger feature: "The Boys" was written by esteemed writer and former Surfing editor Drew Kampion. Chris was one of the four young surfers portrayed, along with Australian Cheyne Horan and Hawaiians Mark Foo and Charley Smith. Several photos I had taken of Chris were featured, including one of him standing next to Oscar's car.

In the weeks that followed, the article earned strong praise and proved to be a turning point for the industry. The surf magazines had previously trended toward publicizing older surfers. But the time had finally come when surfing's youth movement could no longer be ignored. This was where the sport was now headed, and these four surfers stood poised and ready to lead surfing into the future.

Nicknamed the "Boy Wonder From Down Under," seventeen-year-old Cheyne Horan had already built an incredible reputation. He and Chris shared a regular-foot style, bleach-blond hair, and high-caliber surfing. Though they'd grown up on opposite sides of the Pacific Ocean, both surfers had honed their reputations at similar surf breaks. Cheyne was born and raised in Sydney, a hot bed for young competitive surfers. As a kid he competed in club and junior surf events. Victories came often. Just as Chris was being proclaimed as the next big thing in American surfing, so was Cheyne in Australia. Both surfers appeared well on their way to becoming major forces in the sport.

All four surfers were extremely talented, but Chris was the only one who had been through a serious illness. His story was very inspiring to others, and for the first time he spoke openly about his cancer. But he also staunchly refused to use it as an excuse.

"Surfing is the most free and, to me, the most incredible form of self-expression that this

planet has to offer," read one of his quotes. "I want to get established in the pro circuit and make it to all the contests. I'm totally committed."

As the North Shore geared up for another season of powerful winter surf, Chris readied himself to return. He was feeling strong and healthy and figured he could handle any size surf that came his way. In the middle of December, he arrived in Oahu energized and ready to charge. The recent publicity had made him a highly sought-after target by several veteran surf magazine photographers, including Dan Merkel, one of the most prolific surf photographers in the world and senior photographer for Surfing magazine.

When a new swell arrived, Dan arranged to meet Chris and Mark Foo at a photogenic surf break near Pipeline known as Off The Wall. As Chris was leaving, he received a phone call from someone claiming the plan had changed, that he was now supposed to meet Dan at Rocky Point instead. But when Chris arrived, there was no sign of anyone. Since the waves looked good he paddled out anyway, figuring Dan and Mark would be there soon.

Meanwhile, over at Off The Wall, the waves were the best of the entire winter. Shooting from the water, Dan captured several incredible images of Mark Foo and was perplexed as to why Chris hadn't shown up. Every pro surfer yearned to be photographed by someone like Dan Merkel. A few months later, his photos of Mark were published extensively in Surfing magazine, including a cover shot. This one photo session alone served as a significant launching point in Mark Foo's professional surfing career.

Chris had missed a big opportunity, one that would really cost him. The following day when Chris saw Dan, he insisted someone had told him to go to Rocky Point. Finally, a few days later, Chris did get to shoot with Dan during a good swell at Velzyland.

Before he left for Hawaii, Chris's doctors had advised him to avoid spending too much time in the sun. As a result, he was often forced to limit his surf sessions to two hours. Sometimes he wore a thin full wetsuit with short sleeves just to keep the sun off of his body.

Chris also continued his chemotherapy and radiation treatments in Hawaii. On a couple of occasions, Michael Ho and his good friend Hans Hedemann, whose smooth surfing style and deft tube-riding skills Chris admired, drove him across the island to Kaiser Hospital in Honolulu. They saw how taxing the procedures were on his body, and they had a suggestion. Chris was still smoking marijuana anyway. Why not smoke it before and after his treatments to help combat the nausea?

The next time Chris went for his treatment, he didn't become ill afterward. He was elated to have two good friends like Michael and Hans around, and Hans was amazed by Chris's resilience.

Of course, proving his resiliency was Chris's goal. He had received an alternate invitation to the highly coveted Duke

Kahanamoku contest. But when no one dropped out, he lost his opportunity. Chris was disappointed but kept a positive attitude. With a pregnant girlfriend back home, his stay in Hawaii would not be a lengthy one.

Before leaving he talked with surfers like Mark Warren and Larry Bertlemann about the kind of boards they were riding and learned about the new super-lightweight boards that weighed no more than nine pounds. Chris rode a few of them and was astounded by how well they worked. Surfing on lighter boards made all the difference in the world! Crafted by North Shore board shapers Tom Parrish and Bill Barnfield, the boards were revolutionary compared to what Chris had been using.

Chris knew that, in order to reach his goals, he had to be at the forefront of everything within the sport. Upon returning to San Diego, Chris drove to Bill Caster's shaping factory to tell him about the lightweight boards. Bill's eyes widened after each dramatic story Chris told, and soon Bill's boards became much lighter, too.

After spending nearly three weeks in Hawaii, Chris felt re-energized about his future. Seven months after being diagnosed with Hodgkin's lymphoma, he felt everything was getting back to normal. On New Year's night, he celebrated with Jil and appeared as healthy as ever. Having cancer also caused Chris to become more aware of things going on around him, unlike when he was younger and quite single-minded.

But what we noticed even more was the change in his character. Whether it was the illness he had contracted, the true love he felt for Jil, or knowing he would be a father soon, a more unpretentious and humble Chris was emerging. Few of us could even recall the last time he had been in a fight. The year may have come to a close, but for Chris life was just beginning.

Chapter 24

Simmons's Reef and Chemotherapy

Chris eagerly looked forward to the start of the 1978 IPS world tour, but another glorious event would happen first. On January 10, Jil gave birth to a healthy baby boy at Sharp Hospital. Chris described the day as "the proudest moment of my life." The couple named the child Timothy Michael O'Rourke, and Jim Neri was named the boy's godfather.

Shortly after Timothy was born, I went to visit Chris and Jil. I hadn't seen Chris since he returned from Hawaii, and upon seeing Timothy for the first time, I felt tremendously happy for them.

"Would you like to hold him?" Jil asked.

I hesitated. "No, that's okay."

Chris found my reluctance amusing. "What's the matter, Aeder? Are you afraid he's going to throw up or poop on you?"

"Well Chris, before Tim came along, when was the last time you held a baby?" I asked with a laugh.

"Come on, Aeder, it's easy," Chris said.

He lifted Tim from his crib. Chris exuded pure joy while holding his infant son. Behind his smile, though, raged an internal tug of war. Chris still really wanted to be the tough guy. But after contracting cancer, and now with a baby, how could he do that? For the first time in his life, he had to be a responsible person, not just for himself, but for others around him.

Timothy had been brought into the world to very young parents: Chris was still only eighteen and Jil just seventeen.

Raising an infant at such a young age was going to be a major challenge. Everyone was overjoyed, but privately some questioned if they really knew what they were doing.

To Chris and Jil, however, it wasn't even an issue. Chris's doctors had told him the radiation treatments could make him sterile one day. So he suggested to Jil that they try to conceive as soon as possible. Regardless of the circumstances, their child was a product of their love for each other.

If Chris had been humbled by his bout with cancer, the birth of his son had humbled him even further. For Tim's sake alone, he vowed to take a different approach to life. In the past he had rubbed a lot of people the wrong way, and he sought a chance at redemption. Whether he really had become a changed man remained to be seen.

Chris didn't have much time to celebrate Tim's birth. Two weeks later, the second annual Katin surfing contest commenced at Huntington Beach. Most of the top professional surfers in the world were there—184 competitors from the continental US, Australia, Hawaii, South Africa, Brazil, and even Japan. Walking around the event site during the first day, Chris radiated enthusiasm and pride. He was a popular figure; there was a great deal of curiosity about him, and everyone wanted to offer their encouragement.

Chris easily won his first heat that day while surfing for Team Caster. Over the next few days he won or placed highly in several more heats and continued to progress. The final days of the contest drew more than ten thousand spectators. One particular group of surfers stood out among the rest: Peter Townend, Ian Cairns, and Mark Warren hung out together wearing aviator glasses and gold nylon jackets. Embroidered upon the jackets were the words "The Bronzed Aussies."

The concept was the brainchild of Peter and Ian, whose intent was to organize surfing as a team sport. The two outspoken Australians had also been spending a lot of time in California working as surfing stunt doubles in the forthcoming Hollywood movie Big Wednesday.

Most people in the industry wrote off The Bronzed Aussies as brash and full of themselves. But others saw their actions as brilliant foresight. Chris just figured they were trying to advance the sport, and there was certainly nothing wrong with that. Professional surfing needed individuals to step up and take chances. In Chris's view, The Bronzed Aussies were way ahead of their time.

"It's unfortunate that those who try and do different things get ridiculed when they're only trying to improve the sport. People put them down because they are afraid to take big steps themselves. But the truth is those guys are the real pioneers," he told me.

Also in the mix at Huntington was young Aussie Cheyne Horan. Cheyne and Chris hadn't talked much, but there was mutual respect between them. Milling about were notable surfers David Nuuhiwa, Terry Fitzgerald, Rory Russell, and Wayne Lynch. Standing farther away, posing in their new O'Neill wetsuits, were Shaun Tomson and Reno Abellira. It was nice to see such a tremendous mix of worldly surfing talent right there in California.

Unfortunately the surf didn't cooperate. The final day found the international array of surfers forced to compete in windblown, two to three-foot sloppy waves. Chris constantly kept bundled up on the beach trying to stay warm. His doctors had continued to advise him against surfing in cold water, but nothing was going to keep him from competing. He won two more heats and advanced, besting Reno Abellira, the fourth-ranked IPS surfer in the world at the time. A month earlier, the Hawaiian big-wave rider had won the prestigious Smirnoff Pro at Waimea Bay.

When the Katin contest concluded, Chris finished in ninth place overall. He was proud of his achievement and didn't throw any tantrums.

"I've become a lot better about controlling my emotions," he later told a reporter. "I obviously used to be much worse. The fallout from some of the situations I put myself in became pretty messy, so I try not to act that way anymore." It was almost surreal to see Chris learning to take losing in stride.

Larry Bertlemann won the event, with Australians Wayne Lynch and Mark Warren finishing second and third respectively. To the dismay of some surfing purists, the overall team title went to The Bronzed Aussies.

Chris's star continued to rise, but he still had his share of challenges. Several days after the contest, he told me he had felt severe pains in his head while competing. During the contest, he was struck on the head by his own board, and surfing in the cold water at Huntington probably didn't help either. Some mentioned he might be suffering from an acute case of "surfer's ear." At that moment there didn't seem to be much further cause for concern—but there should have been.

Over the next few weeks, the surf in La Jolla was dismal. It was the heart of winter, and the lack of northwest swells was unusual. Chris was anxious to surf, but there was little to ride. Admittedly, I was fine with this since I had a lot of studying to do.

After the lengthy lack of surf, I was elated to receive a phone call from Chris early one February morning. He claimed the waves at Windansea were pretty good and suggested I come take photos. What I noticed most about his request was that it wasn't a demand. There was no forcefulness in his voice, no chiding, and no attitude whatsoever. Clamoring for a change of scenery from my studies, I headed over to Windansea.

But instead of clean wave lines and sunny skies, the surf barely had a pulse, and a thick layer of fog was moving onshore. I spotted Chris standing next to Mark McCoy along the street above Simmons's Reef. I couldn't but help give Chris a little ribbing over the poor conditions.

"Hey Chris, so this is why you dragged me down here? Where's all that great surf you were talking about?"

"There were waves earlier, I swear," replied Mark first.

"The tide is going lower, so maybe it has something to do with that," said Chris, almost apologetically.

We decided to go eat breakfast at John's Waffle Shop and return later when the tide would be higher. My anxiety level was rising; I had three classes later that day and had already concluded that the surf wasn't going to get any better.

Still, I decided to play along, and when we returned to Simmons's Reef a few hours later, the ocean had made one of the most amazing transformations I had ever seen. Pushed by brisk offshore winds, the fog bank had retreated back out to sea well beyond the kelp beds. More importantly, the waves had significantly increased. We stood in awe at nature's dramatic turnaround.

The first wave of the set approached the shallow reef, rose skyward, and exploded into a perfect sparkling right tube.

"Holy shit! I haven't seen waves like that since I was in Hawaii. I knew the higher tide would make it better," said Chris.

Chris ran back to his car like a man possessed. He quickly put on his wetsuit, grabbed his 6' 8"Caster single fin surfboard and ran down the concrete stairway. Seconds later he was in the water.

I set up my camera equipment in anticipation of outstanding photos. The waves were some of the most beautiful I had ever seen in La Jolla. The turquoise-colored water, white sandy beach, and tall palm trees swaying in the offshore winds did make it feel like we were in Hawaii, just as Chris had said.

This was another of those rare "magical" moments in surfing. I was amazed by how rapidly the conditions had changed. But I also knew that the ocean works in mysterious ways, and as quickly as the sea had transformed, the pendulum could swing right back.

Chris quickly paddled for his first wave, a six-foot beauty so crystal clear it looked like a sparkling sheet of glass. He instantly tucked inside a thick lengthy tube ride, emerging to perform two vertical off the lips followed by a punishing roundhouse cutback. Whether it was surfing, or other aspects of his life, everything Chris did always seemed to happen at warp speed. He surfed upon wave after wave with amazing precision. Peering through my Century 650 mm telephoto lens, I noticed his hair was still completely dry!

When Mark finally paddled out, they were the only surfers in the lineup. Not that Chris minded. The waves were all his for the taking, and every few minutes he pulled inside another deep barrel. Chris absolutely lived for this kind of surf: thick hollow waves tailor-made to his style.

An hour into the session, Chris had already captured eight tube rides, and the lineup began to attract other surfers. One of these was Mark's older brother Jeff, along with Dale Stanley, who was a lifeguard at Windansea. The consistent surf offered plenty of waves for everyone.

Then it came, one wave in particular that stood up and identified itself as the wave of the entire magical session. As expected, Chris quickly paddled into it.

The ominous thick slab of liquid rose skyward like a menacing lion. After making the steep drop, Chris turned his focus to what lay ahead. He could see the jagged rock reefs only a few feet below the water's surface, snarling and daring him to take the chance. The tube ride of a lifetime waited, and Chris wasn't about to pass it up. The large cavernous barrel that began to form was so spacious that a dump truck could have fit inside. As the water pitched loudly over his head, Chris entered the tube standing completely upright.

Several seconds passed, and there was no sign of him. Even the other surfers in the water couldn't see him. Watching through my lens, I had lost sight of him, too, but I kept my finger firmly pressed on the shutter button. My camera's motor drive kept firing as the tubing wave rumbled through the lineup.

Figuring that Chris was too deep inside and would never make it back out, Dale Stanley paddled for the leftovers. What happened next shocked everyone. No sooner had Dale stood up and started his bottom turn when Chris suddenly shot out of the curl above him. Everyone watching did double-takes in sheer disbelief—and none more so than poor Dale himself. Startled by Chris's reemergence, he fell off his board.

When Chris's amazing ride came to an end, people sitting in their cars watching from Neptune Street began honking their horns and cheering wildly. Caught up in the euphoria of the moment, Chris thrust both of his arms skyward in ecstasy. Long after his ride had ended, the beach continued to buzz with electricity.

As word of his incredible ride began circulating around the neighborhood, spectators began to gather to watch their hometown surf-star. Chris did not disappoint his local legion of fans. For the next hour, he continued to surf those magnificent waves but never caught another quite like that one. Not that it mattered. His ride for the ages had set a new standard even for him: The longest tube ride ever seen at the La Jolla reefs.

Then a short time later, the pendulum suddenly swung back. The ocean quieted, the offshore winds turned back to onshore, and the thick fog bank returned. Chris and the others paddled back to shore. Like everyone else, I was awed by his performance. This was the first time that I really thought of Chris as being an athlete, or more precisely, as surfers being athletes. The type of skill Chris had just displayed certainly took a lot of athleticism, and as far as I was concerned, I had just seen the best surfer in the entire world.

When Chris came back to the car, I expected him to be boasting, but instead he just wore a genuine smile. And instead of talking about himself, Chris deferred everything to how well his Caster surfboard had performed.

"I can't wait to tell Bill about this. The board worked perfectly out there."

"You were killing it out there, Chris. I can't wait to get these photos developed," I told him.

Before long, a mass of people began milling around Chris, and we lost track of time. Then, Chris looked at his watch and suddenly announced that he had a chemotherapy treatment in an hour.

"Hey Aeder, I forgot to ask you about something. Jil needs to use our car this afternoon, so she can visit with her mom. Can you give me a ride to the hospital?" he asked.

"Are you kidding, Chris? After what you just did out there, I'll give you a ride to the moon!"

I still had classes to attend, but after his remarkable performance, how could I possibly say no? When he began waving a fat joint in my face as an incentive, the deal was sealed. Chris continued to smoke marijuana as a way of combating the nausea caused by his treatments, and it seemed to work.

It didn't take him long to light up the joint. By the time we pulled into the parking lot at Scripps Memorial Hospital, my Volkswagen van was filled with smoke. When Chris opened his door, a white aromatic plume wafted into the air outside. He took one last toke off the joint before handing it back to me.

"This shouldn't take long, just an hour or so. Can you hang out for awhile?" he asked.

"No problem, Chris. All my textbooks are in the car. I'll do some studying while you're in there."

Considering the mind-altering condition I was in, however, brushing up on my studies wasn't going to be easy. An hour later, Chris had not returned, so I went into the hospital to look for him. I had waited inside the cancer treatment center before. The attendant told me Chris was nearly finished, so I sat down and began leafing through a pile of magazines.

If ever I needed a vivid reminder of exactly what Chris was going through, this was it. The room was a mix of both bleakness and hope. Every few minutes, the sliding door opened, and another sick patient emerged: a middle-aged woman thin as a pencil, an elderly man with a huge scar on his neck, and finally, the most painful to see, a completely bald girl no more than twelve years old. Some were vomiting violently. Not wanting to stare, I pretended to read the magazines, but it was hard to ignore the suffering around me. My emotions were roiling, and I felt like crying. Not wanting to bring further grief upon anyone around me, I forced myself to be strong.

I had gone through this same scenario several years earlier, when my mother had breast cancer and had been one of those people. She had defeated it, and now it seemed Chris would do the same. Sitting there waiting, I felt so fortunate to be healthy, but my mind was also filled with an enormous amount of guilt. I contemplated what forces on earth were responsible for causing some people to have cancer while others didn't. I had learned that life could take a serious turn for the worse at any moment. I felt utterly helpless.

The passing minutes seemed like hours. Finally, Chris emerged. I was amazed by his energy level.

"I'm all done. Let's get out of here," Chris said.

"Wow, you don't even look sick. Smoking pot certainly seems to help you," I whispered.

"It totally works. One of my doctors said he might even be able to prescribe it legally for me," Chris said.

"Really? They'll do that?"

On the ride home, he never vomited once or even looked remotely ill. I thought about his day. One moment he's surfing perfect tubes at Simmons's Reef, and the next he's undergoing chemotherapy. It couldn't get more diverse than that.

Chapter 25

Controversy and Another Setback

Chris's surfing, health, and life in general only continued to improve. His treatments would soon end, and the timing could not have been better. The 1978 IPS tour would be starting again soon, and Chris badly wanted to return to Australia. But the recent birth of his son had made him more inclined to stay home. Jil, however, encouraged him to go.

"It's your dream, Chris. You should go for it," she told him.

All indications pointed to Chris having another chance. Ever since he had first been diagnosed with cancer, Chris's wild, arrogant behavior had subsided dramatically. His bout with cancer had been life-altering, but now that his health had improved, I could only wonder how much longer this mood swing would last.

I did not wonder for long. In late February, a clean swell rolled into Big Rock, and Chris's fiery temperament emerged from its long hibernation.

Chris paddled out shortly after sunrise. The waves were a solid six feet; large, cavernous curls that crashed thunderously down upon the shallow reefs. Dominating from the offset, Chris easily stood out in the crowded lineup. The usual Big Rock regulars were all there, but a big surprise came in the form of Hawaiian surfer Rory Russell. A few months earlier, he had bested Gerry Lopez by winning the prestigious Pipeline Masters contest. Having surfed at Pipeline over the last two winters, Chris was familiar with Rory and respected his style.

Now it was time for Chris to impress Rory at Big Rock. Their surfing turned into a friendly tube-riding contest: Rory the goofy foot versus Chris the regular foot.

When Rory finally paddled in, Chris figured he would stay and catch a few more waves. Minutes later, something onshore caught his attention. A surfer in a bright yellow wetsuit ran down to the beach and began paddling out toward the lineup. Chris did not immediately recognize him.

As the surfer inched closer, everyone else let out a chorus of snickers. The hideous yellow wetsuit certainly wasn't going to earn him any goodwill here. Finally Chris realized it was Joey Buran. An arrogant, cocky young kid, Joey had strong professional aspirations. Chris knew that pictures of Joey were beginning to appear in the surfing magazines.

Until now, he had never cared about Joey one way or the other—Chris could surf circles around him. Joey had gained his recognition primarily surfing at beach breaks, and he had a long way to go before catching up with Chris's freakish ability.

But seeing Joey at the Windansea reefs changed all that. Cancer or not, this was his turf, and he had an obligation to protect it. When it came to localism, the tight crew of surfers at The Rock could be a feisty bunch (most of them were regulars at Windansea, too). By wearing the bright wetsuit, Joey had sent the wrong message. All the knee-boarders started laughing while yelling at him to go back to the shore. Feeling the negativity, Joey turned around. But instead of returning to the beach, he planted himself in the channel and tried to stay low-key.

"Look at that idiot," said Chris. "He thinks he can hide over there. But wearing that horrible wetsuit, he can be seen from a mile away."

All the surfers near Chris laughed again.

Joey had never surfed out at Big Rock before. He had no idea that a wave like this, a much smaller version of Pipeline, even existed in California. While scared of the locals, Joey was in awe of the waves. At that moment he didn't mind biding his time over in the channel, watching. He also wasn't aware how badly Chris was fuming inside over his presence. Instead, Joey enjoyed watching him surf. He had seen Hawaiian surfers like Dane Kealoha, Mark Liddell, Buttons Kaluhiokalani, and Reno Abellira, but he never had seen anything from California like Chris O'Rourke before.

For many years, Joey had long admired veteran California surfers like Dale Dobson, Tony Staples, and Mike Purpus. Those surfers, though, had already reached their competitive peak. With the surfing world trending toward a youth movement, Joey understood that Chris was his measuring rod for success. Anyone from here with the desire to be the best had to get by this guy first.

Joey also recalled what his reaction had been upon learning that Chris had cancer:

"That's a tough break for him, but that's a really good break for me."

Selfish and spiteful as it might have seemed, those were his honest feelings. While Joey deeply admired Chris's talents, all he knew about cancer at the time was that most people who got it died. Taking Chris's place atop the order of things was something he dearly wanted to do. If that's the way it should happen, then so be it.

Chris wanted nothing more than to paddle over to Joey right then and there and beat the living snot out of him. But he was a professional now. Doing so could have negative repercussions for him within the surfing industry. He agonized over having to hold back.

Over in the safety of the channel, Joey watched wave after wave explode on the shallow reef. Chris was taking off in the surf farther back than anyone, well behind the exposed dry reef that gave Big Rock its name. After a weightless backside free-fall down the wave's face, he would stand straight up inside the spacious barrel.

Joey grew tired of watching and wanted in on the wave action, too. But if he even tried to paddle for one wave, the locals wouldn't let him have it. Chris never looked his way again. The Big Rock locals had already harassed him enough.

During a lull in the action, Chris gazed toward the shore and noticed a photographer with a long telephoto lens. He realized it wasn't me or any other photographer he knew.

After putting two and two together, it finally dawned on him—it was Chuck Schmid from Huntington Beach. A staff photographer for Surfing magazine, Chuck was the one who had brought Joey here. When they first arrived at Big Rock, Chuck warned Joey about the fierce localism. They took extreme measures by parking their van six blocks away, hoping no one would see them. Windansea, however, has many eyes. Oscar and Ted happened to be walking by and had noticed them.

Out in the water, the bad vibes continued to flow. Joey remained tentative while diligently trying to work his way further into the tense lineup. Although Chris had caught an abundance of waves, by now he had become fed up with Joey's presence. He tried telling himself to stay cool—there had to be another way other than punching his lights out.

Chris caught his last wave and paddled in. He saw me on the bluff and came over.

"Hey Kirk, is that photographer standing over there that Chuck Schmid guy from Huntington?" he asked.

"Yeah, it is," I replied. "Joey Buran and he showed up together."

For the first time in a long time, I saw the anger in Chris's face began to build. Chris didn't really care where surfers like Joey Buran went—as long as they didn't come here to the La Jolla reefs. Bringing along an out-of-town photographer was an added sin.

"Where did they park their car?" Chris asked.

"Not sure," I replied.

Just then Oscar and Ted walked up. They had overheard us talking.

"We saw where they parked. It was way over there on Rosemont Street. They sure looked like they were trying to hide from everyone," said Ted.

"What do these guys think they're doing here? Do they really think they can come down here, have Buran paddle out in a yellow wetsuit, and have a photo shoot right here?" spat Chris.

"Yeah, that's pretty amazing, alright. They park six blocks away, try to stay under the radar, yet Joey paddles out in the brightest wetsuit I've ever seen," I added.

"I'm gonna put an end to this right now," said Chris.

It went against the grain of what surfing localism was all about around Windansea: I don't come to your place, and you don't come to mine, unless you're invited. Selfishness, pride, and ignorance for sure, but in the surfing world, that's just how it was at the time. Chris reasoned that he might have even cut Joey some slack if he had not brought a photographer along.

Seeing Chris vent, I began feeling the same way. His influence had worn off on me; I had developed an animosity toward outsiders, too, particularly other surf photographers who tried to infiltrate "my" area. Chris wanted Joey to leave, and I wanted the photographer out as well.

Out in the lineup, we watched as local surfers Jeff Toomey, Joe Roper, Marshall Myrman, and the Huffman brothers kept Joey from catching any waves. Finally forced to the inside, all he could muster up were the leftovers breaking near the channel. With the crew keeping him at bay, Chris devised his plan.

"Kirk, do you have a pen and paper somewhere?" he asked.

"Sure do," I replied.

I packed up my camera equipment, and we walked over to my car. I handed him the pen and paper, and he scribbled furiously. I didn't know what he wrote, but I knew it would be something good. We drove over to Rosemont Street and quickly spotted their van. Chris jumped out and placed the paper beneath one of the wiper blades. Then he picked up a large rock and made a motion as if he were going to smash one of the windows.

"Whoa, wait a minute, Chris!" I told him. "While I'm in complete agreement with you, doing something like that might be taking it just a tad too far. But ultimately, it's all up to you."

Chris glared at me. "I guess I was wrong about you, Aeder. You're still just a goody-goody."

He might have been pissed at me, but at least their car was still intact. By the time we got back to Big Rock, Chris had a change of heart.

"Sorry about that, Aeder. I'm actually glad I didn't do it, too."

Chris put on his wetsuit and paddled straight back out into the surf, glaring at Joey as he went past him. By now Chuck Schmid was feeling the negative vibes as well and figured it was time to get out of there. He gathered up his cameras and made a hasty retreat. As he neared his van, Chuck could see the piece of paper on the windshield. After looking around to see if anyone was watching, Chuck read the note. What it said sent shivers down his spine.

Chuck hurried back to the beach and frantically tried to get Joey's attention out in the water. Thoroughly frustrated, Joey had had enough anyway. He then noticed Chuck on shore waving him in. Joey didn't know exactly what was transpiring, but he had a pretty good guess. He too figured it was time to get the hell out of there. Chuck told him about the note, and within seconds they were gone.

A few days later, I finally asked Chris what he had written.

"Oh you know...a little violence, a little punishment. Get the hell out of here, we're going to flatten your tires, bust your windshield, and beat the crap out of both of you the next time you try and come back. All that kind of usual stuff," he said calmly.

"And you know something, Aeder? I don't even care if they figure out it was me. The way I look at it, at least I didn't punch anybody out," he continued.

"You're right, Chris, at least you didn't do that," I agreed.

The incident would have significant ramifications for both of us. I also worked for Surfing magazine at the time, but only as a contributing photographer.

A few days later, I took a batch of photos to the magazine's office in San Clemente, and as soon as I saw Larry Moore, his stern expression told me something was amiss. He wasted no time asking if I knew anything about the incident. I sighed and paused for several moments before replying.

"Well, Larry, I live around there, and I was at Big Rock that day, too. So yeah, I know about what happened. At least they didn't get beat up or have their car windows smashed," I said with a lump in my throat.

"Hey Kirk, I know you're in tight with those guys down there. You must know who it was," Larry said.

I had great respect for Larry. His Irish heritage and bright red hair had earned him the nickname Flame. Just like Chris, he had a fiery persona that could be easily ignited. Flame was the toughest and proudest surf photo editor ever. Fair and brutally honest, he was the one who had selected my first surfing pictures ever to be published in a magazine and had always offered very positive advice. So it pained me to have to play dumb now.

"You're right, Flame, of course I know something. What happened to them should not have come as a surprise. That's the way things are at the La Jolla reefs. I'm not the one who makes the rules there," I told him.

"So are you going to tell me?"

"Gosh Larry, I didn't know I was on trial. Does it really matter?" I temporized. "Man, it could have come from thirty or forty different guys. All the locals were there that day. And since everyone pretty much speaks for each other, well that's the way it goes."

Flame was my primary mentor in surf photography, and I had to tread lightly around him. I certainly didn't want to bring out his temperamental side.

"Well, Kirk, this might just be one of the reasons why surfers from your area don't get more publicity in the magazines. And you know something else? This will affect you, too, as a surf photographer. No magazine will want to publish photos of surfers who go around beating up other surfers," he said.

I stood there and absorbed what he told me, yet I still felt the need to refute some of the things he'd said.

"What are you talking about, Flame? No one got beat up. You don't see guys from La Jolla going to Huntington, Newport, or the South Bay to have their photos taken. That's because the waves are really good in La Jolla. It's why surfers from other areas want to come there. If Joey hadn't worn that ugly yellow wetsuit, maybe things would have been different," I said, grinning in an attempt to ease the building tension.

Larry was not thrilled with my justification, but for the time being at least, he chose to move on.

A few days later, Chris began to experience the same kind of headaches he'd had during the Katin contest. He attributed the pain to lack of sleep; he'd been up late at night caring for his son. Coupled with the fatigue from nonstop surfing, this reasoning seemed entirely plausible. He didn't mention the headaches to his doctors right away, and by the time they found out, it was already too late. His life was about to take a sudden turn for the worse.

Chris had not gone surfing in Baja for several months. One week before departing for Australia, he ventured south of the border with Mark McCoy and Tom Castleton, a friend from San Clemente. The surf at Baja Malibu looked good, with four to five-foot waves and not a hint of wind. But as Chris stepped out of the car, he suddenly stumbled and fell to the ground. At first Mark and Tom thought he'd tripped and started kidding him about it. But as he lay motionless on the ground, it became painfully clear that something more serious had happened.

They turned Chris over on his back and saw that he was still conscious. Mark asked him what was wrong, but Chris's face had gone numb and paralysis kept him from responding. He appeared to have difficulty breathing.

"Jesus, what's going on with him?" Tom said in a panic.

They had seen enough. By the time they got Chris into the back seat of the car, he was extremely disoriented. Tom raced back to the border, oblivious to the speed limit. Slowly, Chris regained some movement in his face and was able to speak. He said his face was still numb and he had no energy at all.

After navigating the maze of Tijuana traffic, they arrived at the border, where customs officials learned of the medical emergency and waved them through. Several minutes later, Chris tried to reassure his friends that he was starting to feel better. They wanted to take him straight to the hospital, but Chris insisted on going home. Tom wasn't so sure.

"Hey Chris, don't tell us not to worry about it. You scared the crap out of us. We thought you were going to die!" he said. "I still think we should take you to the hospital. You really don't look so good."

Chris reassured them he really was okay, and they reluctantly drove him home. He turned on the television and lay down on the couch. When Jil returned a few hours later, Chris told her what had happened.

"Why didn't you go straight to the hospital?" she scolded him.

Failing to come up with a reasonable explanation, Chris just shrugged his shoulders, hiding the truth. Australia awaited him, and nothing would stop that.

"Chris, you're so stubborn sometimes. I've had enough of this. We're going to the hospital right now," Jil informed him.

Her instincts proved correct. As they prepared to leave for the hospital, Chris's face went numb again. Jil decided calling 911 and waiting for an ambulance would take too long; she quickly loaded Chris into the car and rushed him to the hospital herself, running red lights along the way.

At the emergency room, a team of physicians took over. Scans and tests were immediately performed. When the diagnosis was announced a few hours later, the news was not good. A large tumor was detected near his brain.

For several months everything had looked so positive, but out of nowhere came this life-threatening setback. Not that Chris had much time to reflect on it. Dr. Kenneth Ott, a neurosurgeon, performed an emergency craniotomy. It was a long, tense procedure, and by the time it was over, there was more bad news. The tumor had only been partially removed, along with a section of Chris's skull. Still, his doctors deemed the operation a success. Now they had to wait for the delicate tissue around his brain to heal, so that a steel plate could eventually be inserted into his head.

Just when it appeared the worst was behind him, Chris found himself back where he had started—only now it was even worse. He vowed that, given the chance, he would never underestimate the warning signs again.

In the weeks following, all he could think about was the IPS tour now taking place in Australia while he remained in the hospital. I was a near daily visitor, and Jil was always by his side. In fact, so many people began visiting him that hospital attendants had to limit the number of people going into his room. The immense support from family and friends was good medicine.

Not surprisingly, in spite of everything he had just gone through, the foremost thing on Chris's mind was getting back on his surfboard. Every time he mentioned the possibility to his doctors, they assumed he was joking. But if the notion of surfing again gave him a goal, then this was a good thing—no matter how farfetched.

Chris wanted to be strong not only for himself, but for his family as well. The onetime wonder boy was an optimist and wanted to prove that he could do it all again. All he needed was another chance.

A few days later, I heard that Chris would soon be discharged. When I went to visit him, Mark McCoy and Ted Smith were already inside. Chris looked tired and fragile, but his spirits were amazingly high. Except for several strands, his hair was all but gone from the combination of brain surgery and renewed chemotherapy treatments. A massive scar was distinctly visible on the right side of his head. Seeing that was heartbreaking, and I fought hard to control my emotions. Chris could sense that I was about to lose it and suddenly made a funny face that helped ease my pain.

"Aeder," Chris whispered. "Get in here and close the door."

Seeing Mark pull a joint from his shirt pocket, I knew what was coming next. After his brain operation, Chris wanted more medicine than the hospital provided.

"Right in here?" I protested. "You guys are nuts. It's a freakin' hospital!"

"Yeah, right here in this room. I will open the windows, and the smoke will blow outside. Chris needs this, and besides, what are they going to do to us anyway?" replied Mark.

"Oh I don't know, maybe call the police, and we all end up in jail!" I barked.

"I won't," said Chris with a grin.

"Relax, Kirk. We brought along a can of air freshener," Ted assured me.

Chris seemed amused by our conversation. Mark sparked up the joint and began passing it around. When it came my way, I hesitated. Then Chris gave me one of those looks.

"Aeder, if I'm doing it, then you're doing it, too."

So I gave in, all the while knowing the strong aroma would be hard to hide. And sure enough, a few minutes later, two nurses walked into the room. Right away they smelled the herb and were not at all pleased. We were caught red-handed.

"I can't believe this! Are you boys smoking grass in here?"

Mark stepped up to the plate.

"Grass? Is that what you called it? Do people really still use that word? Grass? Come on ladies, I believe the term you're looking for is 'pot,'" he said sarcastically.

We started busting up laughing, but the nurses were far from amused. The three of us were quickly removed from his room by security and escorted from the hospital. That evening I called Chris, and we had a good chuckle about it. And two days later he was discharged.

The chance to go back home allowed Chris to get back into a routine. Initially, he spent all of his time with Jil and Tim.

His son was just a newborn and far too young to comprehend what was happening with his father. Watching Tim sleep so peacefully, Chris was overcome with love and admiration. But he also wondered if he would live long enough for his son to get to know him. After his latest setback, he had to be realistic.

A few weeks after returning home, one task began to consume him—finding a hat that would hide the scar on his head. For several days he and Jil drove endlessly around San Diego looking for the right one. He finally settled on a white-rimmed hat with a narrow black band. It didn't take long for this hat to become his trademark, and Chris was recognized wherever he went.

Between medical treatments, Chris embarked upon his own rehabilitation program. Getting his strength back was priority number one. At the condominium near UCSD where they now lived, Chris began paddling his surfboard around the swimming pool. Any activity that built up his arm strength helped. The thought of getting back into the ocean became a powerful motivator; the sea was his sanctuary, and he had to return. While the notion of surfing again must have sounded impossible to those who didn't know him, it all made perfect sense to us.

His head was vulnerable now, and he would have to be cautious. But caution was never in Chris's vocabulary. During a follow-up treatment at the hospital, he reminded his doctors that surfing again was very much on his radar. By now they could see he was serious and advised him against it. But if he was determined to carry out his plan, they said he needed to find something to protect his head.

His doctors had not told him no, but it was hardly a ringing endorsement. Regardless, simply hearing about the possibility was like music to his ears. Chris was now one step closer to paddling back out into the surf.

Chapter 26

Miracle Day

April 1978

Chris's relapse sent shockwaves through America's professional surfing community. No longer could he obliterate another surfer during a contest; other surfers, especially those from California, could now capture center stage.

For Chris, competitive surfing had become a thing of the past. Now his most intimidating opponent was cancer, and he was competing to survive. Frustrated by how his dreams had been thwarted, Chris's animosity toward other aspiring pro surfers from California grew. It was nothing personal. He just couldn't help but wonder, Why me?

Soon, though, Chris realized that anger and stress would not help his situation. Eventually he was able to manifest the negative things that he felt into something positive. Chris still despised the fact that surfers like Joey Buran, Allen Sarlo, Dan Flecky, Chris Barela, and Mike Benevidez were now becoming the darlings of the surf media. They were all healthy with an unlimited future. Chris was sick and, in his mind at least, slipping away not just as a surfer, but as a man. On a level playing field, these other surfers wouldn't stand a chance in hell against him competitively. This was the kind of thinking that fueled Chris's determination even more.

He wanted to return to the ocean as soon as possible. A few weeks later, he did.

"I don't know if I should," sighed Chris.

The cautiousness in his voice was something I hadn't expected; hesitating in the face of a challenge was rare for him. But the rebellious go-for-it attitude seemed to be gone, leaving in its place a subdued, somewhat scared individual—a boy who must quickly become a man and struggle for worth in the eyes of his Maker. With the ocean mist dancing in the onshore wind, Chris was about to test his strength and inner will and, more importantly, surf again.

Would he still be capable of doing the one thing he had always lived for?

It was an early morning in the middle of May. For nearly a week, rain had drenched much of Southern California. Now the storm had moved off, and Chris had decided this day was as good as any. With a large portion of his skull missing, one wrong blow to his head out in the ocean could be fatal. Consequently, Chris heeded his doctors' advice to protect himself from any serious spills.

We had been discussing options until I remembered that, hidden deep inside my garage amid the piles of old boyhood relics, was a white street hockey helmet. This dusty, dinged-up helmet would provide the protection he needed.

I wiped away the cobwebs, polished it up and offered to him, having no idea that it would become Chris's trademark and the most visible symbol of his commitment to the sport that he loved. At the time surfers didn't wear protective headgear; there didn't seem to be a need to. A surfer wearing a helmet looked as out of place as a football player without one. Chris couldn't have cared less about how he looked or what people thought. Surfing was all that mattered.

Chris and I sat hunkered in my car at the Windansea parking lot, gazing at the roiling gray water below us. The conditions were far from ideal; so bad, in fact, that there wasn't another soul in the entire lineup. Even a healthy Chris O'Rourke wouldn't bother paddling out on such a horrible day as this.

Suddenly, Mark McCoy pulled up next to us in his car and hopped out, already dressed in his full wetsuit. Chris and I started to laugh.

"What's wrong Fish-face? Isn't the heater in your car working?" laughed Chris.

Mark smiled and took a few steps toward us.

"Hey buddy," Mark said to Chris. "You want to go surfing?"

Chris didn't need to be asked twice. His face lit up like a Christmas tree, and he quickly began changing into his wetsuit. Then he had to deal with the new part of the routine: fitting the white helmet to his head and tightening the chin strap. Mark and I didn't even bat an eye.

Together they walked down to the sand. At the water's edge, Chris paused and stared out to the sea. He would later comment to me how that moment felt as if his life was beginning all over again. And in many ways, it was.

"Wow, if my doctors could only see me now. They would be freaking out!" Chris said.

Mark paddled out first, with Chris a short distance behind. As Chris paddled he thought hard about his troubled past, about months of lying in hospital beds trying to make himself believe that, in spite of the heavy doubts he harbored, everything would be all right. To stand up and ride a wave again would become his measuring stick for progress. One good wave was all he needed. One good wave might help save his life.

Unfortunately, the first few waves that day were not exactly what the doctor had ordered. Each time, Chris stood up too late and got pitched forward head first. During one underwater thrashing he bumped his shoulder hard on the reef, but luckily not his head. Even with such small waves, crashing hard into the whitewater hurt. He would emerge at the surface coughing and gagging for air, just as he had the first time he had surfed here. Only now the circumstances had changed dramatically.

On a few occasions his helmet came loose and dangled precariously off to one side of his head. While photographing him from the beach, I couldn't help but cringe at the sight.

The last thing he needed was to get hit on the head by his board. Each time Chris wiped out, Mark hurriedly paddled over to assist his friend but was stubbornly waved back. Chris regrouped and paddled back out to try again. Finally he spotted what looked like the right wave. As it approached, Chris paddled farther out into the takeoff zone. He could not escape the names reverberating though his head as he got into position: Buran, Flecky, Sarlo, Buran, Flecky, Sarlo, Buran, Flecky, Sarlo.

Just catch this one wave, he thought. As the wave steepened, Chris stood upright on his board. With a stiff, awkward style, he gingerly rode it through Right Hooker before ending his ride near the beach. Afterward, he gazed toward shore in my direction with an expression of pure amazement.

Again, word spread like wildfire through the Windansea neighborhood. Chris O'Rourke was back. The only difference was that now he wore a helmet. On a weekday, when almost everyone was either working or at school, it was surprising to see the large crowd of onlookers that began to gather. People were genuinely inspired by what was happening in the water.

Other than Chris and Mark, no other surfer even dared to paddle out. This was Chris's moment and his alone, and over the next ninety minutes he caught several more waves. His operations, cancer treatments, and lack of surfing had left his body incredibly rigid. But his balance and poise improved with each wave he rode—not bad for someone with half a skull. And while not a single one of his patented tube rides, vertical off the tops, or slashing cutbacks ever occurred, for this moment at least, he was a champion.

When Chris finally emerged from the ocean, he looked pale and exhausted. The onlookers who were aware of his plight began applauding him. I saw him briefly clutch his head in obvious pain, but by the time he came over to where I was standing, his eyes were gleaming.

"I can still do it, at least kind of anyway. Man, I sure surf like a kook, though. I've got a lot of work ahead of me," he said.

Throughout his entire ordeal, Chris would remember this day as being the most inspirational. Rejuvenated beyond belief, there was no way he would give up now.

Later, as we drove home, he said, "I just love surfing so much. It's such a joy to me, even with the cancer. It's helped make a lot of the terrible things I've done easier to bear and forget about."

When we arrived, Jil came outside holding Tim in one arm and gave Chris a big hug and kiss. Driving away, I looked in the rearview mirror and watched as the three of them continued to embrace—for the moment at least, one happy and thankful family.

Chapter 27

A Bump on the Head Could Kill

After hearing the news, Chris's doctors were not entirely surprised. They knew it was only a matter of time. Chris had gone surfing in cold water, with half of his skull exposed, protected only by a flimsy hockey helmet.

One surf session ultimately led to another, and another, and another. While my hockey helmet had served an immediate purpose, for the long term he would need to upgrade to something thicker and stronger. A sturdier skateboard helmet offered better protection, which was essential since it would still be several months before the steel plate could be inserted into his head.

Despite the risks and protests, Chris was thrilled to be surfing again. Two to three times a week, he paddled out at Windansea. Surfing in bigger waves was definitely out of the question for a while, and he was still trying to adjust to the awkwardness of the helmet. It greatly affected his balance and vision in the water, and every time he went under, he would emerge with water streaming down the front of the helmet into his eyes. He found it hard to locate the next wave and get out of the way.

Regardless, Chris remained undeterred. I understood the magnitude of what he was achieving and continued to photograph him at every opportunity. The shiny yellow helmet made it easy to locate him out in the crowded lineup. With his guns no longer blazing, Windansea had become a much quieter place.

By now Chris's chemotherapy and radiation treatments were just another part of his week.

Hoping that it would combat the debilitating side affects, Jil made sure Chris was now on a very healthy diet. Coupled with consistent surfing, this regimen seemed to help Chris gain weight and build up his strength. Finally, he started surfing in bigger waves again. His confidence grew quickly, but each time he wiped out, everyone watching held their collective breath.

In early May, Chris and I visited the office at Surfing magazine. The editorial staff had asked him to autograph the large white "graffiti wall" located just inside the front office door. It was reserved for only the most established surfers in the world, and Chris was excited. When we arrived, everyone working there came out to greet him. Dave Gilovich, the magazine's editor, handed Chris a large felt pen, and he wrote upon the wall: "Surfing Through Life, Life Through Surfing, Christopher T. O'Rourke."

Afterward Larry Moore walked over and gave Chris a warm hug and pat on the back.

"You're going to be all right, Chris. Stay positive," he told him.

On the way back to La Jolla, Chris let me in on a secret. He had agreed to become a guinea pig of sorts for a new cancer-fighting drug from Japan that contained benzaldahyde.

"Are you already taking it?" I asked.

"Yes. At first the drug makes me feel a little weird, but then I feel really good, just like I used to feel before any of this started happening."

Along with Chris's slowly improving health came the possibility—as outlandish as it might have sounded—that he could one day compete in a surfing contest again. No one around him even dared scoff at the possibility. Amazed by his courage and convictions, not even his biggest surfing rivals in California dared to write him off.

On May 17, Chris and Jil attended the Hollywood premiere of Big Wednesday. Major motion pictures centered on surfing were a rarity, and Chris had eagerly looked forward to going. He mingled with the film's actors: Jan Michael Vincent, Gary Busey, and William Katt. Gerry Lopez also had a small role, and Peter Townend and Ian Cairns had performed the stunt surfing for the film.

The movie's release generated a lot of buzz within the surfing industry. Not since the 1960s' Gidget or Ride the Wild Surf had Hollywood used surfing as a main theme for a movie. At the Big Wednesday premiere, Chris was a hit. In his distinctive hat, he stood out in the crowd. Being there did wonders for his ego, too, making him feel like he was part of the surfing mainstream again. Everyone he met was visibly impressed by his positive attitude. Chris had finally become a surfing celebrity—just not in the manner that he had anticipated.

On June 11, Chris had another reason to celebrate after his brother Bart married his sweetheart, Jenny. Chris was proud of Bart, and their marriage inspired him to one day do the same.

A few weeks later, Chris and Jil attended another gala event. Surfer magazine held its annual Surfer Poll Awards in San Clemente. The affair drew the biggest names in surfing, and Chris was certainly one of them. He talked to friends and competitors throughout the evening, including Jim Banks, Michael Ho, and Shaun Tomson. Shaun was saddened by what had happened to Chris and gave him heartfelt encouragement.

The well wishes didn't stop there. As word circulated about his stellar recovery, letters of support for Chris poured into the offices at Surfer and Surfing. Even Surfing World magazine in Japan published a ten-page color article about him. It seemed as if nearly everyone was sympathetic to his plight and inspired by his courage. Well, almost everyone.

In July, the popular weekly San Diego tabloid known as The Reader published an extensive article about Chris. "A Bump on the Head Could Kill" was a vivid insight into the successes and struggles of his life. Written by staff writer Joe Applegate, the text was genuine, sincere and, under the circumstances, seemingly well-deserved.

So the negative backlash that ensued caught many by surprise. The following week's edition published several harsh letters that strongly criticized Chris. Many went so far as to scold the newspaper's editors for even running the story in the first place. Though Chris had become an inspiration to many, some had not forgotten his volatile past, including those who had once been on the receiving end of his temper tantrums at Windansea. They loudly attributed his illness to karma, saying he had gotten what he deserved.

There was certainly no arguing the fact that Chris had once done some pretty horrible things to others. He was now viewed by some as a Caligua of sorts, part hero and part villain.

Chris was not oblivious to the hoopla; in fact, he read every one of the letters. And while he didn't say so outwardly, I knew the words made him sad. In the days and weeks that followed, he did a lot of soul searching.

Jim Neri told Chris to just forget about it. Jim always had been a steadying influence; after heading off to college, he missed his old friend and often felt guilty for leaving.

"Chris, there will always be people who like to put others down. That's their nature. You can't change the past, so don't let it haunt you. Instead, just live for the future," said Jim.

After a long pause, Chris finally responded.

"You know something, Jim? They're all right. What they said about me was true. I put people down all the time without ever really thinking about it. Shit, I did so many bad things before. I sure didn't know it then, but I do now," he said.

In the coming weeks, however, further media coverage provided a reversal of fortunes. The August issue of Surfer Magazine included a ten-page interview and photo spread entitled "Chris O'Rourke, An Incredible Californian." The article started off with a disclaimer: This interview has not been performed for any reason other than the fact that he deserved it long before his unfortunate bout with cancer.

The article was written by Warren Bolster and gave Chris the opportunity to reflect on some of his mentors, something he had always wanted to do. He also touched upon his significant change in attitude. Asked about his inspirations, Chris was generous with his praise.

"Michael Ho for sure," he said. "Along with surfers from my area like Tom Ortner, Andy Tyler, and David Rullo. Gerry Lopez just blew my mind with his style, the Australians, and Shaun Tomson. Those guys have really influenced me a lot."

All the media attention made him feel like he was on the rebound. His health was still very fragile, but nonetheless Chris declared himself fit and ready to surf in contests again.

He truly had made significant progress, but this seemed like an overly bold statement. There were plenty of skeptics who, although inspired by his accomplishments, doubted he would go very far in another pro contest. But by now I had learned to never count him out of anything. All he needed was a contest within Southern California—and as fate would have it, this would not be far off.

As summer slowly faded, Jim Banks paid Chris a surprise visit. Jim had been staying in Huntington Beach, where he had recently become part of the Bronzed Aussies surf team. He and Steve Jones, another Australian surfer, had replaced Cheyne Horan, who had left the team under a cloud of controversy.

Jim spent a week in La Jolla with Chris and his family. Chris proudly introduced him to all the local surfers at Windansea, and they paddled out and rode the waves together. Jim showed Windansea's finest the latest moves in progressive surfing. Chris did his best to keep up, and Jim was visibly inspired by his friend's performance in the water—especially while wearing a helmet.

On the morning of September 28, Chris and I met at Windansea. By 9am the temperature was already a balmy eighty-five degrees due to the warm Santa Ana winds coming from the inland deserts. I had brought along my Nikonos II underwater camera and looked forward to swimming out into the cool water to shoot photos. I positioned myself in the lineup and waited for Chris to paddle out. Numerous waves passed over me, and sometimes I would open my eyes to see what it looked like. There were clear areas, pockets of whitewater turbulence, rocks, eel grass, and the occasional fish scurrying for cover.

We had a lot of fun shooting photos together. The air was smoky, but we didn't give it much thought since several out-of-control wildfires were burning inland. What we didn't know was that a much more harrowing and tragic incident had just occurred—one that rocked all of San Diego.

As the skies turned darker, Mark McCoy paddled out and told us that there had just been a major airplane crash near the Lindbergh Field airport. A PSA jetliner approaching the runway had collided with a small Cessna that had just taken off, and the remains of both planes had crashed into the North Park community. A dark mushroom cloud could be seen for miles in every direction. Suddenly what we were doing out there in the surf didn't seem very fun at all. A total of 144 people had lost their lives—at the time, the deadliest aircraft disaster in the history of the U.S.

By early afternoon the temperature had hit a sweltering one hundred degrees. After a short break, Chris and I ventured back into the water, but our hearts and minds were definitely elsewhere. Once again, we were acutely aware of the fragility of life.

A few days later, Chris received the news he had been hoping for: A new professional surf contest would be held in Southern California. Bob Hart, a little-known promoter, was planning to stage the California Pro near the Oceanside Pier in North San Diego County. Though not IPS-rated, the contest would still lure most of the big-name surfers in the world.

A few days before the competition, I drove Chris to the Caster shaping factory. Bill had shaped him two new boards for the event and was in his work room carving out yet another, so Chris walked over to speak with Gary Goodrum. Several minutes later, Bill emerged, covered from head to toe with white foam dust. I asked him about the new boards. I had come to appreciate great surfboard design, and Bill's shaping techniques seemed highly advanced. The demand for Caster surfboards was at an all-time high, and he could hardly keep up with the orders.

Bill turned over one of Chris's new boards to show me the bottom.

"You see those little channels? Water flows much faster through them. When Chris does his turns, he will be able to generate even more speed. He actually generates a lot of speed in his surfing already, but given his weaker condition, it's just a little something that will help him even more," he explained.

"Wow, those are pretty cool. How did you come up with that idea, Bill?" I asked, still surveying the board.

When he didn't respond, I noticed he was staring at Chris. Then, he turned and looked at me with an intensely serious expression.

"Kirk," he said quietly, "I know you realize how terrible this thing is with Chris. All we can do is offer him our support. But I can't possibly imagine what's going through his mind right now, what it feels like to have cancer. Never in my wildest dreams."

For some reason his words sent shivers up my spine, but I wasn't exactly sure why.

Bill continued. "All Chris wants to do is go surfing. It's going to be hard keeping him out of the water. I think it's the best thing for him, though. He should just keep doing what he loves to do. In all my life, I have never, ever, seen anyone so addicted to surfing like he is."

Chris walked up in the midst of this conversation, leaving us little time to disguise our solemn expressions. He could easily see that something was up.

"Hey, are you guys talking about me?"

"You're right, Chris, we were. Bill and I were just discussing how well your new boards are going to work. I think you are really going to kick some ass at the contest in Oceanside."

Chris smiled, but he knew that I was lying. We walked outside and fastened the new boards tightly to the roof racks, and Bill shook Chris's hand and wished him good luck. After we drove away, Chris finally spoke up.

"Hey Aeder, I can handle it, you know. I'd rather have you guys just tell me straight,' he said.

"Tell you straight about what, Chris?" I asked innocently.

"You're doing it again right now, Aeder. You know exactly what I mean."

"Yeah, I know. Sorry about that. Watching what's happened to you has been such a radical thing," I said, taking a deep breath. "I thought I had life all figured out, but now I don't have a clue. I just don't know how you are able to stay so positive."

"Well, you let me worry about that. I'm looking for a reason to live, and right now surfing and my family are those reasons. I plan on beating this," he said confidently.

Two days later, Chris paddled out in the small surf at Oceanside in his first competitive heat in nearly nine months. This also marked his first competition wearing the helmet. Before the contest started, many of the competitors approached Chris, not only to wish him well, but to reveal what an inspiration he was for them. He wasn't used to this sort of feedback and was humbled by their gestures.

Many big-name surfers from around the world were competing, including Dane Kealoha, Bobby Owens, Larry Bertlemann, and David Nuuhiwa. Chris's heated rival, Joey Buran, was there, too, along with another emerging young Californian named David Barr. Surfers competed in four-man heats with the top two advancing to the next stage.

Chris had come so far now, doing what many thought he couldn't—competing on the professional level, with half a skull nonetheless. During the opening rounds of the competition, he performed amazingly well. The shifty beach-break waves proved to be a challenge to his strength and paddling ability, but a first and second-place showing kept him advancing.

Over the next several days, Chris continued to advance. The daily surfing was depleting his energy, but he pressed on anyway. This contest was the latest attempt to establish legitimate pro surfing in California. The Katin contest was still active, but the Sutherland Pro, held a year earlier, had turned out to be a one-time event. Everyone had high hopes that the California Pro would stick around longer—or even better, turn into an IPS-rated event. Rumors were already running rampant about the financing for the California Pro being on very shaky grounds, and no one seemed to know much about its promoter, Bob Hart.

On the last day of the event with thirty-six surfers remaining, Bob Hart suddenly announced the contest format would change. At this point, there would have been six heats with six surfers in each, and the top three from each heat would then move into the next round. Hart decided, however, that only the winners of the six remaining heats would advance straight into the finals. The competitors were rightfully confused and angry. What was this all about? The organizer of the event had changed the rules on his own, but what could anyone do?

Now each heat became a do-or-die situation. Up to that point, by far the biggest story of the contest was that Chris was still a participant. In the six-man heat, Chris proved his comeback by winning to reach the finals. Against all odds, he had surfed his way through, quite a stunning achievement.

Returning to the beach, Chris couldn't help but give Joey Buran some ribbing.

"Hey Joey, I just smoked your friend David Barr out there in my heat. Barr is nothing, your friend is nothing, I've got cancer, I'm wearing this silly helmet, and I still smoked your friend. You guys are nothing. Take your friend home—he's done," Chris ranted.

Joey's own heat was coming up next.

Thirty minutes later, it appeared Joey had failed to advance. Then, the unthinkable happened. Bobby Owens, who had won the heat, inexplicably stood upright on his board and rode a wave to shore after the final horn had sounded. A no-no in the rules of contest surfing, this meant instant disqualification for Bobby, and the next highest surfer advanced. Since Joey had finished second, the blunder had opened the door for him.

The final heat of the California Pro took place in glassy three to five-foot wave peaks at Oceanside Harbor's north jetty. Jil, Bill Caster, and a large contingent of Chris's friends stood along the water's edge cheering his every move. And even though Chris had put up a valiant effort to get this far, the well finally had run dry.

Capitalizing on this opportunity, Joey Buran won the event, Larry Bertlemann finished second, and Chris ended up third. In spite of their differences, Joey later admitted he was inspired by what Chris had done. And he wasn't alone. Everyone on the beach applauded his courageous effort.

When Chris emerged from the water, Jil embraced him for a long time.

"I'm so proud of you, Chris," she told him.

Chris then walked over to his son, who was lying on a blanket in the sand. He picked Tim up and kissed him several times on the forehead. Only ten months old, Tim had no idea what was going on around him—but it sure must have been exciting. Chris just wanted to share the moment with him any way he could.

When I went to see Chris a few days later, he looked exhausted but still managed his trademark smile. He also attributed his performance during the contest to a higher power.

"God sent me those waves," he told me.

Sadly, his good fortune didn't extend to his winnings. When he attempted to cash his check from the contest, Chris learned there were insufficient funds; in fact, all of the finalists discovered that their checks were made of rubber. To make matters worse, Bob Hart had disappeared along with all of the contestants' entry fees. So much for California's progress in professional surfing contests.

Everyone associated with the event began calling it "The Bob Hart Ripoff Contest." No one had received their compensation, not even Joey Buran. Given Chris's thin financial situation at the time, the debacle really hurt him. He complained loud and long over what had transpired, but there seemed little he or anyone else could do. The last thing his life needed was more stress. Chris couldn't help but feel snake-bitten. He lived for the dream of becoming a professional surfer, and this was certainly not it.

"Instead of focusing on the lost money, just try and relish the accomplishment. After everything you've gone through, getting third place out of more than one hundred and twenty competitors is an incredible achievement. I remember a time when the money didn't mean a thing to you. It was all about surfing, all about winning, the core of what you stand for," I told him.

Hearing my forthright words certainly caught his attention. Chris's frown immediately disappeared, and he challenged me to a game of backgammon.

"I'll show you what winning is all about, Aeder. I'm going to kick your ass," he said with a smile.

The board game had quickly turned into his favorite. Each time one of his friends visited, Chris couldn't wait to challenge him. Until the next surf contest came along, backgammon and ping-pong were his only competitive outlets.

But the contest saga wasn't over. Joey Buran's victory had been tainted by the scandal, and no one was angrier than he was. So Joey and his mother decided to pursue Bob Hart on their own. By now the promoter had completely disappeared from the radar screen, but their diligence finally paid off. They located him and had him arrested. It took a while, but Bob eventually made full restitution to everyone who was owed money. Because Joey helped Chris get his money, a friendship between them began to grow.

As December approached, surfing was continuing to evolve around the world. Surfers now traveled extensively around the globe in search of perfect surf spots: Indonesia, Europe, South

America, Asia, Fiji, Mexico, Africa. Nowhere was off-limits; any place with a coastline had waves to be ridden.

Professional surfing in the United States was gaining momentum as well. In addition to California, other states such as Texas, Oregon, Florida, North Carolina, and New York all saw a steady increase in surfers. Surfing was expanding in so many positive ways, and Chris was still determined to be there when it all came together. For the first time, he openly acknowledged that other surfers from California were now leading the charge, and he accepted this reality with grace. For now, he simply prayed he could become healthy enough one day to be considered the greatest again.

But every winter, the focus of the surfing world always turned back to Hawaii. Once more his doctors warned Chris about the dangers of going there in his condition. In Hawaii he would be susceptible to infections and tropical diseases, and they strongly recommended he stay home. But Chris could simply not resist the urge, especially when others were willing to foot the expenses for him. He had recently made a few new rich friends who were sympathetic to his situation, and they offered him financial support for travel and medical costs that weren't covered by insurance.

Chris traveled to Hawaii that winter with mixed feelings. It hurt to leave his family behind while he continued to chase his dream. Because he was still forced to wear the helmet, his surfing on the North Shore was limited. In the powerful surf, he had no choice but to take a more conservative approach. Determined to somehow stay in the spotlight, Chris surfed small waves at Rocky Point and Velzyland, accompanied by his good pals Michael and Hans.

During a surf session at Velzyland, several of Michael's Hawaiian buddies were dumbfounded by the sight of such a pale haole surfer wearing a helmet. Surfers from Hawaii weren't used to giving away their waves. But they understood what the former prodigy from California was going through and gladly made an exception.

Attempting to compete in any of the surf contests was certainly out of the question for Chris; with no steel plate in his head, surfing big waves at Pipeline or Sunset simply wasn't going to happen. Chris remained unfazed, and vowed to one day make his name in those fabled breaks.

Two days before Chris returned to California, Jim Banks took him to the Lightning Bolt surfboard factory in Honolulu. Owner Jack Shipley wanted to give Chris some free surfboards and told him to pick out whichever ones he wanted. Chris selected two boards crafted by world-renowned shaper Tom Parrish. By the time Jim and Chris arrived back on the North Shore, it was nearly nightfall. But Chris couldn't wait to surf on one of the shiny new boards. When the two surfers paddled out at Velzyland, it was practically dark. Chris quickly caught a few waves, but soon it became so dark they could no longer see. Then Jim noticed the full moon rising over the ocean.

"Hey Chris, look at that. I think we can still keep surfing after all."

Surfing with his friend under the light of a full moon was an experience Chris would never forget. The next day, he sat on the beach watching Michael and Hans compete in the prestigious Pipeline Masters contest. During the entire time, Chris envisioned himself out there in the lineup, too.

After one of his heats, Michael told Chris, "Next year, brah, you'll be out there with me, too."

Chapter 28

King of Pain

January 1979

Chris started the new year feeling guardedly optimistic about many things: his cancer, his surfing, his life. After all, he'd felt the same way a year before; everything seemed to be progressing positively and then—wham! Yet, in spite of the severity of his brain surgery, Chris had once more come a long way back.

As Tim celebrated his first birthday, the family continued living in a townhouse near UCSD. Money was in short supply, but they were able to manage through a variety of means: Chris's endorsement deals, family donations, and monthly medical welfare checks. With their income limited, Chris asked if I would be interested in renting a room. This worked for everyone; I lived close to school, and the rent money was a bonus for Chris and Jil. I looked forward to being there as a support figure and eagerly anticipated the time when I could shoot surfing photos of him again.

While living with Chris and his family, I reflected upon our friendship and how far it had come. By now I thought I knew everything about his unfortunate situation, but I soon discovered I was wrong. As a roommate, I got an in-depth look into his entire world, and not all of it was pretty.

Sometimes, smoking marijuana was simply not enough to combat the nausea brought on by his chemotherapy. On several occasions, he spent hours in the bathroom throwing up violently. Feeling helpless, I really didn't know how to act or what to do. Like the tides of the ocean, his health rose and fell with each passing day. Jil was committed to doing all she could to improve her Chris's health. An incredibly supportive person, she became the rock that held it all together.

Jil had been forced to grow up very quickly, and she could be as headstrong and stubborn as Chris. She wasn't about to put up with any of his self-pity; instead, she wanted him to remain positive and treated him as a healthy individual. Together they somehow had to stem the tide of what was going on inside him and care for their precious son. Tim was the product of their love for each other and a bond that would tie them together forever.

Shortly after I moved in, Chris's parents moved to North Carolina. Gloria dreaded the idea of leaving her ailing son behind, but Bart Sr. had finally been offered a steady job and felt it was time to move on again. When Chris's parents stopped by to say goodbye, there were tears streaming down Gloria's cheeks—and his.

"I will always love you, Chris. Get better, son."

His brother and sister remained in San Diego. Since Bart was now busy with his own married life, seeing Chris wasn't always on the agenda. Lyn, though, often came to visit him. Jil's mother and two sisters were regulars at the townhouse, too. Support for Chris was certainly strong, and at times it felt like we had a revolving door. People came by all the time, and Chris loved it when they did. But trying to get any studying done was next to impossible for me. When the gatherings became too much, I headed for the college library.

In February, Jim Banks stayed with us for several days. A solid six-foot swell rolled in at Big Rock, and Chris and Jim made the most of the waves with their unique styles. It was a pleasure to photograph such progressive high-caliber surfing. The younger surfers in the water took note of what the pros were doing. They were the next generation of surf kids to emerge from the La Jolla reefs, and they greatly admired Chris.

Occasionally, though, the menacing nature of the Big Rock surf forced Chris to hold back. During his heyday, dropping into a wave late had never been a problem—but it was now. His elasticity and agility had been vastly depleted by his medical treatments, and sometimes when his mind said yes, his body said no. It was extremely frustrating for him.

After witnessing Jim lock into a long tube ride, Chris wanted to do the same. Poised for a late take-off, Chris was forced to pull back at the last second. He slapped the surface of the water and yelled in disgust. I watched his reaction through my lens. The look on his face was agonizing, the kind I hadn't seen in a really long time.

During his stay with us, Jim also began to see the surreal drama that was Chris's life. Here was a guy on the cusp of his twentieth birthday who had cancer, a very young girlfriend, an infant son, mounting bills, an unsure future, and a determination to maintain his status in the surfing world. Jim felt guilty. He was just a young guy right out of school who had made it onto the pro surfing tour. Traveling around the world had become the focus of his life. Simply remaining in the world was the focus of Chris's.

It had been nearly one year since his brain surgery, and he anxiously yearned for his doctors to insert the steel plate. He had grown tired of wearing that darn helmet and looked forward to the day when he wouldn't have to anymore. And as fate would have it, that day soon arrived.

In late March, his doctors decided the time had finally arrived. The thought of another major head operation was daunting, but Chris knew it was a positive step. He anticipated being a complete person again—and being able to surf with complete abandon. He didn't want to hold back on steep waves anymore and envisioned the day when he could again do every maneuver at full throttle. California's other aspiring pro surfers had already written him off, and he was eager to prove them wrong.

"You just watch me, Aeder. I'll show them all," he told me.

Before his surgery, Chris and Jil married in a private ceremony at a small church in San Diego. Hap Brom, pastor of the La Jolla Presbyterian Church, presided over the service. While Chris's long-term fate was still unpredictable, they decided to cross those bridges when they arrived. After witnessing the misfortunes that his own parents had been through, Chris placed importance on the sacredness of marriage and family.

They had kept their plans secret while waiting for the right time. He was twenty years old and Jil just eighteen, so their marriage took almost everyone by surprise. Many family members and close friends didn't know how to react, but after the initial shock wore off, everyone was really happy for them. They were now truly a family, complete in every way.

Chris did not have much time to celebrate. There was no honeymoon or gala wedding party. A few days later, the steel plate was successfully inserted into his head, and he remained in the hospital for a few weeks while doctors monitored his condition.

Each day Chris insisted that he was ready to go home. Finally, they discharged him with strict instructions to take it easy for a while. His doctors knew that keeping Chris out of the ocean was next to impossible, but an infection of his head wound would have serious consequences. So Chris returned to the familiarity of his townhouse and rested.

One day Ted Smith, Mark McCoy, and Tim Senneff came by to see how he was faring. We sat around and talked about surfing, and the more we did, the more eager Chris became. At one point, he stood up and walked over to the closet, where he pulled out a shiny new purple Caster surfboard.

"Check this out, you guys. Bill made me this insane new board and gave it to me as a present after the operation. He called it my 'Comeback Board. On the next swell I'm out there! I'm tired of this fucking bullshit. No more waiting around anymore," he proclaimed boldly.

When the next swell did arrive, it only seemed natural that Chris was the first to paddle out at Windansea. Out of security, I guess, initially he still wore the helmet. But after a few more sessions, he was finally able to surf without it, but he still wanted to protect his nearly bald head from the sun and other possible dangers.

Unfortunately, since he obviously could no longer surf or compete in contests at one hundred percent, Chris's sponsorships with Surfer House and Rip Curl had ended. Yet it didn't take him long to find another sponsor in the form of O'Neill wetsuits. Based in Santa Cruz, the company had a long and storied history in California. Owner Pat O'Neill was stupefied upon hearing of Chris's predicament and eagerly signed him to a contract. Several years earlier Pat had watched him surf against the South Africans during the WSA contest at Steamer's Lane. He felt that Chris typified the consummate California surfer: soul, grace, style, and determination. And the admiration Chris displayed for Pat was mutual.

The timing couldn't have been better. O'Neill had just released a new product onto the market, a soft neoprene head cap designed for surfing the significantly colder waters off Northern California. After wearing the cap during several surf sessions, Chris's confidence skyrocketed. To everyone's astonishment, he had took another giant step forward. But we also had to remind him that, at this stage, surfing was all about having fun. We urged him not to overdo it. Yeah, as if that were going to do any good.

For a short time, Chris did remain cautious, but it went against his nature. The La Jolla reef breaks were challenging places to surf, and the locals rarely backed down to Mother Nature. A few of them often took considerable risks, and sometimes paid the price for it.

One of them was knee-boarder Rex Huffman. A large west swell had steamrolled into Big Rock, and such magical days always attracted a talented crew. Oscar Bayetto, Jeff Toomey, and Craig Eck were all out there along with Rex. Chris had undergone another round of treatments and was too weak to surf in the menacing waves, so instead he stood next to me as I took photos from the beach.

In the surfing world, knee riders did not earn the same respect as stand-up surfers. Rex, however, was the one exception. Of all the surfers in the water, Rex was the most respected and always took a lot of chances. Both Surfer and Surfing magazines had published numerous photos of him. In 1978 he even won a prestigious professional knee-board event held at the Banzai Pipeline that featured the best riders in the world.

Knee-boarding at Big Rock had turned into a family affair for Rex. His younger brothers Eric and Kirk were also upper-echelon riders. The kind of maneuvers Rex executed really opened my eyes to all the possibilities in surfing. There truly were no limits. Rex did things on the waves that regular surfers at the time could only dream about. Since I was still riding an air mat, Rex provided me with a sense of justification: whether standing up, kneeling, lying down, or body-surfing, if you rode the waves, you were a surfer.

But on this day, Rex would pay a heavy price. By early afternoon the swell continued to increase, but with the tide quickly dropping, much of the reef was exposed. A large set was rapidly approaching. None of the surfers had seen it yet, so Chris attempted one of his whistles to get their attention—but that failed.

Finally the surfers realized what was coming and began to paddle in earnest. On the third wave of the set, Rex decided to go. He was tempting fate by taking off extraordinarily far behind the exposed rocks—the very reef that Big Rock is named after. And the odds would finally catch up to him.

Unable to make the late drop, he pitched forward out of control, landing in the impact zone. The lip of the fierce wave hit Rex like a freight train, catapulting him knee-first onto the barnacle-covered reef. As the whitewater began to recede, he was dragged off the sharp reef screaming in pain. Several other surfers quickly brought him to shore and wrapped dry towels around his body to help keep him warm until the paramedics arrived.

Chris and I were amazed by how calm and stable Rex appeared. He even joked with Chris that what had just happened to him was "no big deal."

But it was. Both of his knee caps were completely blown out, and he had serious damage to both legs and several lacerations on his body. It wasn't the first time he had been hurt out there, but it was the worst.

That night, Rex's brother Eric called Chris to tell him that Rex would be okay. The incident certainly gave Chris a wake-up call that even the most advanced surfers could get seriously hurt. He knew that, if he wanted to surf at Big Rock in the future, he would have to rethink his approach out there. It was a frustrating realization—Chris used to own Big Rock. But he owed it to himself and his family, especially after seeing what had happened to Rex.

Jil wasted no time reminding her husband that she didn't want something like that happening to him. She knew what surfing meant to Chris, but there were now limitations to what he could do.

Living with them was an adventure. Each day brought something different, and Chris and Jil certainly had their hands full with young Tim.

Once in the middle of the night, I was awakened by Tim's crying. This was nothing new, but these cries sounded different—full of hysteria and panic. I opened the door of my room and saw all the lights were turned on. Slumped in the corner of the living room was Tim, his eyes filled with pure fear. Each time Chris approached him, the crying and screaming intensified. Clearly Tim didn't want his father anywhere near him. Finally Jil stepped in and got him under control.

"Wow Chris, he sure didn't want you getting close to him. What's happening?" I asked.

"I'm not sure. He just woke up like this, and it got worse and worse. Tim must have had a bad dream," said Chris calmly.

While a bad dream seemed like a plausible answer, to me the situation felt more sinister. Crying babies certainly weren't unusual, but Tim had become frightened beyond belief. For some reason, I just sensed that he had dreamed something about his father's fate—and it must not have been good. For the rest of the time I lived there, Tim never had another nightmare.

Several weeks later, Tim Bessell stopped by. Tim and Chris had been friends for many years, and like so many others, Tim always tried to do the right thing for Chris. Tim surfed at Windansea and was a very talented artist and surfboard shaper. He knew Chris's allegiance to Bill Caster was unbreakable, but that didn't stop him from making a few boards for his friend anyway.

Tim had arranged to drive Chris and Jil north to Costa Mesa to meet with Bob McKnight, a co-founder of the Quiksilver Company in the United States. Tim had known Bob for several years, and given Quiksilver's rapidly expanding role in the American surfing industry, Tim felt it was important for Chris to meet him, too.

The surfwear business in the United States had previously been dominated by companies such as Hang Ten, Ocean Pacific, and Birdwell. But when Quiksilver burst onto the scene with a flashier style that featured brighter colors, unique designs, and smart innovations, they caught the market's attention.

At the company's factory warehouse in Orange County, all of the employees loved to surf, and all of the products revolved around surfing. At first, this consisted of just a handful of items: surf trunks, shorts, pants, and t-shirts. But the stage was set for what would come next.

There were other foreign entries into the market as well. Australian companies like Rip Curl wetsuits and Billabong had made inroads, and Michael Tomson, Shaun Tomson's brother, had started his own clothing company known as Gotcha. To outsiders, it all seemed like a bit of a risk, but these visionaries saw what others didn't. The winds of change were beginning to blow, and people like Bob McKnight were badly needed in order to help fuel pro surfing's rise to respectability, especially in the United States.

Chris had met Bob a few times before, long before he had developed cancer. This time, they spent several hours trading surf stories, something Chris had an endless supply of.

Bob instantly became inspired by Chris, and vice versa. Chris listened intently as Bob described how Quiksilver had essentially started from scratch—something Chris could easily relate to. They discussed nearly everything about surfing: their favorite boards, their favorite breaks and, perhaps most important, what the future held.

Since Chris and his wife seemed like gracious people, Bob was determined to help them. He worked up a sponsorship deal. Quiksilver's arrangement with Chris was meant to be a "feel-good thing" for the company.

For Chris, it was a dream come true. A few years earlier in Australia, he had yearned to become a part of Quiksilver. But the company was already involved with top-flight international pro surfers such as Mark Richards, Jeff Hakman, and Bruce Raymond. The world's most highly regarded surfers came from outside the mainland United States, and there were simply not many dollars left for Californians. At first, Quiksilver took care of three emerging young surfers from Newport Beach: Jeff Parker, Preston Murray, and Danny Kwock. Now it was Chris's turn, and he refused to let his illness deter his enthusiasm.

When their long meeting came to a close that day, Bob couldn't resist asking Chris about something he had always been curious about—his hat. He jokingly told Chris it made him look like a gangster and asked him why he had settled on that particular one.

"Exactly for that reason," Chris told him. "Other surfers don't seem to take me seriously anymore. So if I look like a gangster, then maybe they will."

Chris though could not fully shake the fear that another disaster lurked just around the corner. It also didn't help matters when he occasionally brought them upon himself.

Several days later during a meaty day at Big Rock, he decided it was time to make a statement. It had been a while since he had paddled out in such powerful conditions. Chris loved Windansea, but surfing at the Rock was where he could really show off. Several of his friends had found their way into the lineup before him, including Peter Lochtefeld.

Chris watched Peter pull into a deep tube ride, only to emerge several seconds later. His surfing style was easy to recognize—he always held his left arm out very stiffly. His style looked awkward, but he was one of the best riders out there.

Chris soon caught a couple of small waves and finally got into the rhythm. After paddling into a thick five-footer, his confidence grew. The other surfers always let Chris have any wave he wanted. No longer did he have to battle for his waves, but Chris wished it were for entirely different reasons.

As a big wave approached, Chris realized he was the farthest surfer out on the peak, and it was now up to him. As he paddled for it, he sensed the wave was a little more than he could handle, but the urge inside him was too strong. During those few seconds, a multitude of thoughts raced through his head. Just a few short years ago, he was the undisputed king of competitive surfing in California. Just a few short years ago, he could pull into big backside barrels like this one in his sleep. Just a few short years ago, he was good enough to be pursuing the IPS tour.

Now it seemed there was no reason he couldn't do it again.

"Fuck it, I'm going," he blurted out.

As far as Chris was concerned, this wave was going to be a new beginning. It would be his time again. But in his overzealousness to catch the kind of wave he had not ridden for a long time, Chris paid dearly. Taking off far behind the peak, he failed to get enough speed. The lip of the wave dropped him like a hammer upon a nail, slamming him hard underwater and separating the surf leash from his leg. The impact of the wave sent his board skyrocketing ten feet into the mist-laden air.

Chris found himself in a very bad spot. A surging boil of whitewater pinned him several feet below the surface and showed no indication of letting him up anytime soon. Chris felt for his surf leash but found nothing. Several seconds passed with no sign of him, creating a panic for everyone. Finally, Chris bolted to the surface.

He gasped for air, but the ocean wasn't done with him yet. A second wave slammed him underwater once more. The other surfers paddled to help, but since he was in the heart of the impact zone, the incoming waves had to subside before anyone could reach him.

Amidst a chaotic mass of swirling water, he finally emerged, coughing violently. Mark and Peter hurriedly paddled over and realized he was disoriented. Peter slid off his own board and offered it to Chris, who precariously crawled onto it. Finally out of harm's way, Chris let his friends help him back to shore. He clutched his head in pain and spit up salt water. Numerous deep cuts tattooed his arms.

Watching from the beach, it felt like déjà' vu all over again. The incident was eerily similar to what Rex Huffman had encountered a few months before—exactly the kind of accident we had all warned Chris to avoid. Fortunately, his injuries were not nearly as severe. Mark drove him to the hospital to have his lacerations treated.

As they sped off, we discussed his wipeout. It was by far the worst I had ever seen him suffer. Not long ago, the thought of him taking a spill this bad seemed unimaginable. But not long ago, so was the thought of him having cancer. At that moment I hoped, for Chris's sake, that there would never again be any more horrific wipeouts in his surfing. Or in his life.

When I came home a few hours later, it appeared Chris had recovered from his ordeal. I sensed what he had endured was more emotional than physical. His left arm had required several stitches, but his pride had taken the bigger beating. When I asked what had happened, his reply was vintage Chris:

"Aeder, those two waves kicked the living shit out of me, no doubt about it. It was embarrassing. If it means I can still go surfing, though, I'll take a wipeout like that any time, any day. Maybe the surf will also help kick the crap out of this thing going on inside me, too."

Chapter 29

No Harbor in the Tempest

Summer 1979

The IPS world tour continued sans Chris O'Rourke. Chris knew he couldn't compete like he used to. So instead he shelved his pride and continued to support surfers like Joey Buran, Allen Sarlo, and Dan Flecky, who had now fully emerged as California's most visible competitors.

The 1979 IPS world tour proved to be a trying one. Competition officials were treated to the harsh realities of staging surfing competitions. Two-week waiting periods were often not long enough. At some of the events the wave conditions bordered on mediocrity, and in others, there were no waves at all. For the corporate sponsors, this meant everything in terms of lost media exposure and potential consumer visibility.

Jetting around the world chasing waves was still very much trial and error. And it was not just about the lack of surf; when the contests did take place, the surfers who competed became the focal points of a flawed judging system. Every turn and maneuver they performed was scrutinized and analyzed to the highest degree. Sometimes the judges got it right, and sometimes they didn't. Those surfers on the short end of the stick complained loudly. Rotating judges didn't help, but the solution was not that difficult. Professional surfing learned that it needed to protect its officials and its integrity, just like other sports did.

In spite of the flaws, the tour rolled on. Intense rivalries helped to fuel interest among fans, and the bitterest battle of all was between Mark Richards and Cheyne Horan. After running neck and neck atop the rankings for most of the year, both Australians were locked in a highly contested battle for the world title. Mark was a few years older and had the edge of being a veteran. Cheyne, however, was exceeding expectations faster than anyone expected and was well-positioned for the home stretch. Chris was proud of Cheyne. Before his illness, the two elite surfers were often compared to one another. The general thinking was that, if Cheyne had already progressed this far, then a healthy Chris O'Rourke would not have been far behind.

The fact that American mainland surfers Joey Buran and Dan Flecky were languishing toward the bottom of the rankings came as no surprise. Astute observers of the sport outside the United States remained far from impressed regarding the professional talent mainland America had to offer, and there didn't appear to be much up-and-coming in the amateur ranks either.

Chris still had visions of the IPS dancing in his head. Hoping to build his strength, he continued to surf and exercise as much as possible. Unfortunately, it seemed to have the opposite effect. His body was shrinking, and his skin was becoming dry and weathered. No one around him wanted to admit that Chris appeared to be aging very fast.

A professional surfer's best competitive years were usually before age thirty. Chris was only twenty years old, and it was sad to think that he was now on the downside of his career.

Yet he would soon have one more opportunity to compete. The influx of Australian surf companies into the U.S. market had continued, and still others were eager to join the fray. Stubbies Clothing had also targeted the large American market and needed a launching pad for promotion. Since Stubbies was the sponsor of the highly successful IPS surf contest at Burleigh Heads, the answer was right in front of them. So Stubbies made an interesting decision by announcing sponsorship of a professional surfing contest in California—for surfers from the Golden State only.

The Stubbies California Surfing Trials was conceived by Stubbies founder and chairman Bill Bolmann. The winner and runner-up would earn automatic berths in the more prestigious IPS Australian Stubbies contest the following year.

Reaction among California surfers was surprisingly divided. This was a bit odd, since few other American corporate surf companies were willing to take such a chance. To most, the idea seemed like a good one. A discontented few still voiced concerns that California's surfers didn't need the Australians to show them how to get things done, but the cold hard fact was that they did. Skepticism and divisions still ran amok within California surfing, and now the attitude was again rearing its ugly head.

Fortunately, most of California's professional surfers recognized the tremendous opportunity that had been bestowed upon them. Automatic entries into the Australian Stubbies contest seemed like a pretty good deal, and many of the better pros decided to enter: Dan Flecky, Joey Buran, Dean Hollingsworth, Lenny Foster, Dave Parmenter, and Chris O'Rourke.

When the event commenced in late August, the general sense was that a change for the better was coming. In order for the sport to go forward, the days of bad attitudes and grumpy locals had to be left behind. It had to start sometime, and that time was now.

But it wasn't that easy. The designation of Blacks Beach as the contest site raised a lot of eyebrows. Blacks had hosted a few WSA events, but nothing near this level of competition. Since the locals at Blacks took great pride in their area, almost everyone wondered about potential fallout. Bill Bolmann, however, was willing to take the chance. He knew that quality surf was the one thing the contest required to be successful.

As far as I was concerned, the arguments voiced by many of the local surfers at Blacks had no real merit anyway. They seemed to harbor the delusion that the beach was still some kind of secret spot, but no one could dispute its reputation as one of the premier beach breaks in all of California. All Stubbies asked for were three days and a couple hundred yards of beach. After that they would be gone. Bill obtained the necessary permits from the city. Now the only thing the contest needed was good surf.

On the eve of the competition, Chris's body was stiff, but he would be ready.

"I think I'll use my 6'10". The rails are a little thicker. Bill Caster says I need more buoyancy in the water, especially at Blacks, where there's no defined channel to paddle back out to the waves," he told me.

"Are you worried about that?"

"What, no channels? I've surfed at Blacks a lot before. I'm pretty used to it out there."

"Yeah I know, but that was when you were...healthy," I said hesitantly.

Chris seemed irritated. I sensed there was something else on his mind.

"The contest officials haven't released the heat schedule yet. I just wonder if I'll have a chance to surf against him," he said.

I needed no explanation of whom he meant. The surfing media had proclaimed Joey Buran the new "California Kid." Chris had recently supported him, but the animosity he felt toward Joey still existed on some level. He relished the opportunity to face him again in a heat. Joey's surfing style was still a hard thing for him to tolerate, and there was no other surfer Chris wanted to compete against more.

"You know something, Aeder? I would just like to see all the top guys from here ride the waves with more style and class."

The following morning, amid a dense soupy fog, the Stubbies competition got underway. On several occasions, the contest had to be postponed when the judges couldn't see through the fog. Some heats were held, but eventually the event was called off for the day. In his only heat, Chris placed second and advanced.

On the following day, I arrived at dawn hoping the conditions would be better. Getting to Blacks wasn't easy. Located along a reclusive stretch of coastline, Blacks was bordered by Scripps Pier to the south, and Torrey Pines State Beach to the north. A vertical three- hundred-foot sandstone cliff overlooked the beach. There were several footpaths etched into the hillside, but the easiest way to get there was to walk down a steep paved road. Unless you knew someone with a key to the locked gate at the top, walking was the only option.

The fog rolled in again. I couldn't see the waves as I neared the shoreline, but I heard them breaking loudly off in the distance. As I reached the sand, things started to get interesting. A pile of old surfboards had been deliberately set on fire close to the judging tower. A few were still intact, but others had burned almost completely, creating a smoldering pile of ashes. The stench of resin and burnt fiberglass permeated the early morning air. Over on a large rock etched in coal were these words: "Take you're fucking contest and go home."

The identity of the instigators was anyone's guess (and they needed a grammar lesson). A few disgruntled locals were the obvious choice. Seeing the lineup at Blacks the day before filled with colored wetsuits must have really made them angry. Personally, I had no reaction to it; I had seen plenty of bad stuff at Windansea. Blacks had its local crew, too, so who was I to judge? But in spite of the ominous warning, the Stubbies competition proceeded.

"Kirk, we just can't let a few gasoline-toting maniacs ruin our event," commented Bill Bolmann through his thick Australian drawl.

By now Bill no doubt wondered what he had gotten himself into. Several people began throwing sand onto the fire to help douse the flames. The foul stench hung in the air for the rest of the morning. But the weather soon warmed up, the fog disappeared, and the waves became a little better.

Before his illness, Chris had won a WSA contest at Blacks. But now, as he stood in the cool shade of the judging tower and watched the waves, the place seemed unfamiliar to him. His longtime friend and fellow surfer Mark Brolaski walked over. Back in the days when Chris was still learning the ropes at Windansea, Mark had been a tremendous influence on him. In fact, the entire Brolaski family had taken Chris under their wing.

A student at UCSD like me, Mark surfed at Blacks on every swell and was familiar with the shifting sandbars and lineup. So Chris and Mark talked strategy—where the best place was to paddle out, and whether he was using the right board. Mark still loved being a mentor to Chris and was always happy to help him. As the two talked, a group of young surf kids asked Chris for his autograph. Even in his weakened state, Chris still took competition quite seriously. With a smile, he happily obliged the kids and posed with them for a few photos.

A few minutes later, Chris's heat was announced. He picked up his board and walked down to the ocean's edge, the soft neoprene cap fastened tightly around his head. The midday sun was sweltering, but the cool water provided instant relief. Chris paddled out to the lineup, then sat on his board and rested. There were six surfers in the heat; in order to advance to the next round, Chris had to finish in the top three.

When the heat finally started, Chris feverishly scanned the horizon. He spotted a nice wave breaking to the left and paddled over to catch it. Pushing through his stiffness, he rode the wave and performed several maneuvers. A few minutes later, he caught another wave, and another. Halfway through his heat, I had to admit Chris was doing well—but not great. I felt disappointed that he was underachieving. Was I expecting too much from him? So many times, I kept thinking how the "old Chris" would have annihilated that wave.

His body may have deteriorated, but his ability to read the ocean was as sharp as ever. He could spot a wave and paddle over to it before anyone. Peering through my lens, I could tell the nagging stiffness in his neck hindered him greatly. But each time, Chris was still able to raise his head high enough to see the outside peaks. The smile on his face made me realize he was still having a lot of fun, too—until another mishap occurred.

Out of nowhere the largest set of the day loomed up before him. Chris took several valiant strokes, but he was too far inside. As the first wave descended upon him, Chris instinctively shoved his board aside and headed for the bottom. After a lengthy underwater thrashing, he finally surfaced. His surfboard was gone, and the neoprene cap had been ripped from his head. He ducked under several more large waves, each time surfacing a bit closer to shore. A long and exhausting swim followed, and when he finally reached the sand, he sat down for another rest.

His board had drifted in the current and washed ashore two hundred yards down the beach. I hustled over to retrieve it, wondering how Chris would react to this latest blow. Would his anger quickly surface and his emotions boil over again? Instead, it was just the opposite.

"Aeder, where in hell did that set come from? There wasn't anything close to that size before," Chris asked me, his eyes deep red from the salt water pounding.

"I have no idea at all. When we saw it, we all yelled and whistled, but you never looked back," I replied.

"That's because, with this stupid cap over my head, I can't hear a thing out there," he joked, suddenly shifting moods. "It's also because my neck is so stiff I can't even turn around. I'm so sick of this stuff happening. But at least I found my cap on the swim in."

With only a few minutes remaining in his heat, Chris didn't even bother paddling back out. He had suspected for some time that he could no longer compete against elite surfers, but this moment seemed to confirm it for him. Competition surfing had once been his passion. Stripped of this, what else did he have left? In those few moments, I saw a different kind of person emerging, one who realized it was time to take a new approach to his surfing and his life. A higher order of things awaited him now, and Chris knew he had to take that next step.

Chris never did get the chance to go up against Joey Buran, but one of the other La Jolla surfers still in the running would.

Sure enough, Mark Ruyle surfed against Joey in the next heat. None of us got too excited, though. Mark had little in the way of prior surf contest experience. The Stubbies was his very first one, and he was competing only because of Chris's urging. Mark's surfing at Windansea was very polished, and Chris repeatedly told him he should give surf contests a try.

For the next twenty minutes the two competitors battled it out in the water. Whenever Mark caught a wave, the crowd on the beach cheered; when Joey caught a wave, they booed. Despite his inexperience, Mark overcame his early jitters. In the biggest upset of the event he had defeated Buran in a highly contested close heat.

Spectators loudly applauded the decision, but Joey felt robbed. Visibly upset, he launched into a profanity-laced verbal tirade directed at the judges. He gathered up his surfboards and stormed off down the beach, still lambasting them at the top of his lungs.

"There goes California's top surfer all right. What a joke that guy is," commented someone nearby.

Chris approached Mark, and the two shook hands.

"I honestly don't know how I won, but I got 'em for you, buddy," Mark told him, still in a state of shock.

"Thanks, bro," Chris replied excitedly.

Chris watched as Joey walked away fuming, knowing that only a few years earlier he had acted the same way. Joey's reaction to losing was intense, but for passionate competitors, winning was the only thing that mattered. Chris had often chided Joey over the years, yet he understood his burning desire for success. Losing in a casual manner meant you weren't passionate enough to win.

When the last day of competition rolled around, so did another disturbing incident. Late in the morning, a man armed with a .22 rifle made his way high upon the steep cliffs that overlooked Blacks. One of the contest surfers, Newport's Lenny Foster, noticed him from a distance. By scaling the cliffs himself, Lenny was able to sneak up and subdue the man from behind before any damage was done. Police arrived and arrested the suspect. No one seemed quite sure what his intentions were, but California avoided what could have been a very dark day in surfing history.

The negative incidents that plagued the Stubbies contest highlighted the vast disconnect among surfers not only within California, but across all coasts of the United States. Instead of being isolated from one another, surfers needed to share their ideas and surf culture.

The Stubbies contest at Blacks was pretty much forgettable, but it would prove to be an integral step in the evolution of the sport. The contest also proved that some of California's most talented surfers were not necessarily the best known. Richard Kenvin, a young La Jolla surfer whom Chris had taken under his wing, captured first place. Another San Diego surfer, Jeff Hodges, finished second. Dean Hollingsworth from Carlsbad was in third, followed by Central California's Dave Parmenter in fourth. While Dean and Dave had previous contest experience, Richard and Jeff came entirely out of the blue. Capturing the top two spots meant they were automatically seeded into the prestigious IPS Stubbies Australia contest the following year.

While Chris O'Rourke had once made a fair amount of enemies, he also had the knack for making a hell of a lot of allies. Chris Ahrens was one of them. The two had become friends while surfing at Windansea, and Chris Ahrens, too, had been drawn to Chris O'Rourke like a magnet.

Aware of his friend's desire to surf in a competitive format, Chris Ahrens helped to arrange a one-on-one showdown at Windansea pitting Chris O'Rourke against Dan Flecky. The hour-long competition took place on a hot September day with all of the local surfers there to cheer Chris on. Chris Ahrens and two of his friends acted as judges and vowed to be impartial, as hard as that was going to be.

There was no limit to the number of waves each surfer could ride. One hour later, the two surfers emerged from the ocean. Beneath the Windansea hut, the scores were tabulated, and Chris was declared the winner. The contest was very informal and all for fun—and didn't provide Dan Flecky with much of a chance. He could have surfed circles around Chris and still lost. Under the circumstances, Dan took it all in stride.

Chris continued to be a popular and inspirational figure in surfing communities around the world. Yet Chris wanted more from his life. Though there had been no new cancer flare-ups, he remained fully aware of the disease's unpredictability.

He began to do some serious soul-searching. A few of his friends, most notably Brew Briggs, had long before suggested he take a more religious approach to his life. The advice had taken a long time to sink in, but now Chris wanted to move forward in a completely new direction. The message came to him straight from the teachings of Jesus: Love one another. Chris fully adopted it, committing to treating others only in a way that was pure love. It was pretty powerful stuff.

Of course, at times his patience was tested. Surfing magazine published a special 1970s issue that highlighted the most monumental events of the decade. But when Chris and I noticed the only mention of him was in the letters column, we were furious. There were no photos, write-ups or interviews. After all he had gone through, omitting him from any real coverage felt like a hard slap in the face.

So that afternoon Chris and I jumped into my car and drove north to the Surfing offices. I knew that Flame never liked visitors dropping in unexpectedly, and this time was no different. We hurried in past the receptionist, straight into his office. I could tell that Flame wasn't happy, but he knew right away why we had come. My gut ached in anticipation of what was to come. But right then, I just didn't care. The welfare of my friend came first.

"Hey, you guys can't just barge in here. I'm pretty busy right now, and you should have called first," he said.

"Sorry Flame, but if we were Dan Merkel and Shaun Tomson, I know you would welcome us with open arms," I told him.

"Kirk, what on earth are you talking about?"

"Chris and I are pretty pissed off about that 1970s issue. There's absolutely nothing about Chris in there except that letter. What happened?" I demanded.

"Kirk, I think you're being very selfish, but what can I tell you? Making those decisions is harder than you think. The entire editorial staff had a say," Flame said. "There are only so many pages inside the magazine to go around, and Chris wasn't the only one left out. That was a hard issue to put together. It covered an entire decade of surfing for Christ's sakes! We just ran out of space."

"None of the other surfers had cancer," I added.

"Oh I get it, so that's what this is about," Flame retorted.

"No, that's not what it's all about. The real story about Chris is what his surfing was all about before he got the cancer. That's the Chris you missed out on."

I was shaking my head in disbelief, but I realized I was pushing his limits.

"Flame, maybe I don't understand. Surfing magazine is an American publication. You do a review of the 1970s. There are tons of great stories and photos about how great the surfers from Hawaii, Australia, and South Africa are."

"That's because they are," Flame interrupted.

"I know that. I agree. But even Surfer magazine treats those guys the same way. I just think that, in this case, your magazine left out the best surfer from California, not to mention a monumental story. Chris can't compete like he used to, and we all know that. But his inspirational impact continues to be huge—and he's still surfing," I continued.

During the entire time, Chris stood silently in the corner of Flame's office and never said a word. Maybe he figured our rage was better coming from me. But Larry had heard enough.

"You guys get out of my office right now!"

"Okay Larry, but not until I get all my photos back. I want all the shots in my files. This means I'm not working for Surfing magazine anymore," I added.

"Fine with me," said Flame.

Larry stalked over to a tall metal filing cabinet. He pulled out a file containing all my photos and handed them to me without saying another word. On the way out the door, I felt really bad over what had just happened. It wasn't personal, but I did what I had to do. Departing on bad terms with him had not really been part of the plan. It didn't take long for Chris to speak up.

"Aeder, I've never seen you get that angry before. But you should stand up for yourself sometimes for what you believe."

Once again, I knew he was right.

Chapter 30

Competition and Christianity

December 27, 1979

The controversy stemming from our disagreement with Surfing magazine slowly subsided, but the damage was done. I chalked it all up to politics, but my days as a contributing photographer there were over. So I began working with Surfer magazine instead. Editor Steve Pezman and Photo Editor Art Brewer warmly welcomed me aboard.

Chris, meanwhile, had bigger things to worry about. His doctors had warned him to avoid any kind of stress. But cancer itself is stressful, so that was easier said than done. He required everything in his life to be positive, and surfing certainly qualified. He paddled out in the small waves at Windansea, where he found temporary solace and emerged feeling stoked about life.

He also received an honorary invitation to the Australian IPS contests the following year. The gesture was more symbolic than anything else, but it was appreciated. And except for a few nagging backaches, that night he went to sleep feeling at peace. A simple backache didn't seem like much of an issue.

But like his headaches, it should have. The following morning, Chris's world again began spiraling out of control. He awoke with numbness in his upper body, and he couldn't even get out of bed. Jil immediately called an ambulance, and Chris was rushed to the hospital. Doctors penetrated his skin with small pins, but he never felt a thing. Neurological testing confirmed the worst: another tumor had been detected in his spinal cord.

He immediately underwent emergency surgery. Chris had faced excruciating moments before, but none like this one. Waiting for the doctors to begin felt like an eternity. Fearing the worst, he felt darkness creeping in around him. He wondered if he would survive the operation. And even if he did, the doctors said he might never walk again. Chris realized that, if he couldn't walk, his surfing days were finished, too.

Before the surgery, Jil stayed by his bedside, holding his hands tightly and comforting him however she could. Chris was the one in the life-threatening situation, but few realized how much she was suffering, too. The emotional toll it took upon her at times seemed unbearable. This certainly wasn't how she had imagined their life together. But she remained strong-willed and determined to pull him through.

Dr. Tom Waltz, Head of Neurosurgery at Scripps, performed the surgery on Chris's spinal cord. If the operation wasn't successful, Chris could lose feeling in his legs or become a paraplegic. After several hours of delicate surgery, only seventy percent of the tumor was removed. It was deemed too dangerous to pursue the rest.

Waking up from surgery had become a familiar routine for Chris. Jil and Lyn were by his side, and chemotherapy and radiation treatments would follow. Chris would now have to rely on whatever strength he had left to pull him through. He immediately prayed to God for forgiveness for all the terrible things he had done in the past.

Though his morale was at an all-time low, Chris still clung to a shred of hope. He knew he truly needed a miracle and that perhaps only God could save him now. But he wasn't ready to turn his life completely over to the Lord just yet. After all, wasn't he the tough guy? A complicated battle raged within him.

Ever since his diagnosis two and a half years earlier, the thought of dying weighed heavily on Chris's mind. His soul, however, would never completely give up hope.

"I have to keep believing. Positive thoughts give my body strength," he told me.

All Chris could think about was trying to walk. In the back of his mind, the temptation to surf again was as strong as ever. Could he really do it?

On January 2, 1980, I visited Chris in the hospital. I could only hope the start of a new decade would bring better things his way. His spirits seemed amazingly high, and I knew he wanted me to act as if nothing was wrong. But exclaiming "Happy New Year" didn't seem appropriate. Instead, I asked how he was feeling.

Chris looked fatigued and paused before responding. "I really don't know anymore. I'm so angry at this thing, this disease, for trying to take over my body. It doesn't fight fair. If it was human, I would kick its ass."

"I know you would," I reassured him.

Chris had always shown so much courage, and I wanted to do the same. I had always been able to hold back my tears at the hospital, but now my emotions began to get the best of me. My eyes welled up, and I turned and pretended to look out the window.

"My doctors told me I ought to be thankful just for being alive," he said.

A nurse came in to give Chris his medicine, and I quickly stepped over towards the window and wiped my eyes when he wasn't looking. I no longer knew what to think. Every time he took a step forward, he was soon blindsided by another step back. It was obvious he couldn't go down this path much longer. Things had to take a turn for the better. Time was running out.

After the nurse left, I regained my composure and hung out with him for awhile. We talked about a lot of things, but mostly about surfing.

"Hey, is the food any good here?" I asked.

"You must be joking, Aeder. It sucks! Jil brings me all my food now. I can't stand the crap here."

"What about the nurses? There must be a few hot ones, right?"

A big smile spread across his face.

"Yeah, I've seen a few hot ones. You have any new girlfriends, Aeder? Bring them for a visit sometime," he said with a chuckle.

"Well Chris, now that you mention it, there is a new one. As a matter of fact, her father is a doctor right here at Scripps."

"Tell him to stop by my room. I need all the help I can get," he replied.

"I'll be sure to do that," I said. "Anyway I have to go back to class now. I'll stop by again tomorrow, okay?"

No sooner had I neared the door to leave when Chris spoke.

"Hey Aeder, I just wanted you to know that, in the future when you stop by, there's a big box of tissue right there on the table."

I turned around to look at him.

"Just so you know," he continued with a sly smile.

"How did he know?" I mumbled on the way out.

As I left Chris's room, I saw Brew Briggs walking down the hallway toward me. When Chris was in the hospital, it was always a revolving door with lots of friends and well-wishers. By now the hospital staff had become used to all his visitors. I shook hands with Brew, and we spoke briefly.

Chris's happiness at seeing his newest visitor was short-lived. In the past, Brew had provided Chris with sound religious advice and tried to get him to accept the Lord into his life—and to some degree Chris had.

But this time their conversation took an unpleasant tone. Chris felt Brew was pushing him too far with his religious rhetoric. He asked him to stop, but Brew continued to preach the word of the Bible.

"You know, Chris, I would never force anything upon you. I just feel it's time for you to put your faith in God and let Him show you the way," Brew said.

Brew had tried to get him to read the Bible before and sensed this was the direction Chris really wanted to go. If Chris wasn't going to help himself, then Brew would do it for him—something he knew wasn't going to be pleasant.

Chris looked despondent the entire time Brew read from the Bible. He rarely said a word and tried to ignore what Brew was saying. Finally, Brew decided it was best for him to leave. He placed the Bible on Chris's bedside table and began to walk out of the room. Chris became angry. As Brew closed the door, he heard a loud thud. When he turned back, he was disappointed but not surprised to see the Bible lying on the floor.

"I've tried it already, okay? I've prayed hundreds of times, and it hasn't done me any good! So get that thing away from me, just take it with you and get out of here," Chris demanded.

Brew was sad to hear his friend's words but wasn't about to relent. He placed the Bible back on the table despite the fire burning in Chris's eyes.

"You're not mad at me, and you're not mad at the Lord. You're mad at what's happened to you. This will help you deal with all that. I promise," Brew said. "Just give it some thought, Chris, that's all I'm asking. Besides, what else do you have to do right now?"

Brew was sure his words would ignite another spark. But surprisingly, they didn't. For several minutes after Brew left the room, Chris just stared at the book. Finally, he reached over to pick it up. He read a few pages, and kept reading.

Several days later, Chris was discharged. In the months that followed, through rehabilitation and physical therapy, he slowly developed feeling in both legs again. Every step became precious now. Each movement really did feel like a gift from God, and every morning brought another sunrise, full of sweet promise.

Chris learned not to be bitter about his predicament. He recalled what his grandmother Elbertine had once told him: just keep doing your best, even when things are not looking so good. Under circumstances that were far from normal, Chris had tried to stay positive. His doctors told him it would be a long road back. But back to where? It felt like he was playing with building blocks, and he was always starting from the bottom.

Small steps, though, were the only way. He decided it would help if he lived closer to the beach, so he and Jil found a small upstairs apartment for rent on Bonair Street close to Windansea. Though this meant I had to find a new place, too, the timing actually worked out well. Halfway through college, I needed my own space.

Being near the ocean immediately inspired Chris. He began his own training program, walking slowly to Windansea and back several times each day. Watching the waves was a powerful motivator, and his urge to surf again grew even stronger. Eventually, he began riding a bicycle and gradually built up even more strength by swimming in pools. Each time Chris headed out the door, he told Jil it was purely for exercise. But she knew her husband all too well—the ocean was beckoning. Though the urge to get back in the surf often felt overwhelming, Chris was forced to wait until the time was right.

He was also deeply inspired by people around the world who knew of his illness and supported him. His terrible plight had touched the hearts of thousands.

"All those letters people sent to the magazines and newspapers, along with my family, and all my friends in the surfing community...they tell me I am an inspiration to them, but they have been inspirations to me, inspiring me to keep pushing onward," he told me one night. "It's been a real hard uphill climb with a lot of slipping and falling. I don't think I could have come this far without them."

Chris finally discovered Jesus and very much liked what he saw. In spite of his perilous situation, he found everything started coming a little more easily in life. He regularly began attending church and, in doing so, touched the lives of even more people.

Yet even with his newfound faith, Chris still wondered every single day, "Why me? Why didn't this happen to that person over there, or that person there?" He yearned to be "the man" again at Windansea. As unrealistic as it seemed, it became his unwavering goal.

Chris had been battling cancer for almost three years, and the entire time he'd had a strong contingent of friends who would do anything for him. But we also had to tend to our own lives. Finishing college was important to me, and those times I couldn't be there for him hurt a lot. So I decided to take a one-year hiatus from college to focus on other matters, including spending more time with my friend and traveling.

Chris had told me so many great things about Australia that I decided it was time for me to go there, too. In late March, I went with a group of California surfers to Australia and New Zealand. This included Richard Kenvin and Jeff Hodges, the top two qualifiers from the California Stubbies contest. Mark Ruyle and Jim Neri came along, too. I sensed Chris was disappointed we were going. Australia was the one place he couldn't wait to get back to himself.

"I should be going with you guys," he told me.

I felt guilty leaving him behind, but my surfing photography had really evolved. I looked forward to photographing the world's best in Australia at surf breaks that were nothing short of first-class.

Upon our arrival, we bunked at Neville Hyman's surfboard factory along the famed Gold Coast in Queensland. Neville was a talented, cutting-edge shaper, just like Bill Caster back home. A new swell was on the way, and a few days later, the surf at Burleigh Heads was four to six feet of pure glass. My excitement reached new heights when I saw Australian legends Mark Richards, Mark Warren, and Terry Fitzgerald getting ready to paddle out. Chris was my favorite surfer in the world, but Mark Richards had undoubtedly become number two. "MR" was the IPS world-surfing champion in 1979 and looked to repeat this year.

I set up my equipment and submersed myself in the scene. Thousands of miles from home, I had no other cares except one—I wished that Chris could have been there, too.

Reality quickly set in, though, especially for Richard and Jeff. The IPS Stubbies competition kicked off, and both California surfers were easily eliminated in their first-round heats. Thirty minutes of competitive surfing and they were finished—just like that. Australia's best surfers were very talented and hungry. It wasn't much consolation, but even the Hawaiians and South Africans found it hard to have much success.

Shooting pictures of the contest felt like a dream to me. I shot one heat after the next with all the best surfers in the world: Shaun Tomson, Rabbit Bartholomew, Cheyne Horan, Dane Kealoha, Buzzy Kerbox, and Michael Ho. Yet in spite of all the big names, the ultimate winner of the Stubbies contest was a relative dark horse. Young Australian surfer Peter Harris pulled off one of the biggest upset wins in IPS history by defeating Hawaiian powerhouse Dane Kealoha in the finals. Peter was a low-key, very talented, regular-foot surfer who rarely competed in contests. Like Chris, he was also a devout Christian, and in this event, Peter had his prayers answered.

Meanwhile, back in La Jolla, Chris's faith in God grew stronger with each day. And it wasn't just a passing fancy. Chris truly felt enlightened, excited, and one hundred percent determined to take things in a whole new direction. The frustration of his situation vanished. No longer was he impatient to have things happen quickly. He trusted that, by placing his life into the hands of God, there would come a time when everything would be okay again. He found strength in his family, friends, and the Bible studies conducted inside their small apartment.

Jil, too, had given her life to the Lord. Unwavering in her support for Chris, she soon discovered that it helped her deal better with his situation as well as her own. Thoughts were creeping into her mind that she didn't want to consider, and Bible studies became a positive distraction. Twice a week, their apartment turned into the neighborhood church.

Many of those who attended were among the new crop of young kids who surfed at Windansea—Mikko Fleming, Peter King, Conrad Riggs, Matt Rimel, Drew Littlemore, and Ethan and Eric Shaw. For several years, they had idolized and drawn inspiration from Chris, and during Bible studies, Chris revealed a tremendous amount of guilt for how he had behaved at Windansea during his younger years. The uphill climb he faced made him wiser and brought him closer to the ways of the Lord.

"I feel terrible now about the things I did back then. People wanted to kill me. We would break other surfers' boards on the beach and bust the windshields of their cars. I was like a wild animal on the loose," he told them. "The whole ordeal with cancer has really made me learn a lot, though. About the Lord, it's each individual's choice. All I know is it's right for me."

Sternly, Chris preached to them not to behave like he had. He told them instead to live a cleaner life and, most importantly, to get along with their parents and listen to them.

The young kids weren't the only ones who attended Bible studies; Brew Briggs, Chris Ahrens, and Bob Andrews, his longtime friend from elementary school, were regulars there, too.

Chris and Jil also attended Sunday mass at the Calvary Chapel church in Pacific Beach. Chris couldn't help but notice how all his friends' lives were moving forward so effortlessly. He could only pray that one day it would be like that for him again. By now Chris was a far cry from the person who once terrorized outsiders at Windansea. But the demons of his past would catch up with him one last time.

One day while driving his Volkswagen sedan along La Jolla Boulevard, Chris prepared to make a right turn down Nautilus Street toward Windansea. A car coming from the opposite direction sped through a red light and veered in front of him. Chris clearly had the right of way and was upset the reckless driver had almost caused an accident. Feelings of anger quickly welled inside him—the kind of rage that he hadn't felt in a long time—and up went his middle finger. The driver of the other car quickly pulled over and blocked his path.

When Chris completed his turn, two men were standing in front of his car, and he was forced to stop. Chris hadn't noticed how big the guys were, but he could see it now. His windows were rolled down, and one guy reached inside and grabbed Chris around his neck. His brimmed hat fell off in the skirmish, exposing his bald head. One of the men laughed and called him a skinhead. The other man threw a punch that glanced off Chris's jaw. As Chris continued to struggle, the men tried to drag him out the window while still throwing punches at him.

Chris finally broke free from their grasp and sped away. Shaken and scared, he didn't know where to go, who to tell, or what to do. Worried that the two men might catch up to him, he drove along Neptune Street looking for anyone he knew. But no one was around. So he drove toward Big Rock and parked his car out of sight at Tim Senneff's house.

For several minutes, he sat and tried to calm himself. He was breathing hard, and his pulse rate was through the roof. What exactly was he feeling—anger toward the two men, or frustration at not being able to fight back? Or what it felt like to be on the other side for a change? Finally, he regained his composure and drove on.

Chris circled around the block and drove back to Windansea. He parked the car and walked over to the thatched hut, where he saw Scot Cherry, his former rival. The two had not fought in several years; in fact, a mutual respect had developed between them. Chris was thankful for that, especially since Scot had grown enormously large. Ironically, it was now Scot who was regarded as the number one enforcer at Windansea.

Chris told Scot what had happened. Scot could see that Chris had tears welling in his eyes and was pretty shaken up. In spite of their history, Scot never held a grudge. He realized kids could sometimes do ugly things and be bullies, and he never took it personally. Scot also knew that Chris was the most amazing natural surfing talent to ever come out of La Jolla and was proud of him for that.

As Chris continued to tell Scot his story, he glanced toward the north end of the beach and couldn't believe his eyes. There were the men who had just attacked him.

"Well, I'll be," said Chris. "That's them right over there."

They were about fifty yards away, standing with their surfboards by the water's edge. With no hesitation, Scot hurried over and told them not to go surfing at Windansea. The bigger of the two men started mouthing off, and that was all the incentive Scot needed. He hit the surfer hard in his face, dropping him with one punch. Blood poured from his mouth and nose. The other man tried to assist his friend but was visibly nervous and obviously didn't want any part of Scot.

"Pick up your friend, and get the fuck out of here," Scot told him.

The two left with their tails tucked between their legs. Watching from a distance, Chris wasn't sure how to feel. After all, he was a Christian now. No doubt in the old days, he would have been all in favor of what Scot had just done. But now, he was a man of the Lord, and the incident had truly affected him. Yet Chris knew that he no longer had the strength to stand up for himself, and in light of his history with Scot, it made Chris feel good that someone like him had come to his aid.

Scot had once known what it was like to be in the weaker position. He strongly believed that you had to try and be a good person and do good things. But when somebody crosses you, makes you angry, or hurts someone you care about, the dark side still comes out. In that sense, he and Chris were one and the same.

When I returned from Australia in late April, Chris was the first person I called. Chris told me he had started physical therapy again, along with riding a bike, swimming, and paddling a surfboard in a pool. He had already earmarked the next swell as the one that would mark his return to surfing. I thought to myself, Haven't I already heard this so many times before? Chris acted as if everything in his life was still very normal. As his friend, who was I to doubt him? He had made so many comebacks. Sometimes, it seemed as if he had an endless supply of second chances.

And incredibly, just as he said, on the next small swell he paddled out at Windansea. Aware of the risks, he had planned this carefully and was accompanied by several of the young surfers from his Bible class. Four and a half months after spine surgery, after his doctors told him he might never even walk again, Chris was going surfing.

His neck, however, was even stiffer than before. Simply lifting his head high enough to see if any waves were coming proved to be a challenge. He could hear other surfers chattering around him, a sound he had longed to hear. His eyes glistened. For a brief moment, he felt embarrassed. Had anyone seen? Did it even matter? In the ocean, salt water and tears mixed easily.

He only rode two waves that day, but it was enough. The first surf session led to another, and another, and another. Chris O'Rourke was back at Windansea, but his demeanor had changed remarkably. In the past, Chris paddling up to a stranger at Windansea normally meant trouble. This Chris approached surfers he didn't know with a completely different tone.

"Hey bro, what's your name? Did you know that the Lord loves you?"

Their reaction was one of pure shock and disbelief. Where had all the screaming gone?

Surfing was the easy part; the paddling had become difficult. The physical act easily drained his body of what little energy he had. So the young kids at Windansea devised a plan to help him out. After riding a wave, he held onto their surf leashes and got a free tow back out to the lineup. This made everything much easier. Since his stiff body wouldn't allow him to perform many maneuvers, he just went with the flow of each wave and did whatever he could. The sheer fun of being in the ocean outweighed everything else.

By surfing yet again, Chris had taken another monumental step—one that he attributed to the power of God. When Chris emerged from the water that day, he walked straight over to where I was sitting with my camera. Normally he would have asked me straightaway, "Hey Aeder, did you get a photo of me in that tube?"

What he said instead probably shouldn't have come as a surprise.

"Hey Aeder, how come you never go to church with us?"

I was unsure how to respond. As a child, I regularly attended Sunday school at the La Jolla Presbyterian Church. Over time, my interest in faith had subsided but hadn't gone away completely. Since it had been a while, I figured the timing was right.

"Okay, Chris. Next time I will go with you," I told him.

"That's great! We're going this Sunday. Come to our apartment in the morning, and we'll all go together," he said.

That Sunday, I accompanied Chris, Jil, Tim and six of the young Windansea kids to church. Surrounded by an entourage of devoted friends, Chris seemed more like the star of a famous rock band entering an arena. Nearly everyone sitting in the pews turned around to look. It was clear that he had achieved legendary status in the community. Whether people admired Chris or still hated him, there was no mistaking his strong will to live and surf—and for that alone, he had earned a lot of accolades.

We took our seats, and the sermon began. During the service, I could see the passion in Chris's eyes. He needed a source of hope, and it was quite apparent he had found it. As we left the church, Jil and I were a short distance behind Chris, who was surrounded by all the kids.

"They really love him and make him feel young again," Jil told me.

Her words resonated inside my head. Chris was only twenty-one years old. But after all he had been through, he seemed much older. And as a result, my own outlook on mortality was quite different now.

Chapter 31

Swami's and Gerlach

Chris continued to surf at Windansea throughout the summer. Some days went better than others, but at least he was out in the water. When he wasn't, he was preaching the word of the Lord, undergoing more medical treatments, and doing speaking engagements with children at elementary schools. More than anything else, he enjoyed spending time with his wife and son. Jil picked up a few odd jobs to help out with their finances. They did not have much money, but they were able to get by.

Good news came when Chris was hired to help coach the Nectar Surf team, a rising surfboard manufacturer based in San Diego's North County. Nectar's owner, Gary McNabb, didn't care if Chris's surfing was only a shell of what it used to be. His contest experience was invaluable, and Gary felt that Chris could instill his intense competitive prowess into the young surfers on his team. Chris instantly became a significant source of inspiration and a valuable mentor for a group of surfers that included Greg Mungall and John Glomb. It was also the first time Chris met another young Nectar team rider, Brad Gerlach.

In October, he and Jil attended Bob McKnight's wedding in Newport Beach, where he reunited with many of the world's top professionals. Bob and Chris talked for awhile, but the CEO of Quiksilver sensed Chris's smile disguised what he really felt inside. The spark he had once seen within Chris appeared to be dwindling now.

Windansea was Chris's most accessible surf break, but occasionally he would venture to other locations, most notably Swami's in Encinitas where most of the Nectar team surfed.

Chris liked Swami's because the waves afforded him longer rides than Windansea. But since paddling out was still difficult, he would sometimes grab onto another surfer's leash and get a ride. Chris was well aware that each time he surfed could be his last, and he tried to stay in the ocean for as long as possible.

As the Christmas holidays approached, he received some encouraging news: His latest medical scan detected no new cancerous growths. Still, everyone remained cautiously optimistic about his recovery, especially since we had all heard this before. Chris would still have to be on guard. He continued to pray for a normal life and, God willing, better things to come.

But unknown to us, Chris sensed that soon he was going to die. Personally, I didn't think this was possible. His will to continue living seemed stronger than ever. Yet when I went to visit him one day, the despondent look on his face said otherwise. It really was up to God now.

"Don't stop being somebody, Aeder," he said to me out of the blue. "You should keep doing your photography. Some of the images you take look like postcards, and you'll only continue to get better."

"Thanks, Chris. I do hope to make it my profession someday."

"Learning things at an early age can teach you stuff, so you should definitely try. Keep going to the end, until you know one hundred percent that you are absolutely finished with it," Chris continued.

"Is that how surfing is for you?"

"When I first started surfing, I knew I wanted to do it for the rest of my life. And I still have a lot left," Chris said.

In January of 1981, all of us prayed the New Year would bring more good news for Chris and his family. Jim Neri was still at college in San Luis Obispo; Tim Senneff, Ted Smith, and Mark McCoy had part-time jobs at local restaurants, and Oscar Bayetto had become a very astute businessman. Lyn was still living in San Diego and continued to visit her brother often. Even when we couldn't be with Chris, our thoughts were always with him, and he often remarked how he could feel our prayers.

In early February, Chris received some sad news when his brother informed him that he was temporarily moving to South Carolina. Bart and his wife, Jenny, had a two-year-old son of their own named Terence. They often brought him over to Chris and Jil's apartment, so he could play with Tim. Leaving his sick younger brother was the hardest thing Bart ever had to do, but he knew he had to get on with his own life.

Chris was disappointed to see Bart and his family leave and immediately looked for a distraction to cure his ills. One week later, a solid winter swell pounded the San Diego coastline. Chris paddled out at Swami's with the assistance of fourteen-year-old Brad Gerlach. As the youngest member of the Nectar surf team, whenever Brad needed advice or encouragement, he always came to Chris. Chris realized Brad had tons of potential and was extremely dedicated to his craft. Knowing Brad aspired to become a professional surfer, Chris always tried to steer him in the right direction.

"Brad, if you dedicate yourself to surfing, you can do whatever you want. You have so much more style right now than most of the other surfers from California. You should build on that. Most of the guys getting the publicity right now are not even the best surfers. That needs to change," Chris told him. "Just look at your friend Todd Martin. You are a much better surfer than him. His feet are spread so far apart on the board he looks like a crab! The pro tour right now isn't all about style. But one day it will be, and that's the direction your surfing should be headed in."

Brad listened intently and was deeply impressed by Chris's passion for the sport. Brad knew that Chris really cared. And he thought it was interesting Chris had mentioned Todd Martin. Until then, Brad thought Todd actually had pretty good balance on his board, but Chris had given him a different perspective. This was the first time anyone told Brad he was the better surfer of the two. No one had ever given him this kind of insight and opinion before, and he was greatly inspired by Chris's words. While Joey Buran had come to the forefront as California's next great hope, in Brad's mind, no one represented California surfing better than Chris O'Rourke.

It didn't matter to Brad if Chris was now a shadow of his former self. Gary McNabb had suggested to him that he could still learn a lot from Chris—and now he had, not only about surfing, but about life. Brad had a hard time comprehending Chris's health issues. The prodigy surfer from California was now just a month short of his twenty-second birthday, but his battle with cancer made him look aged and weathered. Brad was shocked to learn his real age.

As the two paddled out together at Swami's, the ocean was so cold that Chris wore a thick 3mm full wetsuit and two of the neoprene caps over his head. Nearing the lineup, they spotted a few of the other Nectar team riders.

But not everyone out in the water that day was friendly. Chris's mere presence immediately caused a stir. A few hardcore locals wasted little time in voicing their displeasure, an obvious indication of previous bad encounters with him. One surfer wanted to fight Chris right then and there but, given his condition, decided to show him some mercy.

"Why is he out here? There's no way I'm giving him any of my waves. I don't care who the hell he thinks he is. He can go back to Windansea for all I care," one local grumbled.

In the past, Chris had no problem paddling right up to another surfer and mixing it up. It was a different time now, a different place, and what seemed like a completely different world. Chris tried not to pay any attention to them, but deep inside the words hurt. Through the Lord, he tried to repent his sins. For now, that's all he could do.

Brad and Chris surfed together for about two hours. Toward the end of their session, Brad noticed Chris's energy level was rapidly declining. Brad helped push Chris into the waves, but he could barely paddle or even raise his hands over his head.

Finally, Chris told Brad he would ride the next wave all the way to the beach.

Chris scanned the horizon one last time. He saw a small wave approaching and started paddling for it. Brad came in to assist, but Chris told him to stay back. Chris felt the wave rise up beneath him, and with every bit of energy he could muster, he rose to his feet, steadied his balance, and trimmed along the face of the liquid wall for nearly two hundred yards. Just before the wave came to an end, Chris crouched down inside the small tube. His ride was certainly no masterpiece. But it was still special. Chris had just ridden the last wave of his life.

Brad caught the next wave behind Chris and followed him to shore. They walked up the beach toward the long wooden staircase that led to the parking lot above. Brad knew Chris was exhausted and offered to carry his board. The suggestion made Chris laugh, stubborn to the end.

As he climbed the steps, Chris saw a small lizard sunning itself. He flashed back to the time when he used to hunt for lizards at Windansea. Ha, ha, got you! He smiled at the memory. He was young and innocent then, but now he felt old and tired. Watching that lizard on the rock, he sensed that his life, and his surfing, had truly come full circle—just as it was meant to be. Becoming the world champion of surfing one day would have been nice, but now his life had a different purpose. God would see him through. The thought relaxed him. And with the waves breaking behind him, Chris continued up the stairs.

Chapter 32

The Joey Buran Factor

Early March, 1981

In his heart, Chris still believed he could compete with the best surfers in the world. His mind and body, however, dictated otherwise.

Chris really didn't know how much time he had left, so every decision he made became that much more important. The one thing Chris really wanted to do was to return to Australia.

And the country wanted him back as well. Chris was named the honorary Team Captain for California. He would have the opportunity to return to Australia for the IPS tour after all—only this time as a coach. He didn't want to simply be an observer, though. He wanted to compete. But how? He prayed to the Lord for the miracle of miracles.

Much of Chris's motivation to become a great surfer again derived from unusual sources—particularly Joey Buran. From the very beginning, Joey's style of surfing vexed Chris. Chris's philosophy was simple: The less body movement, the better. Joey's manner of surfing was the complete antithesis.

There were surfers from California whom Chris admired. Several years before Chris had befriended two surfers from Santa Cruz, Richard Schmidt and Vince Collier, whose surfing styles Chris said he could relate to. He had also become very impressed with young Brad Gerlach.

Then another young surfer caught Chris's eye on a trip to Santa Barbara. One afternoon he and Bob Andrews decided to stop and watch the waves at Rincon, and Chris noticed a small kid tearing the waves apart. Chris learned that he was Tom Curren, the son of longtime and legendary California surf pioneer Pat Curren.

Chris had always felt that California surfers should be faring better in the international surf community. But now, for the first time, he could actually see promise on the horizon in emerging young surfers like Brad and Tom. Chris figured if anyone could lead the way, they could—and it would not be long.

One thing was certain. Professional surfing would continue to evolve, with or without Chris O'Rourke. He knew that going to Australia could be his final chance to maintain any kind of status. Traveling there would hard on his body, and he could only pray something positive would come out of it.

In early March, armed with a few surfboards and wetsuits, Jil drove Chris to the Los Angeles International Airport. There was so much uncertainty in their lives, and it was taking its toll on both of them.

Chris didn't have much time to dwell on it. With his limited mobility, he had been allowed to board his plane early. He never noticed the surfer standing in line right behind him. But Joey Buran had certainly noticed him. Though their relationship had improved, it had been several months since the two had spoken. Given his relationship with God, by now Chris had pretty much buried the hatchet.

Joey, however, wasn't aware of Chris's religious transformation and hoped he didn't have to sit anywhere near Chris on the long flight to Australia. Chris finally noticed him coming down the aisle and sensed Joey's nervousness as he searched for his seat. As fate would have it, they were right next to each other.

Two former rival surfers, their respective lives going in opposite directions, forced to be next to each other on a twelve-hour flight.

In reality, Joey had nothing to worry about. Religion had made Chris a changed man, and harboring negativity only drained his energy further. He was no longer outwardly aggressive, but he could not resist having a little fun with his seatmate. Chris knew he would never get the chance to surf against him in a heat, but sitting next to Joey on an international flight provided other opportunities.

For the next twelve hours, Chris made it a point to get under his skin any way he could. He began by telling Joey how he had found the Lord and how it had changed his life. All the while, Joey kept thinking to himself, "Why is this guy telling me all this? After all, I'm Joey Buran, and I'm a hot surfer. You're Chris O'Rourke, and maybe you need Jesus, but I don't."

Shortly into the flight, Joey knew he had a problem. He was trapped, and Chris wasn't about to let him off the hook. Unable to take his incessant talking any longer, Joey rose from his seat and told Chris he needed to use the bathroom. His real intention was to search for another empty seat on the plane, but the 747 was completely full. Joey had no choice other than to return and sit next to Chris, who by now was eagerly waiting for him.

"So Joey, what are you going to do after surfing?" asked Chris.

"I don't know. I haven't really thought much about it," he replied.

Each time Joey looked over, he saw Chris staring at him.

"So how's it going for you so far?" Chris continued.

Joey just stared straight ahead, wondering why he was asking that.

"You know what I mean, on the tour and stuff. How's it going?" Chris said again.

Joey knew the next several hours were going to feel like an eternity. He began to feel sleepy and closed his eyes. If he were sleeping, perhaps Chris would leave him alone. But then he felt someone tugging lightly on his shirt sleeve. He opened his eyes and saw Chris's face about six inches away.

"Hey Joey, I need some help. Can you put some of this lotion on my back?" Chris asked.

Stunned, Joey took a deep breath. How was he going to get out of this?

"Uh, what's that, Chris, something about lotion? What do you need all that lotion for anyway?" he asked.

"Since my cancer treatments dry out my skin, I have to use this lotion all the time. I can't reach my neck and back. So can you do it?"

Trying not to appear insensitive, Joey put up his best protest but was helpless. Chris turned sideways in his seat and asked Joey to lift up his shirt. Joey reluctantly opened the bottle, poured some lotion into his hands, and began applying it to Chris's back. Though he meant no disrespect, Joey felt as if he were touching death.

It must have been quite a sight. Had Chris been healthy, the two pro surfers would have continued their fierce and bitter rivalry. Life, however, had changed all that. Everything was now reduced to this moment in time: Joey spreading lotion on Chris's back while flying over the Pacific Ocean. Chris continued telling Joey about the ways of the Lord. But this time, for whatever reason, Joey actually listened. He found himself captivated by some of Chris's words and, while it would not take root for several years, a seed was planted.

Still, when the plane finally landed in Sydney, Joey made a hasty departure through the nearest exit.

Chris was met by Jim Banks, and together they took the short flight on to Melbourne. Physically and mentally drained, Chris was nonetheless thrilled to return to the Gold Coast. He was so excited he hardly slept.

The next morning, he went to Burleigh Heads with several other California surfers. The IPS Stubbies contest was still several days away, but everyone was eager to get in some practice. Chris wanted to get out there, too. But with the jet lag from the long flight finally kicking in, he simply had no energy. Instead, he found solace by sitting on the bluff in the shade, watching everyone else. He would rest now and paddle out tomorrow.

Fate, however, had other plans. Chris returned to Burleigh Heads the following day but never entered the water. Out of nowhere, while talking with several of the pros, horrible thoughts crept into his mind, and he became terrified. It suddenly dawned upon him that he was now a long way from his home, his wife and his son—the true anchors in his life.

Chris began to wonder why he had even come. Jil had supported his decision, but what choice did she really have? Chris realized he had been selfish. Jil had been there for him for nearly four years through thick and thin. And this was how he rewarded her? He almost couldn't fault her if she was beginning to waver.

Suddenly, the waves at Burleigh Heads were no longer important. The thought of being away from his family overwhelmed him. He collapsed to the ground and was rushed to the nearest hospital. The doctors were told of Chris's condition but were unable to determine exactly what was wrong with him. Their initial conclusion was that Chris was exhausted and had suffered a panic attack. But there was something more.

Feeling there was nothing more they could do, they recommended he return to the U.S. After finally making it all the way to Australia, three days later Chris was now heading back home. His feet never even touched the ocean.

When Jim Banks heard that his friend had left the country, he didn't know what to think. What had happened? Would he ever see Chris again? Whatever the circumstances were, the contests in Australia marched on, and Chris missed out on the debut of perhaps the most innovative technological concept in surfing history. On April 18, during the Bells contest in Victoria, Australian surfer Simon Anderson revealed the "three-fin thruster" surfboard to the world and forever changed the future of surfing.

Chris had way more important things on his mind—like how much longer he was going to live. After returning to California, he was promptly readmitted to Scripps Hospital. Initially doctors agreed he'd had an anxiety attack. But further tests revealed something much more disturbing. The cancer had returned to his spine yet again, and he would have to endure another operation.

The bad news didn't stop there. Not all of the tumor could be removed. In a sea of bad dreams, this was the worst possible nightmare.

"That's enough," Chris decided.

He told his doctors there would be no further treatments. His frail body simply couldn't take it any more.

When Lyn heard the news, she was heartbroken. She immediately called her parents and brother back east to break the sad news. Chris's mother began to cry. Jil, too, was devastated. Little Tim was still too young to comprehend what was really going on.

"Timmy just thinks Daddy lives in the hospital," Jil would say.

For the woman who braved her soul to help her husband, this latest setback seemed all too inevitable. Jil had seen him overcome so many things before, but now she sensed that it wasn't going to happen any longer. She was scared, but as a believer in Christ the Lord, she remained optimistic that another miracle was out there somewhere.

Chris thanked God that he still had a wife and a son who were healthy. He spent the next two weeks in the hospital and then went home. He had refused further treatment, and there was nothing more his doctors could do. They estimated he had three to six months to live.

As Lyn drove her brother home from the hospital, it was clear Chris had begun to accept his fate.

"Lyn, even with all this pain, I am still alive, at least for now. I'm going to die, but it's okay. Having found the Lord really has helped me to deal with all of this," he told her.

While Chris may have given up, others refused to do so. His physicians at Scripps told Chris he could resume his treatments at any time. The surfing community of San Diego came forward to help as well. A group of surfers organized an international funds drive for him and raised a significant amount to help pay his bills. The worldwide surfing media covered him extensively. I produced a ten-page color article that was published in Surf

Magazine Japan, along with an eight-page feature for Breakout, a new California-based publication.

"The Friends of Chris O'Rourke Foundation" was spearheaded by Ed Wright and Chris Ahrens. The two men determined that any chance he had at survival required a new environment, so Ed invited Chris and his family to move into his home in Encinitas. Most of the time, Chris couldn't walk or sit up for longer than five minutes. There was little flesh or muscle left on his bones. Chris Ahrens was there to help him nearly every day.

With Chris having ruled out chemotherapy, the foundation devised an alternative approach of their own and actively sought professional help from people in the holistic health field. Chris was put on a rigorous diet that consisted purely of fruits, vegetables and massive amounts of vitamins. The idea was to surround him with a healing environment while rejuvenating any good cells remaining in his body.

When I visited, I found his spiritual enlightenment inspiring. In spite of approaching his darkest hours, he somehow pulled it all together. For awhile, he was vintage Chris, cracking jokes and complaining mightily about his nutrition regimen.

"I ate something yesterday that tasted like camel food. But it did make me feel better. These guys seem to know what they're doing. I am so lucky and can only say God bless to all of them," he told me.

The effort that Ed Wright and Chris Ahrens put forth was nothing less than extraordinary. They put their own lives on hold to try and save his. Finally, though, Ed and his family began to feel the strain of having the O'Rourkes in their home. So he began searching for a new place for them to live.

Soon, however, Chris contracted pneumonia. Lyn knew her brother had no choice other than to return to Scripps. His doctors candidly told her that only a miracle would save him now—and it would need to come soon. She stayed the entire first night with him, and the two talked for hours.

"It feels like drowning," he told her.

"Well, Chris, as a surfer I guess you would know. And I'm sorry," she said, starting to cry.

"It's funny because I'm scared to death of drowning. This one time at Blacks, on a really big day, I was held down for such a long time. It was dark and turbulent, and I was really scared."

Chris looked at his sister with clear blue eyes that instantly pierced her heart.

"I'm going to die, Lyn. I wasn't sure before. Now I'm sure," he said.

"Don't say that, Chris." Lyn's heart was pounding, and her palms were wet.

"It's okay. I have done everything in life I wanted. Lots of people never get to do anything they want and live to be really old," he said. "Hey, do you remember what a jerk I used to be? I've decided that, even though I have truly changed as a person, I still had to pay a price for all the bad things I did in the past."

"I used to have such a bad attitude. Then I was the one who became the geek," he continued. "Do you remember that one time when I got out of the hospital? My head was shaved, and I had stitches across my skull. I looked like Frankenstein's monster! Some guy at Swami's said to me, 'Hey man, where did you get your tan?' So I told him on the moon."

"Are you scared?' asked Lyn.

"No. Well, maybe a little. But being afraid hasn't stopped me before."

That much was certainly true.

Lyn noticed Chris's hat on the table. She recalled how he had always worn that hat like a crown, covering what he lacked, celebrating what he had. In spite of everything that had happened, he genuinely had enjoyed his life.

The following morning, I stopped in for a visit. As usual, Chris appeared upbeat. He smiled and joked, and we talked a lot about surfing.

"Hey Aeder, remember that one time I saw you at the Shores after school? You were such a little jock-head back then," he said.

We both laughed.

"Yeah, I guess I was. But I will admit to you, Chris, when I first saw people surfing, I thought it was kind of a stupid thing, too," I replied.

"You know something, Aeder? There was a time when I thought that, too. I couldn't figure out what the big deal was. I told my brother that surfing was for goons. Then I realized that all those waves in the ocean shouldn't go to waste, that someone should be riding them in the final moments of their lives, and that person should be me," he said proudly.

For several moments, we both reflected on what he had just said.

"When I was young, I learned about life by trial and error. Judging from where I am now, I must have made a lot of mistakes," Chris said.

"Don't say that, Chris," I told him, trying to ease the pain he felt inside.

"Hey is Mark Richards still your favorite surfer?" he asked, changing the subject and mood.

"No, he's number two now. Some kook from California is at the top of my list. His last name is Irish...O'Rourke, or something like that," I smiled.

We both laughed a bit more, something that was not easy for him. Sometimes his laughing would turn into coughing, and I could tell he had a lot of pain in his chest.

"Hey Chris, I'm sorry, but I have to go to class now. I'll come again soon, okay? Hang in there, buddy."

"I'm trying, Aeder, I'm really trying," he sighed.

It was the last real conversation I would ever have with him.

That night as I drifted off to sleep, I reflected upon everything he had been through in his life: the family turmoil of his younger years, the surfing, the competition, the localism, his new family, and all the unfortunate setbacks. Full of ups and downs, his was a hard life for me to imagine. And it was coming to an end far too soon.

Chapter 33

Undercurrents

May 26, 1981

Soft beams of early morning sunlight filtered through the thin white curtains as Chris opened his eyes. It had been a long night with only snatches of restless sleep and waking nightmares. He was happy to see the morning finally arrive and to have survived for one more day.

Suddenly, Chris felt blindsided by uncertainty. Where was he again? Turning his head on the starched cotton pillowcase, he saw the machines next to his bed. Then he remembered—he was in the hospital attached to machines that kept him up all night with their endless whirring, beeping and blinking.

Despite the beads of sweat drenching his face and neck, he felt cold—a combination of fever and fear. The fear came most often when he was alone in his room, listening to the machines, listening to his own pulse. Being scared was nothing new. He'd been afraid countless times before, but he'd never shown it. Ask the surfing crew at Windansea. He'd fought his way into the peak by not showing fear. He'd battled his way through every swell, every wave, every stupid parking lot brawl, every spitting confrontation with the outsiders. Through it all, he'd been so angry, so desperate to establish his place in the hierarchy. It had always been his nature to fight—just like he had fought the terrible thing going on inside his body for the past four years.

He tried to sit up but was too weak and exhausted. He fell back onto the pillows. He remembered when his body used to do everything he wanted it to do——and so many things even he didn't know it could do. At one point in his life, he had had such strength, balance, and grace. Well, those sure as hell were gone now. All that remained were the guts.

Coughs wracked his body. Pneumonia, the latest in a long series of setbacks, had now invaded his weakened lungs. He was engaged in a final grand battle for his body and soul, and he was tired of the fight.

"I pray to you, Lord, either give me my good health back or take me from this world. I'm no use to my wife and son like this."

He suddenly found it difficult to breathe, as if he were in the midst of a two-wave hold down underwater. He'd always come up for air. He never felt more alive than when he was in the ocean.

But now, he felt life slipping away.

In the distance, he heard a familiar voice.

"Chris, you're awake! I was so worried. How are you feeling, honey?"

He turned his face away from the bright light of the window and peered into the room. Jil sat slumped in a chair, weary after another sleepless night.

Chris tried to speak, but his voice was weak and hoarse. Seeing him struggling to breathe, Jil leaned in close. Chris reached for her hand, and she took hold of his firmly.

"What are you trying to tell me, Chris?"

He found it so hard to even think clearly, let alone speak.

"I just wanted to tell you...how much I hate these hospital rooms," he gasped, gulping for air. "And...I also want to tell you...how much I love you."

Jil's tears bounced silently off the stiff sheets.

"Chris, I love you, too."

Like all of us, Jil had seen Chris win so many times. But she knew he was losing this battle.

"Fight it, Chris. Don't slip away," Jil told him, fighting to smile through her tears. "I'll go get the doctors and tell them you're awake, ok?"

She headed for the door when Chris spoke again.

"Jil, I love you more than anything else in the whole world, and...I'm not ready to die just yet."

With tears streaming down her face, Jil couldn't bear to turn around. She hastily set out to find the doctor.

As she made a hasty retreat out the door, Chris's eyes followed her.

She returned with two physicians just as Chris's anger swelled one last time. He somehow picked up a large crystal vase full of flowers and hurled it against the wall, sending hundreds of wet glass shards across the floor. Indignation surged like an electric current throughout his withered body. This final act of defiance took all his energy, and Chris collapsed back onto his bed.

The lines on the monitor screens all went flat.

More physicians hurried in to revive him. The next few moments for Jil were a blur of shock, remorse, panic, and pandemonium. Her mind was reeling. Please God, bring him back to me. Seconds seemed like minutes, minutes like hours. Then, Jil finally heard the words she was praying for.

"We've got a pulse. We've got him back."

Chris was only slightly conscious but heard the commotion around him. He struggled to speak.

"I'm back? Back from where, Jil?"

Confusing thoughts leapt into Chris's mind.

That afternoon, I was in the midst of finals week at UCSD, and I hadn't seen Chris for a week. I knew he was back in the hospital, but his tenacity had always been strong. Every time he went into the hospital, he always came right back out. He seemed almost indestructible. Knowing how Chris had always defied the odds, I had little reason to think this time was any different.

After lunch, I decided to take a much-needed break from the books. I needed to stimulate my senses, and the ocean was the obvious choice. The sun blazed as I made the short drive north from La Jolla to Torrey Pines State Beach in Del Mar. A westerly swell of waves was breaking near the shore; small, but good enough to go body-surfing. I ran across the soft wet sand and submerged myself in the cool water. Feeling that first wave break over my body, I knew this was what I needed. I gazed out to sea and saw a large pod of dolphins splashing and playing around. Free and uninhibited, they rode the waves like surfers could only dream of doing. I thought of Chris. He would be here right now, if he only could.

I body-surfed a perfect wave nearly all the way to shore. Rejuvenated, I turned and watched the dolphins as they moved swiftly down the coast before finally disappearing from sight. It seemed odd how at that very moment the mood of the entire day began to change. Out of nowhere, a thick fog bank formed near shore. The gray curtain of humidity reduced visibility to nearly nothing. A cold onshore wind ruffled the ocean's surface and drove me from the water.

Walking toward the beach parking lot, I shivered almost uncontrollably. I quickly got into my car, turned on the heater, and began changing into my clothes. Another eerie feeling washed over me. Was it just the fog and wind? Or could something else explain that pit in my stomach? Something certainly seemed amiss, but I had no idea what.

In just a few days, I would complete my third year of college. Maybe I'm just feeling guilty about taking a break from studying, I thought. But on the drive back to La Jolla, just past the Torrey Pines Golf Course, I felt that strange sensation again. The order of the world as I knew it was being altered somehow. Alongside the road ahead, towering eucalyptus trees cast ominous late afternoon shadows, flickering bands of light and darkness.

I thought of Chris for a second time. There seemed no doubt that these strange feelings had something to do with him. Was he trying to send me a message?

Rapidly approaching the intersection of Genesee Avenue and Torrey Pines Road, I faced a crossroads. Should I turn right and resume studying, or go straight and head to Scripps Hospital? The strange force beckoned again. The decision was made for me.

Less than a minute later, I crossed over the freeway and could see the hospital looming in the distance. I thought about how my mother had been treated for cancer there and won. Chris hasn't been as fortunate. His battle had changed my entire outlook on life.

It was the same for all of us—Mark McCoy, Jim Neri, Tim Senneff, Ted Smith, Mark Ruyle, and Oscar Bayetto. We were entirely different people now compared to the first time we met him. If ever I was having a bad day, all I had to do was think about how Chris handled all the adversity that came his way. That set me straight real quick.

A few minutes later, I pulled into a parking spot close to the tall brick medical building. The hospital was over three miles from the sea, but the thick fog bank had followed me all the way here. I walked briskly towards the entrance, feeling the cold sea breeze blowing strongly. The winds whipped up a carpet of dry leaves that swirled around my legs. The start of summer was less than a month away, but suddenly it seemed more like winter. I quickened my step.

Over the past four years, I had visited Chris here so many times I lost count. Sometimes I would sneak in a pint of ice cream and Milano cookies and watch his eyes light up. I was continually amazed at how he always seemed to end up in the same room. The routine it took for me to get there never varied: straight through the main lobby, take the elevator to the third floor, turn right and go down the hall past the attendant's station to room 312.

This time, however, my journey felt much different.

I slowly pushed the door open. To my surprise, the room was empty. I walked back to the nurse's station and found two attendants shuffling through a stack of medical charts.

"Excuse me. Can you please tell me what room Chris O'Rourke is in?"

They exchanged brief, grim looks.

"Mr. O'Rourke is in the intensive care unit, two floors up," one explained. "But I'm afraid you can't go in there. I'm sorry to tell you this, but...it is not looking good for him right now."

Not looking good? Was that as bad as it sounded? I felt myself go numb. Where had all the dolphins gone?

"Sir?" she asked. "Are you a family member? Sir?"

In my sudden, mindless stupor, it took me several seconds to respond.

"No, no, I'm not a family member. I am his friend. Is there anyone else there with him?"

"His wife, sister, and one or two others," she replied.

"If you don't mind, could you tell them that Kirk is here? And ask if it is okay for me to come inside?"

The attendant picked up a telephone, and after a lengthy conversation, I was allowed to proceed. At the ICU, another attendant greeted me.

"It's okay. You can go in there now," she said softly.

Chapter 34

Return to the Sea

"Honey, Kirk is here," Jil said.

I was in some sort of time warp. An entire lifetime passed. Yet there was no mistaking what was taking place before me now. Chris was hooked up to a respirator, and his breaths came intermittently with only a faint pulse on the monitor. With tears streaming down her face, Jil held his hands tightly. Chris often told me that Jil's resilience and strength enabled him to survive as long as he had.

The entire scene appeared so surreal, as if I were watching a movie.

"Be strong, my brother. The storm is almost over," Lyn whispered to him.

For now I could only stare at my friend helplessly. I tried to envision him in a better place, somewhere with an endless supply of waves. After everything he had been through, Chris certainly deserved that. My mind was reeling.

Chris, do you know where we are? You've always been a prisoner of your own soul. There is no going back, only forward, yet my own life seems to begin and end with you, too. What am I going to do now? You suffered, that's for sure, but you shouldn't be denied. And you won't.

"Hey Kirk, could you go call some of his other friends? Everyone should know what's going on," Lyn said softly, waking me from my stupor.

I quickly found the nearest phone. The first person I called was Tim Bessell, then Mark McCoy, Eric Huffman, and Tim Senneff. They each called others, who then did the same. As word spread, a steady stream of friends began to arrive. Some went into his room while others waited outside the door.

Several rows of his friends and supporters formed around his bed. Some of us stood stoically by; others wept openly. Then one of the machines Chris was hooked up to started beeping. I looked at one of the monitors; there was no pulse. A doctor and nurse rushed in and quickly asked everyone who was not family to leave the room. At first no one moved—it was so hard to leave—until the doctor's request became a demand.

Before leaving, I looked back at Lyn, who nodded at me as if to say it was all going to be okay. Nearly fifty people had gathered in the hallway. Time stood still, and we all offered a vigil of prayers. Heartfelt cries echoed from within the room.

Just before Chris passed away, Lyn noticed a tear flowing from his right eye, stretching down the length of his cheek. Like the last wave in a set, our friend's long odyssey had finally come to an end.

As tears filled her eyes, Jil whispered into his ear. "I love you Chris, and I'm really sorry."

It was Lyn who noticed that one of the machines attached to him turned back on. Although Chris had been dead for several minutes, Jil's words appeared to revive him, if only for a couple of seconds.

"My God Jil, he was trying to answer you," said Lyn.

By the time Jil turned back to look, the lines had already gone flat again, this time for good. She stayed by his side for several minutes and then left the room, sobbing uncontrollably. We tried to comfort her as best we could. It all seemed like a bad dream. The disbelief that Chris had finally passed continued to linger among us.

Right then, I couldn't help but question the purpose of life. Rather than prolong Chris's agony for four years, why couldn't he have just died right away? What had been the purpose of all this? Why had God allowed it to happen?

What I didn't realize until much later was that there had been a purpose in it all. Chris wanted me and everyone else to know it, too. His brief life had sent a message to us—not just in the surf community but all over the world—that giving up in life is never an option. He had always lived for the moment, and while he hadn't exactly been an angel in his younger years, at the end he had turned into one for all of us. And from this day forward, we knew Chris would watch over all his friends and family.

As tears continued to be shed, a nurse advised Lyn that, while her brother had passed away, the hospital staff could not officially pronounce him deceased until the doctor arrived. I asked Lyn if it would be alright for me to go back inside his room.

"Of course, Kirk," she said.

Intent upon giving final respect to my great friend, I opened the door. Except for Chris's lifeless body on the bed, the room was now completely empty. Tears welled in my eyes like never before, running down my cheeks like open fire hydrants. Nothing I had ever felt before in my life had prepared me for this. At least he was now in a state of bliss.

"You're home now, Chris. I hope the surf is six to eight feet, perfect, and you get all the waves you want," I said quietly.

I touched his lifeless body one last time and didn't want to let go. The moment lasted only seconds, but it was very special for me. On a day when all of life's youthful innocence had come crashing down, I discovered that we really aren't immortal after all. It was a profound realization of how complex life and death could really be. Chris would not want us to be sad, though. He wanted us to see the beautiful side of his life—along with the fighting spirit that exists within all of us.

During those first few hours after his death, we all grew up quickly. Several of us milled around the hospital, reluctant to leave. Finally, one by one, we began to depart. Lyn stayed to meet Chris's parents, who were flying in from North Carolina. She would have to break the news to them that their youngest son didn't make it.

Chris's brother Bart and his grandmother Elbertine stayed behind in North Carolina. The news would be tragic for them, too, especially for Elbertine. In her lifetime, she had lost her husband, her son, and now her grandson. No woman should ever have to go through that. Jim Neri received the news of his best friend's death, too, and immediately began driving down the coast from San Luis Obispo.

That evening when I finally left the hospital, my mind was completely numb. Driving back home was a blur, but I recalled briefly stopping by my girlfriend Diana's house in the Shores. I rang the doorbell. When her mom opened the door, she took one look at my face and knew.

"Uh-oh, you look like you have some very sad news. I'm sorry, Kirk."

Later that night, between attempts to regain my composure, I called various people to spread the news—my parents, Don Craig at Rip Curl, and shaper Bill Barnfield in Hawaii. Sleep wasn't easy, but I was able to get a little rest. The next morning upon awakening I prayed his death had all just been a bad dream. But I knew that it wasn't.

A few days later, the official cause of his death was released. In his weakened physical state, pneumonia brought on by cancer had taken his life.

Several days later, Chris's funeral took place at the La Jolla Presbyterian Church. Lyn, Jil, and Jim organized the service. One of Chris's favorite songs, "The Secret of Life" by James Taylor, was played as well-wishers walked down the aisles. The lyrics seemed very appropriate:

The secret of life is enjoying the passage of time...such a lovely ride.

Chris's parents were present, but his brother Bart was still grieving hard and did not attend. The church was filled to capacity with a mix of his family, friends, and people who had never met him, yet knew of his heroic will to survive. Many people stood in the pathway outside. Standing room only at his funeral—Chris would have been impressed. I felt proud for him that so many people attended.

His cremated ashes had been placed inside a plain brown box, so Jim and Lyn searched for something that would better reflect his spirit. Jim located some Christmas wrapping paper and quickly covered the box. Lyn and Jim figured Chris would have gotten a kick out of that.

In spite of the solemn occasion, we celebrated his brief time on earth. A number of people spoke, but every time I tried to stand up and say something, I sat right back down. It was just too hard. Jil stood remarkably strong. When the church ceremony concluded, everyone went to Windansea. The tears quickly turned to cheers when we paddled his ashes out into the lineup at Right Hooker. Nearly seventy surfers formed a tight circle around Jim, who held the small box of Chris's ashes.

We held our hands together so tightly that not even the tug of the ocean swells could pull us apart. All of our crew was there: Tim Bessell, Eric Huffman, Ted Smith, Mark McCoy, Bob Andrews, Mark Brolaski, Tim Senneff, and many others. Hundreds lined the shore. Chris's remarkable story had drawn them all there.

Out in the ocean, Jim began to speak.

"All of us are here for a reason. Chris was your friend, as he was mine. He wants none of us to ever forget what happened. So live the rest of your lives knowing that he is in a better place now. And every time you paddle out, not just here at Windansea, but in every ocean around the world, any wave you surf upon, he will there be with you. Chris doesn't want us to be sad, but to proudly move forward in each of our lives."

No sooner had Jim finished speaking than the cloudy skies overhead revealed a faint patch of blue, which slowly became larger. A large flock of pelicans glided by in perfect flight formation and dipped their wings simultaneously as if offering their salute. A few dolphins broke the water's surface outside the wave lineup. They all felt like signs.

Jim opened the box and emptied his ashes. At first, the particles clung tightly to the surface, and then gently descended to mix with the undercurrents of the sea. Many of us placed flowers into the water, creating a field of color. Chris's physical being was gone, but his soul still felt very much alive. And he was finally at peace.

During the entire time we had been out there, not one set of waves had passed through. But just as Chris's ashes finally dropped out of sight, a few bumps formed outside the lineup, then a few more. Moments later a non-stop set of waves poured in that seemed to go on forever. We rode them to honor Chris, hooting at the top of our lungs.

Finally, I paddled in. Tim Bessell and Eric Huffman emerged from the water, too, and came over to where I was standing.

"How nice was that?" said Eric.

"That was so beautiful. And man, how about that set of waves! Where did that come from? That had to be Chris," Tim replied.

Soon the rest of the crew had gathered around, too. For a long time, we all just stared at the ocean. Not a word more was said. We gave each other hugs and pats on the back. Cancer may have robbed professional surfing of a world-class athlete, but more importantly, it had robbed us of our friend and the most genuine person we would ever meet.

Chris made a difference, that much was sure. Talented yet tormented, by the end of his short life, he made us all better people, each in our own way.

Over time, I emerged from my shell and transformed into a more confident person. Tim Senneff turned to competitive surfing as a tribute and, like Chris, found Jesus Christ. Mark McCoy found his passion in music, diligently pursued it, and ended up as the guitarist for Iggy Pop's band. Jim Neri followed his dream of becoming an architect, something Chris had once suggested. Oscar Bayetto changed his name to Ozstar De Jourday and became one of the best real estate agents in La Jolla. Ted Smith became more resilient in his endeavors. Mark Ruyle married and started a family.

Chris's exit from this world was as tumultuous as his entry: dark and stormy. In the days and weeks following his funeral, the outpouring of community support, especially from those who never even knew him, was astounding. The list of lives Chris had touched around the world was long and diverse, ranging from the most novice of surfers, to his peers, to people who had nothing to do with surfing at all. He had engaged life in only one way: straight on. Lyn summed it all up best:

"My parents' struggles with their own lives had a huge impact upon Chris. His brief time on this earth had all seemed so biblical, so redemptive to me. It goes far beyond surfing, or even the fight to survive against all odds. I felt that when Chris died, everyone else's lives began. His story would not have been complete by living, but by dying," Lyn told me. "His friends, and others he didn't even know, saw him as an inspiration and a redemptive figure. We all saw life differently because of his presence in it, like a Jesus figure that compels people to continue his story throughout time. Chris once said to me, 'I wonder if maybe through my suffering somebody else's stripes will be healed.' He was referring to the Jewish Prophet Isaiah who mentioned about the coming Messiah by saying, 'Through his stripes they will be healed,' while referring to the Hebrews."

Chris always seemed to be reaching out for that brass ring but landing in the dirt instead. Yet even when life was slipping away, he somehow still showed a lot of grace and clarity. Chris may not have lived long, but he did live passionately and in the moment—in much the same way a unique wave rises once to a peak of power, beauty, and destructive force and then collapses to become a memorable mist, both intense and unforgettable. Sometimes God takes a man to deeper water not to terrify but to cleanse him.

A month after Chris's passing, Cheyne Horan won the IPS Gunston 500 surfing contest at Jeffrey's Bay in South Africa. While accepting his trophy, Cheyne delivered an inspiring speech about the late Chris O'Rourke. He dedicated the win to him and asked that Chris's battle inspire the world's surfers for a long time to come.

Every year in every sport, whether team or individual, there can only be one world champion. Once he faced exclusion, but now Chris is finally redeemed. He wasn't able to achieve his dream, but Chris did become a champion in another way— through his deft ability to rise, and rise again.

THE END

Surfing Champ Chris O'Rourke Dies
Cancer Finally Claims 22-Year-Old La Jollan

By NANCY RAY, *Times Staff Writer*

LA JOLLA — Chris O'Rourke, the 22-year-old champion surfer, lost his battle with cancer Tuesday.

He died at Scripps Memorial Hospital where he was being treated for pneumonia and complications from his most recent cancer surgery.

During the last four years, O'Rourke had undergone operations to his spine, spleen, lungs, and brain in his fight to stem the spread of cancer through his body.

Between operations and chemotherapy treatments, he continued the surfing career that had vaulted him into world competition at the age of 14.

O'Rourke's physician, Dr. Richard E. Anderson, said recently that the young man's will to live and to return to surfing had helped him overcome the physical and mental effects of Hodgkin's disease, cancer of the lymph glands.

As recently as March, O'Rourke had judged an Australian surfing competition, but had to return to Scripps for treatment when a recurring spinal tumor paralyzed him from the waist down.

After his release from the hospital four weeks ago, O'Rourke began a regimen of massive doses of vitamins and a vegetarian diet under the guidance of holistic medicine adherents.

Two surfing friends, Craig Wright and Chris Ahrens, started a fund drive for O'Rourke to help pay the expenses of the alternative treatments.

A benefit for O'Rourke was held Wednesday at the La Paloma Theater in Encinitas and another live concert by surf guitarist Dick Dale will be held at the La Paloma June 5 as part of the Encinitas Flower Festival.

Friends of O'Rourke say the concert is still scheduled but has been changed to a memorial for the surfer.

Ahrens and Wright plan to show slides of Chris competing in surfing events during the June 5 show.

Funds raised will be used to pay for O'Rourke's funeral and to care for his wife and son, Ahrens said.

"He had a terrific attitude," Ahrens said. "Just the day before he died in the hospital, he opened

Please see O'ROURKE, Page 12

Chris O'Rourke, A Champion, Fought For Life All The Way

By GREG GROSS
Staff Writer, The San Diego Union

A common euphemism for death by cancer is to say that its victim succumbed to the illness.

For the past four years, family members and friends watched as a painful lymph nodal cancer known as Hodgkin's disease reduced Chris O'Rourke from a muscular 18-year-old U.S. surfing champion to a bedridden 22-year-old paraplegic, paralyzed below the waist and able to breathe only with effort.

O'Rourke's response was to do upper-body exercises in his bed at Scripps Memorial Hospital, regale an increasing number of visitors and friends, and to tell his sister on Monday, "I can lick this thing so easily."

It can be said that La Jolla's Chris O'Rourke died quietly Tuesday evening from complications due to Hodgkin's disease. It cannot be said that he succumbed.

"It wasn't that he wasn't ready to die; he was," his sister, Lyn, said. "But as long as he was alive, he was going to fight to live."

A graduate of La Jolla High School, O'Rourke had begun surfing when he was 9, building a reputation and carving out his own "territory" among the waves off La Jolla's Windansea Beach before he was 13.

By the time he was 18, he was acknowledged as one of the world's top surfers, winning the U.S. championship in 1976 and 1977. He had several sponsors who supported his travels to the world's best beaches to meet the best surfers in international competition.

But just prior to a competition in Australia, O'Rourke's wife, Jill, discovered the lump on his neck that doctors diagnosed as Hodgkin's disease.

During his four years of treatment, during which he was in and out of hospitals, O'Rourke underwent eight major operations, including spinal, spleen and brain surgery. After the brain operation, he donned a hockey helmet and went out surfing.

His physical state deteriorated rapidly during the last two months, but to the last, O'Rourke never abandoned his search for a solution to his illness, trying treatments of holistic medicine and "natural" diets with friends who were skeptical about the worth of conventional cancer therapies.

He also refused to stay in the Scripps seventh-floor cancer ward, preferring the pediatric unit instead.

(Continued on B-5, Col. 1)

Chris O'Rourke

Child of the Storm

by Jim Neri
October, 1981

Of winter winds was born
The Child of the Storm
A wave wise ocean boy
To ride the sea with joy

The first of many lines
Who raced ahead of time
O'er trackless miles of brine
Between the sun and sea

A pulse of energy
Of liquid harmony
Without never any doubt
What he was meant to be

Fierce willed and temper short
Secure in place and sport
To earn him great rapport
With those who know the tide

But such is give and take
Those first are first to break
And left to their fate
Are not who decide

So on the reef was torn
The child of the storm
A wave wise ocean boy
Who rode the sea with joy

Aftermath

"I just hope that professional surfing grows because the surfers need it so much. They've put their lives into this sport."
—Chris O'Rourke, 1978

♦ ♦ ♦

Chris had eight major operations, which included surgery on his spine, brain, arms, and spleen, and countless chemotherapy and radiation treatments. He continued to surf through almost all of them. One particularly unfortunate part of Chris's situation was his allergic reaction to Penicillin and Dilantin, two drugs that really could have helped him.

♦ ♦ ♦

For a long time after his passing, I had little interest in continuing my pursuit of surf photography. With Chris no longer part of my world, there was little inspiration. Each time I went to Windansea, the waves looked empty to me. Soon I began to realize Chris would not want me to quit altogether, as he had once conveyed to me. I resumed taking photos of surfing, but not with the same fervor—and rarely at Windansea.

♦ ♦ ♦

In 1984, the IPS changed its name to ASP (Association of Surfing Professionals). The pro tour that travels around the world today continues at a significantly higher level for both men and women. California's Tom Curren went on to win three world titles. During the 1980s, Tom's influence upon Kelly Slater, a young prolific surfer from Florida, was undeniable. Kelly has since rewritten the record books by winning an amazing eleven world titles and counting. Another American surfer, the late Andy Irons from Hawaii, also won three world titles. Surfing is now flourishing as a professional sport like never before.

◆ ◆ ◆

In 1985, I moved to Hawaii. My surfing photography would live on, just not around La Jolla. But I did name my photojournalism company after him. IMOCO Media (In Memory of Chris O'Rourke) still exists, and the photo credit has appeared in numerous magazines and publishing companies around the world. And after all these years, I'm still listed as a Contributing Photographer for Surfer Magazine.

◆ ◆ ◆

In 1985, Gloria O'Rourke started acting strangely. At first, Lyn and Bart thought their mother had begun drinking again. But the sad fact was she had started to lose her mind. A year later, Gloria was institutionalized, where she lived for the next fourteen years. Her husband, Bart, developed Parkinson's disease, became confined to a wheelchair and died five months later. In an odd twist of fate, it wasn't Parkinson's that killed him, but pneumonia, the same as his son.

◆ ◆ ◆

Among the individuals mentioned in this story, Chris was not the only one who would tragically succumb to the ravages of cancer. Bill Caster passed away from colon cancer in March 1987, Mark McCoy from stomach cancer in 1995, and Surfing magazine photo editor Larry 'Flame' Moore from a brain tumor in October 2005. Another well-known professional surfer not mentioned here, Rell Sunn from Hawaii (the Queen of Makaha), passed away from breast cancer in January 1998.

◆ ◆ ◆

And, in an ironic twist of fate, Joey Buran, once Chris's hated rival, went on to become a minister in a Southern California church where he remains today. He states that Chris's incessant conversations with him on their flight to Australia triggered his faith. Joey has also coached the United States surfing team on several occasions. Both Joey Buran and Brad Gerlach had very successful professional surfing careers.

◆ ◆ ◆

In 1998, a video/DVD titled Changes was released onto the market by Walking On Water Film Productions. The documentary about Christian surfers featured Skip Frye, Tom Curren, Joey Buran, Tim Curran, CT Taylor, board shaper John Carper, and the late Chris O'Rourke. The film also provided an insider's look at Windansea, one of the most localized surf spots in the entire United States. Since Chris's passing, however, localism at Windansea has subsided dramatically.

◆ ◆ ◆

Quiksilver went on to become a $2.5 billon company that today still operates like a little family operation. Bob McKnight remains the company's CEO, and his passion for surfing is undeniable. The Quiksilver Foundation focuses on supporting agencies that provide for children, science, education, the ocean and environment. Educating people about caring for their planet is its goal.

Providing Hope Against an Unpredictable Enemy

If Chris O'Rourke were surfing today, he'd likely be riding a much thinner, lighter board. His wetsuit would be constructed from ultra-elasticized material that enhances flexibility and stretches with movement. On really cold days, he could insert a battery-powered heating panel inside the suit for extra warmth. And thanks to advanced radar and satellite technology, he'd know days in advance where the next huge swell was going to hit, and the best time to catch it.

Just as technology has significantly improved the sport that Chris O'Rourke lived and loved, it has done the same for the disease that took his life. As a medical oncologist, I have been treating patients with Hodgkin's disease—now known as Hodgkin's lymphoma—for more than twenty years. We are no closer today to understanding what causes this disease than we were thirty years ago, nor are we able to screen for it. But we have made rapid and remarkable advancements in its diagnosis, treatment and supportive care. As a result, a disease that killed about sixty percent of patients in the 1970s is now highly treatable—and highly survivable.

When Chris developed Hodgkin's in 1977, the protocol for diagnosing the disease and determining how far the cancer had advanced—a process called staging—included a chest X-ray, a bone marrow aspiration and biopsy, and surgical removal of a lymph node and the spleen, which also were biopsied. Today, instead of a chest X-ray and spleen removal, we use non-invasive and far less toxic positron emission topography (PET) scans to create a 3-D image of the body. We inject a small amount of radioactive glucose (sugar) into the vein; cancerous cells attract glucose, so glucose concentrations on the scan tell us where to find the cancer.

We might also remove a lymph node, but instead of a biopsy, we now apply a panel of fifty antibodies that definitively tells us what type of cancer our patient has. If the PET scan is negative, we may do bone marrow aspiration and biopsy.

The staging results dictate the course of treatment for Hodgkin's lymphoma; the higher the stage, the more advanced the cancer.

Stage I is limited to one lymph node or a single organ.

Stage II affects a single organ or tissue and two different lymph nodes, but is still limited to an area of the body either above or below the diaphragm.

Stage III is found in lymph nodes both above and below the diaphragm.

Stage IV is the most advanced, with cancerous cells in one or more organs and tissues as well as lymph nodes.

For stage I and some stage II cases in which the cancer is in one area only, we would most likely use radiation therapy. For stages II, III and IV, we use chemotherapy almost entirely, as it travels through the bloodstream to reach all areas of the body. Today, there is less concern about long-term toxicity with chemotherapy than with radiation; once reserved for cancer in its most advanced stages, chemotherapy now is much safer and has fewer side effects than in the past. In addition, we now have much better supportive care, including improved medications to block side effects, such as low blood counts and infection. And thanks to newer medications and integrative therapies such as acupuncture, problems like nausea and vomiting have been nearly eliminated. As a result, safer, more effective chemotherapy regimens are becoming the treatment of choice for Hodgkin's patients, even with less advanced disease.

Should chemotherapy fail, however, the next step may be "salvage therapy" involving an autologous stem cell transplant. Developed in the 1980s, this treatment involves removing the patient's own stem cells and treating them to kill any cancer. The stem cells are then stored while the patient receives high doses of chemotherapy to kill resistant cancerous cells in the body. After the chemotherapy treatment, the stem cells are injected back into the patient.

Because of such incredible advances in medicine and technology, most young people like Chris O'Rourke who develop Hodgkin's lymphoma today have a much brighter future. Today, ninety percent of those with Hodgkin's lymphoma have at least a five-year survival rate, and most go on to have successful careers, healthy families, and full lives.

Will we get to one hundred percent? Probably not. Cancer comes in many forms, with a wide range of treatments and success rates. For some Hodgkin's lymphoma patients, treatment simply does not work.

It is always hard to lose a patient. It is especially hard to lose a patient like Chris: young, vibrant, full of life with an incredible future ahead. Fortunately, it doesn't happen often—but when it does, we are left wondering how to make sense of such a loss.

It is this search for meaning and understanding that led me on a very personal journey during the summer of 2009. I traveled to Assisi, Italy, to study the effect of spirituality in health care. For thousands of years, people have used prayer to help the ill. We don't know how or if it works. We do know—and clinical studies have shown—that simply sitting at the bedside of a sick person and providing a healing presence is a hugely strong spiritual intervention. There is more research on the role of prayer in health care and healing underway. If nothing more, prayer may help give meaning to those who lose loved ones like Chris O'Rourke, and reason to believe that all of our lost loved ones have completed the journey they were meant to have in this world and have moved on to the next.

> —James Sinclair, MD, Medical Director of the Stevens Cancer Center at Scripps Memorial Hospital La Jolla

Acknowledgments

While growing up in La Jolla, I had some of the best times of my life. Though for the past twenty-seven years I've called Hawaii—the birthplace of surfing—my home, a few times each year I still return to La Jolla and reminisce with my old friends. Chris's name always comes up and seems to bring his spirit back to life. Nearly everyone I interviewed for this book said the same thing about him: He liked to drive fast! It's easy to understand why. His entire life was accelerated. He really only had a chance to live for the moment.

This book would not have been possible without the assistance of the following individuals; Ray Allen, Dr. Richard Anderson, Jim Banks, Jeanne Bellezzo, Tim Bessell, Brew Briggs, Shauna Buffington, Joey Buran, Scot Cherry, Chrome Digital, Ozstar DeJourday (formerly Oscar Bayetto), Paul Diamond, Sam George, Brad Gerlach, Dave Gilovich, Dr. Richard Hall, Hans Hedemann, Ernie Higgins, Michael Ho, Cheyne Horan, Eric Huffman, Rick Irons, Drew Kampion, the La Jolla Historical Society, Tim Lynch, Steve Malcolm, Matthew Martin, Kelly McLaurin, Willy Morris, Bob McKnight, Bob Mignogna, Robert Mitchell, Jim Neri, Bart O'Rourke, Lyn O'Rourke, Tom Ortner, Leslie Osment, Rikki Pearson, Mike Purpus, Dennis Reiter, Dave and Marlene Reynolds, Peter Townend, Allen Sarlo, Tim Senneff, Eric Shelky, John Silverwood, Dr. James Sinclair, Ted Smith, Shaun Tomson, and Peter Townend.

A big mahalo to all of you.

Bibliography

Ahrens, Chris. "Caster Was Truly A Quality Individual." *Del Mar Citizen*, March 11, 1987.

Applegate, Joe. "A Bump on the Head Could Kill Chris O'Rourke." *The San Diego Reader*, August 3, 1978.

Balch, Donald. "The First International Challenge US-South Africa." *Surfer Magazine*, V. 16, #2.

Bolster, Warren. "Profile: Chris O'Rourke." *Surfer Magazine*, V. 17 #2.

Bolster, Warren. "Malibu 1973, The U.S. Surfing Championships." *Surfing Magazine*, Feb/March, 1974.

Dinder, Karen. "Cancer-Stricken Surfer Gets Help From Friends." *Coast Dispatch*, May 6, 1981.

Gerschler, Tony. "A Taste of Juice." *Surfing Magazine*, Feb/March, 1976.

Grissim, John. "Bertlemann Boogies, B.A.'s Grab Team Title." *Surfing Magazine*, June/July 1978.

Gross, Paul. "The Callow Formalizing of California." *Surfer Magazine*, March 1977.

Harvey, Richard. "Wandering and Pondering." *Surfer Magazine*, March 1977.

Hill, Robert. "Tennyson's Poetry ('Crossing The Bar'), New York, W.W. Norton & Company, 1999.

Kempton, Jim. "The 1977 Sutherland California Pro." *Surfer Magazine*, Feb/March 1978.

Naughton, Kevin. "The Last South of Summer." *Surfer Magazine*, V. 16, #5.

Newman, Maria. "Champion S.D. Surfer Lies Stricken In Grip of Life-Sapping Cancer." *San Diego Union,* May 19, 1981.

McKnight, Ken. "Even Hodgkin's Disease Is No Wipeout." *The San Diego Union,* August 16, 1979.

Mc Neal, Laura. "Sea Changes: God and Localism at Windansea." *San Diego Reader,* January 27, 2000.

Petix, Mark. "Friends of O'Rourke Keep Him Believing." *Del Mar Citizen,* May 13, 1981.

Safady, Richard. "The Monster from New Zealand." *Surfer Magazine,* V. 16, #5.

Wander, Brandon. "WSA, WISA, & WHOOSHA." *Surfing Magazine,* Feb/March 1976.